Praise for *New York Times* bestselling author Brenda Jackson

"Brenda Jackson writes romance that sizzles and characters you fall in love with."

—*New York Times* and *USA TODAY* bestselling author Lori Foster

"Jackson's trademark ability to weave multiple characters and side stories together makes shocking truths all the more exciting."   —*Publishers Weekly*

"There is no getting away from the sex appeal and charm of Jackson's Westmoreland family."

—*RT Book Reviews* on *Feeling the Heat*

"What is it with these Westmoreland men? Each is sexier and more charming than the one before.… Hot, sexy, smart and romantic, this story has it all."

—*RT Book Reviews* on *The Proposal*

"Jackson has a talent for creating the sexiest men and pairing them off against feisty females. This story has everything a hot romance should have."

—*RT Book Reviews* on *Hot Westmoreland Nights*

Praise for Kristi Gold

"Kristi Gold's *The Pregnancy Negotiation* (4.5) is a fun, sexy and breezy exploration of parenthood, families, love and growing up."   —*RT Book Reviews*, RT Top Pick

"Gold turns up the steam in this intriguing, haunting tale that will have readers flipping pages into the wee hours."

—*RT Book Reviews* on *House of Midnight Fantasies*, 4.5 stars, Top Pick

"Kristi Gold pens great sexual chemistry, quick dialogue, and wonderful secondary relationships in this terrific keeper!"

—*RT Book Reviews* on *Dr. Desirable*, 4.5 stars, Top Pick

TEXAS TEMPTATION

NEW YORK TIMES BESTSELLING AUTHOR

Brenda Jackson

Kristi Gold

Previously published as *Bane* and *An Heir for the Texan*

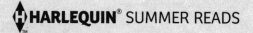

HARLEQUIN® SUMMER READS

ISBN-13: 978-1-335-00527-4

Texas Temptation
Copyright © 2018 by Harlequin Books S.A.

First published as Bane by Harlequin Books in 2015 & An Heir for the Texan by Harlequin Books in 2017.

Recycling programs for this product may not exist in your area.

The publisher acknowledges the copyright holders of the individual works as follows:

Bane
Copyright © 2015 by Brenda Streater Jackson

An Heir for the Texan
Copyright © 2017 by Kristi Goldberg

This edition published by arrangement with Harlequin Books S.A.

For questions and comments about the quality of this book, please contact us at CustomerService@Harlequin.com.

Printed in U.S.A.

www.Harlequin.com

Brenda Jackson is a *New York Times* bestselling author of more than one hundred romance titles. Brenda lives in Jacksonville, Florida, and divides her time between family, writing and traveling.

Email Brenda at authorbrendajackson@gmail.com or visit her on her website at brendajackson.net.

Books by Brenda Jackson

Harlequin Desire

The Westmorelands

Zane
Canyon
Stern
The Real Thing
The Secret Affair
Breaking Bailey's Rules
Bane

The Westmoreland Legacy

The Rancher Returns
His Secret Son
An Honorable Seduction

Visit the Author Profile page at Harlequin.com for more titles.

BANE

Brenda Jackson

To the man who will always and forever be
the love of my life, Gerald Jackson, Sr.

So, then, my beloved brothers, let every man be swift to
hear, slow to speak, and slow to anger.

—James 1:19

Westmoreland family had gathered in the sitting room to watch a holiday movie with the kids, and the men had gone upstairs for a card game.

"Yes, come on in, Bane."

Bane stopped in front of Dillon's desk. He knew Dillon was studying him with that sharp eye of his, taking in every detail. And he could imagine what his brother was thinking. Bane was not the same habitual trouble-maker who had left Westmoreland Country five years ago to make something of himself.

Bane would be the first to admit that a lot in his life had changed. He was now military through and through, both mentally as well as physically. Since graduating from the naval academy and becoming a navy SEAL, he'd learned a lot, seen a lot and done a lot...all in the name of the United States government.

"I want to know how you're doing," Dillon inquired, interrupting Bane's thoughts.

Bane drew in a deep breath. He wished he could answer truthfully. Under normal circumstances he would say he was in prime fighting condition, but that was not the case. During his team's last covert operation, an enemy's bullet had nearly taken him out, leaving him flat on his back in a hospital bed for nearly two months. But he couldn't tell Dillon that. It was confidential. So he said, "I'm fine, although my last mission took a toll on me. I lost a team member who was also a good friend."

Dillon shook his head sadly. "I'm sorry to hear that."

"Me, too. Laramie Cooper was a good guy. One of the best. We went through the academy together." Bane knew Dillon wouldn't ask for specifics. Bane had explained to his family early on that all his covert ops were classified and linked to national security and couldn't be discussed.

Dillon didn't say anything for a minute and then he asked, "Is that why you're taking a three-month military leave? Because of your friend's death?"

Bane eased down in the leather armchair across from Dillon's desk. When their parents, aunt and uncle had gotten killed in a plane crash over twenty years ago, Dillon, the eldest of the Denver Westmorelands, had acquired the role of guardian of his six brothers—Micah, Jason, Riley, Stern, Canyon and Bane—and his eight cousins—Ramsey, Zane, Derringer, Megan, Gemma, the twins Adrian and Aidan, and Bailey. As far as Bane was concerned Dillon had done an outstanding job in keeping the family together and making sure they each made something of themselves. All while making Blue Ridge Land Management Corporation, founded by their father and uncle, into a Fortune 500 company.

Since Dillon was the eldest, he had inherited the main house in Westmoreland Country along with the three hundred acres it sat on. Everyone else, upon reaching the age of twenty-five, received one hundred acres to call their own. Thanks to Bailey's creative mind, each of their spreads were given names—Ramsey's Web, Zane's Hideout, Derringer's Dungeon, Megan's Meadows, Gemma's Gem, Jason's Place, Stern's Stronghold, Canyon's Bluff and Bane's Ponderosa. It was beautiful land that encompassed mountains, valleys, lakes, rivers and streams.

Again, Bane thought about how good it was to be home, and safe here talking with his brother.

"No, that's not the reason," Bane said. "All my team members are on leave because our last operation was one from hell. However, I'm using my leave for a specific purpose, and that is to find Crystal."

Bane paused before adding somberly, "If nothing else,

Coop's death showed me how fragile life is. You can be here today and gone tomorrow."

Dillon would never know that Bane wasn't just referring to Coop's life, but also how close he'd come to losing his own more than a few times.

Bane watched as Dillon came around and sat on the edge of his desk to face him, unsure of how his brother had taken what he'd just said about finding Crystal. Especially since she was the main reason Dillon, and the rest of Bane's family, had supported his decision to join the navy. During their teen years, Bane and Crystal had been obsessive about each other in a way that had driven her family, as well as his, out of their wits.

"Like I told you when you came home for Jason's wedding..." Dillon said. "When the Newsomes moved away they didn't leave a forwarding address. I think their main objective was to put as much distance between you and Crystal as they could." He paused, then said, "But after your inquiry, I hired a private investigator to locate their whereabouts, and I'm not sure if you know it but Carl Newsome passed away."

Bane shook his head. Although he definitely hadn't been Mr. Newsome's favorite person, the man had been Crystal's father. She and her dad hadn't always seen eye to eye, but Crystal had loved him nonetheless. "No, I didn't know he had died."

Dillon nodded. "I called and spoke to Emily Newsome, who told me about Carl's death from lung cancer. After offering my condolences, I asked about Crystal. She said Crystal was doing fine, working on her master's degree at Harvard with plans to get a PhD in biochemistry from there, as well."

Bane tipped his head to the side. "That doesn't surprise me. Crystal was pretty smart. If you recall she was two grades ahead and was set to graduate from high school at sixteen."

What he wouldn't bring up was that she would have done just that if she hadn't missed so many days of school playing hooky with him. That was something everyone, especially the Newsomes, blamed him for. Whenever Crystal had attended school steadily she'd made good grades. There was no doubt in his mind she would have graduated at the top of her class. That was one of the reasons he hadn't tried to find her for all these years. He'd wanted her to reach her full potential. He'd owed her that much.

"So you haven't seen or heard from Crystal since that day Carl sent her to live with some aunt?"

"No, I haven't seen her. You were right at the time. I didn't have anything to offer Crystal. I was a hothead and Trouble was my middle name. She deserved better and I was willing to make something of myself to give her better."

Dillon just stared at him for a long moment in silence, as if contemplating whether or not he should tell him something. Bane suddenly felt uneasy. Had something happened to Crystal that he didn't know about?

"Is there something else, Dil?"

"I don't want to hurt or upset you Bane, but I want to give you food for thought. You're planning to find Crystal, but you don't know what her feelings are for you now. The two of you were young. First love doesn't always mean last love. Although you might still care about her, for all you know she might have moved on, gotten on with her life without you. It's been five years. Have you considered that she might be involved with someone else?"

Bane leaned back in his chair, considering Dillon's words. "I don't believe that. Crystal and I had an understanding. We have an unbreakable bond."

"But that was years ago," Dillon stressed. "You just said you haven't seen her since that day Carl sent her away. For all you know she could be married by now."

Bane shook his head. "Crystal wouldn't marry anyone else."

Dillon lifted a brow. "And how can you be so sure of that?"

Bane held his brother's stare. "Because she's already married, Dil. Crystal is married to me and I think it's time to go claim my wife."

Dillon was on his feet in a flash. "Married? You? Crystal? B-but how? When?"

"When we eloped."

"But you and Crystal never made it to Vegas."

"Weren't trying to," Bane said evenly. "We deliberately gave that impression to send everyone looking for us in the wrong direction. We got married in Utah."

"Utah? You have to be eighteen to marry without parental consent and Crystal was seventeen."

Bane shook his head. "She was seventeen the day we eloped, but turned eighteen the next day."

Dillon stared at him. "Then, why didn't the two of you say something? Why didn't she tell her parents that she was your wife or why didn't you tell us? You let them send her away."

"Yes, because I knew that although she was my wife, I could still be brought up on kidnapping charges. I violated the restraining order from that judge when I set foot on her parents' property. If you recall, Judge Foster was pissed about it and wanted to send me to the prison farm for a year. And knowing Mr. Newsome, had I mentioned anything about me and Crystal being married, he would have demanded that Judge Foster send me away for even longer. Once I was gone, Newsome would have found a way to have our marriage annulled or forced Crystal into divorcing me. She and I both knew that so we decided not to say anything about our marriage no matter what... even if it meant being apart for a short while."

"A short while? You've been apart for five years."

"I hadn't planned for it to be this long. We figured her old man would keep her under lock and key for a while. We were prepared for that seven-month separation because it would give Crystal a chance to finish high school. We hadn't figured on him sending her away. But then something you said that day stuck with me. At the time I had nothing to offer Crystal. She was smart and deserved more than a dumb ass who enjoyed being the town's troublemaker."

Bane didn't say anything for a minute before adding, "I told you earlier that I hadn't seen Crystal, but what I didn't say is that I managed to talk to her after she left town."

Dillon frowned. "You made contact with Crystal?"

"Only once. A few months after she was sent away."

"But how? Her parents made sure no one knew where she'd gone."

"Bailey found out for me."

Dillon shook his head. "Now, why doesn't that surprise me? And how did Bailey find out where Crystal was?"

Bane held his brother's gaze. "Are you sure you want to know?"

Dillon rubbed his hand down his face. "Does it involve breaking the law?"

Bane shrugged his shoulders. "Sort of."

Bailey was their female cousin who was a couple of years younger than Bane and the baby in the Denver Westmoreland family. While growing up, the two of them, along with the twins, Adrian and Aidan, had been extremely close, thick as thieves, literally. The four used to get into all kinds of trouble with the law. Bane knew that Dillon's close friendship with Sheriff Harper was what had kept them out of jail.

Now the twins were Harvard graduates. Adrian had a PhD in engineering and Aidan was a cardiologist at Johns Hopkins Research Hospital. And both were happily married. Bailey, who had her MBA, was marrying Walker Rafferty, a rancher from Alaska, on Valentine's Day and moving to live on his spread. That announcement had definitely come as a shock to Bane and everyone else since Bailey had always sworn she would never, ever leave Westmoreland Country. Bane had met Rafferty today and immediately liked the ex-marine. Bane had a feeling Rafferty would not only handle Bailey but would make Bane's cousin happy.

"So if you knew where she was, what stopped you from going to her?" Dillon asked, holding Bane's gaze.

"I didn't know where she was and I made Bailey promise not to tell me. I just needed to talk to her and Bailey arranged a call between me and Crystal that lasted about twenty minutes. I told her about my decision to join the navy and I made her a promise that while we were apart I would honor our marriage vows, and for her to always believe that one day I would come back for her. That was the last time we talked to each other."

Bane remembered that phone call as if it had been yesterday. "Another reason I needed to talk to Crystal was to be certain she hadn't gotten pregnant during the time we eloped. A pregnancy would have been a game changer for me. I would not have gone into the navy. Instead, I would have gone to her immediately."

Dillon nodded. "Do you know where she is now?"

"I didn't know up until a few hours ago. Bailey lost contact with Crystal a year and a half ago. Last week I hired someone to find her, and I got a call that she's been found. I'm heading out in the morning."

"To where?"

"Dallas, Texas."

One

Leaving her job at Seton Industries, Crystal Newsome quickly walked to her car, looking over her shoulder when she thought she heard footsteps behind her. She tried ignoring the sparks that moved up her arms, while telling herself she was probably getting all worked up for nothing. And all because of that note someone had left today in her desk drawer.

Someone wants the research you're working on. I suggest you disappear for a while. No matter what, don't trust anyone.

After reading it she had glanced around the lab. Her four colleagues seemed preoccupied, busy working on their individual biochemistry projects. She wondered who'd given her the warning and wished she could dismiss the note as a joke, but she couldn't. Especially not after the incident yesterday.

Someone had gotten inside her locker. How the person had known her combination she wasn't sure, since there hadn't been any signs of forced entry. But whoever it was had taken the time to leave things almost exactly as she'd left them.

And now the anonymous note.

Reaching her car, she unlocked the door and got inside, locking it again behind her. After checking her surroundings and the other cars parked close by, she maneuvered out of the parking lot and onto the street. When she came to a stop at the first traffic light, she pulled the typed note from her purse and reread it.

Disappear? How could she do that, even if she wanted to?

She was currently working on her PhD as a biochemist, and was one of five chosen nationally to participate in a yearlong research program at Seton Industries. Crystal knew others were interested in her research. Case in point: just last month she'd been approached by two government officials who wanted her to continue her PhD research under the protection of Homeland Security. The two men had stressed what could happen if her data got into the wrong hands, namely those with criminal intent. She had assured them that even with the documented advances of her research, her project was still just a theoretical concept. But they had wanted to place her in a highly collaborative environment with two other American chemists working on similar research. Although their offer had been tempting, she had turned it down. She was set to graduate from Harvard with her PhD in the spring and had already received a number of job offers.

But now she wondered if she should have taken the

men's warning seriously. Could someone with criminal intent be after the findings she'd already logged?

She glanced in her rearview mirror and her heart pounded. A blue car she'd noticed several traffic lights back was still there. Was she imagining things?

A short while later she knew she wasn't. The car was staying a few car lengths behind her.

Crystal knew she couldn't go home. The driver of that blue car would follow her. So where could she go? Who could she call? The four other biochemists were also PhD students, but she stayed to herself the majority of the time and hadn't formed relationships with any of them.

Except for Darnell Enfield. He'd been the one intent on establishing a relationship with her. She had done nothing to encourage the man and had told him count-less times she wasn't interested. When that hadn't de-terred him, she'd threatened to file a complaint with the director of the program. In anger, Darnell had accused her of being stuck-up, saying he hoped she had a lonely and miserable life.

Crystal had news for him. She had that already. On most days she tried not to dwell on just how lonely the past five years had been. But as far as she was concerned, Loneliness had been her middle name for further back than five years.

Born the only child to older, overprotective parents, she'd been homeschooled and rarely allowed to leave the house except to attend church or accompany them to the grocery store. For years, her parents wouldn't even allow her to go outside and play. She remembered when one of the neighbor kids had tried befriending her, the most she could do was talk to the little girl through her bedroom window.

It was only after their pastor had encouraged her parents to enroll Crystal in public school to enhance her social skills that they did so. By then she was fifteen and starving for friends. But she'd discovered just how cruel the world was when the other girls had snubbed her and the guys had made fun of her because she'd been advanced in all her studies. They'd called her a genius freak. She had been miserable attending school until she'd met Bane.

Brisbane Westmoreland.

The man she had secretly married five years ago on her eighteenth birthday. And the man she hadn't seen since.

As a teenager, Bane had been her best friend, her sounding board and her reason for existing. He'd understood her like no other and she'd felt she had understood him. Her parents made the four-year difference in their ages a big issue and tried keeping them apart. The more her parents tried, the more she'd defied them to be with him.

Then there was the problem of Bane being a Westmoreland. Years ago, her and Bane's great-grandfathers had ended their friendship because of a dispute regarding land boundaries, and it seemed her father had no problem continuing the feud.

When Crystal came to another traffic light she pulled out a business card from her purse. It was the card those two government officials had left with her. They'd asked her to call if she changed her mind or if she noticed any funny business. At the time she'd thought their words were a scare tactic to make her give their offer more consideration. But could they have been right? Should she contact them? She replaced the card in her purse and looked at the note again.

No matter what, don't trust anyone.

So what should she do? Where could she go? Since her father's death, her mother was now a missionary in Haiti. Should Crystal escape to Orangeburg, South Carolina, where her aunt Rachel still lived? The last thing Crystal wanted was to bring trouble to her elderly aunt's doorstep.

There was another place she could hide. Her childhood home in Denver. She and her mother had discovered, after going through her father's papers, that he'd never sold their family homestead after her parents moved to Connecticut. And even more shocking to Crystal was that he'd left the ranch to her. Had that been his way of letting her know he'd accepted that one day she would go back there?

She nibbled her bottom lip. Should she go back now? And face all the memories she'd left behind? What if Bane was there? What if he'd hooked up with someone else despite the promises he'd made to her?

She didn't want to believe that. The Bane Westmoreland she had fallen in love with had promised to honor their wedding vows. Before marrying someone else he would seek her out to ask for a divorce.

She thought about the other promise he'd made and wondered if she was the biggest fool on earth. He'd vowed he would come back for her. That had been five years ago and she was still waiting. Was she wasting her life on a man who had forgotten about her? A lot could have happened since he'd made that promise. Feelings and emotions could change. People could change. Why was she refusing to let go of teenage memories with a guy who might have moved on with his life?

Legally she was a married woman, but all she had to show for it was a last name she never used and a husband who'd left her with unfulfilled promises. Her last contact with him after her father had sent her away was when he'd called to let her know he was joining the navy. Did he expect her to wait until he got tired of being a sailor, moving from one port to the next? What if an emergency had come up and she'd needed him?

She knew the answer to that without much thought. Had an emergency arisen, she could have reached him through his family. Although the Westmorelands had no idea where she lived now, she'd always known where they were. She could have picked up the phone and called Dillon, Bane's eldest brother, if she'd ever truly wanted or needed to contact Bane. Several times she'd come close to doing that, but something had always held her back. First of all, she knew the Westmorelands blamed her for a lot of the trouble Bane had gotten into.

As teens, her and Bane's relationship had been obsessive and she didn't want to think about the number of times they'd broken the law to be together. She'd had resorted to cutting school, and regardless of what her parents had assumed, the majority of the time it had been her idea and not his. Nothing her parents or his family said or did had torn them apart. Instead, their bond had gotten stronger.

Because of the difference in their ages, her parents had accused Bane of taking advantage of her, and her father had even put a restraining order in place and threatened Bane with jail time to keep him away from her. But that hadn't stopped her or Bane from being together. When they'd gotten tired of their families' interference, they had eloped.

She reached inside her shirt and pulled out the sterling-silver heart-shaped locket Bane had given her instead of a wedding ring he couldn't afford. When he'd placed the locket around her neck he'd said it had belonged to his deceased mother. He'd wanted her to have it, to always wear it as a reminder of their love. His love. She swallowed a thick lump in her throat. If he loved her so much, then why hadn't he kept his promise and come back for her?

Her mother had mentioned that Bane's eldest brother, Dillon, had called a year ago when he'd heard about her father's death. According to her mother, the conversation had been brief, but Dillon had taken the time to inquire about how she was doing. According to her mother the only thing he'd said about Bane was that he was in the navy. Of course her mother thought her daughter was doing just fine now that Bane was out of her life, and the Westmorelands probably felt the same way since she was out of Bane's. What if her mother was right and Bane *was* doing just fine without her?

Drawing in a deep breath, Crystal forced her thoughts back to the car following her. Should she call the police for help? She quickly dismissed the idea. Hadn't the note warned her not to trust anyone? Suddenly an idea popped into her head. It was the start of the holiday shopping season and shoppers were already out in large numbers. She would drive to the busiest mall in Dallas and get lost in traffic. If that didn't work she would come up with plan B.

The one thing she knew for certain was that she would not let the person tail her home. When she got there, she would quickly pack her things and disappear for a while. She would decide where she was going once she got to the airport. The Bahamas sounded pretty good right about now.

What would Seton Industries think when she didn't show up for work as usual? At present that was the least of her worries. Staying safe was her top priority.

Half an hour later she smiled, satisfied that plan A had worked. All it took was to scoot her car in and out of all those tenacious shoppers a few times, and the driver of the blue car couldn't keep up. But just to be certain, she drove around for a while to make sure she was no longer being tailed.

She had fallen in love with Dallas but had no choice except to leave town for a while.

Sitting in the SUV he had rented at the airport, Bane tilted his Stetson off his eyes and shifted his long legs into a more comfortable position. He checked his watch again. The private investigator's report indicated Crystal was employed with Seton Industries as a biochemist while working on her PhD, and that she usually got off work around four. It was close to seven and she hadn't gotten home yet. So where was she?

It *was* the holiday season and she could have gone shopping. And she must have girlfriends, so she could very well be spending time with one of them. He just had to wait.

None of his family members had been surprised when he'd announced he was going after Crystal. However, except for Bailey, who knew the whole story, all of them were shocked to learn he'd married Crystal when they had eloped. His brother Riley had claimed he'd suspected as much, but all the others hadn't had a clue.

Bailey had given Bane a huge hug and whispered that it was about time he claimed his wife. Of course others, like Dillon, had warned Bane that things might be differ-

ent and not to expect Crystal to be the eighteen-year-old
he'd last seen. Just like he had changed over the years,
so had she.

His cousin Zane, who was reputed to be an expert on
women, had gone so far as to advise Bane not to expect
Crystal to readily embrace her role as loving wife or his
role as long-lost husband. Zane had cautioned him not
to do anything stupid like sweeping her off her feet and
carrying her straight to the bedroom. They would have
to get to know each other all over again, and he shouldn't
be surprised if she tried putting up walls between them
for a while.

Zane had reiterated that regardless of the reason, Bane
hadn't made contact with his wife in almost five years
and doubts would have crossed Crystal's mind regarding
Bane's love and faithfulness.

He had appreciated everyone's advice. And while he
wished like hell he could sweep Crystal off her feet and
head straight for the nearest bedroom when he saw her,
he had enough sense to know they would have to take
things slow. After all, they had been apart all this time
and there would be a lot for them to talk about and sort
out. But he felt certain she knew he would come back for
her as he'd promised; no matter how long it had taken
him to do so.

He was back in her life and didn't intend to go anywhere. Even if it meant he lived with her in Dallas for a
while. As a SEAL he could live anywhere as long as he
was ready to leave for periodic training sessions or covert
operations whenever his commanding officer called. And
as long as there was still instability in Iraq, Afghanistan
and Syria, his team might be needed.

Thinking of his team made him think about Coop.

It was hard to believe his friend was gone. All the team members had taken Coop's death hard and agreed that if it was the last thing they did, they would return to Syria, find Coop's body and bring him home. His parents deserved that and Coop did, too.

For the longest time, Bane had thought he could keep his marriage a secret from his team. But he found it hard to do when the guys thought it was essential that he got laid every once in a while. Things started getting crazy when they tried fixing him up with some woman or another every chance they got.

He'd finally told them about his marriage to Crystal. Then he wished he hadn't when they'd teased him about all the women they were getting while he wasn't getting any. He took it all in stride because he only wanted one woman. His team members accepted that he intended to adhere to his wedding vows and in the end they all respected and admired him for it.

Now the SEAL in him studied his surroundings, taking notice. The one thing he appreciated was that Crystal's home appeared to be in a safe neighborhood. The streets were well lit and the houses spaced with enough distance for privacy yet with her neighbors in reach if needed.

The brick house where she lived suited her. It looked to be in good condition and the yard was well manicured. One thing he did notice was that unlike all the other houses, she didn't have any Christmas decorations. There weren't any colorful lights around her windows or animated objects adorning her lawn. Did she not celebrate the holidays anymore? He recalled a time when she had. In fact the two most important days to her had been her birthday and Christmas.

He'd made her birthday even more special by marrying her on it. A smile touched his lips when he recalled
how, over the years, he had bought her birthday cards and
anniversary cards, although he hadn't been able to send
them to her. He'd even bought her Valentine's Day cards
and Christmas cards every year. He had stored them in a
trunk, knowing one day he would give them to her. Well,
that day had finally arrived and he had all of them packed
in his luggage. He had signed each one and taken the
time to write a special message inside. Then there were
all those letters he'd written. Letters he'd never mailed
because he hadn't a clue where to send them.

He'd made Bailey promise not to tell him because if
he'd known how to get to Crystal he would have gone to
her and messed up all the effort he'd made in becoming
the type of man who could give her what she deserved
in life.

Five years was a long time and there had been times
he'd thought he would lose his mind from missing her
so much. It had taken all he had, every bit of resolve he
could muster, to make it through. In the end, he knew
the sacrifice would be worth it.

He figured he would give Crystal time to get into the
house before he got out of the car and knocked on the
door, so as not to spook her. No need to give her neighbors anything to talk about, either, especially if no one
knew she was married. And from the private investigator's report, her marital status was a guarded secret. He
understood and figured it wouldn't be easy to explain a
husband who'd gone AWOL.

His phone rang and a smile tugged at the corner of his
mouth when he recognized the ringtone. It was Thurston
McRoy, better known to the team as Mac. All Bane's

team members' names had been shortened for easy iden-
tification during deployment. Cooper was Coop. McRoy
was Mac. And because his name was Brisbane, the nick-
name his family had given him was already a shortened
version, so his team members called him Bane like everyone else.

"What's up, Mac?"

"Have you seen her yet?"

He had spoken to Mac on his way to the airport to let
him know his whereabouts, just in case the team was
needed somewhere. "No, not yet. I'm parked outside her
place. She's late getting off work."

"When she gets there, don't ask a lot of questions and
please don't go off on her as if you've been there for the
past five years. You may think she's late but it might
be her usual MO to get delayed every once in a while.
Women do have days they like to get prettied up. Get
their hair and nails done and stuff."

Bane chuckled. He figured Mac would know since he
was one of the married team members. And Mac would
tell them that after every extended mission, he would go
home to an adjustment period, where he would have to
get to know his wife all over again and reclaim his position as head of the house.

When Bane saw car lights headed toward where he
was parked, he said, "I think this is her pulling up now."

"Great. Just remember the advice I gave you."

Yours and everybody else's, Bane thought. "Whatever.
I know how to handle my business."

"See that you do." Then without saying anything else,
Mac clicked off the phone.

As Bane watched the headlights get closer, he couldn't
stop the deep pounding of his heart. He wondered what

changes to expect. Did Crystal wear her hair down to her shoulders like she had years ago? Did she nibble her bottom lip when she was nervous about something? And did she still have those sexy legs?

It didn't matter. He intended to finally claim her as his. His wife.

Bane watched as she pulled into her yard and got out of the car. The moment his gaze latched on to her all the emotion he hadn't been able to contain over the years washed over him, putting an ache in his gut.

The streetlight shone on her features. Even from the distance, he could see she was beautiful. She'd grown taller and her youthful figure had blossomed into that of a woman. His pulse raced as he studied how well her curves filled out her dark slacks and how her breasts appeared to be shaped perfectly beneath her jacket.

As he watched her, the navy SEAL in him went on alert. Something wasn't right. He had been trained to be vigilant not just to his surroundings but also to people. Recognizing signs of trouble had kept him alive on more than one mission. Maybe it was the quickness of her steps to her front door, the number of times she looked back over her shoulder or the way she kept checking the street as if to make certain she hadn't been followed.

When she went inside and closed the door he released the breath he only realized now that he'd been holding. Who or what had her so antsy? She had no knowledge that he was coming, so it couldn't be him. She seemed more than just rattled. Terrified was more like it. Why? Even if she'd somehow found out he was coming, she had no reason of be afraid of him. Unless...

He scowled. What if she assumed he wasn't coming

back for her and she'd taken a lover? What if she was the mother of another man's child? What if…

He cleared his mind. Each of those thoughts was like a quick punch to his gut, and he refused to go there. Besides, the private investigator's report had been clear. She lived alone and was not involved with anyone.

Still, something had her frightened.

After waiting for several minutes to give her time to get settled after a day at work, he opened the door to the SUV. It was time to find out what the hell was going on.

With her heart thundering hard in her chest, Crystal began throwing items in the suitcase open on her bed. Had she imagined it or had she been watched when she'd entered her home tonight? She had glanced around several times and hadn't noticed anything or anyone. But still…

She took a deep breath, knowing she couldn't lose her cool. She had to keep a level head. She made a decision to leave her car here and a few lights burning inside her house to give the impression she was home. She would call a cab to take her to the airport and would take only the necessities and a few items of clothing. She could buy anything else she needed.

But this, she thought, studying the photo album she held in her hand, went everywhere with her. She had purchased it right after her last phone call with Bane. Her parents had sent Crystal to live with Aunt Rachel to finish out the last year of school. They'd wanted to get her away from Bane, not knowing she and Bane had married.

Before they'd returned home after eloping, Bane had convinced Crystal it was important for her to finish school before telling anyone they'd gotten married. He'd told her that if her parents tried keeping them apart that he would put up with it for a few months, which was the time it would take for her to finish school. They hadn't counted on her parents sending her away. But still, she believed that Bane would come for her once the school year ended, no matter where she was.

But a couple of months after she left Denver, she'd gotten a call from him. She'd assumed he was calling to let her know he couldn't stand the separation and was coming for her. But his real purpose had been twofold. He'd wanted to find out if she had gotten pregnant when they eloped, and he'd told her he'd enlisted in the navy and would be leaving for boot camp in Great Lakes, Illinois, in a few weeks. He'd said he needed to grow up, become responsible and make something out of himself. She deserved a man who could be all that he could be, and after he'd accomplished that goal he would come for her. He'd also promised that while they were apart he would honor their wedding vows and she'd promised him the same. And she had.

She'd figured he would be in the navy for four years. Preparing for the separation, she'd decided to make something of herself, as well. He deserved that, too. So after completing high school she'd enrolled in college. She had taken a placement test, which she'd aced. Instead of being accepted as a freshman, she had entered as a junior.

Sitting on the edge of the bed now, she flipped through the album, which she had dedicated to Bane. She'd even had his name engraved on the front. While they were apart she'd kept this photo journal, chronicling her life without him. There were graduation pictures from high school and college, random pictures she'd taken just for him. She'd figured that by the time she saw him she would have at least two to three years' worth of photos. She hadn't counted on the bulky album containing five years of photographs. The last thing she'd assumed was that they would be apart for this long without any contact.

She thought of him often. Every day. What she tried not to think about was why it was taking him so long to come back for her, or how he might be somewhere enjoying life without her. Forcing those thoughts from her mind, she packed the album in her luggage. Her destination was the Bahamas. She had done an online bank transfer to her "fun" account, which had accumulated a nice amount due to the vacations she'd never gotten around to taking. And in case her home was searched, she'd made sure not to leave any clues about where she was headed.

Was she being impulsive by heeding what the note had said when she didn't even know who'd written it? She could report it, what happened to her locker and that she'd noticed someone following her to those two government officials. If she couldn't trust her own government, then who could she trust? She shook her head, deciding against making that call. Maybe she'd watched too many TV shows where the government had turned out to be the bad guy.

Crystal thought about calling her mother and Aunt Rachel, and then decided against it. Whatever she was involved with, it would be best to leave them out of it. She would contact them later when she felt doing so would be safe. Moments later, she had rolled her luggage out of her bedroom into the living room and was calling for a cab when her doorbell rang.

She went still. Nobody ever visited her. Who would be doing so now? She crept back into the shadows of her hallway, hoping whoever was at the door would think she wasn't home. She held her breath when the doorbell sounded again. Had the person on the other side seen her enter her house and knew she was there?

Moments passed and the doorbell did not sound again. She sighed in relief—and then there was a hard knock. She swallowed. The person hadn't gone away. Either she answered it or continued to pretend she wasn't there. Since the latter hadn't worked so far, she rushed into her bedroom and grabbed her revolver out of the nightstand drawer.

She'd grown up around guns, and thanks to Bane she knew how to use one. This neighborhood was pretty safe, and even though she'd figured she'd never need to use it, she had bought the gun anyway. A woman living alone needed to be cautious.

By the time she'd made it back to the living room, there was a second knock. She moved toward the door, but stopped five feet away. She called out, "Who is it?" and tightened her hands on the revolver.

There was a moment of silence. And then a voice said, "It's me, Crystal. Bane."

Crystal Gayle? She sucked in a deep breath. Nobody called her that but her parents…and Bane. When she was young, she had hated being called by her first and middle names, which her father had given her, naming her after his favorite country singer. But Bane had made her like it when he'd called her that on occasion. Could it really be him at the door?

Lowering the gun, she looked out the peephole. Her gaze connected to a gorgeous pair of hazel eyes with a greenish tint. They were eyes she knew. It *was* Bane.

She was about to open the door when she remembered the note. *Trust no one.* But this wasn't just anyone, she reasoned with herself. This was Bane.

She unlocked the door and stepped back. Soft porch light poured into her foyer as Bane eased open the door. He'd always been tall and lanky, but the man entering her house appeared a lot taller than she remembered. And he was no longer slender. He was all muscles and they were in perfect proportion to his height and weight. It was obvious he worked out a lot to stay in shape. His body exemplified endurance and strength. And when her gaze settled on his face, she drew in a deep, sharp breath. He even looked different. Rougher. Tougher.

The eyes were the same but she'd never seen him with facial hair before. He'd always been handsome in a boyish sort of way, but his features now were perfectly masculine. They appeared chiseled, his lips sculpted. She was looking into the most handsome face she'd ever seen.

He not only looked older and more mature, but he also looked military—even while wearing jeans, a chambray shirt, a leather bomber jacket, Western boots and a Stetson. There was something about the way he stood, upright and straight. And all this transformation had come from being in the navy?

He closed the door behind him, staring at her just as she was staring at him. Her heart pounded. A part of her wanted to race over to him, tell him how glad she was to see him, how much she had missed him…but she couldn't. Her legs refused to move and she knew why. This Bane was like a stranger to her.

"Crystal."

She hadn't imagined it. His voice had gotten deeper. Sounded purely sexy to her ears. "Bane."

"You look good."

She blinked at his words and said the first thing that came to her mind. "You look good, too. And different."

He smiled and her breath caught. He still had that Brisbane Westmoreland smile. The one that spread across a full mouth and showed teeth that were perfectly even and sparkling white against mocha-colored skin. The familiarity warmed her inside.

"I am different. I'm not the same Bane. The military has a way of doing that to you," he said, in that husky voice she was trying to get used to hearing.

He was admitting to being different.

Was this his way of saying his transformation had changed his preferences? Like his taste in women? He was older now, five years older, in fact. Had he shown up on her doorstep tonight of all nights to let her know that he wanted a divorce?

Fine, she would deal with it. She had no choice. Besides, she wasn't sure if she would like the new Bane anyway. He was probably doing her a favor.

"Okay," she said, placing her revolver on the coffee

table. "If you brought any papers with you that require my signature, then give them to me."

He lifted a brow. "Papers?"

"Yes."

"What kind of papers?"

Instead of answering, she glanced at her watch. She needed to call a cab to the airport. The plane to the Bahamas would take off in three hours.

"Crystal? What kind of papers are you talking about?"

She glanced back over at him. And why did her gaze automatically go to his mouth, the same mouth that had taught her how to kiss and given her so much pleasure? And why was she recalling a lot of those kisses right now? She drew in a deep, shallow breath. "Divorce papers."

"Is that why you think I'm here?"

Was she imagining things or had his voice sounded brisk? She shrugged. Why were they even having this conversation? Why couldn't he just give her the papers and be on his way so she could be on hers? After all, it had been five years. She got that. Did it matter that she had spent all that time waiting for him to show up?

"Crystal? Is that why you think I'm here? To ask for a divorce?" He repeated the question and she noticed his tone still had a brusque edge.

She held his gaze. "What other reason could there be?"

He shoved his hands into the pockets of his jeans and braced his legs apart in a stance that was as daunting as it was sexy. It definitely brought emphasis to his massive shoulders, the solidity of chest and his chiseled good looks.

"Did you consider that maybe I'm here to keep that promise I made about coming back for you?"

She blinked, not sure she'd heard him correctly. "You aren't here to ask for a divorce?"

"No. What makes you think I'd want to divorce you?"

She could give him a number of reasons once her head stopped spinning. Instead, she said what was in the forefront of her mind. "Well, it has been five years, Bane."

"I told you I'd come back for you."

She placed her hands on her hips. "Yes, but I hadn't counted on it being *five* years. Five years without a single word from you. Besides, you just said you've changed."

The look in his eyes indicated he was having a hard time keeping up with her. "I *have* changed, Crystal. Being a SEAL has a way of changing you, but that has nothing to do—"

"SEAL? You're a navy SEAL?"

"Yes."

Now she was the one having a hard time keeping up. "I knew you'd joined the navy, but I figured you'd been assigned to a ship somewhere."

He nodded. "I would have been if my captain in boot camp hadn't thought I would be a good fit for the SEALs. He cut through a lot of red tape for me to go to the naval academy."

That was another surprise. "You attended the naval academy?"

"Yes."

Jeez. She was realizing just how little she knew about what he'd been doing over the past five years. "I didn't know."

He shifted his stance and her gaze followed the movement, taking in his long, denim-clad, boot-wearing legs.

"Bailey said the two of you lost contact with each other a couple of years ago," he said.

Now was the time to come clean and say losing contact with Bailey had been a deliberate move. The periodic calls from his cousin had become depressing since they'd agreed Crystal wouldn't ask about Bane. Just as he wouldn't ask Bailey any questions about Crystal.

That had been Bane's idea. He'd figured the less they knew about the other's lives, the less chance they had of reneging on their promise not to seek the other out before he could meet his goals.

During one of those conversations Bailey had informed her Bane had set up a bank account for her, in case she ever needed anything. She never had and to this day she'd never withdrawn any funds.

"Even if Bailey and I had kept in touch, she would not have told me *what* you were doing, just *how* you were doing. That was the agreement, remember, Bane?"

"You could have called Dil," he said as he raked his gaze over her.

He was probably taking note of how she'd changed as she'd done with him. He could clearly see she was no longer the eighteen-year-old he'd married, but was now a twenty-three-year-old woman. Her birthday had been two weeks ago. She wondered if he'd remembered.

"No, I couldn't call your brother, or any other member of your family for that matter, and you know why. They blamed me for you getting into trouble."

Crystal glanced at her watch again. He'd said he was here to fulfill his promise. If he was doing it because he felt obligated then she would release him from it. Although asking for a divorce might not have been his original intent, she was certain it was crossing his mind now. Why wouldn't it? They were acting like strangers instead of two people who'd once been so obsessed with each other they'd eloped. Why weren't they all over each other? Why was he over there and she still standing over here? The answer to both questions was so brutally clear she had to force tears from her eyes.

Like he said, he had changed. He was a SEAL. Something other than her was number one in his life now. More than likely it had been his missions that had kept him away all this time. He'd chosen what he really wanted.

"Crystal, I have a question for you."

His words interrupted her thoughts. "What?"

"Why did you come to the door with a gun?"

It had taken every ounce of Bane's control not to cross the room and pull his wife into his arms. How often had he dreamed of this moment, wished for it, yearned for it? But things weren't playing out like he'd hoped.

Although he'd taken heed to Zane's warning and not swept her off her feet and headed for the nearest bedroom, he hadn't counted on not getting at least a kiss, a hug…something. But she stood there as if she wasn't sure what to make of his appearance here tonight. And he still couldn't grasp why she assumed he wanted a divorce just because he'd told her he'd changed. He'd changed for the better, not only for himself but also for her. Now he had something to offer her. He could give her the life she deserved.

Crystal nibbled her bottom lip, which had always been an indication she was nervous about something. Damn, she looked good. Time had only enhanced her beauty, and where in the hell had all those curves come from?

She had changed into a pair of skinny jeans, a pullover sweater and boots. She looked all soft and feminine. So gorgeous. Her hair was not as long as it used to be.

Instead of flowing past her shoulders it barely touched them. The new style suited her. How had she managed to keep the guys away? He was certain that with her beauty there had been a number of men who'd come around over the years.

Even now Bane's hands itched to touch her all over like he used to. He would give anything to run his fingers across the curve of her hips and buttocks and cup her breasts.

"The gun?"

Her question pulled his concentration back to their conversation. Probably for the best, since the thought of what he wanted to do with his hands was turning him on big-time. "Yes. I watched you get out of your car to come into the house and you seemed nervous. Is something going on? Is some man harassing you or stalking you?"

She lifted a brow. "A man stalking me? What makes you think that?"

He held her gaze. "I told you. I noticed you were nervous and—"

"Yes, I got that part," she interrupted to say. "But what makes you think any man would stalk me?"

Had she looked in the mirror lately? If she'd asked him *why* he thought she was being stalked, then he could have told her that his SEAL training had taught him how to zero in on certain things. But her question had been what made him think *any man* would want to stalk *her*. That was a different question altogether. He could see a man becoming obsessed with her. Hadn't Bane?

"You're a very beautiful woman. You've always been beautiful, Crystal. You're even more so now."

She shook her head. "Beautiful? You're laying it on thick, aren't you, Bane?"

"No, I don't think so. Level with me. Is there some man stalking you? Is that why you had the gun? And what's with the luggage? You're going someplace?"

She broke eye contact with him to shrug. "The gun is to protect myself."

Bane had a feeling that wasn't all there was to it. When he'd first walked into her house he'd seen the luggage, but his mind had been solely on her, entranced with her beauty. This older version of Crystal sent his heart pounding into overdrive. It had been a long time. Too long.

He turned his concentration back to what she'd just told him. "You have the gun to protect yourself... I can buy that, although this seems to be a pretty safe neighborhood," he said. "But that doesn't explain why you were ready to shoot. Has your home been broken into before?"

"No."

"Then what's going on?"

Even after all this time he still could read her like a book. She had a tendency to lick her lips when she was nervous, and unconsciously shift her body from side to side while standing on the balls of her feet. He could tell she was trying to decide how to answer his question. That didn't sit well with him. In the past, he and Crystal never kept secrets from each other. So why was she doing so now?

"After all this time, you don't have the right to ask me anything, Bane."

You're wrong about that, sweetheart.

Without thinking about what he was doing, he closed the distance separating them to stand directly in front of her. "I believe I do have that right. As long as we're still legally married, Crystal, I have every right."

She lifted her chin and pinched her lips together. "Fine. Then, we can get a divorce."

"Not happening." He rubbed his hand down his face. What the hell was going on here? Not only was this reunion not going the way he'd wanted, it had just taken a bad turn.

He looked at her, somewhat bewildered by her refusal to answer his question. "I'm asking again, Crystal. What's going on with you? Why the gun and the packed luggage?"

When she didn't answer, standing there with a mutinous expression on her face, he then asked the one question he hadn't wanted to ask, but needed to know. And he hoped like hell he was wrong.

"Are you involved with someone who's causing you problems?"

Three

That question set Crystal off. She took the final step to completely close the distance between them. "Involved with someone? Are you accusing me of being unfaithful?"

"Not accusing you of anything," he said in a tone that let her know her outrage had fueled his. "But I find it odd you won't answer my question. Why are you acting so secretive? You've never acted that way with me before."

No, she hadn't. But then the Bane she used to know, the one she'd loved more than life itself, would not have forgotten her for five years. He would have moved heaven, hell and any place in between to have her with him so the two of them could be together.

"You're not the only one who's changed. Just like you're not the same, I'm not the same."

They faced off. She didn't see him move, but suddenly his body brushed against hers and she drew in a sharp breath. The touch had been electric, sending a sizzle through her. Suddenly, her mind was filled with memories of the last time they'd touched. Really touched. All over. Naked. Those memories were enough to ignite a fire in the pit of her stomach.

"You may not be the same," he said, breaking into the silence between them, speaking in a low tone, "but you kept your wedding vows."

He spoke with such absolute certainty, she wondered how he could be so sure. But of course he was right. "Yes, I kept them."

He nodded. "And before doubt starts clouding that pretty little head of yours, let me go on record to say that I might not be the same, but I kept my wedding vows, as well."

There was no way. Not that she didn't think he would have tried, but she knew when it came to sex, some men classified it as a *must have*. She of all people knew how much the old Bane had enjoyed it. There was no reason to think the new and different Bane wouldn't like it just as much. Just look at him. He was more masculine, more virile—so macho. Even if he hadn't targeted women, they would definitely have targeted him.

"Now that we have that cleared up…"

Did they? "Not so fast," she said, trying to ignore it when his body brushed against hers again. Had it been intentional? And why hadn't one of them taken a step back? "What kept you sane?"

"Sane?"

"Yes. You know. From climbing the walls and stuff. I heard men need sex every so often."

He smiled and the force of it sent her senses reeling.

"Remind me to give you all the details one day. Now, back to our earlier topic, why did you come to the door with a gun and why the packed bags?"

They were back to that?

But then maybe they should be. She needed to call a cab and get to the airport. And just like she didn't want to involve her mother and Aunt Rachel in whatever was going on, she definitely didn't want to involve Bane. Maybe she should have lied and said she was involved with someone else. Then he would have gotten angry and left, and she would be free to do as the note advised and disappear. Whatever was going on was her issue and not his.

She nibbled her lips as she tried coming up with something that would sound reasonable. Something that wasn't too much of a lie. So she said, "The reason for the packed luggage is because I'm taking a trip."

He looked at her as if to say *duh*. Instead, he held her gaze and asked, "Business or pleasure?"

"Business."

"Where are you headed?"

If she told him the Bahamas, he would question if it really was a business trip, so she said, "Chicago."

"Fine. I'll go with you."

She blinked, suddenly feeling anxiety closing in on her. "Go with me?"

"Yes. I'm on leave so I can do that," he said calmly. "Besides, it's time I got to know you again, and I want you to get to know me."

She drew in a breath, feeling her control deteriorating. Those hazel eyes had always been her weakness.

She knew she was a goner when he asked in a husky

voice, "You do want to get to know me all over again, don't you, Crystal Gayle?"

Getting to know Brisbane Westmoreland the first time around had been like a roller coaster, and she'd definitely enjoyed the ride. There was no doubt that getting to know the new Bane would be even more exhilarating. Now she could enjoy the ride as a woman in control of her own destiny and not as a girl whose life was dictated by her parents. A woman who was older, mature and could appreciate the explosiveness of a relationship with him.

As if he knew what she was thinking and wanted to drive that point home, he caressed the side of her face with the tip of his finger. "I definitely want to get to know you again, Crystal."

Then he brought her body closer to his. She felt his erection pressing hard against her middle and a craving she'd tried to put to rest years ago reared its greedy head, making her force back a moan. When his finger left her face to tug on a section of her hair, sensations she hadn't felt in years ran rampant through her womb.

She stared into his eyes. Hazel eyes that had literally branded her the first time she'd gazed into them. Eyes belonging to Bane. *Her* Bane. And he had admitted just moments ago to keeping their vows all this time. That meant he had five years of need and hunger stored inside him. The thought sent heated blood racing through her veins.

Then he shifted. The movement nudged his knees between hers so she could feel his hard bulge even more. Intentional or not, she wasn't sure. The only thing she was certain about was that if she didn't get her self-control back, she would jump his bones without a second thought. And that wasn't good. She didn't even know him anymore.

He leaned in slowly—too slowly, which let her know this side of Bane wasn't different…at least when it came to this. He'd always let her establish the pace, so as not to take advantage of the difference in their ages and experience levels. She'd always known she hadn't been Bane's first girl, but he'd been her first guy. And he'd always handled her with tenderness.

Bane was letting her take the lead now, and she intended to take it to a whole other level. At that moment, she didn't care that they'd both changed; she wanted his hands on her and his tongue in her mouth. To be totally honest, she needed more but she would settle for those two things now…even if she knew there probably wouldn't be a later.

He bent his head closer, and she refused to consider anything other than what she wanted, needed and had gone five years without. She clutched tight to his shoulders and leaned up on tiptoes to cover his mouth with hers.

Bane wasn't sure what was more dangerous. Storming an extremist stronghold in the middle of the night, or having his way with Crystal's mouth after all these years of going without her taste. But now was not the time to dwell on it. It was time to act.

The way their mouths mated seemed as natural as breathing, and he was glad time had not diminished the desire they'd always shared.

When she slid her tongue inside his mouth, memories of the last time they'd kissed flooded his mind. It had been on their wedding day, during their honeymoon in a small hotel in Utah. He recalled very little about the room itself, only what they'd done within those four walls. And they'd done plenty.

But now, this very minute, they were making new memories. He had dreamed about, thought about and wished for this moment for so long. She took the kiss deeper and he wrapped his arms around her waist and pulled her closer, loving the feel of her body plastered against his.

He loved her taste. Always had and always would. When she sucked on his tongue, his heartbeat thundered in his chest and his erection throbbed mercilessly behind his zipper. He was tempted to devour her and tried like hell to keep his self-control in check. But it became too much. Five years without her had taken its toll.

Suddenly he became the aggressor, taking her mouth with a hunger he felt all the way to the soles of his feet. He wanted her to feel him in every part of her body. And when he finally caught her wriggling tongue, he feasted on it.

The one thing that had consumed his mind on their wedding day was the same thing consuming his mind right now. Crystal was his. Undeniably, unquestionably and indisputably his.

He thrust his tongue even deeper into her mouth. He knew he had to pull back; otherwise he would consume her whole. Especially now, when he was filled with the need to do the one thing he shouldn't do, which was to sweep her off her feet and head for the nearest bedroom. He had wanted this moment for so long… Kissing her filled him with sensations so deliciously intoxicating that he could barely think straight.

Bane knew he was embarking on a mission more dangerous than any he'd gone on as a SEAL. Crystal had al-

ways been both his weakness and his strength. She was
an ache he'd always had to ease. Some way, somehow, he
had to show her, prove to her, that any changes he'd made
over the past five years were all good and would benefit both of them. Otherwise, the time they'd spent apart
would have been for nothing. He refused to accept that.

Reluctant to do so but knowing he should, Bane ended
the kiss. But he wasn't ready to release her yet and his
hands moved from her waist to boldly cup her backside.
And while she was snuggled so close to him, his hands
moved up and down the length of her spine before returning to cup her backside again. Now that she was back
in his life, he couldn't imagine her being out of it again.

That thought drove him to reiterate something he'd
said earlier. "I'm going to Chicago with you."

Slowly recovering from their kiss, Crystal tilted her
head back and gazed up at Bane. Her lips had ground
against his. Her tongue had initiated a dance inside his
mouth that had been as perfect as anything she'd ever
known. And he had reciprocated by kissing her back
with equal need. Waves of passion had consumed her,
nearly drowning her.

But now she had reclaimed her senses and the words
he'd spoken infiltrated her mind. She knew there was no
way he could go anywhere with her. She was about to
open her mouth to tell him so when her cell phone rang.
She tensed. Who could be contacting her? She seldom
got calls.

"You plan on getting that?" Bane murmured the question while placing a kiss on the side of her neck.

She swallowed. Should she? It could be the airline calling her for some reason. She had left them her number in

case her flight was delayed or canceled. "Yes," she said, quickly moving away from him to grab the phone off the table, right next to where she had laid the gun. Seeing the weapon was a reminder of what she had to do and why she couldn't let Bane sidetrack her.

She clicked on her cell phone. "Hello?"

"Don't try getting away, Ms. Newsome. We will find you." And then she heard a click ending the call.

Crystal's heart thumped painfully in her chest. Who was the caller? How did the person get her private number? How did the person know she was trying to get away? She turned toward Bane. Something in her eyes must have told him the call had troubled her because he quickly crossed the room to her. "Crystal, what's wrong?"

She took a deep breath, not knowing what to do or say. She stared up at him as she nervously bit her lip. Should she level with Bane and tell him everything that was going on? The note had said not to trust anyone, but how could she not trust the one and only person she'd always trusted?

"I don't know what's wrong," she said quietly.

She pulled away to reach for her purse and retrieve the note. "I got this note at work today," she said, handing it to him. "And I don't know who sent it."

She waited while he read it and when he glanced back up at her, she said, "Yesterday someone broke into my locker at work, and I noticed someone following me home today."

"Following you?"

"Yes. I thought maybe I was imagining things at first, but when the driver stayed discreetly behind me, I knew that I wasn't. I deliberately lost the car in all the holiday shoppers at one of the busiest malls."

"What about that phone call just now?" he asked, studying her.

She told him what the caller had said. "I don't know who it was or how they got my number."

Bane didn't say anything for a minute. "Is that the reason for the packed bags? You're doing what the note said and disappearing?"

"Yes. Those guys said craziness might start happening and—"

Bane frowned. "What guys?"

"Last month while I was eating lunch at a restaurant near work, I was approached by two government men. They showed me credentials to prove it. They knew about the project I'm working on at Seton and said Homeland Security was concerned about my research getting into the wrong hands. They offered me a chance to work for the government at some lab in DC, along with two other chemists who're working on similar research."

"And?"

"I turned them down. They accepted my answer, but warned me that there were people out there with criminal intent who would do just about anything to get their hands on my research. They gave me their business card and told me to call them if any craziness happened."

"Have you called them?"

"No. After reading the note I wasn't sure who I could trust. At this point that includes Homeland Security."

"Do you still have the business card those guys gave you?"

"Yes."

"May I see it?"

"Yes." She reached for her purse again. She handed

the card to him and watched him study it before snapping several pictures of it with his mobile phone.

"What are you doing?"

He glanced over at her. "Verifying those guys are who they say they are. I'm sending this to someone who can do that for me." He then handed her back the card. "Just what kind of research are you working on?"

She paused a moment before saying. "Obscured Reality, or OR as it's most often called."

"Obscured Reality?"

She nodded. "Yes. It's the ability to make objects invisible."

Four

Bane lifted a brow. "Did you say your research was finding a way to make objects invisible?"

"Yes. Although it hasn't been perfected yet, it won't be long before I perform the first test."

Because he was a SEAL, Bane was aware of advances in technology that most people didn't know about, especially when it came to advanced weapons technology. But he'd never considered that objects could become invisible to the naked eye. He could imagine the chaos it would cause if such a thing fell into the wrong hands.

"And you think this note is legit?" he asked.

"If I doubted it before, that phone call pretty much proved otherwise. That's why I'm leaving."

He nodded. "And that's why I'm going with you."

She shook her head. "You can't go with me, Bane, and I don't have time to argue with you about it. I need to get to the airport."

Argue?

It suddenly dawned on him that in all the years he and Crystal had been together, mostly sneaking around to do so, they'd never argued. They had always been of one accord, always in sync with their thoughts, plans and ideas. The very concept of them not agreeing about something just couldn't compute with him. Of course it would be logical not to be in complete harmony since they were different people now.

Even so, him going with her was not up for discussion.

"How were you planning to get to the airport? Drive?" he asked her.

She shook her head. "No. I was going to call a cab and leave my car here."

"Then, I will take you. We can talk some more on the way."

"Okay, let me close up everything. Won't take but a second."

His gaze followed her movements as she went from room to room turning off lights and unplugging electrical items. Her movements were swift, yet sexy as hell and his body responded to them. She'd always had a cute shape, but this grown-up Crystal was rocking curves like he couldn't believe.

Earlier she had asked how he'd maintained his sanity without sex. He wondered how she'd maintained hers. They had enjoyed each other and he was convinced the only reason she hadn't gotten pregnant was because when it came to her, he'd always been responsible. A teenage pregnancy was something neither of them had needed to deal with.

She leaned down to pick up something off the floor

and the way the denim stretched across her shapely back-side sent heat rushing through him. He drew in a deep breath. Now was not the time to think about how hot his wife was. What should be consuming his mind was finding out the identity of the person responsible for her fleeing her home. Whoever was messing with her would definitely have to deal with him.

"At least I'm going where there's plenty of sunshine."

His brow furrowed. Did she honestly think there was sunshine in Chicago this time of the year? She met his gaze and he knew from the uh-oh look on her face that she'd unintentionally let that slip.

He was reminded now that although they'd never ar-gued, they had lied quite a few times. But never to each other. Mainly the fibs had been for their families. They'd gotten good at it, although Dillon would catch Bane in his lies more often than not.

Crossing the room, Bane stopped in front of her. "You lied to me about where you're going, didn't you?"

She took a deep breath and he could hear the beats of her heart. They were coming fast and furious. Bane wasn't sure whether her heart was pounding because he was confronting her about the lie or because his nearness unnerved her like hers did him. Even when he should be upset about her lying to him, all he wanted to do was lean in closer and taste her again.

"Yes, I lied. I'm not going to Chicago but to the Baha-mas. But when I lied about it, it was for your own good."

"For my own good?" he repeated as if making sure he'd heard her right.

"Yes. In the past I was the reason you got into trouble. Now you're a SEAL and I won't be responsible for you getting into more trouble on my account."

He stared at her. Didn't she know whatever he'd done in the past had been of his own free will? During those days he would have done anything to be with her. There was no way he could have stayed away as her father had demanded. Her parents hadn't even given them a chance just because Bane's last name was Westmoreland. Although Carl Newsome had claimed Bane's age had been the major factor, Bane often wondered if that was true.

Everyone knew how much he'd loved Crystal. Members of his family had thought he was insane, and in a way he had been. Insanely in love. Hadn't his brother Riley even told him once that no man should love any female that much? Bane wondered if Riley was singing that same tune now that he was married to Alpha. Bane doubted it. All it took was to see his brother and Alpha together to know Riley now understood how deeply a man could love a woman.

"Crystal?" he said, trying to keep his voice on a serious note because he knew she actually believed what she'd said. "Stop thinking you're the reason I was such a badass back in the day. When I met you I was already getting into trouble with the law. After I hooked up with you, I actually got in less trouble."

She rolled her eyes. "That's not the way I remember it."

"You remember it the way your parents wanted you to remember it. Yes, I deliberately defied your father whenever he tried keeping us apart, but it wasn't as if I was a gangster or anything."

A smile curved his lips as he continued, "At least not after meeting you. With you I was on my best behavior. You even nailed the reason I behaved that way. You're the one who pointed out it had everything to do with the loss of my parents and aunt and uncle in that plane crash. The depth of our grief overpowered me, Bailey and the twins, and getting into trouble was our outlet. That just goes to show how smart you were even back then, and your theory made sense. Remember all those long talks we used to have?"

She nodded. "Yes, by the side of the road or in our private place. Our family thought all those times the sheriff found us that we were making out in your truck or something. And all we'd been doing was talking. I tried telling my parents that but they wouldn't listen. You were a Westmoreland and they wanted to think the worst. They believed I was sexually active when I wasn't."

He recalled those times. Yes, they had been caught parking, and cutting school had become almost the norm, but all they'd done was spend time together talking. He'd refused to go all the way with her until she was older. The first time they'd had sex was when she'd turned seventeen. By then they'd been together almost two years.

At least Dillon had believed Bane when he'd told his brother he hadn't touched her. However, given their relationship, it would have been crazy to think they wouldn't get around to making love one day, and Dillon had had the common sense to know that. Instead of giving Bane grief about it, his older brother had lectured him about being responsible and taking precautions.

Bane would never forget the night they'd finally made love. And it hadn't been in the backseat of his truck. He had taken her to the cabin he'd built as a gift for her seventeenth birthday. He'd constructed it on the land he was to inherit, Bane's Ponderosa.

It was a night he would never forget. Waiting had almost done them in, but in the end they'd known they'd done the right thing. That night had been so unbelievably special and he'd known she would be his forever. He knew on that night that one day he would make her his wife.

In fact it had been that night when he'd asked her to marry him once she finished school, and she'd agreed. And that had been the plan until her parents made things even worse for them after she'd turned seventeen.

Crystal had retaliated by refusing to go to school. And when her parents had threatened to have him put in jail if he came on their property, he and Crystal had eloped. He hadn't counted on her parents sending her away the moment Sheriff Harper found them.

Bane had come close to telling everyone they'd gotten married; no one had the right to separate them. But something Dillon had said about the future had given him pause.

Once he'd revealed they were married, he'd known Crystal would not go back to school. And he of all people had known just how smart she was.

That was when he'd decided to make the sacrifice and let her go. That had been the hardest decision he'd ever made. Lucky for him, Bailey had put her pickpocketing skills to work and swiped old man Newsome's cell phone to get Crystal's aunt's phone number.

"I need to go, Bane," Crystal said, intruding into his memories. "I'll give you my number and we can talk when I get to where I'm going."

Then in a rush, she added, "I'll call to let you know when I arrive in the Bahamas so you'll know I'm okay."

He stared at her. Evidently she didn't get it and it was about time that she did. "Crystal," he said in what he hoped was a tone that grabbed her absolute attention. When she stared at him he knew it had. "If you think I'm going to let you disappear on your own, then you really don't know me. The old Bane did let you disappear when your father sent you away. But at the time I figured it was for your own good. But those days are over. There's no way in hell you're disappearing on me again."

From her blistering scowl he could tell she didn't appreciate what he'd said. When she opened her mouth to reply, he quickly held up his hand. "I know it's been five years and that we have changed. But there's something with us that hasn't changed."

"What?" she asked in an annoyed tone.

"No matter what happens, we're in this together. That's how things have always been with us, right?"

"Yes, but that was then, Bane."

"And that's how it is now. We're married," he said, touching the locket he'd given her on their wedding day. Just knowing she was still wearing it meant everything to him. "We're in this together, Crystal. Got that?"

For a minute Crystal didn't say anything and then through clenched teeth, she snapped, "Yes, I got it."

There was no way she could *not* get it when he'd spoken so matter-of-factly. She'd never liked being bossed around and he knew that, which was why he'd never done it before. They had understood each other so well. And in the past they'd made decisions together, especially those that defied anyone trying to keep them apart, whether it was her family or his.

But this Bane was difficult to deal with. Didn't he understand it was not in his best interest to go anywhere with her?

Without saying anything else she walked away, leaving him standing in the middle of her living room while she went into the kitchen to check the locks on the back door. She needed time alone. Time away from him. His unexpected arrival had torpedoed her world.

As soon as she was out of his view, she leaned against the kitchen counter and released a sigh as blood pounded through her body. The man she'd loved was back after five years. One moment she'd been rushing around, trying to disappear, and the next she was opening the door for Bane. They had been separated for so long she'd thought... What?

That he wasn't going to come for her. But if she'd really thought that then why hadn't she gotten on with her life?

There were a lot of other whys she needed answered. Why had he decided to become a SEAL? Placing his life at risk with each mission? Better yet, why had he wanted to be involved in something that would keep him from her longer? And why had he shown up today of all days, when her normal life was turned upside down?

On top of everything else, he wanted to take over, as if he'd been here all the time. As if she didn't know what she was doing. As if she hadn't taken care of her own business for the past five years without him.

"Need help in there?" he called out.

Crystal gritted her teeth. "No, I've got this." She crossed the kitchen floor to check the locks on the back door.

What did he expect of her? Of them?

And of all things, within ten minutes of being inside her house they had kissed. A kiss she'd initiated. He might have made the first move by lowering his head, but she had been the one to make the connection. The memory of their mouths locking and tongues tasting had her feeling all hot inside. It had definitely proved they were still attracted to each other. That kiss had snatched all her senses and made her weak in the knees. She was certain she could still taste him on her lips.

She pushed a strand of hair back from her face and walked out of the kitchen and stopped in the living room. Bane's back was to her as he stood in front of her fireplace, staring at the framed photographs on her mantel. Except for one picture of her parents, all the rest were of him or of her and him. Most had been taken when they'd dated and the others when they'd eloped.

He turned around and their gazes met. She almost forgot to breathe. Was that heat in her stomach? And why was her heart beating a mile a minute? She drew in a deep breath wondering what he was thinking. Had he remembered each and every moment in those pictures? Did he remember how in love they'd been? Did he realize, married or not, they were different people now and needed to get to know each other all over again?

Should they?

Could they?

She broke eye contact to look at where her luggage had been. Then she glanced back at him. "You've taken my bags out already?"

"Yes."

"I didn't hear anything. Not even the door open."

A smile tugged at the corner of his lips. "That's the way a SEAL operates."

Five

"I was sorry to hear about your dad, Crystal," Bane said, after easing the car onto the interstate. "Although the two of us never got along, he was still your father."

He felt her gaze on him, and he wanted to take his eyes off the road and look at her but decided not to. She was gorgeous and every time he gazed at her he felt desire seep into his bones. He needed to keep his self-control so he could convince her that he was coming with her when she left town.

"Thanks. Sending me away to live with Aunt Rachel widened the chasm between us but we made amends before he died...as best we could, considering everything." She was quiet for a moment before continuing, "He even told me he loved me, Bane. And I told him I loved him, as well. Dad leaving me the ranch was a shocker because he said he would be selling it to make sure I never had a reason to return to Denver. But after he died I found out he had left it to me. I wasn't aware he still owned it and assumed he'd sold it like he said he would do."

Bane had assumed Mr. Newsome had sold it, as well. Whenever he came home, Dillon had mentioned that the Newsome place was still deserted, but Bane had assumed the repairs needed around the place hadn't made it an easy sale. But there was something else he'd wanted to tell her. "It's admirable that you're working on your PhD, Crystal. For someone who claimed they hated school, that's quite an accomplishment."

"No big deal. Since I didn't have a life I decided to go to school full-time. All year-round. Nonstop. And when I took a placement test, there were classes I didn't have to take. My parents were happy that I was focusing on my studies again."

And not on him, he thought, and then asked her the question that had nagged at him since he'd first seen her tonight. "How did you do it?"

"Do what?"

"Keep the guys away. You're a very beautiful woman so I'm sure plenty tried hitting on you."

He glanced over and saw the compliment had made her blush. He meant it. She had the kind of beauty he'd never been able to explain with words.

"The guys stayed away because they thought I was gay."

Bane almost swerved into another lane. Placing a tight grip on the steering wheel, he glanced over at her again. "They thought what?"

"That I was gay. I didn't have a boyfriend so what else were they to think? The rumor started in college when I refused all their advances, even the guys on the football team, who were in such high demand on campus. They figured if I wasn't into them, then I must be into females."

"Why didn't you tell them you were a married woman?"

"What good would that have done with a husband who never came around?"

He could imagine how she'd felt knowing a rumor was circulating about her. One that was false.

"I thought about you every day, Crystal."

"Did you?"

He heard the skepticism in her tone. Did she not believe him? He was about to question her when she said, "This isn't the way to the airport, Bane."

"We aren't going to the airport."

"Not going to the airport? And just when did you decide that?"

"When I noticed we were being followed."

They were being followed?

Crystal glanced over at Bane. "How do you know?"

"Because although the driver is trying to be inconspicuous, that blue car has been tailing us for a while."

"Blue car?"

"Yes."

Her muscles trembled. "The car that followed me earlier was blue. But how would he know to follow you when we're not in my car?"

"Evidently someone saw us getting into mine."

The feel of goose bumps moved up her neck. "If the person saw us leave that means he knows where I live."

"Pretty much. But don't worry about it."

His calm unnerved her. How could he tell her not to worry? It was her home they were talking about. Whoever was after her would probably trash her house looking for something that wasn't there.

As if Bane read her mind, he said, "The reason I told you not to worry is because Flip is watching your place for me."

She stared over at him. "Someone you know is watching my house?"

He exited off the interstate. "Yes. David Holloway is one of my team members, who happens to live here in Dallas. His code name is Flipper because he's the best diver on the team. I contacted him when my plane landed to let him know I was in town. I called him again when I took out your luggage. I noticed a strange car in the driveway across the street."

Crystal was trying hard to keep up. He didn't live in her neighborhood, so how could he tell when some car was out of place? "How did you know it was a strange car?"

"I sat in front of your place for two hours waiting for you to come home and it wasn't parked there then," he said, turning another corner.

She noticed they were driving in an area she wasn't familiar with and wondered where in the heck they were going. "That's it? You figured it was out of place because it hadn't been there earlier?"

"That was enough. I'm trained to take stock of my surroundings."

Evidently, she thought. "And this Flipper guy went to my house after we left?"

"He got there just as we were leaving. Flip and his brothers will be keeping an eye on the place while you're gone."

She arched a brow. "Brothers?"

Bane looked over at her when he brought the car to a stop at a traffic light. "Yes, he has four. All SEALs. Your place is in good hands for now."

She was glad to hear that, but she couldn't help wishing the only hands her house was in were hers. Granted, she leased it rather than owned it, but it was the only house she'd lived in since moving to Dallas. When she noticed him glancing in the rearview mirror and grinning she asked, "What's so funny?"

"Ambush. I deliberately had the driver of the blue car follow us here and Flip's brothers were waiting."

"How did they know?"

"When Flip's brothers noticed I was being followed, they followed the blue car. Then one of Flip's brothers passed the blue car and got in the front of us to lead me off the interstate. The others went ahead and were ready to stop the guy at that intersection back there."

Nervousness danced around in her stomach. "So now we can continue to the airport?"

"No," he said, pulling the car into what appeared to be the parking lot of an abandoned warehouse. After parking the car and turning off the lights, he grabbed the mobile phone he'd placed on the dashboard. He glanced down at it for a minute before looking back at her. "There might be others looking for us there."

"Why would you think that?"

He pushed back in the seat to stretch out his legs. "Remember those two men who approached you about coming to work for Homeland Security?"

"Yes, what about them?"

"It seems *they* are the bad guys."

Bane wished he could kiss the shocked look right off Crystal's face, beginning at her eyes and moving slowly downward to her lips.

"That's not possible," she said. "I saw their credentials."

"Whatever credentials they had were faked. The department they claimed to work for under Homeland Security doesn't even exist."

"Are you sure?"

"Positive. I texted a copy of that business card to a friend at Homeland Security and a few minutes ago he verified what I'd suspected."

He watched her nibble her bottom lip and wished seeing her do so didn't have such an arousing effect on him. He had to stay focused. "The mystery of that note bothers me."

"How so?"

"Did the person who wrote it have your best interest at heart, or did he or she advise you to disappear for a reason, hoping when you did it would make it easier for those guys to find you?"

She lifted a brow. "You think someone at Seton Industries, the person who put that note in my desk, is in cahoots with those two guys?"

"You have to admit that's a strong possibility. You said someone broke into your locker. Who would have access to that area other than another employee?"

Bane didn't like this. He and Crystal should be at her place talking about their future and how they would get beyond the five years they'd spent apart.

He started to say something else when his mobile phone rang with Flipper's ringtone. He grabbed it off his dashboard. "What you got, Flip?"

"A bunch of crazies, man. No sooner than you and the blue car pull off, a black sedan pulled up and two goons got out. It was like watching a scene out of *Men in Black* with both of them dressed in black suits and all. Not sure how they planned to break into your wife's place but there's no doubt in my mind that was their intent. Until…"

Bane lifted a brow. "Until what?"

"Until they noticed the infrared beam Mark had leveled in the center of their chests. I guess knowing we could blow their guts out freaked them, especially since we could see them but they couldn't see us. I've never seen two men run back to their car so fast."

Bane shook his head. "You and your brothers are having fun with this, aren't you?"

"Yes, I guess you can say that."

Flip would. Although Bane hadn't met any of Flipper's brothers, he'd heard about them. They had inherited their thirst for excitement and danger from their father, who'd retired as a SEAL. "What about the driver of the blue car?"

"He got out and hauled ass. Left the car running. You said not to shoot anybody so my brothers let him go. Sure you don't want to involve the cops?"

"Not yet." Bane told Flipper about who he figured the men in black were.

"Impersonating government officials isn't good," Flipper said.

Bane had to agree. He glanced over at Crystal and saw she'd been trying to follow his conversation. "You're right. But at least you put the fear of God in them. However, don't be surprised if they come back."

"We'll be ready. Take care of yourself and your lady."

Bane nodded. "I intend to."

He had barely clicked off the phone when Crystal asked, "They broke into my house?"

Her shoulders sagged and he wished he had told Flipper it was okay for his brothers to shoot the bastards after all. He hated that she was going through this. "No, but that had been their intent. Flipper and his brother ran them off." There was no need telling her the method they'd used to do so. "They'll be back if they believe you have information or data stored somewhere in your house."

"I don't."

"I doubt they know that, and the first place they'll look is your computer."

"So what now? Where do we go?"

He checked his watch. It was late. "Find a hotel."

She narrowed her eyes. "Why?"

Not for the reason I want, he thought, again remembering the last time he'd been in a hotel room with her. The memory of her naked on that bed and all they'd been doing before the sheriff had shown up was what had kept him sane during dangerous missions.

"We're going to a hotel to sleep and put a plan of action in place, Crystal. As much as I want to make love to you, I've got a feeling the want isn't mutual."

Which meant it would be a long night.

with him would definitely be like old times, but she was no longer a teenager who thought she could never get enough of Bane Westmoreland. She was a woman on the run with a husband she no longer knew. "We're too old for parked cars, Bane."

"I know. That's why I suggested a hotel."

She turned toward him. It was time to burst his bubble. "If we go to a hotel we get separate rooms."

"Why? We're married."

She tried to ignore the sexiness of his voice. And she definitely didn't need to notice the electricity sizzling in the air between them. Yes, they were married, but hadn't it already been established that things had changed? That *they* had changed? For starters, she was no longer a dreamer but a realist. And he was no longer the guy who claimed she would always be his love for life. Apparently the navy had booted her aside.

"Legally yes, we are married, but that's about all. Five years is a long time. We've already established that we're different people now. You may not like the new me, and for all I know I may not like the new you."

"I don't *like* you, Crystal. Never have. I fell in love with you the first time I saw you."

Now, why would he go and say something like that? If he really felt that way, wouldn't he have come back long before now? And why was she now remembering that day when she had been walking home from school, minding her own business, and he'd passed her on his motorcycle. He'd made a U-turn and the moment he'd stopped his bike, taken off his helmet and turned those hazel eyes on her, she'd been lost. So if he wanted to say that he'd fallen in love with her the moment he'd first seen her, she could certainly make that same claim about him.

But there were still those five years apart between them.

"Will it make you feel better if there were two beds in the room?"

Crystal took a breath. *Not really.* Even after being separated for five years she still found him captivating. Even now, tingles of awareness were invading her entire body. She couldn't look at any part of him without getting naughty thoughts. Being in close quarters with him all night would only be asking for trouble. She shook her head. "Doubt that will work, Bane."

He shrugged broad shoulders. "It will have to work, because I don't plan on letting you out of my sight until we get to the bottom of what's going on."

Her gaze narrowed on him. She was about to tell him that when it came to her he didn't make any decisions, when his cell phone went off again. He quickly reached for it. "Yes?"

Crystal studied his face. Whatever the caller was saying was making him angry. She could tell by the fire she saw forming in the depths of his eyes, the tightening of his jaw and the way his fingers gripped the phone. And she couldn't miss the abrasive tone of his voice.

She was certain the call was about her, which was why his gaze flicked to her time and time again. Gone was that hot and steamy I-can't-wait-to-get-some-of-you look in his eyes. It had been replaced with a look that clearly said that if pushed, Brisbane Westmoreland was liable to hurt somebody.

She pushed her hair back from her face and silently tapped her fingers on the car's console. She couldn't wait for the call to end so she could find out what was going on.

As soon as she heard him click off the phone she

turned, ready to inquire, but he held up a finger to silence her. Already he had clicked someone else's number. He then quickly barked the words into his phone. "Code purple. Will enlighten everyone in a few."

As soon as he disconnected the call she asked, "What was that about?"

He didn't say anything for a long moment. He just stared at her as if he was trying to make up his mind about something.

She frowned and said, "And don't you dare think about not telling me what's going on, Bane."

Bane had contemplated doing just what she'd accused him of. But he knew he couldn't. Crystal was too intelligent, too quick to figure out things. Besides, she needed to know what they were up against and the caution they would have to take.

But more than anything, he needed her to trust him and to believe that he would never let anyone touch a single hair on her head.

"Bane?"

He took a deep breath. "First, give me your cell phone."

"My cell phone?"

"Yes."

She stared at him for a second, then went into her purse to retrieve her phone. He took it and then got out of the car. Throwing the phone on the pavement and ignoring her shocked gasp, he used his foot to stomp it into pieces.

"Are you crazy? What do you think you're doing?" she asked in outrage after getting out of the car to save her phone. Of course it was too late.

"I'm destroying your phone."

She placed her hands on her hips and glared up at him. "I see that. What I want to know is why."

"There's a chance a tracking device is on it."

"What are you talking about?"

"Things are more serious than I thought or what you might know, Crystal."

She stiffened her spine. "Well, I've got news for you. I don't know anything other than what I received in that note today and that my locker was tampered with and a blue car has been following me."

He glanced around. "Come on, let's get back inside the car. I'll tell you what I know."

She looked down at her smashed phone in disgust before going around the front of the SUV to get back inside. As soon as they had gotten inside the car, she said, "Tell me."

She touched his arm and a surge of desire rushed through him. Evidently it shone in his eyes because she quickly snatched her hand away. "Sorry."

He grabbed her hand, entwined their fingers and met her gaze. "Don't ever apologize for touching me."

Instead of a response, she nervously swiped her tongue across her bottom lip and his own tongue tingled, dying to mate with hers. Since he figured he couldn't kiss her anytime soon, he would tell her what she wanted to know. What she needed to know.

Ignoring the thud in his chest from holding her hand in his, he said, "My contact at Homeland Security did some more digging, even went so far as to tap into classified information. It seems you've been watched for a while."

She lifted a brow. "By who?"

"Mainly the government. They are aware of the research you're working on."

She shrugged. "I figured they were. Seton sent periodic reports to them as part of national security. Besides, the funding for my research was a grant subsidized by the government."

"Well, it seems the report got into the hands of someone it shouldn't have. To make a long story short, a plan was devised to kidnap you and the two other biochemists working on similar projects. They were to take the three of you to a lab underground somewhere and force you to work together and perfect a formula they'd use to their advantage."

Crystal shook her head. "That plan is preposterous."

Bane wished she wouldn't do that. Shake her head and make her hair fan across her face and place more emphasis on her dark eyes. Momentarily he lost his concentration. He couldn't afford any distractions now. There was too much at stake. "Whoever came up with the idea evidently didn't think so. And now you're the missing link."

She leaned back and frowned. "What do you mean I'm the missing link?"

His hand tightened on hers. "The other two chemists were abducted yesterday. One was leaving his home for work and the other chemist was leaving the gym around noon. The plan was to kidnap the three of you within hours of each other. However, their plan to grab you was foiled. But since they are determined to get their hands on the formula, they won't give up."

The spark in her eyes told him she clearly understood what he was saying. She was vital to these guys' plans and they didn't intend to fail. That spark also told him something else. She would like to see them try to grab her. He still had the ability to read her mind sometimes. She still had the spunk he'd always admired in her.

He swallowed hard when she eased her hand from his and broke eye contact to gaze out of the car's windshield. She was thinking, trying to come up with her own plan. One that didn't include him. More for his safety than anything else, he figured. And while she was spending that time thinking, he was spending his time feeling possessive, protective and proactive. If anyone thought they would grab her from him, then they didn't know Bane Westmoreland.

She looked back at him and because he had a feeling he knew what she was about to say, he cut her off before she could start. "I won't leave you unprotected, so forget it."

When she just continued to look at him, he added, "I need you to trust my ability to keep us safe."

A ripple of awareness floated between them and he tried to ignore it. Knowing he had her trust was more important at the moment.

"It's going to be hard, Bane," she said softly. "I've been on my own for a long time."

Five years. And not for the first time he wondered if he'd done the right thing in staying away. She had been his wife, yet he'd left her believing that living apart was the best thing for both of them. That they'd both needed to grow up and mature. Especially him. And he had. But what if he hadn't shown up today? What if she'd gotten kidnapped like those other two chemists? What if—

"I will trust you in this, Bane."

Her words intruded into his thoughts. He nodded. He was more than ready to be the husband she deserved, but he had to show her that she could trust him. Not just to keep her safe, but to build a life with her.

"So…" she said with a heavy sigh. "What now?"

A smile touched his lips. "Now we show them that together we're a force to reckon with."

A force to reckon with.

Crystal couldn't help but smile. That was how Sheriff Harper used to describe them. Nothing, not even the threat of jail time, could keep Bane from her or her from him. They'd been that fixated on each other.

Bane's cell phone signaled a text massage had come through and he grabbed the phone off the dashboard. Out the car window she saw they were parked in an unlit area. The only illumination was from the stars and moon overhead. Bane read the text with his full attention while her full attention was on him. She couldn't help but admire the way his wide shoulders fit his leather jacket and the casual way he sat in his seat. He had pushed the seat back to accommodate his long legs. And speaking of those long legs…

She loved how they looked bare, whenever he went swimming, and when they were covered in jeans, like they were now. Or when he rode his motorcycle or one of the horses from his family ranch. She'd known how to ride when she met him, but with his help, she had perfected the skill. He'd also taught her how to ride a motorcycle, shoot a gun and climb mountains. She had shared his love for the outdoors and they would spend time together outside whenever they could.

She swept her gaze over him from head to toe, thinking he was definitely sheer male perfection, the epitome of every woman's fantasy. It was only when he'd cleared his throat that she realized he had finished reading the text and had caught her ogling him.

"Yes? Did you say something?"

He chuckled. "No. Just wanted you to know that our ride will be here in a few minutes."

She lifted a brow. "Our ride?"

"Yes. We're changing vehicles. Chances are the people looking for you have already ID'd this one, so we need to swap it out."

"So who's bringing us another vehicle?" she asked, glancing out the window. Other than a huge vacant building, the parking lot was empty.

"Flip's dad."

She frowned. "His dad?"

"Yes. He's an ex-SEAL."

Moments later Crystal heard the sound of another vehicle pull up and noted the driver had turned out the headlights. Bane looked over at her.

"That's our ride."

Seven

Bane gathered their belongings out of the SUV so they could place them in the trunk of the car Mr. Holloway had delivered.

Flip favored his father. Same shade of blue eyes and blond hair, although the older man had streaks of gray. It was easy to tell the man had been a SEAL. A commanding officer. He was still alert and wore an intense look on his face. And it was quite obvious that even at the age of sixty-five, he was in great shape physically. He was ready for anything and could probably still hold his own.

"Don't need to know where you're headed. The less people who know the better. Just be safe," the older man said, handing Bane the keys.

"I will, and thanks for everything, Mr. Holloway. I owe you and your family."

Mr. Holloway waved off his words. "No, you don't.

David told me and his brothers what happened during your last mission when you saved his life. Besides, any friend of my boys is a friend of mine. If you get in a pinch, just give us a call."

Bane didn't plan on getting in a pinch, but figured it was best to accept the offer just the same. "I will, and thanks."

Crystal was already seated inside the new car with her seat belt snapped in place. The older man followed Bane's gaze. "I understand that's your wife who you haven't seen in a while."

Bane nodded as he looked back at the man. "Yes, that's right."

"And she waited for you to come back for all that time?"

Bane nodded, remembering what Crystal had told him. She had kept her promise like he'd kept his. "Yes, she waited."

The older man smiled. "Then, you're a very lucky man. Take care of yourself and your wife."

His wife. He liked the sound of that. He was ready to finally claim her as his wife—but he had to keep her safe first. "I will. Again, thanks for all you and your sons have done. Are still doing." He knew Flip and his brothers would be keeping an eye on Crystal's place for a while.

"Don't mention it." Mr. Holloway gave him a supportive pat on the shoulder before getting into the SUV to drive off.

Bane quickly walked to the car, got inside, closed the door and locked it.

Crystal glanced over at him. "Where to now?"

He could hear the exhaustion in her voice. It was close

to eleven. Probably past her bedtime. "A hotel, but not here in Dallas. Get some sleep. We'll be riding for a while."

"Okay."

She didn't ask where they were headed and as he started the ignition, he watched her lower her seat into a reclining position. He couldn't stop his appreciative gaze from sweeping over her, taking in how the denim molded to her hips and thighs. At eighteen she'd had a slender figure. Now she was amazingly curvy with a small waist. Forcing his eyes off her, he adjusted the car's temperature to a comfortable setting. It had gotten pretty cold outside.

As he pulled out of the parking lot he saw her starting to doze off. She looked just as beautiful with her eyes closed as she did when they were open. This was what he had dreamed about, what he had craved. The two of them together again.

Bane had driven a few miles and had made it to their first traffic light when he heard the sound of her chuckle. He glanced over at her and saw that her eyes were closed, yet a smile had formed on her lips. Was she having a dream or something? No sooner had that thought entered his mind than she opened her eyes, saw him looking at her and shifted upright in her seat. "What's wrong?" she asked.

"Nothing is wrong with me. You chuckled in your sleep just now."

A smile touched her lips. "I wasn't asleep. Just resting my eyes. And I got to thinking that this is getting to be the norm for us."

"What?"

"Being on the run. The last time we were together we eloped and were running from Sheriff Harper. Remember?"

"Yes, I remember." How could he forget? They had intentionally led everyone on a wild-goose chase thinking they were headed to Vegas when they'd married in Utah.

"Now we're on the run from heaven knows who."

"Doesn't matter. We're together again," he said.

She didn't say anything, and when the traffic light changed, he moved forward. After a while he figured she'd dozed off…or as she put it, had gone back to resting her eyes, when she asked, "For how long, Bane?"

Grateful for another traffic light, he brought the car to a stop and glanced over at her. "How long?"

"Yes, how long will we be together before you leave? Before I'm all alone again? You're a SEAL. That means you'll be gone a lot, right?"

He hesitated for a moment, giving thought to how he would respond. If she thought he would allow her to use his being a SEAL against him, against them, then she was definitely wrong. "Yes, I might be gone on missions whenever my CO calls."

"Your CO?"

"Commanding officer."

"And what if he calls now? You'll have to go, won't you?"

He tightened his grip on the steering wheel. Was she trying to insinuate that when it came to her he wasn't dependable? "Unless there's a national threat of some kind, it won't happen. I'm on military leave. My entire team is."

"Why?"

Now, this was where things got kind of sticky. He had to let her know that parts of his job weren't up for discussion, but he'd save that heart-to-heart conversation for later. Right now he merely said, "We were due one." That was the truth, although he wasn't telling her everything.

"You take risks. Put your life in danger."

Now it was his turn to chuckle.

"What's so funny?" she asked.

"I was just thinking that right now it's not my life that's in danger. I'd say we both have unusual occupations."

"There's nothing unusual about mine. I just happen to be working on research that's pretty sensitive."

He smiled, figuring that was one way of looking at it. "I guess you can say I work on things that are pretty sensitive, as well."

"There's no comparing what we do so don't even try, Bane."

Okay, so she had a point. But still, like he'd told her, he wasn't the one in danger now. "I'm well trained in what I do. Six months ago I made master sniper." That had been a major accomplishment for someone who was new on the team. But Bane's skills as a sharpshooter were what had caught the eye of his chief in boot camp. When he discovered Bane could hit a bull's-eye target with one eye closed, the man had put the thought of becoming a SEAL in Bane's head. The chief had made the captain aware of Bane's skill and the captain had pulled a lot of strings to get him into the naval academy.

"Master sniper? That doesn't surprise me. You were the one who taught me and Bailey how to shoot. And you always held your own against JoJo."

Yes, he had, he remembered proudly. And the Westmorelands sure knew how to shoot. He hadn't been surprised when he'd gotten home and everyone had told him about that grizzly bear Bailey had taken down in Alaska last month. And Crystal had been just as good a shot as

Bailey. Only person better than those two was JoJo, who was now married to his brother Stern.

"And you want me to think your job isn't dangerous, Bane?"

"I admit it's dangerous, but it's also rewarding."

He heard her snort before she said, "I can see you think it's rewarding because it gives you an excuse to kick ass in the name of your country."

He laughed, and considering everything, it felt good to laugh. Especially with her. She always had a knack for bringing humor to any situation, although he was convinced what she'd just said hadn't been meant to be funny.

"You're making a career out of it, though, aren't you?"

Was she seriously asking or did she think she had everything figured out already? "Not sure. It's a decision we will have to make together."

"Oh, no, don't pull me into this, Bane. I won't let you blame me for making your life miserable."

Making his life miserable? What was she talking about? "Define what you mean."

"Gladly. I can see you as a SEAL, and a darn good one. What I don't see is you going into the office at Blue Ridge Management every day. You'd go stark crazy sitting behind a desk. And you'd never forgive me if you saw me as the reason you had to go work there."

She knew him well and was right about his not wanting to work at his family's company. Although his brothers—Dillon, Riley, Canyon and Stern—as well as his cousin Aidan were a perfect fit for Blue Ridge Land Management, he wasn't.

"I could join Jason, Derringer and Zane in their horse-training business," he said. Honestly, he couldn't imagine doing that, either. He didn't have the same love of horses that his brother and two cousins had.

"Bailey told me about their company the last time we talked."

"But she wouldn't tell you anything about me," he said in a gruff tone.

Crystal frowned at him. "That was the rule, Bane, and need I remind you that it was your idea." She broke eye contact with him to glance out the side window.

Yes, it had been. And it was time they talked about it. He suddenly felt the tension flowing in the car between them and didn't like it. "You know why I made my decision, Crystal."

"The decision to desert me?"

He quickly swerved off the road and whipped into the parking lot of what looked like an all-night truck stop. He pulled in between two tractor trailers, which concealed them from the view of anyone driving by. He brought the car to a stop and turned off the ignition.

"Are you trying to kill us, Bane?" she asked, trying to catch her breath.

Instead of answering, he unsnapped his seat belt and turned toward her. "I know you didn't just say that I deserted you."

Crystal could tell Bane was furious. She'd seen him angry before, but his anger had never been directed at her. Now it was. He was glaring at her to the point where the color of his eyes seemed to take on a Saint Patrick's Day green. But she had a feeling it was not her lucky day. Not backing down, she lifted her chin. "And what if I did?"

"Then, we need to talk."

"Too late for that. Nothing you say will make me change the way I feel."

"Then, you need to tell me why you feel that way."

He really didn't know? She would find the whole thing amusing but instead she wanted to cry. She had loved him so much. He had been her world. The yang to her yin. The one person she'd thought would never hurt her or let her down. But he had.

"Crystal?"

Fine, if he wanted to pretend he didn't know why she felt the way she did then she'd tell him. "I understand why you let my father send me away after we eloped but—"

"It was for the best. You were going to drop out of school, Crystal. I couldn't let you do that. I couldn't interfere with your education. It was November. All you had to do was make it to June to graduate."

"I know all that," she snapped. "So I let my father think he was calling the shots when he sent me to live with Aunt Rachel." The memory of that day still scorched her brain whenever she thought about it. "I figured I could put up with it because you would come and get me in June after I finished high school."

She saw the look in his eyes, knew the exact moment he figured out where she was going with this. She took a deep breath and plunged forward. "When you finally called me in January, I thought it was to tell me you couldn't live without me and had decided to come for me early. And that I could finish school back in Denver while we lived together in the cabin you had built for me. As man and wife."

"Dammit, Crystal, I know you. If I had come for you early, you would have come up with all kinds of excuses not to go back to school. Plus, I wouldn't have been able to support you. I wasn't old enough to claim my land or my trust fund. When I finished high school, my income came from working odd jobs. I walked off the job Dillon gave me at Blue Ridge at the end of the first week. I didn't like my supervisor telling me what to do. I was a Westmoreland. My family owned the damn company and I figured that gave me the right to do whatever the hell I wanted."

"I would have gone back to school, Bane. I promised you that I would. And as far as you not having a stable income, we would have made it work."

"You deserved more."

"I thought I deserved you. I was your wife."

"Why can't you understand that I needed to make something of myself?" he asked in an agitated tone. "As your husband, I owed that to you. Why can't you see that you deserved better than what I was at the time? I was an undisciplined man without any goals in life. I enjoyed defying authority."

"Those things didn't matter to me, Bane."

"They should have."

She narrowed her gaze at him. "Your family got to you, didn't they? Convinced you we didn't belong together. So you told no one we were married. No one but Bailey."

She watched him rub his hands down his face in frustration. As far as she was concerned, he had no right to be frustrated. She was the one he'd forgotten about when he'd chosen a career as a SEAL over her.

"You're wrong about my family, Crystal. They knew how much I loved you, but they saw what we refused to see. They knew we couldn't keep going the way we were headed. So I made a decision that I felt was best for us.

And I want to believe that it was. Look at you now. You not only finished high school, but you went on to college and got your master's degree and are working on your PhD. You were always smart and I was holding you back. Had I been selfish enough to claim you as my wife, I would have taken you to that cabin and made a pitiful life for you there. And it would have been just our luck if you'd gotten pregnant. What sort of future would our kid have had?"

She quickly turned her face away so he wouldn't see the tears in her eyes, but she hadn't been quick enough. Bane knew her. He could read her when she didn't want to be read. And she knew he was doing it now when he reached out, used his finger to turn her face back toward him. He studied her features intently.

Moments later he narrowed his gaze. "What's wrong? What aren't you telling me, Crystal?"

She knew she had to tell him. There was no reason to keep her secret any longer. "That day when you called and told me you had decided to go into the navy, you asked me if I was pregnant and I told you no."

He didn't say anything for a minute and a part of her knew he'd already guessed what she was about to say. "But you lied, didn't you? You *were* pregnant, weren't you?" he said in an accusing tone.

She didn't say anything for a long moment and then answered, "I didn't lie. When you asked, I wasn't pregnant…any longer. I had miscarried our baby, Bane. A few days before. The day you called was the day Aunt Rachel brought me home from the hospital."

Eight

Bane literally buckled over as if he'd been kicked in the gut. In a way he had. He drew in a deep breath as if doing so would ease the pain. It took a few moments for him to get himself together, and when he looked over at Crystal, she was sitting up straight in her car seat and the first thing he noticed were the tears streaming down her face.

His breath caught. He'd always been a sucker for tears...especially hers. But a part of him couldn't ignore that she'd been pregnant with their child and hadn't told him. Although he hadn't known where her parents had sent her, other than to live with some aunt, she had known how to reach him. And she hadn't even tried.

He recalled the days he had waited by the phone, figuring she would get around to contacting him somehow to let him know where she was. And when she hadn't, he'd figured her parents had probably talked the same sense into her that Dillon had talked into him. It was then and only then, that he had made the decision to follow Dillon's advice and make something of himself before going to claim her.

Trying to pull himself together and keep the anger out of his voice, he asked, "How could you not tell me?"

She looked over at him. "I didn't tell you because you'd already made up your mind about what you wanted to do."

"Dammit, Crystal, I only went into the navy because—"

"You thought I deserved more. You've said that."

A muscle in his jaw ticked. When had she developed such a damn attitude? He felt anger beginning to roll around in his stomach and he worked hard to control it because he'd never lost his temper with her. "Yes, I said it and I will keep on saying it."

Neither of them spoke for a while and the silence between them was thick, full of the tension he knew they both felt. "When did you know you were pregnant?" he finally asked her.

Tears reappeared in her eyes and she swiped them away. "That's the thing, Bane. I didn't know. I was late but I'd been late before, you know that. So I really didn't think anything about it. I was trying to fit into a new school and was focusing on my studies. It was nearing the end of January and I was looking forward to you coming to get me by June. Silly me, I figured even if you didn't know where I was that you would look for me until you found me.

"Anyway, I got really bad stomach pains one night. When I went to the bathroom I noticed I was bleeding profusely and woke up my aunt. She took me to the emergency room and after checking me over, the doctor told me I'd been pregnant and had lost the baby. They kept me in the hospital overnight because I'd lost a lot of blood."

She swiped at her eyes again. "How can a woman be pregnant and not know it? How could I have carried your baby—our baby—in my body and not know it? That seemed so unfair, Bane. So unfair. The doctor was a nice woman. She said miscarriages weren't uncommon and usually happen within the early weeks of pregnancy. I figured I'd gotten pregnant on our wedding night so I was less than eight weeks along. She assured me it wasn't because of anything I did, and that my next pregnancy should go smoothly."

A deep pain sliced through Bane. It had been his baby as well, and at that moment he mourned for the loss of a life that would never be. A baby that had been a part of him and a part of her. He wanted to reach out and pull Crystal into his arms. Hold her. Share the pain. He felt he had every right to do that. But then he also felt she'd put an invisible wall between them and he would need to tear it down, piece by piece.

"I'm sorry about our baby," he said, meaning every word. It was true he'd gotten careless on their wedding night. It had been the first time they'd ever spent the entire night together, wrapped in each other's arms, and he had been so overjoyed he'd gotten carried away and hadn't used a condom. "I never deserted you, Crystal. I could no more do that than cut off my arm. Do you have any idea what I went through when we were apart?" he asked softly. "How much I suffered each day not knowing where you were?"

"I called you."

"When?"

"As soon as I could get away from my parents. They

kept an eye on me during the entire plane trip to South Carolina, but when the plane landed I went into the ladies' room and asked some woman to use her cell phone. It was around five hours after we parted."

Bane frowned. He hadn't gotten her call. But then he figured it out. "I know the reason why you couldn't reach me," he said, remembering that day. "I was at the cabin, and there's no phone reception out there."

He paused and then added, "After Sheriff Harper told me you'd left Denver, I stormed out of the police station and got into my truck and went to your parents' place and found it deserted. I drove around awhile, getting angrier by the minute. Somehow I ended up at the cabin and I stayed there for two whole days. On the third day Riley came and convinced me to go home with him."

She nodded. "That's probably why I still couldn't reach you the next night, either. I waited until everyone had gone to bed and sneaked downstairs and used my aunt's phone. I couldn't get you, which was just as well because Dad caught me trying. He got upset all over again, and said he knew I would try calling you and figured it was time for me to know the truth."

Bane frowned. "What truth?"

"That he and your brother Dillon had met when we first went missing and made a deal."

"What kind of a deal?"

"The two of them agreed that when we were found, Dillon would keep you away from me and Dad was to keep me away from you."

"That's a damn lie!" Bane said bluntly, feeling red-hot anger flow through him.

"How can you be so sure?"

Her question only infuriated him more. "First of all,

Dil doesn't operate that way. Second, Dillon wasn't even in Denver when we eloped. He was somewhere in Wyoming following up on leads to learn more about my great-grandfather Raphel. Ramsey called Dil but he didn't get home until after we were found."

Bane angrily rubbed his hand over his head. "I can't believe you fell for what your dad said. You knew how much he despised the Westmorelands. Did you honestly think he and Dillon sat down and talked about anything?"

She lifted her chin. "I didn't want to believe it but…"

"But what?"

"I called you twice and you didn't take my calls."

"I didn't take them because I didn't get them," he said.

"Well, I didn't know that."

"You should have."

"Well, I didn't. And when you finally called me…two months later…it was to tell me you were going into the navy and it would be best for us to go our separate ways."

His frown deepened. "The reason it was two months later was because it took me that long to find out where you'd gone. And Bailey had to pickpocket your dad's phone to find out then. And as far as saying it was best for us to go our separate ways, that's *not* what I said."

"Pretty much sounded like it to me."

Had it? Frustrated, he leaned back in his seat, trying to recall what he'd said. Joining the navy had been a hard decision, but he'd made it after talking to his cousin Dare, who'd been in the marines. He'd also talked to Riley's best friend Pete. Pete's brother, Matthew, had joined the navy a few years before, and Pete had told Bane how much money Matthew had saved and how the military had trained him to work on aircrafts. Bane had figured going into the navy would not only teach him a skill but also get him out of Denver for a while. Being there without Crystal had made him miserable.

As he recalled all he'd said to her that day, he could see why she'd assumed it was a break-up call, considering the lie her father had told her. His only saving grace had been the promises he'd made to her that he would keep his wedding vows and would come back for her. That made him wonder...

"You think I deserted you. Did you not believe me when I told you that I would come for you once I made something of myself? And that I would keep my wedding vows?" he asked.

She glanced out the window before looking over at him. "Yes, at the time I believed you, although I sort of resented you for putting me out of your life even for a little while, for whatever the reason."

Her words took him by surprise. How could she think he would do such a thing? And she had said, "at the time I believed you." Did that mean at some point in time she had stopped believing? Now he wondered if he'd made a grave mistake not keeping the lines of communication open between them.

"I never put you out of my life and I had every intention of coming back for you. That never changed, Crystal. I thought about you every day. Sometimes every hour, minute and second. I longed for you. I went to bed every night needing you. There were days when I wasn't sure I could go on without you and wanted to give up. That's why I made sure Bailey didn't tell me where you were. Had I known, I would have given up for sure and come after you. And had you told me about your miscarriage, nothing would have stopped me from coming for you. Navy or no navy."

Unable to stop himself, he released his seat belt and reached out and unfastened hers before pulling her across the console to hold her in his arms.

Crystal buried her face in Bane's chest. She couldn't stop her tears from flowing and was surprised she had any tears left to shed. She'd figured she had gone through all of them when the doctor had broken the news to her that day that she had lost her baby. And then getting Bane's call, the same day she'd come home from the hospital, had been too much.

Her aunt Rachel had been wonderful and understanding, the one to hold Crystal each time she wept. And when she'd begged her aunt not to tell her parents about the baby, her aunt had given Crystal her word that she wouldn't. Whether it had been his intention or not, his phone call that day had made her feel as if he was turning his back on them and their love. Deserting her. It had been her aunt who had persuaded her to pull herself together and make decisions about her life…with or without Bane. So she had made them without him. But each time Bailey had called after that, a part of her had hoped it was Bane instead of his cousin. Then, when it had gotten too much for her to deal with, she'd had her number changed.

After listening to Bane's words just now, she remembered all too well how she had thought about him every day, sometimes every hour, minute and second, as well. He had longed for her, gone to bed needing her, and she had done the same for him. At one point she had been tempted to go to Denver to find him. But then she'd known he wouldn't be there and hadn't a clue where he would be. And at some point, how had he expected her not to doubt he still cared when he hadn't contacted her in five years?

"I'm fine now, Bane," she said, pushing back from him and wiping away her tears.

He looked down at her with an intense scrutiny that sent shivers through her body. "Are you, Crystal? Are you fine? Or will you hold it against me for wanting to give you the best of me?"

"I thought I already had the best of you, Bane. You didn't hear me complaining, did you?"

He didn't say anything and she used that time to scramble out of his lap and back into her seat. She stared out the window and could see from the reflection in the glass that he was staring at her.

Without turning back around to him, she asked, "Have you decided where we're going?"

He started the ignition. "Yes, I know where we're going."

Instead of telling her where, he pulled the car out of the parking spot and headed back to the main road.

Nine

"I'll take the bed closer to the door, Crystal," Bane said, dropping his luggage on the floor by the bed.

Instead of answering him, she merely nodded and rolled her luggage over to the other bed. Figuring that she had missed dinner, he'd stopped at an all-night diner to grab orders of chicken and waffles. Then he had driven four hours before finally settling at this hotel for the night. During that time she hadn't said one word to him, not a one. And her silence bothered the hell out of him. How could she be upset with him for wanting to give her a better life? How could she think he'd deserted her? It now seemed that not keeping in contact with her had been a mistake, but what she failed to understand was that she was his weakness.

She said she would have been satisfied with him just the way he was. Flaws and all. But she deserved more.

Deserved better. No matter what she thought, he would always believe that. He would admit he had been separated from her longer than he'd planned, and for that he would take the blame. Five years was a long time to expect her to put her life on hold. But that was just it. He hadn't expected her to put her life on hold. He had expected her to make something worthwhile out of it, like he had been doing with his. And she had. She had finished high school, earned both bachelor and master's degrees and was now working on her PhD. All during the five years he'd been gone. Why couldn't she understand that when he'd decided to go into the navy, he'd believed that he was giving them both the chance to be all that they could be, while knowing in the end they would be together? They would always be together. Although he'd loved her more than life, he had been willing to make the sacrifice. Why hadn't she? Had he been wrong to assume that no matter what, their love would be strong enough to survive anything? Even a long separation?

"I need to take a shower."

His heart nearly missed a beat upon hearing the sound of her voice again. At least she was back to talking to him. "All right. I figure we'll check out after breakfast and head south."

"South?"

"Yes, but that might change depending on any reports I get from people I have checking on a few things."

"Is that what that Code Purple was all about?"

So she had been listening. "Yes. That's a code for my team. It means one of us is in trouble and all hands on deck."

"Oh, I see."

She then opened her luggage and dismissed him again.

He placed his own travel bag on the bed and opened it. The first thing he came to was the satchel containing all the cards and letters he'd saved for her over the years. He had looked forward to finally giving them to her. But now…

"You haven't heard anything else about my home, have you?"

He looked over at her. Although she'd taken several naps while he'd been driving, she still looked tired and exhausted. However, fatigued or not, to him she looked beautiful. "No. Flip has everything under control."

She nodded before gathering a few pieces of clothing under her arms and heading for the bathroom, closing the door behind her. Deciding he would really try hard to not let her attitude affect his, he took the satchel and walked over to place it on her bed. It was hers. He had kept it for her and had lived for years just waiting for the day when he could give it to her. He wouldn't let the bitterness she felt keep him from giving it to her.

His phone beeped, letting him know he'd received a text message. He glanced at his watch. It was two in the morning. He pulled his phone from his jacket and read Flip's message. All quiet here.

He texted back. Let's hope things stay that way.

He tried to ignore the sound of running water. He could just imagine Crystal stripping off her clothes for her shower. He would love being in there with her, taking pleasure in stepping beneath the spray of water with her, lathering her body and then making love to her. He would press her against the wall, lift her up so her legs encircled his waist and then he would ease inside her. How many nights had he lain in bed and fantasized of doing that very thing?

To take his mind off his need to make love to his wife, he glanced around the hotel room, checking things out in case they needed to make a quick getaway. This room was definitely a step up from the one they'd shared on their wedding night. He'd taken her to a nice enough hotel in Utah, but tonight's room was more spacious. The beds looked warm and inviting and the decor eye-catching.

Crystal had accompanied him inside when he'd booked the room. He could feel her body tense up beside him when he'd told the hotel clerk he wanted one room. He'd then heard her sigh of relief when he'd added that he wanted a room with two beds.

He lifted a brow when his cell phone went off and he recognized the ringtone. It was a call from home. Dillon. He pulled his phone out of his back pocket again. "Yes, Dil?"

"You didn't call to let us know you'd made it to Dallas. Is everything okay?"

How could he tell his brother that no, everything wasn't okay? "Yes, I made it to Dallas. Sorry, I didn't call but things got kind of crazy."

"Crazy? Were you able to find Crystal?"

"Yes, went straight to her place but…"

"But the warm, cozy, loving reception that you had expected isn't what you got."

He shook his head. His brother could say that again. "I figured we would have to work through some issues, but I didn't expect her to open the door with a loaded gun in her hand, her luggage packed and a bunch of bad guys trying to kidnap her."

There was a pause and then Dillon said, "I think you need to start from the beginning, Bane."

* * *

Crystal toweled herself off and tried not to think of the man on the other side of the door. The man she had shared her first kiss with. Her body. The man who had been her best friend. The one who'd defied her father's threat of jail time just to be with her. And the man who was her husband.

She glanced at herself in the mirror. Did Bane see the changes? Did he like what he saw? She couldn't attribute her figure to spending time in the gym or anything. The changes had just happened. One day she was thin and then the next, right after she'd turned twenty, the curves had come. The guys at college had noticed it, too, and tried causing problems. That was when she wished she'd had a wedding ring on her finger that would have deterred their interest. Instead, she had this, she thought, glancing at her locket.

She brought it to her lips and kissed it. It had been what had kept her sane over the past five years. She would look at it and think of Bane and remember the promise. Even on those days she hadn't wanted to remember or thought he'd possibly forgotten.

Her heart began thumping in her chest when she recalled how he had looked at her a few times tonight. The last had been when she'd told him she was going to take a shower. Nobody could turn her on quicker with a mere look than Brisbane Westmoreland. When he had leveled those hazel eyes on her, she could feel her skin get flushed. He was the only one in his family with that eye color, which he'd inherited from his great-grandmother.

She slid into a pair of sweats and then pulled on an oversize T-shirt. Looking into the mirror again, she nervously licked her lips as she thought of Bane. *What a man. What a man.* She even used her hands to fan herself. A number of times on the ride tonight she had pretended to be asleep just so she could study him without him knowing she was doing so. If his eyes weren't bad enough, he had an adorable set of lashes. Almost too long to be a man's. He had taken off his jacket and she couldn't help but appreciate the breadth of his shoulders. Bane was so well toned that it was obvious he lifted weights or something. SEALs were known to stay in shape. If it was required of them, then he was passing that test with flying colors.

Knowing she had spent more time than she needed in the bathroom, she gathered up her clothes in her arms and slowly opened the door. She saw Bane sitting at the desk staring at a laptop.

A laptop? How many times in the past when she'd tried showing him how to surf the net had he claimed he was technology challenged and just couldn't get the hang of using a computer? She sniffed the air and picked up the smell of coffee. Evidently he'd made a pot while she was taking a shower. Coffee was something she'd never acquired the taste for. She preferred hot chocolate or herbal tea.

Crystal cleared her throat. "I'm finished."

"Okay."

He didn't even turn around, but kept his back to her as he stared at the computer screen. Shoving the clothes she'd taken off earlier into the small travel laundry bag, she turned to put it into her luggage and saw the satchel on the bed. She picked it up. "You left something on my bed."

It was then that he looked over his shoulder at her and at that moment she wished he hadn't. Having those hazel eyes trained on her was sending spikes of desire up her spine. "I put it there. It's yours."

She lifted a brow. "Mine?"

"Yes." He turned back to his computer.

She glanced down at the satchel. "What's in it?"

Without turning back around to her he said, "Why don't you look inside and see?"

Bane returned his attention to the computer screen, or at least he pretended to. He'd known the moment Crystal had walked out of the bathroom. Hearing the door open had sent all kinds of arousing sensations through him. The last thing he needed was to glance over at her. His control wasn't all that great. Going without her for five years was playing havoc on his brain cells. Although he kept his eyes glued to the computer, he could hear her ease the leather strap of his satchel open. His wife never could resist her curiosity, and he'd known it.

"There are cards in here. A lot of cards and envelopes," he heard her say. Yet he still refused to turn around.

"Yes. I remembered your birthday, our wedding anniversary, Valentine's Day and Christmas every year. Although I couldn't mail them to you, I bought them anyway and tucked them inside my satchel. I knew one day, when we got back together again, I'd have them for you."

He could hear her shuffling through all those sealed envelopes. "There are letters in here, as well," she said.

"Yes. Most of the other guys had wives or significant others to write home to, but again, I couldn't do the same for you. So I got in the habit of writing you a letter whenever you weighed heavily on my mind." He hoped she could tell from the number of letters he'd written that she'd consumed his mind a lot of the time.

"Thanks, Bane. This is a surprise. I hadn't expected you to do this…for me."

This time he couldn't help but turn around when he said, "I would do just about anything for you, Crystal."

It never ceased to amaze him how easily he could make her blush. At least that hadn't changed. He could actually feel her gaze moving across his face as she held his stare and he wondered if she could feel him doing the same thing. Suddenly, she broke eye contact with him while drawing in a deep breath. He could see the nipples of her breasts pressing against the T-shirt she had on. It was supposed to fit large on her, but she still looked sexy as hell wearing it.

She glanced back down at the satchel. "I can't wait to read the cards and letters."

He nodded and then turned his attention back to his laptop just when the shrill ring of his mobile phone got his attention. He grabbed it off the desk. "This is Bane."

He nodded and his jaw tightened as he listened to what his friend was telling him. Nick Stover, who used to be a member of his SEAL team, had decided to leave the field and go work for Homeland Security when his wife gave birth to triplets. Bane appreciated his friend's inside scoop. But what he was telling him now had his temper rising.

When Nick was done, Bane said, "Okay. Thanks for letting me know so I can get in touch with Flip."

He clicked off the phone and immediately called Flipper. There was no doubt Crystal had stopped whatever she was doing to listen to his conversation. He would have to tell her what was going on. But first, he had a question for her. He turned around and saw her staring at him.

"Is there anything in your home you want saved?"

She frowned. "What?"

"I asked if there's anything in your house that you want to save."

He could tell by the look on Crystal's face that she was trying to figure out why he would ask her such a thing. Before he could explain himself further, he heard Flip pick up the phone. "This is Bane." He knew Nick had already relayed the same information to Flip that he'd just told him.

"Yes, there are some things she wants to save." Since Crystal hadn't answered his question, just continued to look at him like he'd grown a set of horns or something, he said to Flip, "I know for certain she'll want to save all the photographs on her fireplace mantel."

Crystal crossed the room to stand next to him. "Hold it! Why are you telling him that, Bane? What's happening to my house?"

Bane spoke into the phone. "I'll call you back in a sec, Flip." He then clicked off the phone and placed it back on the desk.

He regretted having to answer her question, but knew he had to. "In a couple of hours or so, your house will get burned down to the ground."

Ten

Crystal felt the room spinning and wondered if she was about to fall flat on her face. Bane was obviously wondering the same thing because he was out of his chair in a flash and had grabbed hold of her arm to steady her.

"I think you need to sit down, Crystal," he said, trying to ease her down into the chair he'd just vacated.

"No. I won't sit down," she said, telling herself she'd just imagined what he'd said about her house burning down. There was no way he could have said that. But all it took was to see the concerned look on his face to know she hadn't imagined anything at all.

"Why would anyone want to burn my house down?" She just couldn't fathom such a thing.

"Actually, it's not just anyone. The order came from Homeland Security."

Shock took over her features. "Homeland Security? Why would the government do something like that?"

"I told you about those other two chemists who were kidnapped. And now the kidnappers are trying to get their hands on you. It's a serious situation, Crystal, and you're talking about national security. As long as there's a possibility something is in your house connected to the project you're working on, then—"

"But I told you there wasn't. I never bring work home."

"The Department of Homeland Security can't take any chances. Without you the bad guys will try to piece together what they need, and DHS can't let them do that."

"Fine. Get them on the phone."

"Get who on the phone?"

"Someone at Homeland Security. Evidently you have their number. If they don't believe you, then maybe they will believe me."

"I can't do that."

"Why not?"

There was a moment of silence before he said, "Because right now we can't trust anyone. Not even Homeland Security. At least until they find out what's going on. Evidently, there's a mole within the organization. Otherwise, how else would your project come under such close scrutiny?"

He moved around her to the cabinet that held the coffeepot, poured a cup and took a sip. He leaned back against the cabinet and added, "Homeland Security has no idea where you are. All they know is the bad guys haven't nabbed you yet because they're still trying to find you. Obviously, the person who sent you that note is one of the good guys and figured out what was about to go down, which is why he or she told you to disappear. For all they know, that's what you did."

He took another sip of his coffee. "So beside those

framed photographs over your fireplace, is there anything else in your house you want to save?"

Crystal drew in a deep breath. Technically, it wasn't her house since she was leasing it. But it was where she'd made a home for the past year, putting her own signature on it with the decorating she'd done. What she'd liked most about her home was the screened-in patio. She could sit out there for hours and read. That made her realize that all the furniture she did own would probably be destroyed because it was too big to move out without attracting attention. The impact of that made her slide down in the chair. It was still warm from when Bane had sat in it.

"We don't have much time, Crystal."

She sat upright, glad she'd already packed her marriage license and placed it inside the photo album she'd kept for Bane. "My family Bible," she said with resolve. "It's in the nightstand drawer. And there are more pictures in a small trunk under my bed."

"Okay."

He returned to the desk and when he reached for his phone, his arm brushed against hers. The feel of their skin coming into contact made her draw in a sharp breath. He looked at her, holding her gaze for a minute, and she knew he'd felt the sizzle, as well. He continued to hold her gaze, letting her know she had his full attention while he talked on the phone. "Flip, check the nightstand drawer next to her bed and grab her family Bible. And there's a small trunk under her bed."

Moments later he clicked off the phone. "I see you haven't outgrown that."

"What?"

"Blushing."

"Was I supposed to outgrow it?"

He smiled. "I have no complaints. In fact I've always enjoyed watching you blush."

She tried to give him a small smile, but in all honesty, she had very little to smile about right now.

"I didn't ask if you wanted a cup of coffee. Since you didn't order a cup at that diner earlier tonight, I figured you're still not a coffee drinker."

She nodded. "And I see that you still are."

"Yep."

She frowned and broke eye contact with him to look at the cup he held in his hand. "Too much caffeine isn't good for you."

He chuckled. "So you've always said."

"And so I know. Especially now that I've become a biochemist. It's not good for your body."

Why had she said that? And why after saying it did her gaze automatically move up and down his solid frame? Bane Westmoreland was so overwhelmingly sexy. He'd always possessed a magnetism that could draw her in. The man was such a perfect hunk of carved mahogany, it was a crying shame.

She moved her gaze off his body and up to his face, thinking his facial hair gave him a sexier look. He gave her a roguish smile and she could feel her cheeks flush. "Looking at me like that can get you in a lot of trouble, Crystal Gayle," he murmured in a deep husky voice.

He was standing close, so close she could inhale his scent. Manly. Deliciously provocative. "Then, I won't look at you," she said, cutting her eyes elsewhere. Namely to her bed and all the cards and letters she'd pulled out of the satchel. "I don't need any more trouble than I'm already in. It's pretty bad when you have the government burning down your house. I'd like to see how they explain their actions to the insurance company."

"They won't have to. They will handle it in a way that makes it look like an electrical fire or something. It definitely won't appear intentional."

She lifted her chin. "Still, I don't like it." She eased up out of the chair, assuming he would step back and give her space. He didn't, and it brought their bodies within touching distance of each other.

"You look good in your T-shirt and sweats, by the way," he said softly. They were standing so close the heat of his words seemed to fan across her face.

She looked down at herself, thinking he had to be kidding. Both garments were old and ratty looking, but she remembered her manners and glanced up and said, "Thank you."

The moment she looked into his face, she wished she hadn't. The intense desire in the hazel eyes staring back at her was so profoundly sensual she felt a tug in the middle of her stomach.

Setting his coffee cup down, he moved closer. Before she knew what he was doing he reached out and placed his hands at her waist. But he didn't stop there. As he inched his hands upward and gently caressed the curve of her body, he said, "I can't get used to these. Where did all these curves come from?"

She shrugged. "Wish I knew. I just woke up one morning and they were there." Why wasn't she telling him to keep his hands to himself? Why did his touch feel so good?

He chuckled. "Only you would think these curves were an overnight thing."

Although a part of her wished he didn't do that, she

kind of liked the way he would subtly remind her that they had a past. And she needed that because at times he seemed like such a stranger to her.

"Well," she said, making a move to scoot around him. But he held tight to her waist and when he began lowering his head, she could just imagine how their tongues would mingle.

The moment he took hold of her mouth, his lips ground against hers and she was powerless to do anything but kiss him back.

Bane loved kissing Crystal. Always had and figured he always would. Their kisses weren't just hot, they were flaming red-hot, and in no time he was shivering with desire. And like in the past, he had to taper his lust; otherwise he would have her spread out on that bed in no time. And he doubted she was ready for that just yet.

So he enjoyed this. The way she was provocatively returning his kiss. The way his mouth seemed to be in sync with hers, feeding off hers with a hunger he felt in every part of his body. As when he'd kissed her earlier tonight, it felt as if he'd finally come home to the woman he loved. He had been hungry for her taste for five years. He'd tried to remember just how delicious it was and knew his memories hadn't come close. The intensity was clouding his mind and he could tell she wasn't holding back, pouring everything into the kiss like he was doing.

She suddenly pulled her mouth away and drew in a deep breath. When she licked her bottom lip, he was tempted to kiss her again, take his own tongue and lick her lips.

"We should not have done that, Bane," she said softly. And the look of distress in her eyes touched him.

"Don't see why not. You're my wife."

"I don't feel like your wife."

"That can be remedied, sweetheart," he said in a provocative drawl.

"I know," she said, looking at him with a serious expression. "But sleeping with you won't make me feel as if I know you any better. I need time, Bane. I don't need you to rush me into anything."

"I won't."

She crossed her arms over her chest and he wished she hadn't done that when he saw her nipples pressed against her T-shirt. "Then, what was that kiss about just now?"

He smiled. "Passion. You can't deny you felt it. I want you so much, Crystal." He saw uneasiness line her pupils. "Relax, baby. You will let me know when you're ready. One day you will realize that no matter how long it's been, I'm still your husband."

She shook her head. "But we haven't seen each other in five years."

He frowned. Was she saying that because she wasn't sure she still loved him after all this time? He refused to believe that. "Trust me, Crystal," he heard himself say softly. "After reading all my cards and letters to you, I have no doubt you'll see what I mean."

His cell phone rang and when he turned to pick it up, she used that time to quickly move away from him and back to the bed.

"This is Bane." He nodded a few times. "Okay, Flip. Thanks and I owe you." He then clicked off the phone.

He looked over at her. "That was Flip. He wanted to

let me know he collected all the items you wanted saved. And by the way. Did you know your house was bugged?"

Crystal was experiencing one shock after another. First Bane returned after five years. Then she was on the run from men who wanted to kidnap her. Then the government wanted to burn her house down. And now she was being told it was bugged?

"That's not possible. Nobody I work with has ever been invited to my home. They consider me a recluse."

Bane nodded. "Where did the stuffed giraffe come from?"

She frowned. "The stuffed giraffe?"

"Yes."

She thought for a minute. "It was a gift from one of my coworkers, who took a trip to South Africa earlier this year. She brought everyone souvenirs back."

"Who was this generous person?"

"A biochemist by the name of Jasmine Ross."

"Well, yours was given to you with a purpose. Flip saw it on your dresser and figured it would be something you'd want to keep, as well. When his sensor went off he knew it contained an audio bugging device. He proved his suspicions true when he gutted it. I guess someone thought they could catch you saying something about your research on the phone or something."

"Well, they were wrong." Things were getting crazier by the minute and she couldn't believe it. "Were there others?"

Bane shook his head. "Flip and his brothers combed the rest of the house and didn't detect anything. Now you see why Homeland Security wants to burn it down to the ground?"

No, she still didn't see it. "They could have found another way."

"Evidently not."

She didn't like Bane's attitude, as if he was perfectly fine with someone torching the place where she lived. Turning her back to him, she angrily began shoving all the cards and envelopes back into the satchel. She was in no mood to read anything now. All she wanted to do was get into bed and rest her brain.

"I'll take my shower now."

"Fine." Crystal was tempted to turn around but refused to do so. She planned to be in bed and dead asleep by the time he came out of the bathroom.

When she heard the bathroom door close she released a deep sigh. How were she and Bane going to share a hotel room without...

She shook her head. The thought of them making love was driving her nuts. All of a sudden the memories of their last time together were taking hold of her. They had been happy. They had just gotten married and thought the future was theirs to grab and keep.

When she heard the water from his shower she couldn't help but recall when they had showered together. All the things he had taught her to do. Bane had been the best teacher, and he'd always been easy and gentle with her.

As she drew the bedcovers back and then slid beneath them, she tried to not think of Bane. Instead, she thought of her house and how at that very minute it could be going up in flames.

Eleven

Twenty minutes later Bane walked out of the bathroom and glanced over at the bed where Crystal lay sleeping. Or was she? He found it amusing that she was pretending to be asleep while checking out his bare chest and the way his sweats rode low on his hips. He had no problem with her ogling him; she could even touch him if she liked. Better yet, he would love for her to invite him to her bed. He would love to slide between the sheets with her.

Intending to give her more to look at, he decided he might as well get on the floor and do his daily exercises. He'd begin with push-ups after a five-minute flex routine that included bending to touch his toes. Maybe a vigorous workout would work out all the desire that was overtaking his senses and at the same time arouse her enough that she would want him to make love to her. It was worth a try.

Less than thirty minutes into his exercises he wondered if she realized her breathing had changed. He most certainly had noticed. Now he was off the floor and running in place. His sweats had ridden even lower on his hips and his bare chest was wet from sweat. Now for a few crunches.

"What you're doing doesn't make sense, Bane."

He forced himself not to smile. "I thought you were asleep," he said, lying, when he knew she'd been peeking through a slightly closed eye at him.

"How could I sleep with all that racket you're making down there on the floor?"

"Sorry if I disturbed you. And what doesn't make sense?"

"For a person to take a shower only to get all sweaty again."

He chuckled. "I'll take another shower. No problem."

She had shifted in bed to lie on her side and look over at him. "You did three hundred push-ups. Who does that?"

"A SEAL who needs to stay in shape." Evidently she'd been counting right along with him but had missed a few. "And I did three hundred and twenty-five." He wondered where her concentration had been when he'd done the other twenty-five.

"Whatever. I just hope that's the last of it."

"For tonight. I do the same thing each morning. But I'll try to be a little quieter so as not to disturb you."

The sound of him exercising wasn't what was disturbing her, Crystal thought, trying not to let her gaze roam all over Bane. Jeez. How could sweat look so good on a man? It was such a turn-on. All that testosterone being worked up like that. Rippling muscles. Bulging biceps. Firm abs. Mercy! She'd gone without sex for five years and it had never bothered her before. But now it did. Only because the man here with her now was Bane.

She had pretended to be asleep when he'd come out of the bathroom. But seeing him bare chested and wearing sweats was just too much. She had tried closing her eyes and holding them shut. Tight. But the sounds of him grunting sent all kinds of fantasies through her mind and she'd begun peeking. And definitely getting an eyeful. If she didn't know better she'd think he'd deliberately gone after her attention.

"I've worked up an appetite. Do you want something?"

She had worked up an appetite watching him as well, but it wasn't for food. She definitely wanted something, but it was something she'd best do without—it was just too soon since Bane had come for her, and she needed to stay focused until she was out of danger. "No thanks. I'm still full from those waffles and chicken we ate earlier. But you can order room service if you like. The hotel clerk did say the kitchen was open twenty-four hours." But who wanted to eat at four in the morning?

He glanced at the clock on the nightstand separating the beds. "I think I'll order something up. Nothing heavy. If I do it now, it will probably arrive by the time I get out of the shower. But if they come while I'm in the shower, don't open the door for anyone. They can wait a few minutes. If they can't, then they can take it back to the kitchen."

She wondered if all that was necessary. But then all she had to remember was her house was probably getting burned to the ground about now. "Fine." She hoped by the time he got out of the shower for a second time that night she would be asleep for real. But that hadn't worked during his first shower—the sound of running water and picturing him naked beneath that water had kept her awake.

She watched as he moved over to the desk and picked up the phone to order a steak dinner with potatoes. At four in the morning? She lifted a brow. Hadn't he said nothing heavy? If that wasn't heavy then what was his definition?

And speaking of heavy...

Why had her breathing suddenly gone that way? Could it be because her gaze had now landed on the perspiration dripping off his hard chest, past those chiseled muscles, and making a path toward the waistband of his sweats? And why did the thought of licking it before the drops of sweat could disappear beneath the waistband actually appeal to her?

He had grabbed more clothes and was about to go into the bathroom when his cell phone rang. "That's Nick," Bane said, turning and heading back toward the desk.

Crystal felt a tightening of her stomach. It seemed that whenever this guy Nick called, he was the bearer of bad news. "Maybe they changed their minds about burning down my house."

The look Bane gave her all but said not to count on it. "Yes, Nick?"

She saw the tightening of Bane's jaw and the dark and stormy look in his eyes. And when he said, "Damn" three times she felt uneasy and suspected the news wasn't good.

"Thanks for letting me know. We're on the road again. Contact Viper. He'll know what to do."

Crystal had eased up on the side of the bed. As soon

as he clicked off the phone she was about to ask what was wrong when he asked, "Where's your jacket?"

She lifted a brow. "My jacket?"

"Yes."

"Hanging up in the closet. Why?"

"It has a tracking device on it."

"What!"

Already Bane had reached the closet and jerked her jacket off the hanger. She watched in horror as he took a pocketknife and ripped through a seam. "Bingo." He pulled out a small item that looked like a gold button.

She drew in a deep breath and met Bane's gaze when he looked over at her. "Does that mean…"

"Yes. Someone has been keeping up with our whereabouts all this time, and chances are they know we're here."

"But how did someone get my jacket?"

"Probably at work. Do you keep it on during the day?"

"No. I always take it off, hang it up and put on my lab coat."

He nodded. "Then, you have your answer. And I suspect the person who put this tracker in your coat is the same person who gave you the stuffed giraffe." He rubbed his hands down his face. "Come on. Let's pack up and get the hell out of here."

"But what about your food? Your shower?"

"I'll stop somewhere later to grab something, but for now we need to put as much distance between us and this place as we can. As for my shower, you'll just have to put up with sharing a car with a musky man."

"I can handle it." She was already on her feet and pulling out her luggage. She considered how Bane hadn't expected all this drama when he'd come looking for her.

"I'm sorry, Bane." She glanced over at him and saw he was doing likewise with his luggage.

He paused in tossing items into his duffel bag and looked back at her. "For what?"

"For being the cause of so much trouble. I guess you hadn't figured on all of this."

"No, but it doesn't matter, Crystal. You're my wife, and I will protect you with my life if it came to that."

She shivered at the thought and hoped it didn't. But still, the words he'd just spoken had a profound impact on her. She pushed several locks of hair back from her face to focus on Bane as he continued to pack. Surprisingly, it wasn't Bane's sexiness that was wearing her down, but his ability to still want her in spite of everything.

"Ready?"

She nodded. "Yes."

"We need to be aware of our surroundings more than ever and make sure we aren't being tailed. There's a pretty good chance someone is sitting and waiting for us in the parking lot, which is why I'm putting plan B in place."

"What's plan B?"

"You'll see."

After Bane checked up and down the hallway, they left the hotel room, moving quickly toward the stairwell instead of the elevator. She followed his lead and didn't ask any questions. And when they came to a locked door that led to the courtyard, he used what looked like a knitting needle to pick the lock.

"Still doing that, I see," she said.

He shrugged. "Not as much as I used to."

In no time the lock gave way and she saw they were in the courtyard, which was located on the other side of the building from the parking lot. "How will we get to our car?"

"We won't."

She was about to ask what he meant when suddenly a white SUV pulled up, tailed by a dark sedan. Since Bane didn't seemed alarmed by the two vehicles, she figured he knew the occupants. When the door to the SUV opened and a big bruiser of a man got out, she saw Bane's lips ease into a smile.

When the man came to a stop in front of them, Bane said. "Crystal, I want you to meet Gavin Blake, better known as Viper. Another one of my teammates."

Bane wasn't bothered by the way Viper was checking out Crystal. He was curious, as most of his teammates were. They had wondered what kind of woman could keep a man faithful to a wife he hadn't seen in five years. Bane could tell that Viper, a known ladies' man, was in awe, if his stare was anything to go by.

Moments later, Viper switched his intense gaze from Crystal back to Bane. "She's beautiful, Bane."

"You forgot to check out my teeth," Crystal said, frowning.

Viper let out a deep laugh. "And she has a good sense of humor," he added. "I like that. She's definitely a keeper."

"Yes, she is." Bane had known that the first day he'd met Crystal. "Did you check out the parking lot?"

Viper nodded. "Yes, and it was just like you figured. A car with two men inside is parked beside the one you were driving. I phoned in the description and the license plates to Nick, and according to him, it's the same vehicle an eyewitness saw in the area when one of the other biochemists was kidnapped. So you did the right thing by having Nick call me."

Viper nodded toward the SUV. "Here's your new ride. Chances are those guys don't know you're onto them. They probably planned to snatch your wife the minute you checked out of the hotel tomorrow morning."

"Like hell."

"That's what I said," Viper said, chuckling. "I figured they don't have a clue who they're messing with. I'm going to keep those guys busy while you and your lady get a head start. This ought to be fun."

Bane frowned. "Don't enjoy yourself too much."

"I won't. I brought my marine cousin with me to make sure I stay out of trouble. At least as much as I can," Viper said, handing Bane the keys to the SUV. "Do you have a plan from here?"

Bane nodded. "Yes. My brother is calling in family members with connections to law enforcement."

Viper nodded. "That's good. There's nothing like family backing you when you're in a pinch." He then turned his attention back to Crystal and smiled. "It was nice finally getting to meet you. You have a good man here. And, Bane, if you need my help again, just call." With those words, Viper walked away and got inside the dark sedan before the driver pulled off.

Bane watched him leave before turning his attention to Crystal. "Come on, let's get the hell out of here before those guys sitting in the parking lot figure out we're one up on them." He opened the trunk and placed their luggage inside.

"Do you want me to drive, Bane? You have to be tired."

He smiled when he opened the SUV's door for her to

get in. What he was enduring was nothing compared to missions he and his teammates typically encountered. "No, I'm fine. We're together, and that's all that matters to me."

We're together, and that's all that matters to me.

A half hour later, as Bane took the interstate with a remarkable amount of ease for a man who hadn't gotten much rest, Crystal couldn't help but continue to recall those words. Shouldn't that be all that mattered to her, as well? The one thing she knew for certain was that she was glad he was here with her. No telling what her fate would be if he wasn't. She wouldn't have known where to go or what to do. Her plans had been to head for the Bahamas, not knowing someone would have been there, waiting for her at the airport to grab her before she could get on the plane.

But Bane had known. Through his intricate network of teammates, he'd been able to stay one step ahead of the bad guys. What had gone down at the hotel was too close for comfort. She would never have known a tracker had been sewn inside her jacket.

She was surprised Jasmine Ross was involved. The woman was a few years older than she and seemed perky enough. Jasmine had even tried to befriend her a few times, but Crystal hadn't been ready to become the woman's friend. She hadn't thought anything about the stuffed giraffe, since Jasmine had given everyone working in the lab a gift. And as for her jacket, Crystal hung it on the coatrack like everyone else, so Jasmine had access to it. She could have sneaked off with it and placed a tracker inside without being detected.

Crystal wondered what would entice a person to be on

the wrong side of the law. What was in it for the woman? Crystal didn't want to think about what those other two chemists were enduring against their will. They'd been separated from their families and probably didn't know if anyone would find and rescue them. Were they even still in this country?

"You okay over there?"

She glanced at Bane. As far as she was concerned, she should be asking him that. At least she'd gotten a couple hours of sleep earlier tonight. "Yes, I'm fine. What about you?"

He chuckled. "I'm great."

To a degree, she believed him. Bane was definitely in his element. This was a different Bane. More in control. Disciplined. Not impulsive, irresponsible or reckless. The Bane she remembered would have gone out to the parking lot to confront those guys, ready to kick ass. The old Bane had an attitude and detested anyone telling him what to do, especially when it involved her. That was why he'd butted heads with her father countless times and defied the law.

And defied his family. She recalled how often his brother Dillon had sat them down and talked to them, urging her to stay in school. He had lectured them to stop acting impulsively and to start thinking of someone other than themselves.

Deciding to continue the conversation with the goal of keeping him awake, she asked, "So what's going on with your family? Are your brothers and cousins still single?"

His laugh was rich and filled the car's interior. The sound filled her as well, and she wondered how the deep throatiness of his voice could do that to her. "Not hardly.

In fact, after Valentine's Day when Bailey ties the knot, that will take care of everyone."

"Bailey is getting married?"

"Yes, and she's moving to Alaska. Her husband-to-be owns a huge spread on an island there."

Crystal was shocked. "Bailey always swore that she would never marry and move away."

"Well, evidently Walker Rafferty was able to change her mind about that. I got a chance to meet him over Thanksgiving. A pretty nice guy. Ex-marine."

The man must really be something if Bane approved of him. As the youngest two Westmorelands, Bane and Bailey had been close growing up. They'd done a lot of things together. Even got into trouble. "I'm happy for her."

"So am I."

She then listened as he brought her up-to-date on his other siblings and cousins and the women and men they had married. His cousins Zane and Derringer, and his brother Riley were also shockers. She remembered they had reputations around Denver as being ladies' men.

She shifted to get comfortable in her seat as Bane continued to fill her in on his family. She loved hearing the sound of his voice and could tell he was proud of everyone in the Westmoreland family. He also told her about more cousins his family had tracked down in Alaska with the last name of Outlaw.

As she continued to listen to him, she didn't think to question where they were headed. Like he'd said earlier, they were together, and that was all that mattered. She felt safe with him, and at the moment she couldn't imagine being anyplace else.

Twelve

"I'm taking the bed closer to the door again."

"All right."

Bane tossed his duffel bag on the bed and glanced around the hotel room. This one was roomier than the last and the bed looked inviting as hell. The first thing he intended to do was take a shower. He had driven for nine hours and he had to hand it to Crystal, she had tried keeping him company by engaging him in conversation about his family and his job as a SEAL. He had explained that due to the highly classified nature of what he did, there was a lot about his missions he couldn't divulge. She understood and seemed fascinated by what he had been able to tell her.

He glanced over at her and could tell she was exhausted, as well. It was daylight outside but he figured as long as they kept the curtains drawn the room would have the effect of nighttime. Right now he doubted his body cared that it was just two in the afternoon. As long as he could get a little sleep, he would be ready for the next phase of his mission to keep his wife safe.

He turned to place his cell phone on the nightstand. He'd received text messages from Flip letting them know Crystal's house had been burned down to the ground, which probably infuriated those thinking she had data stored somewhere inside it. And then Viper had texted to say that before turning those guys in the parking lot over to Homeland Security, he and his cousin had given them something to think about. Bane hadn't asked for details, thinking it was best not to know. But he figured the men wanting Crystal had to be insanely mad when their plans were derailed time and time again. Hopefully, if those guys were the same ones who had kidnapped the other two chemists, it would be just a matter of time before they were found.

"Do you want me to order you something to eat? That way when you get out of the shower your food will be here," Crystal asked.

He glanced back over at her. "That would be nice. Thanks."

"Anything in particular you want?"

It was close to the tip of his tongue to answer and say, *Yes, you. You are what I want.* Instead, he said, "Whatever looks good. I'm game." Grabbing some fresh clothes out of the duffel bag, he went into the bathroom and closed the door behind him. And then he leaned against it and drew in a deep breath.

Needing a shower was just an excuse. What he really needed was breathing space away from Crystal. Sharing a room with her, being in close proximity to her after all this time was playing havoc on every part of his body. Every time he looked at her he was filled with desire so deep, the essence of it seemed to drench his pores. And he couldn't ignore the sensations he felt knowing they were finally together after being apart for so long.

The sound of his phone alerted him to a text message from Nick. Pulling the phone out of his back pocket, he quickly read the lengthy text before placing his phone on the vanity.

Stripping off his clothes, he stepped into the shower. A cold one. And he didn't so much as flinch when the icy cold water bore down on his skin. Instead, he growled, sounding like a male calling out for a mate he wanted but couldn't have.

Deciding to focus on something else to get his mind off Crystal for the time being, he mentally ran through all the information Nick had texted him. Crystal's co-worker, Jasmine Ross, was nowhere to be found. Rumor within Homeland Security indicated she'd had help from inside, and for that reason Nick agreed with Bane's way of thinking to not let anyone, especially Homeland Security, know of his connection to Crystal. Right now everyone was trying to figure out where she'd gone.

The plan was for him and Crystal to stay put at this hotel until tomorrow. Then they would drive overnight to the Alabama and Georgia line and meet with some of his family members. Namely his cousins Dare, Quade, Cole and Clint Westmoreland. Dare, a former FBI agent, was currently sheriff of College Park, a suburb of Atlanta. Clint and Cole were former Texas Rangers and Quade still dabbled from time to time in secretive assignments for a branch of government connected directly to the White House.

Bane stepped out of the shower and began toweling himself off, ready to have something to eat and then finally get some sleep. After slipping into a pair of jeans and a T-shirt, he grabbed his phone and slid it into his back pocket. He then opened the bathroom door and walked out to find Crystal pacing the hotel room. "What's wrong?"

She paused and looked over her shoulder at him. "What makes you think something is wrong?"

"You're pacing."

"So I was." She moved to the desk and sat down in the black leather armchair. "Too much nervous energy, I guess. I don't want to bother you."

"You aren't bothering me," he said, moving to his duffel bag to discard the clothes he'd just taken off. "I just don't want you to wear yourself out."

"You're worried about me wearing myself out? You? Who barely got any sleep or ate a decent meal in the past twenty-four hours?"

"I've survived before on less."

"Well, I prefer not hearing about it."

He wondered if she was ready to hear what Nick had texted him earlier. "Jasmine Ross is missing."

"Missing?"

"Yes. Nick thinks she might have suspected DHS is onto her and went into hiding." At that moment there was a knock on the door, followed by a voice that said, "Room service."

"Great timing," Bane said as he headed for the door. Deciding not to take any chances, he grabbed his gun off the table and then looked through the peephole before opening the door.

After the attendant had rolled in a cart loaded down

with a variety of foods, arranged everything and left, Bane smiled over at Crystal. "The food looks good. You're joining me, right?"

She nodded. "Yes, I'm joining you."

"I doubt if I can eat another bite, Bane," Crystal said, sliding her chair back from the table. Her goal had been to make sure he got something to eat and not the other way around. But he'd had other ideas and had practically fed her off his plate. She recalled how they used to do stuff like that years ago. Until now, she hadn't realized just how intimate it was.

"Mmm, you've got to try this. The piecrust is so flaky it nearly melts in your mouth," he said, reaching over and offering her his fork with a portion of apple pie on it.

It slid easily between her lips and she closed her eyes and moaned. He was right. It was delicious. In fact, everything was. Instead of ordering an entrée, she had chosen a variety of appetizers she thought he might like. And from the way he'd dived in, he had been pretty hungry. She was glad he had enjoyed all her selections.

She watched him finish off the last of the pie and tried ignoring the way her own stomach fluttered. He even looked sexy while he ate. Seriously, how totally ridiculous was that? Sighing, she glanced around the hotel room, deciding she could handle looking at just about anything right now except Bane. More than once she'd noticed him looking at her and had recognized that glint in his eyes. He'd always had that look when he wanted her. And why was she having such a hard time getting past that look?

"It's hard to believe the sun is about to go down already."

She glanced over at him and saw he was looking out the window. She had opened the blinds while he was taking a shower so the room wouldn't look so dark. The light coming through the window had helped, but now they would be losing that daylight soon.

"We'll make the twenty-four-hour mark in a few hours."

She lifted a brow. "Twenty-four-hour mark?"

He smiled and stared at her for what seemed like a minute or two before saying, "We will have spent the past twenty-four hours together. That's a pretty good start, don't you think?"

Pretty good start? Considering everything, he could think that? "I suppose." She glanced at her watch. "Now it's my turn to shower. I plan on getting into bed early."

"So do I."

She glanced at him and saw gorgeous hazel eyes staring back at her across the rim of a coffee cup. She couldn't help but return his stare. Okay, what was going on here and why was she encouraging it? He shouldn't be looking at her like that and she certainly shouldn't be returning the look. She should be saying something…or better yet, shouldn't she be getting up from her chair and heading for the bathroom? Yes, that was exactly what she should be doing.

She cleared her throat before easing to her feet. And because she felt she needed to say something she said, "Umm, I think I'll take a tub bath instead of a shower. I feel the need to soak my body in bubbles for a while." She frowned. Seriously? Wasn't that too much information?

She knew it probably had been when she saw his smile. It wasn't just any old smile but one that was so sexy it had sparks of desire shooting all through her.

"Sounds nice. Mind if I join you?"

Why had he had to ask her that? And why had his gaze just lowered to her chest just now? And why were her nipples stiffening into buds and feeling achy against her T-shirt? "You took a shower earlier. Besides, you'd be bored to tears."

His rich chuckle filled the room. "Bored to tears? In a bathtub with you? I seriously doubt that, sweetheart. In fact, I know for sure that won't be the case."

She raked her eyes over him from head to toe. She had a feeling that wouldn't be the case as well, but would never confess that to him. "But I'm sure such a macho SEAL wouldn't want to smell like vanilla," she said, moving quickly to the bed where she'd laid out a change of clothes.

Grabbing the items off the bed, she dashed into the bathroom and closed the door behind her.

Bane took the last sip of his coffee as he continued to stare at the closed door. Did he have his wife running scared? He grinned, thinking how he'd at least asked about taking a bath with her…even if she'd turned him down. Already he heard the sound of running water and his mind was beginning to work overtime, conjuring up all kinds of fantasy scenarios involving Crystal's naked body and a bathtub full of bubbles.

He had it bad. Yes, he most certainly did. But hell, that could be expected. He was a full-grown man who hadn't shared a woman's bed in five years, and the woman he'd been holding out for was behind that closed door without a stitch of clothes on, playing with bubbles and smelling like vanilla.

He shifted his gaze from the closed door to glance

out the window. He might as well get up and close the blinds, since it was getting dark outside. However, instead of moving, he continued to gaze thoughtfully out of the window. He wondered how long it would be before he could officially bring Crystal out of hiding. According to Nick's text messages, two arrests had been made, but so far those guys weren't talking.

Just then, his phone went off. He picked it up when he recognized the ringtone. "Yes, Bay?"

"Just checking on you and Crystal. Dillon told us what's going on."

Bane leaned back in his chair. "So far so good, considering someone had sewn a tracker inside Crystal's jacket. Luckily, we were able to stay ahead of them anyway."

"Dillon said you're headed south. Why not come home to Westmoreland Country?"

"Can't do that. The last thing the family needs is for me to deliver trouble to everyone's doorstep."

"We can handle it, Bane."

"It's not the old days, Bay. My brothers and cousins have wives and kids now. We're dealing with a bunch of crazies and there's no telling what they might do. I can't take the chance."

"Then, come to Kodiak. Walker told me to tell you that you and Crystal are welcome there. We're leaving for home tomorrow and won't be returning to Westmoreland Country until a week before Christmas."

Bane smiled. "Did you hear what you just said?"

"About what?"

"Kodiak, Alaska. You said that you and Walker were leaving for *home* tomorrow. It's strange hearing you think of anywhere other than Denver as home."

Bailey chuckled. "I guess I'm beginning to think of wherever Walker is as home for me."

Bane nodded. "You really love the guy, don't you?"

"Yes. Now I know how you and Crystal felt all those years ago. Especially the obsession. I can't imagine my life without Walker." She paused a moment and then asked, "And how are things going with you and Crystal? You guys still love each other, right?"

"Why wouldn't we?"

"The two of you haven't seen each other in five years, Bane. That's a long time to not have any kind of communication with someone."

Yes, it was, but he'd known the moment he'd seen Crystal that for him nothing had changed. But could he say the same about her feelings for him?

Before his cousin could ask him any more sensitive questions, he said, "I need to make a call, Bay. Thank Walker for the offer and tell him if I decide to take him up on it, I'll let him know."

"Okay. Stay safe and continue to keep Crystal safe."

"I can't handle my business any other way."

He ended the call, then stood and closed the blinds before wheeling the table and dishes out into the hall. Once back inside he reached for his phone, figuring now was a good time to check in with Nick before calling it a night. His friend picked up on the second ring. "What's going on, Nick?"

"Glad you called. I was about to text you. Jasmine Ross has been found."

Crystal drew in a deep breath as she slid into her bathrobe. She felt good and refreshed. Soaking in the tub for almost an hour had definitely relaxed her mind. Hopefully Bane was asleep by now and she would be soon, too. They both needed a good ten hours' worth before heading out again.

Opening the bathroom door she allowed her eyes to adjust to the semidarkness. The first thing she noticed was that Bane was not in bed sleeping as she had hoped but was sitting at the desk with his back to her.

He turned around when he heard her and she could tell from the look on his face that something was wrong.

"Bane? What's going on?"

He stood and stuck his hands into the pockets of his jeans. "I talked to Nick a short while ago."

Nick, who was usually the bearer of bad news, she thought, tightening the belt of her robe around her. "And?"

"They found Jasmine Ross."

"Really?" she said, moving toward Bane with a feeling of excitement flowing through her. "That's good news, right? Hopefully Jasmine will confess her part in all this and work out a plea deal or something. Maybe they'll get her to tell them where those other two chemists are being held."

"Unfortunately, Jasmine won't be telling anyone anything."

Crystal frowned. "Why?"

"Because she's dead. She was shot in the head and dumped in a lake. A couple of fishermen came across her body a few hours ago."

Thirteen

"Here. Drink this."

Crystal's fingers tightened on the glass Bane placed in her hand, and she fought hard to hold it steady. Jasmine was dead? Suddenly everything seemed so unreal. So unbelievable.

She glanced down into the liquid. It was alcohol, and the smell alone was so strong it had her straightening up a little in her chair. "Whoa. What is it?"

"Scotch."

She lifted an arched brow. "Where did Scotch come from?"

"I ordered it from room service after I talked with Nick. I figured you'd need a glass."

"I don't drink, Bane."

"You need to drink this. It will help with the shock of what I told you."

Crystal nodded, took a sip and frowned. Like coffee,

liquor was a taste she'd never acquired. She drew in a deep breath as her gaze flickered around the room.

"She brought it on herself, Crystal," she heard Bane say. "Evidently, the woman didn't have any problem setting you up. Don't forget she placed a bugging device in a gift she gave you and a tracker inside your jacket."

"I know, but it's still hard to believe she'd do something like that. She was nice most of the time. At least she pretended to be," Crystal said, leaning forward to place her glass on the desk. One sip had been enough for her. "How could she have gotten mixed up in something so devious?"

Bane shrugged. "Who knows what makes people do what they do? Unfortunately, she got in too far over her head. And the people she thought she could trust saw her as a threat instead of an asset."

Shivers passed through Crystal, and when Bane touched her arm she nearly jumped out of her skin. "You okay?" he asked softly.

She tipped her head all the way back to gaze up at the ceiling before lowering it to look at him. "Not really. It was bad enough to know one of my coworkers was involved in heaven knows what, but then to find out she lost her life because of it is a little too much."

"Are you sure you're okay?"

She glanced at Bane. "Yes, pretty much. But I think I'll go to bed now and try to get some sleep."

Crystal stood up. Without saying anything else and feeling Jasmine's death weighing her down, she moved across the room, threw back the covers and slid into bed. She turned her back to Bane so he wouldn't be able to see her tears.

Bane came awake with a start. First there was a small whimper from the bed next to his. Then he heard a rumbled, emotional plea. "Please don't! Don't shoot him. Please don't."

It took only a second to realize Crystal was thrashing around in her bed having a bad dream. He was out of his bed in a flash and flipped on the small lamp on the nightstand, bathing the room in a soft glow. He sat on the edge of her bed, gently shaking her awake. "Crystal, it's okay. Wake up, baby. You're having a bad dream. Wake up."

He watched as her eyes flew open just seconds before she threw herself into his arms. Automatically he held her tight and used his hands to gently stroke her back. "It's okay, Crystal."

"Bane."

She whispered his name against his neck and the heat from her breath set off a fire in the pit of his stomach. Her arms tightened around him and he refused to let this moment pass. She needed him and he wanted to be needed.

"I'm here, baby."

She pulled back slowly, meeting his gaze and holding it. "It was an awful dream. They came for us, and you wouldn't let them take me. You put yourself in front of me. To protect me. And the man raised his gun to shoot. They were going to shoot you and I felt so helpless."

He slid one hand to the back of her neck and used the other to push several strands of hair back from her face. He saw fear in her eyes, and more than anything he wanted to take that look away. "It was just a dream, Crystal. No one is here but us, and no one is going to shoot me."

"B-but I…"

"Shh, baby. It's okay. I'm okay. We're okay."

He leaned in close to kiss the corners of her lips but she tipped her head at an angle and his mouth landed over hers. Instinctively, she parted her lips at the moment of impact and he swept his tongue inside her mouth to kiss her fully.

They'd kissed a couple of times over the past twenty-four hours, but nothing like this. There had been a hunger, but tonight this was about taking care of an ache. He deepened the kiss to taste her more fully as desire quickened inside him. She whimpered, and the sound was so unlike the one that had awakened him earlier. This one sent sensations jolting through him, filling him with the awareness of a sexual need that he felt all over.

And when she reached up and wrapped her arms around his neck it became the kind of kiss that curled a man's toes and made his entire body get hard. She tangled her tongue with his in a way that made every cell in his body come alive and he could only moan out loud.

A swirl of heat combined with a heavy dose of want overtook him as he continued to ply her mouth with hungry, languorous strokes of his tongue. There was only so much of her he could take without craving more, and his desire for more was nearly eating him alive, driving him insane.

And he didn't want to just kiss her. He wanted to make love to her the way a husband would want to make love to his wife. He wanted to taste her all over. Feel his hands touching every inch of her. And reacquaint himself with being inside her.

Exploring her mouth this way was making his already aroused body that much more unrestrained. It was hard to remain in his good-guy lane and stay in control. Especially when she was returning his kiss with just as much bone-melting fire as he was putting into it. Explosive chemistry was something they'd always shared. Noth-

ing had changed. The taste of her was incredibly pleasurable as always. To his way of thinking, even more so.

Unable to take any more, he broke off the kiss and
pressed his forehead to hers while releasing pent-up
breath from deep in his lungs. "Crystal." He wasn't sure
why he needed to whisper her name at that particular
moment, but he did.

"I'm here, Bane."

Yes, she most certainly was, he thought, breathing
hard. He briefly considered giving her another kiss before tucking her under the covers and returning to his
bed, but for some reason he couldn't do that. He wanted
to continue holding her in his arms, so she would know
she was safe here with him.

Bane shifted their bodies so they were stretched out
together in the bed, and as they lay there beside each
other, he wrapped his arms around her. "Sleep now," he
whispered softly, trying to ignore how the angle of her
backside was smacked up against his groin. He had a
hard-on and there was no way she couldn't feel it.

She began writhing around in the bed trying to get
comfortable, and each time she did so he felt his engorged erection get that much harder. Finally, after grit-
ting his teeth a few times, he reached out and cupped a
firm hold to her thigh. "I wouldn't do that too often if I
were you," he warned.

"Why? Because you want me?"

With a guttural hiss, he positioned her body so that
she was lying flat on her back. He loomed over her and
looked down into her eyes. "What do you think?"

She broke eye contact with him for a mere second before returning his gaze. "I think I might not be as good
with that as I used to be."

"Why would you think that?"

"It's been a while. Five years."

A smile curved his lips. "Are you saying that because you think that I might not be as good as I used to be, as well?"

Surprise leaped into her eyes and she exhaled sharply. "No. That never crossed my mind."

"Good. And just for the record, the thought that you're not as good as you used to be never crossed mine, either."

"Not even once?"

He stared at her in the lamplight. Her features were beautiful, the look in her eyes intense as she waited on his answer. "Not even once," he said, meaning every word. "But I have been wondering about something, though," he added, breathing her scent deep into his nostrils.

She lifted a brow. "What?"

"Can my tongue still make you come?"

Bane's words caused Crystal to squeeze her eyes shut as sensations, namely memories of him doing that very thing, assailed her. She always thought Bane's mouth should be outlawed. And it didn't take much to recall everything he used to do, while licking her from the top of her head to the bottom of her feet, paying close attention to those areas in between.

Especially those areas in between.

"Open your eyes, sweetheart."

She did and her gaze met his. Held it. She felt the sexual tension mounting between them, easing them into a comfortable and mutual existence where memories were surrounding them in ways they couldn't ignore or deny. And at the exact moment his fingers shifted from her thigh to settle between her legs, she knew just what he'd found.

A woman who was hot and ready.

Crystal wasn't exactly sure when the amount of time they'd been apart no longer mattered to her. The only thing that mattered was that he still wanted her after so long. That he hadn't been with another woman just like she hadn't been with another man. It was as if her body was his and his was hers. They had known it, accepted it and endured the loneliness. She hadn't wanted any other man but him, and now her body was demanding to have what it had gone without for quite some time.

"Do you know how many times I lay in bed at night and envisioned touching you this way, Crystal?" Bane whispered.

He shifted his hand and his fingers began moving, sliding inside her, and automatically her thighs eased apart. "No, how many?" she asked, loving how the tip of his fingers stroked up and down her clit.

"Too many. Those were the times I had to take matters into my own hands. Literally. That's how I kept from going insane. But I like this better," he said as he continued working his fingers inside her, causing a deep ache to spread through her. "The real thing. No holds barred."

No holds barred. As he stroked the juncture between her thighs, Crystal couldn't recall the last time she had felt so electrified. For so long, she had mostly ignored her body's demands, except for those rare occasions when she couldn't and had resorted to self-pleasure the way he had.

But Bane's fingers were not toys. They were real, and what they were doing to her was as real as it could get. The sensations being generated inside her were so intense she actually felt air being ripped right out of her lungs with every breath she took. Her heart rate had picked up, and she felt as if she was being driven off the edge, falling headfirst into one powerful wave of pleasure.

"You like this?"

Before she could answer, he reached down, sliding his free hand beneath her shirt and settling it on the center of her stomach. She felt the heat radiating from his touch and began writhing. "Hey, it's okay, baby. It's just me and my touch. I want to put my imprint on you everywhere," he whispered.

Did he think his imprint wasn't already there? She was convinced his fingertips had burned into her skin years ago. And when he pushed her T-shirt up, she felt a whoosh of air touch her skin, especially her breasts. She wasn't wearing a bra and could feel the heat of his gaze as he stared down at the twin globes.

"Hmm, beautiful. Just as I remembered. Do you have any idea how much I used to enjoy sucking these?"

Yes, she had an idea because he used to do so all the time. At one point she'd been convinced his mouth was made just for her nipples. And now, when he used his tongue to lick his lips just moments before lowering his head toward her breasts, she could actually feel a fire ignite inside her. She felt her nipples harden even more. And all it took was one look into his eyes to know he was about to devour her alive.

He buried his face in her chest and took her nipple easily between his lips. Then he began sucking hard. She wasn't sure if it was his fingers working inside her below or his mouth torturing her nipples that would do her in first. When it happened, she had a feeling it was both.

"Bane!"

An orgasm tore through her immediately and she

couldn't hold back the scream. But he was there, capturing her mouth with his, smothering her deep moans with his kiss. Still, he didn't let up, his fingers continuing to work her, rebuilding a degree of passion within her that she could not contain. And when he released her mouth, he began licking her skin from the base of her chin, all over her breasts, down past her stomach all the way to where his mouth met his fingers. He pulled his fingers out of her only to lift her hips to bring the essence of her toward his mouth. The moment his tongue slid inside her she shuddered, filled to the rim with flames of erotic desire.

She pushed on his shoulders but he wasn't letting up. It was as if he was a hungry beast who intended to get his fill, and when another orgasm ripped through her, she cried out his name again. For a fraction of a second, she was convinced she had died and gone to heaven.

But she was quickly snatched back to earth when she felt him lower her hips and remove his mouth from her. Then she watched through languid eyes as he stood and began stripping off his clothes before reaching down to practically tear off hers. A raw, primitive need was overtaking him. It stirred the air, and she could see it in the passion-glazed eyes staring down at her. She felt the heat in every part of her body.

"That was just the beginning," he whispered as he slid a condom on his engorged erection. "Just the beginning."

And then he was back, spreading her thighs, looming over her, and when their gazes met, she saw what she'd always seen when he'd made love to her. Love. Pure, unadulterated love. Bane still loved her and she knew at that moment that no matter what they'd gone through and what they were going through now, she still loved him, as well.

She reached out and slid her hands up his back, feeling the deep cords of his muscles and flinching when she came to several scars that hadn't been there before. But before she could even imagine what story those scars told, he was taking her mouth again, pulling her in and consuming her with a need that was demanding her full concentration. On them. On this. Never had she been filled with such overwhelming desire, need and passion. She wanted him. Her husband. The man who had been her first and only best friend. The man who'd always had her back and had defied anyone who'd tried keeping them apart.

He ended the kiss to stare down at her. "You ready?"

She looked up at him, dragging in a deep whoosh of air filled with their heated scents. "Yes, I'm ready."

And then, holding tight to her hips, spreading her thighs even wider, he slid inside her.

Bane pushed into Crystal all the way until he couldn't go any farther, not sure where his body began and hers ended. The only thing he knew was this was home. He was home. He had been gone five years and that was five years too long. But now he was back and intended to remind her just how good they were together. Remind her why she was his and he was hers.

His blood was boiling, and at that moment it seemed as though all of it had rushed to the head of his erection buried deep inside her. He felt compelled to move, to mate, to drown even deeper into her sweet, delicious depths. He felt her inner muscles clamp down on him, begin milking him, and he threw his head back and growled. Then he began moving, pumping into her, thrusting over and over again until her climax hit so hard that he was convinced they would have tumbled to the floor had he not been holding on to her tight.

"Bane!"

"Crystal!"

Never had he wanted any woman more than he wanted her. Nothing had changed. But in a way, things *had* changed. They were older, wiser and in control of who they were and what they wanted. No one could dictate when and where they could love. The sky was now their limit. And as he continued to rock his hips against hers, thrusting in and out of her, working them both into yet another orgasm, he knew that this was just the beginning, just like he'd told her.

He wanted her to feel every hard, solid inch of him; he wanted to rebrand her, reclaim her. And when another climax hit them both, this one more earth-shattering and explosive than the last, he met her gaze just moments before claiming her mouth, kissing her with a hunger he knew she felt. The ecstasy was bone-deep, mind-blowing, erotic.

And when he released the kiss and she screamed his name once again, he knew that no matter what, Crystal Gayle Newsome Westmoreland was his destiny. He knew it with all his heart.

Fourteen

Crystal slowly opened her eyes and squinted against the bright morning sun coming through the open window blinds. She shifted her gaze to Bane, who was down on the floor doing push-ups. She watched and listened to him keeping count. He was up to three hundred and eighty and his entire body was glistening with sweat. She dragged in a deep breath, thinking the man had more energy than anyone she knew.

That was just the beginning...

He had been deadly serious when he'd issued that warning last night. He had proved that yes, he could still make her come with his tongue. Nothing had changed there. And what he was packing between those fine legs of his wasn't so bad, either. She had barely recovered from one orgasm before he'd had her hurling into another. She didn't recall him having the ability to do all that before. At least not in such rapid succession.

She switched her gaze to the clock on the nightstand and saw that it was almost nine. She had slept late and didn't have to wonder why. It had been a late night and early morning with Bane. He had the ability to make her body want him over and over again, to satisfy her each and every time.

This morning she felt sore, but at the same time she felt so gratified and contented she had to force back a purr. She couldn't stop smiling as she shifted in bed to stretch out her limbs, feeling the way her body was still humming with pleasure. If his goal had been to make up for all their lost time, he definitely had succeeded.

"Good morning. It's nice seeing you smile this morning."

She glanced back at Bane. His deep, husky voice sent erotic shivers down her spine. He had finished exercising and was standing across the room with a cup of coffee in his hand. His feet were braced apart, his sweats hung low on his hips and his chest was bare.

"Good morning to you, too, Bane. You gave me a lot to smile about last night," she said honestly.

"Glad you think so."

From his smile she knew he was pleased by her admission. She saw no reason to pretend regret when there wasn't any. And Bane of all people knew there had never been a shy bone in her body. However, seeing him two days ago after all those years had given her pause. She had to take things slow and get to know him all over again. It would be a process and, as far as she was concerned, making love was part of the process.

"I wanted to wait for you to wake up before ordering breakfast," he said, placing the coffee cup aside to come sit on the edge of her bed.

She pulled herself up, being careful to keep the bed-sheet over her naked body. "You didn't have to do that. I'm sure with everything…and especially those exercises…that you must be hungry."

"Starving."

"Then, let's order."

"Okay, but this first."

He leaned down and pulled her into his arms. It didn't bother her one iota that her naked body was revealed in the daylight. She recalled having a problem with Bane seeing her naked before since she'd always thought she didn't have enough curves to show off. Now she did.

He kissed her and she wrapped her arms around his neck and returned the kiss. She could feel every hard inch of him, all solid muscles, and immediately thought back to last night. Her pulse began hammering inside her veins. Only his kisses had the ability to do that to her. If she didn't put a halt to things, she was liable to short-circuit. Like she had last night.

Typically, she wasn't a demonstrative person, not in the least. However, last night had been a different story. She could blame it on the fact that she'd gone a long time without having sex, and once she was getting some, she was like a woman starving for more and more. Bane was a man who had no problem delivering, and she had experienced one orgasm after another. Yes, she could definitely say last night had been off the charts in more ways than one.

She broke off the kiss at the sound of her stomach growling. She chuckled. "I guess that's my tummy's way of letting me know it needs to be fed."

"Then, I'll order breakfast," Bane said, standing and

reaching for the phone on the nightstand. "Anything in particular that you want?"

"Pancakes if they have them. Blueberry ones preferably. Maple syrup and bacon. Crisp bacon. A scrambled egg would be nice and a glass of orange juice."

He looked at her and grinned. "Anything else?"

"Umm, not at the moment. And while I'm waiting, I'll take a shower and put on some clothes."

"If you want to walk around naked, I wouldn't mind."

After last night she could definitely see where he wouldn't mind. "I'd rather put on clothes."

"Your choice."

As he placed their order, she slipped out of bed and looked around for the clothes he'd taken off her last night. But she didn't see them. When she found his T-shirt under a pillow she slid it over her head.

"Nice fit."

She looked down at herself. "It will do in a pinch." She looked back at him. "Any calls this morning?"

"No. I think we got enough excitement yesterday."

She nodded as she began pulling clean clothes from her luggage. "What are the plans for today?"

"We stay here most of the day and rest up. When it gets dark then we'll leave."

"And go where?"

"We'll meet up with my cousins Quade, Dare, Clint and Cole near the Alabama-Georgia border."

She nodded, recalling having met those particular cousins at a family get-together around the time that the Denver Westmorelands had discovered they had relatives living in Georgia, Texas and Montana.

Crystal glanced over her shoulder. Bane was back to doing his exercises, and the woman in her couldn't help

but admire the way his muscular hips rocked while he ran
in place. Drops of perspiration trickled off his face and
rolled down his neck and shoulders toward his bare chest.

She drew in a deep breath as she imagined her tongue
licking each drop and the way his skin would taste. But
she wouldn't stop there. She would take her hands and
run them all over his body, touching places she might
have missed out on last night, although she doubted there
were any. She had been pretty thorough.

But still…

What if there were places she had missed and—

"Anything wrong?"

She blinked and realized she'd been standing there
staring. Swallowing deeply she said, "No, nothing is
wrong." She wanted to turn and rush off toward the bathroom to take her shower, but for some reason she couldn't
get her feet to move. It was if they were glued to the floor.

Now he was the one staring at her. She could actually
feel his gaze on every part of her. Any place it landed
made her body sizzle. She closed her eyes to fight off the
desire that threatened to overwhelm her but when she saw
it was no use, she opened them again and let them roam
over every single, solid inch of him. He was so muscular, and so big and hard. She glanced down at his middle.
Umm, did she say big and hard?

She drew in a deep breath when she saw him moving slowly toward her. She wanted to back up but again
her feet wouldn't cooperate. All she could do was stand
there and watch all six foot three of him gaining ground
on her. She felt herself breathing faster with every step
he took and her hands actually began shaking. Her fingertips were even tingling, but what she noticed most of

all was how the juncture of her thighs seemed to throb like crazy.

When had her desire for him become so potent? Had making love to him all night suddenly turned her into a lustful woman? A woman whose needs dictated how she behaved with him? She could only imagine. But then she thought, no, she really couldn't. She hadn't been with a man taking up her space and time for so long, she wasn't sure how to deal with Bane now.

"Are you sure nothing is wrong, Crystal?" Bane had come to a stop directly in front of her. He was standing so close it wouldn't take much to reach out and touch him, feel those hard muscles, that solid chest glistening with sweat.

"Nothing's wrong, Bane. I'm fine."

He gave her a knowing grin, which put her on notice that he knew she was lying. She wasn't fine. Thanks to him she had gotten a taste of what she'd been missing for five years, and just how well he could still deliver. But it was more than just sex when it came to him. She'd always known it, ever since they'd held out those two years before even making love.

During that time they had developed a closeness and an understanding she knew very few couples shared. She had thought that maybe it hadn't survived their separation, but it seemed to have. Of course she knew better than to expect everything to go back to the way it had always been between them. They weren't the same people. They still needed to work out a few things, make adjustments and get a greater understanding of who they were now. But it could be done.

"May I offer a suggestion?" he asked her.

She licked her lips. It was either doing that or giving in to temptation and leaning over and licking him. "What?"

"Let's shower together."

Now, why had he suggested that? All kinds of hot and searing visions begin flooding her brain. "Shower together?"

"Yes. I suggested that same thing the night before last but you sort of turned me down."

Yes, she had. "I wasn't ready."

He took a step closer. "What about now, Crystal? Are you ready now? After last night, are you ready to give your husband some more playtime?"

It wasn't his request that caused her mind to shatter. It was his reference to himself as *her* husband. Because at that moment it hit her that he was hers and had been since her eighteenth birthday, probably even before then.

Bane had always told her she was his, regardless of what her parents or his family thought about it. And she had believed him. At no time had she doubted his words. Until that day he'd called to tell her he had decided to go into the navy. But now he was back and was letting her know that although he might have changed in some ways, he was the same in the way that mattered to her. He was still hers.

"That shower isn't very big," she decided to say. "And it might get messy with water sloshing all over the place."

"I'll clean it up," he said.

His smile made her weak in the knees, it was so darn sexy. "Well, if you don't mind doing that, then who am I to argue?" And without saying anything else, she forced her feet to move and walked toward the bathroom. But she didn't close the door behind her. When she turned toward the vanity to look in the mirror, out of the corner of her eye she saw that he was still standing in the same spot staring at her. So she figured that she might as well give him something to look at.

"Down boy," Bane muttered under his breath, trying to get his hard-on under control as he watched Crystal strut off toward the bathroom. As he stood there watching, she proceeded to wash her face and brush her teeth. When had seeing a woman doing basic morning tasks become a turn-on? He could answer that easily. The woman was his wife, and the times he'd seen her do those things had been few and far between.

So he watched her and began getting harder. He couldn't help noticing how his T-shirt clung to her breasts as she leaned toward the sink to rinse out her mouth, how the hem of the shirt had inched up and barely covered her thighs. The same thighs he'd ridden hard last night.

And back to her breasts… He could clearly see how hard the buds were and how well defined the twin globes looked. They were a nice size and nice shape. And he knew for certain they had one hell of a nice taste. As far as he was concerned everything about Crystal was nice. The word *nice* wasn't good enough. He could come up with a number of better ways to describe his wife. *Shapely. Sexy. Mesmerizing. Hot. Tasty.*

Did he need to go on? He doubted it. Instead, as he stood there and watched her take a washcloth to wet her face, he was suddenly turned on in a way he'd never been turned on before. Hell, it was worse than last night, and he hadn't believed that could be possible.

Feeling like a man who needed his wife and needed her now, he moved toward the bathroom. She had to know he was coming, but she didn't turn and look his way. Instead, she began removing his T-shirt and then tossed it aside. By the time he reached her she was naked.

Bane moved behind her and looked into the mirror, holding her gaze in the reflection. He moved closer and took hold of her backside, settling his groin against it. Perfect fit. And when he began grinding, feeling his engorged erection working against her buttocks, the contact nearly sent him over the edge. He broke eye contact with her in the mirror to lean over to lap her shoulder, licking it from one end to the other, taking a few nibbles of her flesh in between. He liked the way her skin tasted this morning. Salty. Womanly.

"I haven't taken a shower yet," she whispered in a voice that let him know the effect his mouth had on her.

"We'll eventually get around to it. No rush."

Then he remembered there was a certain spot on her body, right underneath her left ear, that when licked and sucked could make the raw hunger in her come out. So he licked and sucked there and immediately her body began shivering in a way that sent a violent need slamming through him.

"Bane…"

"I know, baby," he whispered. "Trust me, I know. And I want you just as much. Now. I need to be inside you. Bad. I got five years of want and need stored up just for you."

"And last night?" she asked in that same sexy whisper.

"Just the beginning. One night can't alleviate everything. To be honest, I doubt one hundred nights can."

"Oh, my."

"Oh, yes."

And with that said, he turned her around to face him,

lifted her off her feet and sat her on the vanity. "Spread your legs for me, Crystal."

As if they had a will of their own, her thighs parted. He pulled a condom pack out of the side pocket of his sweats and moved back only far enough to ease the sweats down his legs.

"You don't have to use that unless you want to," she said softly. "After I lost the baby my aunt suggested I go on the pill. More to help keep me regulated than anything else."

He nodded. So in other words she was letting him know that this time or any time they felt like it, they could go skin to skin, flesh to flesh. Just the thought made his entire body feel as if it was on fire. "Then, I won't use one."

With his pants out of the way, he got back into position between her spread legs. His shaft was ready, eager to mate and greedier than he'd ever felt it to be. He cupped himself to lead it home.

"Let me."

He looked up and gazed into her eyes. The thought that she'd asked to guide him inside her almost made him weak in the knees. "All right."

When she reached out and took hold of him, he felt himself harden even more in her hands. And then she led him to her center, and it was as if a thousand watts of electricity jolted through her nerve endings to him. And instinctively he pushed forward, thrusting into her hard and deep, all the way to the hilt. Reaching out, he grabbed hold of her hips, and began moving inside her like crazy.

Needing even more of a connection with her, he leaned forward to capture her lips with his. She had the minty taste of whatever mouthwash she'd used and he intended to lick the taste right from her mouth. She returned the kiss and he deepened it as much as he could while thrusting even more deeply into her body. Setting the same rhythm for both, the same beat. The same drive.

And the beat went on. He could hear her whispering in a choppy breath for him not to stop. So he didn't. He couldn't. It seemed that everything was out of his control. He was out of control. His entire body was ablaze for her.

"Bane!"

She screamed his name and tightened her legs around his waist. He thrust harder in response and before he could catch his next breath, his body exploded. But he wasn't done.

"Hold on, Crystal. I'm coming again."

"Bane!"

He threw his head back and sucked in a deep gulp of air that included a whiff of her scent. He practically lifted her hips off the vanity as he pushed deeper, and he came again with a primal need that made his entire body tremble. Now he knew that this woman who'd gotten under his skin so many years ago, who'd been his world, still was. And would always be so.

Fifteen

There was a knock on their hotel room door. "That should be dinner."

Crystal felt an immediate sense of loss when Bane separated his limbs from hers. Had they gone through breakfast and lunch? A part of her knew they had but the only thing she could recall with clarity was their seemingly nonstop lovemaking sessions. They'd only taken time out to grab something to eat and indulge in a couple of power naps in between.

She watched as he quickly slid into his jeans. When he grabbed his gun off the desk and inserted it into his waistband, it was a stark reminder of the situation they were in. There was a group of people out there who wanted her, and Bane was just as determined that they would not get her.

"Yes?" Bane asked as he looked out the door's peephole.

"Room service."

"Just a minute." He looked over his shoulder at her. "Decent?"

She was pulling his T-shirt over her head. "Now I am." But she still slid beneath the covers and pulled the bedsheet practically up to her chin.

He opened the door to a smiling young woman who couldn't help roaming her gaze all over Bane as she pushed a cart into their hotel room. "Everything you ordered, sir."

"Thanks."

Once the woman left, Crystal slid out of bed and glanced at the food. The cart was set like a table for two. Bane was finally getting his steak and potatoes, and as far as she was concerned, he deserved it. She was certain he'd worked up an appetite over the past few hours.

"I need to wash my hands first."

"So do I."

"But not together. I'll go first," she said, racing off toward the bathroom and closing the door behind her. Every time she and Bane entered the bathroom together they ended up making out all over the place. He had taken her on the vanity and in the shower just before breakfast. And then again in the shower right before lunch.

After washing her hands she quickly dried them off before opening the bathroom door, only to find him standing right there waiting. "My turn now," he said, grinning. "If you want to keep me company, I won't mind."

Yes, she just bet he wouldn't. "No thanks. I'll be okay out here waiting for you. I promise not to start without you."

"I won't be long because I'm sure you're hungry, too,"

he said with a grin. He went into the bathroom and closed the door behind him.

Crystal rubbed her hand down her face. Jeez. This new Bane was almost too much for her. He'd always had a pretty hefty sexual appetite, but in the past, due to her lack of experience, he'd always kept that appetite under control. Now it was obvious he wasn't holding anything back. In a way she couldn't help but smile about that because now he was treating her as an equal in the bedroom. He'd taken off the kid gloves and wasn't treating her like a piece of china that could easily break.

"I'm back."

She glanced up and thought that yes, he was back, looking sexy as ever and easily transforming her into one huge bundle of sexual need. "Umm, maybe I should change clothes. Keeping on your T-shirt might not be a good idea."

He moved around her toward the cart. "Don't know why you think so. Besides, we'll both be changing soon enough since we'll be moving out in a few hours."

That was right. He had mentioned that to her. They'd be meeting up with his cousins. When she approached the cart, Bane pulled out a chair for her. She wasn't surprised. One thing about those Westmoreland men, they might have been hell-raisers a time or two, but they always knew how to act proper and show respect.

"Thanks, Bane," she said, taking her seat.

"You're welcome." He leaned down and placed a kiss on her lips. "Eat up."

"Do you know what the plan is after we meet with your cousins?"

He took a sip of coffee and shook his head. "Not sure.

Quade has connections with the White House. He may have some insight into the mole at Homeland Security."

Crystal didn't say anything as she began eating, but she couldn't help wondering what could be done to keep her safe. She doubted Bane could continue to protect her on the run. What if he had orders for an assignment? Then where would she be?

"You're frowning. You think the food isn't good or something?"

She glanced over at him. "The food is good," she said of the grilled chicken salad she'd ordered. "I was just wondering about something."

"What?"

"What happens if you get that phone call?"

"What phone call?"

"The one from your commander that you're needed on one of those covert operations."

He shrugged. "Like I told you, my team and I are on military leave for a while. However, if something comes up, I'll let my commander know I can't go. You're my wife and I won't be going anywhere until I know for certain that you're safe."

"Because of your sense of duty and obligation?" she asked, needing to know.

He stared at her as a moment of silence settled between them. Then, he spoke. "I'm not sure what it's going to take for you to realize something, Crystal."

"What?"

"That you're more than an obligation to me. I love you. Always have and always will. That's why I joined the navy five years ago instead of hanging around in Denver and getting into more trouble. In all honesty, I think had I claimed you as my wife back then we might very well be divorced by now."

His words almost snatched the air from her lungs. "Why do you think that?"

"Because there is more to life than what we had back then."

"We had love."

"Yes," he agreed. "And it was our love that would have held things together for a while. But I could see things eventually falling apart. I had a high school education and barely two years of college, and you were determined not to go back to school to get a diploma. All you wanted was to be my wife and the mother of my kids."

"And you saw something wrong with that?" she asked, not sure what he was getting at.

"No, not at the time. But think about it. How far would we have gotten on our own without finally asking your family or mine for help? And eventually I would have resented having to ask anyone for handouts. Granted, I had my land, though legally it didn't belong to me until I turned twenty-five, which meant we would have had to live in the cabin, but only if Dillon agreed to it. But then I doubt the cabin would have been enough. I would have wanted to build a house just as big as my brothers'. One large enough to raise our kids in."

He paused a moment before adding, "And we talked about having a house full of kids without really giving any consideration to how we would take care of them."

She nodded. Although a part of her didn't want to admit it, she knew what he was saying was true. After her miscarriage she had cried for months because she'd lost his baby. After all, they'd talked so often of having a child together one day. But neither had talked about how they would take care of one financially. She'd known the Westmorelands had money, and her young, immature mind had assumed that whatever she and Bane needed his family would eventually take care of. He was right; all she had wanted to do was marry him and have his babies. And she had hated school. Or so she'd thought. The kids had been mean and hateful and resented her ability to ace every test with flying colors. After a while she'd gotten tired of being the class star and having the haters on her back. She'd finally convinced herself that going to school was a waste of her time. Her family had blamed Bane for that decision but it had been hers and hers alone.

She glanced over at him. He had gotten quiet again as he cut into his steak. *Her Bane.* And then a part of her finally got it. He had loved her back then and he loved her now and had told her so several times since he'd walked through her front door. Bane had wanted to give her a better life five years ago because he loved her enough to believe that she and his kids deserved the best of anything. And to give them that, he had made sacrifices. And one of those sacrifices had been her. But she could finally say she understood why he'd made them.

He had wanted to grow up, but he'd also given her a chance to grow up, as well. And she had. She knew how to think for herself, she had two college degrees and was working on her PhD. That had been a lot to accomplish in five years' time and she had done it thanks to him. He had practically forced her to realize her full potential.

"That steak was good."

She glanced over at his plate. It was clean. "You want some of my salad?"

He shook his head and grinned. "No, thanks. I'm good."

Yes, she agreed inwardly. Bane Westmoreland was definitely good. "Bane?"

He pushed his plate aside and glanced over at her. "Yes?"

"I've finally taken my blinders off, and do you know what I see?"

He leaned back in his chair and stared at her. "No. What?"

"A man who loves me. A man who truly loves me even after five years of not seeing me or talking to me. A man who was willing to give me up to give me the best. And for that I want to give you my thanks."

Instead of the smile she'd expected, she watched as a muscle twitched in his jaw. "I really don't want your thanks, Crystal."

No, he wouldn't want her thanks, she thought. He would want her love. Pushing her chair back, she eased from her seat and went to him. Ignoring the look of surprise on his face, she slid down into his lap and turned around to face him. Wrapping her arms around his neck she leaned up and slanted her mouth over his.

He let her kiss him but didn't participate. That was fine with her because she needed him to understand something with this kiss. She'd know the moment he got it, the moment he understood. So she kissed him, putting everything she had into it, and when she heard his breathless moan, she knew he'd almost gotten it. He then returned her kiss with as much passion as she was giving and she felt his hand slide down to her thighs before moving underneath the T-shirt to caress her naked skin.

She knew things could turn sexual between them real quick if she didn't take control. If she didn't let him know what was on her mind…and in her heart. So she pulled back, breaking off the kiss. But that didn't slow up his hands, which were still moving. One was still underneath her T-shirt and the other was sliding up and down her back, stroking the length of her spine.

"I love you, too, Bane," she whispered against his lips. "I guess you can say I never knew how much until now. And you never stopped loving me like I never stopped loving you. I get that now."

"No, baby. I never stopped loving you," he whispered back against her lips. Then he tightened his arms around her as he stood with her and headed toward the bed.

After placing her there, without saying a word he tucked his fingers into the hem of the T-shirt she was wearing and took it off her.

She watched him step back and ease his jeans down his thighs and legs. Her gaze roamed up and down his naked form. Good thing she wasn't wearing any panties or they would be drenched. She wanted him just that much. And she could tell from the look in his eyes that he wanted her with all the passion he'd stored up for five years. He'd told her as much a number of times, had proved it last night and all day today. She saw it now while looking at his engorged erection and could hear it in his breathing.

He came back toward the bed, and before he could make another move, she reached out and wrapped her fingers around his swollen sex. It fit perfectly in her hand. "Nice," she said, licking her lips.

She heard Bane groan deep in his throat before saying, "Glad you think so."

"I do. Always have thought so."

When she began stroking him with her fingers, even using her fingernail to gently scrape along the sensitive skin, he threw his head back and released a growl that seemed to come from deep within his gut. And when she leaned down and swirled her tongue over him, she felt his fingers dig through her hair to her scalp. That drove her to widen her mouth and draw the full length of him between her lips.

Pleasure ripped through Bane to all parts of his body. Crystal was using her mouth to build a roaring fire inside him. A fire that was burning him from the inside out. And when she used her fingers to stroke the thatch of curly hair covering his groin, he could feel his erection expanding in her mouth. That pushed her to suck on him harder and he fought hard not to explode right then and there. Instead, he reached down and entwined his fingers in the silky strands of her hair before wrapping a lock around his fist. And then he began moving his hips, pumping inside her mouth. The more he did so the more she stroked him before using those same fingers to gently squeeze his testicles.

Was she trying to kill him? Did she have any idea what she was doing to him? Did she know how hard it was to hold back and not come in her mouth? He knew if he allowed her to continue at this rate, she was liable to soon find out.

"Crystal," he whispered, barely able to get her name past his lips as his heart raced and blood pulsed through his veins. "Stop, baby. You need to stop now."

She was ignoring him, probably because he hadn't said it with much conviction. And honestly, there was no way he could with all the pleasurable sensations tearing through him. Her desire to please him this way meant more than anything because even with her inexperience she was doing one hell of a job making him moan.

When he could no longer hold back, he shouted her name and tried pushing her away, but she held tight to his thighs until the last sensation had swept through his body. He should have felt drained but instead he felt even more needy. Desperate to get inside her body, he jerked himself out of her mouth and eased her back on the bed.

He felt her body shudder the moment he entered her. She was wet, drenched to the core, which made it easy to thrust deep, all the way to her womb. Then he positioned them so that her legs were wrapped around his waist and back.

He stared down into her face. "I love you. I love your scent. I love your taste. I loved making love to you. I love coming inside you. And I love being buried inside you so deep it's unreal. Heaven. Over-the-top wonderful."

"Oh, Bane."

He was certain she would have said more, but when he began moving, she began moaning. He lifted her hips and began thrusting in and out of her with rapid strokes, taking her over and over again, and intentionally driving her over the edge the way she'd done earlier to him.

He couldn't get enough of her, and when she screamed his name and he felt the heels of her feet dig deep into his back, he knew she was coming. However, he refused to go there yet. But it was the feel of her inner muscles clamping down on him, trying to pull everything out of him that was the last straw, and he couldn't hold back his explosion any longer.

"Crystal!"

He was a goner as he emptied himself completely inside her, filling her in a way that had his entire body shuddering uncontrollably. He could feel her arms wrapped around him and could hear her softly calling his name. Moments later when the earth stopped shaking and his world stopped spinning, he managed to lift his head to stare down at her before crashing his mouth down on hers.

And the words that filled his mind as he kissed her with a hunger he couldn't contain were the same ones he'd said a number of times recently.

This is just the beginning.

Sixteen

"Wake up, sleepyhead."

Crystal slowly opened her eyes and looked out the car's windshield. They were parked at what appeared to be a truck stop decorated with a zillion Christmas lights that were blinking all over the place, although she could see the sun trying to peek out over the mountains.

They had checked out of the hotel around six the night before, which meant that they'd been on the road for twelve hours or so. They'd only stopped twice for bathroom breaks. Otherwise, most of the time she'd been sleeping and he'd been driving. She had offered to share the driving time, but he had told her he could handle things and he had.

He probably figured she needed her rest and she was grateful for that. Before getting dressed, the two of them had taken a third shower. The third in a single day, but all that physical activity had called for it. Besides, she enjoyed taking showers with Bane. He could be so creative when they were naked together under a spray of water. The memories of all they'd done had her body tingling.

Pulling herself up in her seat, she glanced over at him. "We're here already?"

"Yes, but plans changed. Instead of meeting up at the Alabama-Georgia line, we're meeting here."

She glanced around and lifted a curious brow. "And where is here exactly?"

"North Carolina."

North Carolina? No wonder they were surrounded by mountains so huge they reminded her of Denver. "Why the change?"

"They preferred meeting at Delaney's cabin but didn't say why. My guess is because it's secluded, and the way Jamal has things set up, you can spot someone coming for miles around."

"I see." And honestly she did. She had met his cousin Delaney once and recalled hearing how she'd met this prince from the Middle East at a cabin in the North Carolina mountains. To make a long story short, the two had fallen in love and married. "I read an article about her in *Essence* a couple of years back."

"Did you?"

"Yes. And she and her prince are still together."

"Yes, they are. Only thing is that now Jamal is king. He gave the cabin where they met to Delaney as a wedding gift. Since she lives outside the country most of the time, she's given us permission to use it whenever we like."

Bane's phone went off and he quickly pulled it out of the pocket of his jacket and answered it. "This is Bane."

After a few seconds he said, "We're here." Then several moments later he said, "Yes, I recall how to get there. I'll see you guys in a little while."

After he hung up the phone he glanced over at her. "I know this has to be both taxing and tiring for you, Crystal, but hopefully the guys and I will come up with some sort of plan."

She nodded. "Still no word on the whereabouts of those other two chemists?"

"No. None. I spoke to Nick while you were sleeping and he's not sure what the hell is going on now. It seems that with the revelation of a mole in the agency, everyone is keeping their lips sealed."

Crystal figured that didn't bode well for her, since Nick had been Bane's source of information from the inside. She bit back an exasperated sigh and leaned back against the headrest.

"Everything is going to be all right," Bane said, reaching over and taking her hand in his. Not waiting for her to respond he asked, "Did you enjoy yourself yesterday and last night?"

That brought a smile to her lips as the pleasant memories washed over her. Hot and spicy memories that made her nipples suddenly become hard and sensitive against her blouse. "Yes, I did. What about you?"

"Yes, I thought it was nice. Best time I've had in a long time."

She was glad he thought so because she definitely felt the same way. The chemistry they'd always shared had been alive and kicking. It didn't even take a touch between them. A look sufficed. At one point he'd lain across his bed and she'd lain across hers with the television going. She had been trying to take a power nap and had felt his gaze on her. When she'd looked over at him and their eyes connected, she couldn't recall who had moved first. All she knew was that the glance had sparked a reaction between them. A reaction that had them tearing off their clothes again.

He brought her hand to his lips and kissed her fingers. "I can't wait to get you back home."

"Home?" She thought of her house that had been set on fire.

"Yes, back in Denver."

She nodded. Although she realized there was nothing back in Dallas for her now, it had been a long time since she'd thought of Denver as home. "What's the hurry?"

"I can't wait for everyone to see you, and to finally introduce you to them as my wife. And we'll have a house to design and build."

Instead of saying anything, she met his gaze and couldn't ignore the flutter that passed through her stomach or the way her pulse quickened at that precise moment. She watched his gaze roam over her, and noticed how his eyes were drawn to her chest. Specifically, the hardened buds pressing against her blouse.

Releasing her hand he turned on the car's ignition. "Come on. We better find Delaney's cabin, and if I figure right, it's about a half hour drive from here. If it was left up to me we'd check into another hotel and have another play day."

Crystal glanced over at him. His eyes were on the road and he was concentrating on their surroundings. She should be, too, but at the moment she couldn't help but concentrate on him.

Brisbane Westmoreland had always seemed bigger than life to her. The past five years hadn't been easy for either of them, but they were back together and that was all that mattered. Now, if they could only stop the men who were trying to kidnap her, everything would be great.

When he brought the car to a stop at a traffic light he glanced over at her and smiled. "You okay, baby?"

She nodded, smiling back at him. Releasing her seat belt, she leaned toward him and placed a quick kiss on his lips. "You're here with me, and as far as I'm concerned that's all that matters now."

She rebuckled her seat belt and sat back. Satisfied.

"What the hell?" Bane muttered through clenched teeth.

Crystal looked over at him and then sat up straight in her seat and glanced out the SUV's window. "What's wrong, Bane?"

He shook his head and stared out at all the cars, trucks and motorcycles that were parked in front of the cabin they'd pulled up to. "I should have known."

"Should have known what?"

"That it would be more than just Quade, Dare, Clint and Cole meeting us today. Some Westmorelands will find just about any excuse to get together."

Chuckling, he brought the car to a stop and turned off the ignition before unbuckling his seat belt. He then reached over and unbuckled hers. "Before going inside, there's something I need to give you."

"What?"

"This," he said, pulling a small black velvet box from his jacket. When he flipped open the lid, he heard her breath catch at the sight of the diamond solitaire ring with a matching gold wedding band.

"Oh, Bane, it's beautiful."

"A beautiful ring for a beautiful woman," he said, taking the ring out of the box and sliding it on her finger. "It looks good on you, as if it's where it belongs."

She held up her hand and the diamond sparkled in the sunlight. "But when did you get it? How?"

He smiled. "I got it in New York. I had a layover there for a couple of days due to bad weather, and to kill time I checked out some of the jewelry stores. When we got married I couldn't afford to give you anything but this," he said, reaching out and touching the locket she still wore. "I figured it was time I get you something better. It was time I put my ring on your finger."

He got quiet for a moment and then said, "You don't know how much it bothered me knowing you were out there not wearing a ring. I wondered how you were keeping the men away."

"I told you what they thought."

Yes, she had, which he still found hard to believe, but at least it had kept the men at bay.

He lifted her hand and brought it to his lips and kissed it. He then leaned over and lowered his head to kiss her. And he needed this kiss. He hadn't made love to her in over twelve hours, and it was too long.

How had he gone without her for five years? That showed he had willpower he hadn't known he had.

And the one thing he liked most about kissing her was the way she would kiss him back, just like he'd taught her all those years ago to do. Some women's mouths were made for kissing, and he thought hers was one of them. She tasted just as good as she looked and smelled. And that was another thing about her: her scent. His breath would quicken each and every time he took a sniff of her.

His cousin Zane swore that a woman's natural scent was a total turn-on for most men. It had something to do with pheromones. Bane wasn't sure about all that, but the one thing he did know was that Crystal's scent could literally drive him over the edge. And her scent was a dead giveaway that she wanted him regardless of whether she admitted it or not.

There was a loud knock on the truck's window, and he broke off the kiss to glare at the intruder, who said, "Knock it off, Bane."

Rolling his eyes, Bane returned his gaze to Crystal, mainly to focus on her wet lips. "Go away, Thorn."

"Not until I check you over to make sure you're all in one piece. I'm on my way to a benefit bike race in Daytona and in a hurry, so get out of the car."

Bane shook his head as he eased his car seat back. But then in a surprise move he reached across and pulled Crystal over the console and into his arms. He opened the door with her in his arms and got out.

"Bane! Put me down," Crystal said, trying to wriggle free in his arms.

"In a minute," he said, holding her a little longer before sliding her down his body so her feet could touch the ground.

He then turned to Thorn. "Good seeing you, Thorn."

"Good seeing you, too," Thorn said, giving Bane a bear hug. Thorn then reached out to Crystal and pulled her to him, as well. "You too, Crystal. It's been a while."

Bane watched the exchange and knew Thorn's comment had surprised her. Thorn Westmoreland was the celebrity in the family, a well-known, award-winning motorcycle racer who as far as Bane was concerned also built the baddest bikes on earth. He had several movie stars and sports figures as clients.

Crystal and Thorn had only met once at a Westmoreland family reunion, but Bane knew that when it came to his family, Crystal had assumed they saw her as the reason he'd gotten into trouble all those times.

"Thanks, Thorn. It's good seeing you again, as well," Crystal said, as Bane pulled her closer to his side. "How is your family?"

"Fine. Tara's inside along with all the others."

"And just who are *all* the others?" Bane asked.

No sooner than he'd asked that question, the door to the cabin opened and his family members began filing out. The one person Bane hadn't expected to see was Dillon. His older brother stepped out onto the porch along with their cousin Dare. Bane shook his head, not for the first time, at how much Dillon and Dare favored each other.

Bane smiled as his family kept coming out of the cabin. There was Dare and Thorn's brother Stone, and Quade's brother Jared. And besides Dillon, Bane saw his brothers Riley and Canyon, as well as his twin cousins, Aidan and Adrian. He'd just seen the latter four in Denver for Thanksgiving.

"Hey, what's going on?" he asked chuckling. "Last time I looked, Crystal and I were on the run and not dropping by to socialize."

"Doesn't matter," his cousin Dare said, grinning. "We all wanted to see for ourselves that the two of you were okay."

"And we're ready to take anyone on who thinks they can snatch Crystal away from us," Riley said.

"From *us*?" Bane asked, looking at his brother. He

knew that of all his siblings and cousins, Riley had been
bothered the most by Bane's relationship with Crystal.
Riley was afraid that Bane's quest to find her might prove
painful if she hadn't waited for him those five years the
way Bane had waited for her.

"Yes. *Us*. She's a Westmoreland and we take care of
what's ours" was Riley's response.

Bane looked over at Crystal and pulled her closer to
his side. "Yes, she is a Westmoreland."

Quade came forward. "Most of the men arrived yesterday. Figured we would get some fishing in while we
waited for you to get here. The women showed up this
morning and are out back on the porch frying the fish.
First we eat breakfast, then we talk about putting a plan
together. There're a couple of others we're waiting on."

Bane wondered who the others were but didn't ask.
Instead, he said, "Fried fish in the morning? Hey, lead
the way."

Crystal had never felt as much a part of the Westmoreland family as she did now. And she knew she had the
women to thank for that. They had oohed and aahed over
her ring, telling her how much they liked it and how good
it looked on her finger. And they had congratulated her
on her marriage to Bane and officially welcomed her to
the family.

This was her first time meeting Dillon's wife, Pam.
In fact, the last time she'd seen Dillon, he was a single
man on a quest to find out more about his great-grandfather Raphel. It seemed that pursuit had landed him right
on Pam's doorstep, and it had meant nothing to Dillon
that Pam was engaged to marry another man at the time.

And then there was Tara, Thorn's wife, whose sister,

Trinity, was married to Bane's cousin Adrian. Crystal thought it was pretty neat that two sisters were married to two cousins. And the same thing went for Pam and her sister, Jillian. Jillian was married to Bane's cousin Aidan. Crystal also enjoyed getting to know Dare's wife, Shelly, Stone's wife, Madison, Jared's wife, Dana, and Canyon's wife, Keisha.

Quade's wife, Cheyenne, was back home in Charlotte with their triplets—a son and two daughters. The girls had dance class today; otherwise, he said his wife would have come with him.

All the women were friendly and the men were, as well. Crystal fought back tears when they welcomed her to the family in a toast. And when Bane's brother Dillon pulled her aside and said that as far as he was concerned, she'd always been part of the family, and that he was glad she and Bane were back together again, she had to excuse herself for a minute to compose herself. Coming from Dillon, that had meant everything.

After going inside for a quick second to get a beer out of the refrigerator, Bane found her sitting on the dock by the lake. Without saying anything, he pulled her up into his arms. "You okay, baby?"

She looked up at him and nodded. "Yes. Everyone is so nice to me."

He smiled and reached out and caressed her cheek. "And why wouldn't they be nice to you? You're a nice person."

"B-but you and I used to cause your family so many headaches. We did some crazy stuff and got into a lot of trouble."

"Yes." He nodded. "We did. But look at us now, Crystal. I finished the naval academy and I'm a SEAL, and you're just a few months shy of getting your PhD. I think Dr. Crystal Westmoreland will sound damn good, don't you?"

Swiping tears away from her eyes, she said, "Yes. I think so, as well."

"All I'm saying is that you and I have changed, Crystal. We aren't the same people we were back then. We're older, better and more mature, although I'll admit we still have a lot of growing to do. But above all, what didn't change was our love for each other. That's the one thing that remained constant."

Crystal knew Bane was right. Their love *had* been the one thing to remain constant. "I love you, Bane," she whispered.

"And I love you back, baby."

Standing on tiptoe, she slanted her mouth over his, doubting that she could or would ever tire of kissing him. And when he wrapped his arms around her and returned her kiss, she knew she could stay in his arms like that forever. Or maybe not, she thought, when she began feeling weak in the knees.

It was the sound of a car door slamming that made them pull their mouths apart. They both turned to look toward the clearing at the people getting out of the cars that had just pulled up. There were three men and a woman. The only person Crystal recognized was the woman. It was Bane's cousin Bailey.

"I'll be damned," Bane said. "That guy… The one in the black leather jacket sure does look like—"

"Riley," she finished for him. "Riley doesn't have a twin, so who is he?" she asked staring.

"That has to be Garth Outlaw. I never met him but I'd heard how he and his five siblings look just like the

Westmorelands. And they *are* Westmorelands. I told you we found out that my great-grandfather Raphel had a son he hadn't known about who was adopted by the Outlaws as a baby."

"Well, if anyone doubts Garth Outlaw is related to your family all they have to do is put him and Riley side by side."

"That's true," Bane agreed. "And the man with Bailey is her fiancé, Walker Rafferty. I wonder why they decided to come here instead of flying back to Alaska. When I talked to her the other day that's where they were headed. And I have no idea who the third guy is. The one in the dark suit."

Bane took Crystal's hand in his. "Come on. Quade is beckoning us to join them."

A few moments later when they reached Quade, introductions were made. Just as Bane said, Riley's lookalike was one of their newfound cousins from Alaska, the Outlaws, and the man with Bailey was her fiancé, Walker. However, the third man, the one in the dark suit, was just what Crystal had figured him to be—a government man. She wasn't surprised when Quade said, "Bane and Crystal, this here is Hugh Oakwood. He was recently appointed by the president to head a special agency under the Department of Defense."

Bane raised a brow. "Department of Defense? I don't understand why this would involve the DOD. Their primary concern is with military actions abroad. The Department of Homeland Security's role is to handle things domestically."

Hugh Oakwood nodded as he glanced from Bane to Crystal. "Typically that would be true, but what's going on here isn't typical. We think we're dealing with an international group. And it's highly likely that some of our own people at Homeland Security are involved. That's why the president has authorized my agency to handle things."

The man glanced around and saw he had an audience. Clearing his throat, he asked, "Is there someplace where we can talk privately?"

Quade spoke up and said, "Yes, come this way, Hugh. I got just the place."

Seventeen

Bane had heard that after Jamal had purchased the cabin for Delaney, he'd hired a builder to quadruple the size of it to expand the kitchen, add three additional bedrooms, three more bathrooms, a huge family room and a study. The spacious study was where they were now.

He couldn't imagine anyone getting any studying done in here. Not with the gorgeous view of the mountains and the lake. And if those two things didn't grab you then there was the room itself, with its oak walls and beautiful rustic decor. A floor-to-ceiling bookshelf took up one wall and another wall consisted entirely of a large plate-glass window.

Bane sat beside Crystal on a sofa facing the huge fireplace. Dillon, Quade, Clint, Cole and Dare grabbed chairs around the room. It seemed that Hugh Oakwood preferred standing, which made perfect sense since he had the floor. It was obvious that everyone was interested in what he had to say.

The man turned to Crystal. "I read the report and you, Dr. Westmoreland, have a brilliant mind."

Bane noticed that everyone's gaze had settled on Crystal and she seemed uncomfortable with all the attention she was getting. They were realizing what he'd always known. His wife was a very smart woman.

Crystal blushed. "I wouldn't say that. And officially I'm not a doctor yet."

"I *would* say that. And it's only a matter of months before you get your PhD. After going over all your research, at least what I have access to, there's no doubt that you'll get it," Oakwood said. "And if you don't mind, although I noted you've never used the Westmoreland name, I prefer using it now."

"No, I don't mind," she said. "Bane and I decided years ago to keep our marriage a secret."

Oakwood nodded. "That in itself might be a blessing in disguise. Because no one knows of your marriage, the group that's looking for you has no leads as to where you might be right now."

He paused a moment, then said, "In your research you've basically come up with a formula to make items invisible. Similar testing and research have been done by others, but it seems you might have perfected it to the degree where it's almost ready to use."

"So what does all this mean?" Bane asked.

"It means that in the wrong hands it can be a threat to national security. Right now one particular terrorist group, PFBW, which stands for People for a Better World, sees it as a way to smuggle things in and out of countries undetected."

"Things like what?"

"Drugs, bombs, weapons, you name it. Right, Dr. Westmoreland?"

Crystal nodded. "Yes. Although there's quite a bit of research that still needs to be done before that can happen."

Oakwood nodded. "PFBW have already nabbed the other two chemists, as you all know, and would have grabbed you if your husband hadn't intervened."

"I got that note from someone as a warning," Crystal said.

"Yes, you did. PFBW started recruiting members a few years ago. But we managed to infiltrate the group. That's the only way we know what's going on. When you join, you join for life and the only way to get out is death. We're lucky that our informant hasn't been identified so far."

He paused a minute and then added, "The best we can figure is that although Jasmine Ross started out as part of the group, somewhere along the way she had a change of heart and is the one who slipped you that note. It seems that she tried to disappear as well but wasn't as lucky as you. They found her."

And Bane was sure everyone in the room was aware of the outcome of that. "My wife can't continue to hide out and be on the run forever."

"I agree," Oakwood said. "The problem we're facing is not knowing who we can trust in Homeland Security. The one thing we do know is that PFBW still wants you, Dr. Westmoreland. You're the missing link. The other chemists' work can only go so far. You have researched a key component they lack, and it's your work that's needed to put their scheme in place."

"Sorry, but they won't be getting her," Bane said through clenched teeth as he wrapped his arms around Crystal's shoulders.

"That's why we have a plan," Oakwood said, finally taking a chair.

"What's the plan?" Bane asked, removing his arm from around Crystal to lean forward.

From the looks exchanged between Quade and Oakwood, Bane had a feeling whatever plan Oakwood had come up with, he wasn't going to like it.

Bane was off the sofa in a flash. "No! Hell no! No one is using my wife as bait!"

Crystal reached out and touched Bane's arm. "Calm down, Bane. It doesn't sound too bad."

Bane stared down at her. "They want to set you up someplace and then tell PFBW where you are so they can grab you and—"

"When they do come for me, it sounds as if Oakwood and his men will be ready to arrest them."

Bane rolled his eyes. As a SEAL, he of all people knew things didn't always go as planned. "But what if something goes wrong? What if they fail to protect you? What if—"

"Their mission is successful?" Crystal asked, still trying to calm her husband down. "I have to take the chance their plan will work. Like you said, I can't be on the run for the rest of my life."

Bane pulled her up into his arms. "I know, baby, but I can't take a chance with your life. I can't have you back just to lose you."

Crystal heard the agony in his voice, but she needed to make him understand. "And I can't have you back just to lose you, either, but every time you'll leave to go on covert operations as a SEAL I'll face that possibility."

"It's not the same. I'm trained to go into risky places. You aren't."

He was right; she wasn't. "But I'll be well guarded from a distance. Right, Mr. Oakwood?"

The man nodded. "Right. And we do have an informant on the inside."

A muscle twitched in Bane's jaw. "Not good enough," he said, bracing his legs apart and crossing his arms over his chest. "She won't be alone. I will be with her."

Oakwood shook his head. "That won't work. The people looking for her expect her to be alone."

Bane frowned. "Damn their expectations. I refuse to let my wife go anywhere alone. At some point they'll suspect she had help. They probably already do from the way we've successfully eluded them up to now. I don't like your plan, Oakwood, and the only way I'll even consider it is if I'm the one protecting my wife."

"May I make a suggestion?" Everyone in the room glanced over at Quade.

"What's your suggestion, Quade?" Crystal asked when it was obvious neither Bane nor Oakwood was going to. Tension was so thick in the room you could cut it with a knife.

"Oakwood ran his idea by me earlier and knowing Bane like I do, I figured he wouldn't go along with it, so I came up with a plan B, which I'm hoping everyone will accept. It still requires using Crystal as bait, but at least Bane will get to stay with her."

Oakwood stared at Quade for a moment and then said, "Okay, what's your plan?"

Quade stood. "Before I explain things, I need to get

two other people in here who will be instrumental to the success of this plan. The three of us discussed it last night and feel it will work."

He then went to the door, opened it and beckoned for someone. Moments later, Bailey's fiancé, Walker Rafferty, and the Westmorelands' newfound cousin Garth Outlaw entered the room.

Crystal studied Walker and could see how Bailey had fallen for him. He was a looker, but so was Bane. In Crystal's mind, no man looked better. And Garth Outlaw looked so much like Riley it was uncanny. And she found out that like Walker, Garth was an ex-Marine.

Garth began talking. "Quade brought me up-to-date as to what's going on. If you want to set a trap by using Crystal as bait then I suggest you do it in Alaska."

"Alaska?" Bane asked, frowning. "Why Alaska?"

"Because the Outlaws happen to own a cabin on Kodiak Island and it's in a very secluded area. But it's also secured and the cabin has an underground tunnel," Garth said.

Quade moved forward. "If word intentionally leaks out as to where Crystal is, then the people wanting her won't lose any time going after her."

"In Alaska?" Now it was Crystal's turn to ask doubtfully.

"Yes, in Alaska," Oakwood said, rubbing his chin, as if giving plan B serious thought. "They will check things out to make sure it's not a trap, though. Why would Dr. Westmoreland escape to Alaska? The dots will have to connect."

"They will," Garth spoke up and said. "I understand Crystal attended Harvard. Coincidentally, my brother

Cash went there at the same time. He was working on his master's degree. Who says their paths didn't cross?"

"I'm following you," Oakwood said thoughtfully. "The people looking for Dr. Westmoreland will assume that their paths *did* cross, and that in desperation, Dr. Westmoreland, you reached out to Outlaw and he offered you safe haven at a cabin he owns in Alaska."

"Exactly," Quade said. "And from what Garth says, this cabin will be perfect. It's in a secluded location on Outlaw property, and the underground tunnel will provide an escape route if needed."

"And in addition to all of that," Garth said, smiling, "thanks to those strong Westmoreland genes, Bane and Cash look alike. Probably just as much as me and Riley resemble each other. That will work in our favor if someone knows Crystal had help and has gotten a glimpse of the guy she's been seen with. They would expect that same guy to be there with her, still protecting her. They will think it's Cash when it will be Bane."

Dillon spoke up. "That plan will work if no one knows that Crystal is married to Bane. Are you guys absolutely certain no one knows?"

"So far that's a guarded secret," Oakwood said. "I checked and Dr. Westmoreland never indicated Brisbane Westmoreland as her husband on any official school records or other documentation. I wasn't even aware of the marriage until Quade brought it to my attention. However, on the other hand," he said, shifting in his chair, "Brisbane Westmoreland has always indicated on any of his official paperwork that he was married and Crystal Newsome Westmoreland is listed as his wife."

Bane shrugged. "I needed to make sure Crystal was taken care of if anything ever happened to me," he said, pulling her closer to him and placing a kiss on her fore-head. "I also have medical coverage on her as well, just in case she ever needed it, and I established a bank account in her name."

"All traceable if someone really started to dig," Dare said. It was obvious his former FBI agent's mind was at work.

"Let's hope no one feels the need to dig that far," Clint Westmoreland said. He then looked over at Oakwood. "Can't that information be blocked?"

"Yes, but because I don't know who's the mole at Homeland Security and how high up in the department he or she is, blocking it might raise a red flag," Oakwood said. "Our main goal is to try to flush out the mole. Right now he is a danger to our national security. To know he might be someone in authority is even more of a reason for concern."

Neither Bane nor Crystal said anything as everyone looked over at them. The decision was theirs.

"It's a big decision. You might want to sleep on it," Cole suggested.

Crystal stood. "Thanks, but there's no need to sleep on it. And I appreciate everyone wanting to help me. However, what concerns me more than anything is that those people want me alive, but they won't think twice about taking out Bane if he gets in their way. For that reason, I prefer that Bane not be with me."

"Like hell!"

When Bane stood up to object further, Crystal reached out and placed a finger over his lips. "I figured that would be your reaction, Bane." She shook her head. "There's no way you'll let me put my life at risk without trying to protect me, is there?"

He removed her finger from his lips and stared down at her with an unwavering expression on his face. "No."

She released a deep breath. "Then, I guess that means we'll be together in Alaska."

A gusty winter's breeze caused Bane to pull his jacket tighter as he wrapped his arms around Crystal and they walked inside the hotel. It was late. Close to midnight. After making the decision that they would be traveling to Alaska, they'd needed to put in place concrete plans. Crystal had trusted him to handle things and asked to be excused to join the ladies who'd been outside sitting on the patio.

In a way he was glad she'd left when she had, because more than once he'd ripped into Oakwood. Too often it appeared that the man was so determined to find out the identity of the mole at Homeland Security that he was willing to overlook Crystal's safety. And Bane wasn't having that.

It had taken Dillon, Quade and Dare to soothe his ruffled feathers and remove the boiling tension in the room by assuring him that Crystal's safety was the most important thing. Only after that could they finally agree on anything.

He still didn't like it, but more than anything he wanted to bring those responsible to justice so that he and Crystal could have normal lives...something they hadn't had since the day they married.

"You've been quiet, Bane," Crystal said a short while later after they'd checked into the hotel and gone to their room.

"Been thinking," he said, glancing around at the furnishings. They were staying at the Saxon Hotel, and it was as if they'd walked right into paradise.

Dare had offered them the use of one of the bedrooms

at Delaney's cabin, but since some of his kin also planned
to stay there for the night, he had opted out. He preferred
having Crystal to himself, and was not up to sharing
space with anyone, not even his family. After he said that
he and Crystal would spend the night at a hotel in town,
Quade had offered him his room at the Saxon Hotel. The
penthouse suite.

It just so happened Quade's brother-in-law was Dom-
inic Saxon, the owner of the luxurious five-star Saxon
Hotels and the Saxon Cruise Line. Quade had a standing reservation at any Saxon Hotel, but since his wife,
Cheyenne, hadn't accompanied him on this trip, he preferred hanging out with his cousins and brother at the
cabin, figuring a card game would be taking place later.

"Wow! This place is simply gorgeous," Crystal said.

Bane leaned back against the door as she walked past
him to stand in the middle of the hotel room and glance
around.

"Yes, it is that," he said, thinking the room wasn't the
only gorgeous thing he was looking at. Before leaving the
cabin she had showered and changed clothes. Now she
was wearing a pair of dark slacks and a pullover sweater.
Whether she was wearing jeans and a T-shirt or dressed
as she was now, as far as he was concerned, she was the
epitome of sexy.

Since her original destination had been the Bahamas,
most of the items she'd packed were summer wear. Luckily she and Bailey were similar in size and height, so
Bailey had loaned Crystal several outfits that would be
perfect for the harsh Alaska weather.

"Come on, let's explore," she said, coming back to
him, grabbing his hand and pulling him along.

He wished this could have been the kind of hotel he'd

taken her to on their wedding night. As far as he was concerned, it was fit for a king and queen. There was a state-of-the-art kitchen, and according to the woman at the check-in desk, the suite came with its own chef who was on call twenty-four hours a day.

Then there was the spacious living room with a beautiful view of the Smokey Mountains. He figured the furnishings alone in the place cost in the millions. There was a private bar area that came with your own personal bartender if you so desired, and a connecting theater room that had box-office movies at the press of a button.

But what really had his pulse racing was the bedroom, which you entered through a set of double doors. The room was huge and included a sitting area and game nook. He was convinced the bed was created just for lovemaking. Evidently Crystal thought so, as well. He watched as she crossed the room to sit on the edge of the bed and bounced a few times as if to test the mattress.

"It will work."

He lifted a brow, pretending he didn't know what she was referring to. "Work for what?"

"For us. I think that last hotel probably had to replace the mattresses on the beds after we left."

He chuckled, thinking he wouldn't be surprised if they had. He and Crystal had definitely given both beds major workouts. He continued to stare across the room at her. There was just something about seeing Crystal sitting on the bed that was causing a delicious thrill to flow through him. When their gazes met and held, he decided there was something missing from the picture of her sitting on the bed.

Him.

Eighteen

Crystal leaned back on her arms and gazed through watchful eyes as Bane moved from the doorway and headed in the direction of the bed. Straight toward her.

As much as she tried, she couldn't dismiss the flutter in her tummy or the way her pulse was beating out of control. All she could do was watch him, knowing what he had in mind, because it was what she had in mind, as well. He was taking slow, sexy and seductive steps with an intensity that filled the room with his sexual aura. There seemed to be some kind of primitive force surrounding him and she could only sit there, stare and feel her panties get wet.

As if he knew what she was thinking, what she wanted, without breaking his stride he eased his leather jacket from his shoulders and tossed it aside. Next came his shirt, which he ripped from his body, sending buttons flying everywhere. And without losing steam he jerked his belt through the loops and tossed it in the air to land on the other side of the room.

Without a belt his jeans shifted low on his hips, and she couldn't keep her eyes from moving from his face to his chest to trace the trail of hair that tapered from his chest down his abdomen to disappear beneath the waistband of his jeans.

And then there was what he was packing between those muscular thighs of his. She had seen it, touched it and tasted it. And what made her body tingle all over was knowing it was hers.

She studied Bane's face and saw the intensity etched in his features. A few more steps and he would have made it to the bed. And to her. It seemed the room was quiet; nothing was moving but him and he was a man with a purpose.

By the time he reached her she was a ball of desire, and his intoxicating scent—a mixture of aftershave and male—wasn't helping matters. Her head began spinning and she could actually feel her nipples tighten hard against her sweater, and the area between her legs throbbed mercilessly.

"Do you know what I love most about you?" he asked her in a low, husky voice.

"No, what?" She was barely able to get the words out.

"Every single thing. I can't just name one," he said, gazing down at her. "And do you know what I was thinking while standing there watching you sit on this bed?"

"No, what were you thinking?" He was asking a lot of questions and she was providing answers as best she could. Her mind was struggling to keep up and not get distracted by the masculine physique standing directly in front of her. Shirtless, muscular and sexy as sin.

"I was thinking that I should be on this bed with you."

"No problem. That can be arranged. Join me."

She watched his eyes darken. "If I do, you know what's going to happen."

"Yes, but we're making up for lost time, right?"

"Right."

"In that case." She slowly scooted back on the bed. "Join me," she invited again.

In an instant he was bending over to remove his shoes and socks. Straightening, his hands moved to the snap of his jeans and she watched as he pulled his jeans and briefs down his legs.

When he stood stark naked looking at her, he said, "You got too many clothes on, Crystal."

A smile touched her lips. "Do I?"

"Yes."

She chuckled. "And what, Bane Westmoreland, are you going to do about it?"

Hours later Crystal opened her eyes and adjusted to the darkness. The only light she could see was the one streaming in through the bedroom door from the living room. The bed was huge but she and Bane were almost on the edge, chest to chest, limb to limb. She didn't want to wake him but she needed to go to the bathroom.

He wasn't on top of her but he might as well have been. With his thigh and leg thrown over hers, he was definitely holding her hostage. When she tried untwining their limbs to ease away from him, his eyes flew open.

"Sorry, didn't mean to wake you."

He stared down into her eyes and she stared back into

his. They were sleepy, drowsy, satisfied. He tightened his hold on her. "And where do you think you're going?"

"The bathroom."

"Oh."

He released his tight hold on her and rolled to the side. "Don't be gone too long. I'll miss you."

She smiled when he closed his eyes again. She quickly searched for her clothes but didn't see them anywhere and didn't want to turn the lamp on to look for them further. So she decided to cross the room in the nude, something he'd done plenty of times.

Moments later after coming out of the bathroom, she decided to go through her luggage to find something to put on. Their bags were just where they'd left them, not far from the door. She was able to see in the light coming from the sitting room, so it didn't take her long to open her luggage and pull out one of her nightgowns. After slipping it on she noticed the satchel Bane had given her.

Not feeling sleepy, she decided now would be a perfect time to read. Opening the satchel, she saw Bane had placed the letters and cards in stacks so she could read them in order. He had also banded them together and labeled them. She grabbed the ones marked My First Year.

She decided to sit on the sofa in front of the fireplace. Using the remote, she turned it on and the bright glow and the heat gave her a warm cozy feeling.

Settling on the sofa with her legs tucked beneath her, she opened the first letter and began reading…

Crystal,

I made it to the navy training facility in Indiana. The other recruits here are friendly enough but I miss my brothers and cousins back home. But more than anything, I miss you. A part of me knows I need to do this and make something of myself for you, as well as for myself, but I'm not sure I can handle our separation. We've never been apart before, and more than once I wanted to walk out and keep walking and return to Denver and confront your parents to find out where they sent you. I want to let them and everyone know you are my wife and that I have every right to know where you are.

But on those days I feel that way, I know why I am enduring the loneliness. It's for you to reach the full potential that I know you can reach. You are smart. Bright. And you're also pretty. I want you to make something of yourself and I promise to make something of myself, as well.

Not sure if you will ever read this letter but I am hoping that one day you will. Just know that you will always have my heart and I love you more than life itself and I'm giving you space to come into your own. And the day I return we will know the sacrifice would have been for the best.

Love you always,
Your Bane

Crystal drew in a deep breath and wiped a tear from her eye. *Her Bane.* Putting the letter back in the envelope, she placed it aside and picked up a Valentine's Day card. She smiled after reading the poem and when she saw how he'd signed the card, "Your Bane" once again, she felt her heart flutter in her chest.

She kept reading all the cards and letters in the stack.

In them he told her how his chief had noted how well
he could handle a gun, and how he could hit a target
with one eye closed or while looking over his shoulder.
"Show-off," she said, grinning as she kept reading. His
extraordinary skill with a weapon was what had made
him stand out so much that his chief had brought it to
the attention of the captain who had recommended him
for the SEAL program.

She also noted that although her birthday and their
wedding anniversary were the same day, he'd bought her
separate cards for each. By the time she had finished the
first stack she felt she knew how that first year had gone.
His first year without her. He had been suffering just as
much as she had. He had missed her. Yearned for her.
Longed for her. She felt it in the words he'd written to her,
and she could just imagine him lying down at night in his
bunk and writing her. He'd told her about the guys he'd
met and how some of them had become friends for life.

Crystal was halfway through reading the second stack
of cards and letters when she heard a sound. She glanced
up and saw Bane standing in the doorway.

"You didn't come back. And I missed you."

At that moment all she could think about was that the
man standing there was *her Bane*. Putting the stack of
cards and letters aside, she eased to her feet and crossed
the room to him. They had been through a lot, were still
going through a lot, but through it all, they were together.

When she reached him she wrapped her arms around
his waist and said the words that filled her heart. "I love
you, Bane."

"And I love you." He then swept her off her feet and
into his arms. "I'm taking you back to bed."

"To sleep?" she asked.

"No."

She smiled as he carried her back into the bedroom. Once there he eased her gown off her and tossed it aside before placing her back in bed. "I began reading your letters and cards," she said when he joined her there. "Thank you for sharing that period of time with me. And I kept something for you, as well. A picture journal. I'll give it to you when we get to Alaska."

He stroked a hand down her thigh. "You're welcome, and thanks for keeping the journal for me."

And then he leaned down and kissed her and she knew that like all the other times before, this was just the beginning.

Nineteen

"I can't believe this place," Crystal said, after entering the cabin and glancing around.

Bane knew what she meant because he could barely believe it, either. The cabin was huge, but it wasn't just the size. It was also the location and the surroundings, as well as how the cabin has been built with survival in mind.

They had arrived in Kodiak, Alaska, a few hours ago after spending another full day in North Carolina. They had been Garth's guests on his private jet owned by Outlaw Freight Lines. Garth's three brothers—Cash, Sloan and Maverick—had met them at the tiny airport. Their brother Jess, who was running for senator of Alaska, was currently on the campaign trail and their sister, Charm, had accompanied their father to Seattle on a business trip. Garth had joked that it was business for their father and a shopping expedition for their sister.

As far as Bane was concerned, Garth hadn't been lying when he'd said that there was a strong resemblance between him and Cash. The similarity was uncanny in a way. And the similarities between the Westmorelands and the Outlaws didn't end there. In fact, Sloan closely resembled Derringer, and Maverick favored Aidan and Adrian. The Outlaws had easily accepted their biological connection to the Westmorelands, but according to Garth, their father had not. He was still in denial and they didn't understand why.

After making a pit stop at Walker's ranch to drop off Bailey and Walker, Garth and his brothers had driven them on to the Outlaw cabin, which was deep in the mountains and backed up against the Shelikof Strait, a beautiful waterway that stretched from the southwestern coast of Alaska to the east of Kodiak.

"Let us show you around before we leave," Garth said. He and his brothers led them from room to room, and each left Bane and Crystal more in awe than the last. And then the Outlaw brothers showed them the movable wall that led to an underground tunnel. It was better than what Bane had expected. It was basically a man cave with living quarters that included a flat-screen television on one of the walls. The sofa, Bane noted, turned into a bed. The pantry was filled with canned goods. Then there was the gun case that probably had every type of weapon ever manufactured.

"Our grandfather was a gun collector," Sloan Outlaw explained. "Our father didn't share his passion so he gave them to us to get rid of. He has no idea we kept them. As far as we were concerned, they were too priceless to give away."

"Of course, over the years we've added our own favorites," Maverick said, grinning, pointing to a .458 caliber Winchester Magnum, a very powerful rifle. "That one is mine. Use it if you have to."

A short while later, after the tour of the cabin ended, they had returned to the front room. Bane looked over at Cash, the cousin whose identity he would assume for a while. "Hope I'm not putting you out, man."

Cash smiled. "No problem. I need a few days away from Alaska anyway. A couple of friends and I are headed for Bermuda for a few days. Hate how I'll miss all the action."

The plan was to lead the group looking for Crystal to assume that she was in the cabin with Cash, an old college friend. But in order for that plan to work, in case someone went digging, the real Cash Outlaw needed to go missing for a while.

Oakwood would be calling in the morning to give Bane the final plans and let him know when word of Crystal's whereabouts would be leaked so they could be on guard and get prepared. The DOD already had men in place around the cabin. They had been there when Bane and the group arrived. Other than Garth, no one had noticed their presence, since they blended in so well with the terrain.

A short while later Bane and Crystal were saying goodbye to everyone. After Bane closed the door behind him, he looked across the room at Crystal. He thought she was holding up pretty damn well for a woman who in the next twenty-four hours would be the bait in an elaborate trap to catch her would-be kidnappers. As soon as the DOD purposely leaked her whereabouts, it would set things in motion.

"I like them."

He saw her smile. "Who?"

"Your cousins."

"And what do you like about them?" he asked, moving away from the door toward her.

"For starters, how quick they pitched in to help. They didn't have to offer us the use of this place."

"No, they didn't. Garth and his brothers paid a visit to Colorado the week before Thanksgiving to meet the Denver Westmorelands and from there they headed south to visit with the Atlanta Westmorelands. Dillon told me I would like them when I met them and I do."

He drew her into his arms. "If we pull this off we'll owe them a world of thanks. This place is perfect, and not just because of the underground tunnel. There's also the location, the seclusion. I can see someone hiding out here, and I'm sure the people looking for you will see it, too."

"I wonder when Oakwood will send his men," she said thoughtfully, looking up at him.

Bane chuckled. "They're already here."

Surprise appeared on her face. "What? Are you sure?"

"Pretty much. I haven't seen them but I can feel their presence. I noticed it the minute we pulled up in the yard. And because Garth is an ex-Marine, he did, too."

"He said something to you about it?"

Bane shook his head. "He didn't have to. He knew what to look for." Bane didn't say anything for a minute and then he said, "Nothing can happen to you, Crystal. I won't allow it. Do you know what you mean to me?"

She nodded and reached up to place her arms around his neck. "Yes, I know." And she really did. Reading those cards and letters had left her in awe at the magnitude of his love for her.

"Good." And then he leaned down and captured her mouth with his.

* * *

Later that night, just as before, Crystal untangled herself from Bane and slid out of bed. At least she tried. But Bane's arms tightened around her. "Where are you going?"

"To read. I'm on stack three now."

He rolled over in bed so they could lie side by side. "Interesting reading?"

"I think so," she said. "It means a lot knowing you were thinking about me." Reading those cards and letters, especially the letters, had helped her to understand that he loved being a navy SEAL and that his teammates were his family, as well.

"I always thought about you," he said huskily. He rubbed her cheek. "Sleepy?" he asked her.

"No. I plan to read, remember? So let me go."

"Okay, just as long as you're where I can see you."

"I'll just be in the living room."

He shook his head. "Not good enough. I want you in here with me."

She was about to argue with him, remind him the cabin was surrounded by the good guys, but instead she said, "Okay, I'll read in bed if you're sure I won't disturb you."

"I'm sure. I'm wide-awake, as well."

He released her. After slipping back into the gown that he'd taken off her earlier, Crystal padded across the room to pull the third stack out of the satchel.

While getting the cards and letters, she pulled out the photo album she had packed. Going back to the bed, she handed it to him. "Here. This is my gift to you."

Bane took it. "Thanks, baby." He then got into a sitting position and began flipping through the photo album.

He came across their marriage license and smiled. When she saw his smile, she said, "We were so young then."

"Yes," he agreed. "But so much in love."

"We still are," she said, settling into position beside him. In amiable silence, he turned the pages of the photo album while she read his cards and letters. "This is your high school graduation picture?" he asked.

She glanced up from reading the letter to look over at the photograph he was asking about. "Yes. And all I could think about that day was that because of you, I had done it. I had gotten the very thing I thought I hadn't wanted and was actually pretty happy about it."

He looked at several more pictures, and when he came to her college graduation picture he said, "Isn't it weird that Cash was there on campus at the same time you were?"

"Yes. I can't imagine what my reaction would have been had I ran into a guy on campus who reminded me of you. So personally, I'm glad our paths didn't cross."

She was about to go back to reading her cards and letters when Bane's cell phone went off. He reached for it. "This is Bane."

Crystal tried reading his expression while he talked with the caller but she couldn't. The only clue she had that he was angry was the way his chin had tightened. And then when he asked the caller in an angry tone, "How the hell did that happen?" she knew something had made him furious. A few moments later he ended the call and immediately sent several text messages.

"What's wrong, Bane?"

He looked over at her and paused before saying anything, and she figured he was trying hard to get his anger in check. "That was Oakwood. Someone in his department screwed up."

He threw his head back as if to get his wrath under control and said, "Your location has already been leaked. The only good thing is that whoever they suspected as the mole took the bait, and he and his men are headed here believing that you're hiding with Cash."

"And the bad thing?" she asked, knowing there was one.

Bane drew in a deep fuming breath. "Whoever this guy is, he's evidently pretty high up there at Homeland Security. He contacted the person in charge of Oakwood's men and gave an order to pull out because a special task force was coming in to take over."

Crystal frowned. "Are you saying Oakwood's men are no longer outside protecting us?"

"That's exactly what I'm saying. But I don't want you to worry about anything. I got this," Bane said, getting out of bed and slipping on his jeans. "What I need for you to do is to go and get in the tunnel below."

"Is that where you'll be?"

"No," he said, picking up his Glock and checking his aim. "I might need to hold things down for a while. Oakwood ordered the men to return and hopefully they'll be back soon."

Crystal didn't want to think about what could happen if they didn't. Bane expected her to be hiding out below, where she would be safe, while he single-handedly fought off the bad guys until help arrived. "I prefer staying up here with you. I may not be as good a shot as you, but thanks to you I'm not bad."

He frowned. "There's no way I can let you stay here with me."

"I don't see why not," she said, sliding out of bed to begin dressing, as well. "To be honest with you, I feel pretty safe."

He shook his head. "And why are you feeling so safe?"

She looked over at him and a smile spread across her lips. "Because I'm not here with just anyone protecting my back. I'm here with Badass Bane."

Twenty

A short while later, Crystal studied the arsenal of Bane's personal weapons spread out on the table and glanced over at him. "I thought a person couldn't travel on a plane with one weapon, much less a whole suitcase full of them."

He met her gaze. "They can't."

She lifted a curious brow. "Then, how did you get through the security checkpoint when you flew to Dallas?"

"I didn't. Bailey figured I might need them and brought them with her to the cabin. I'm glad she did. And there was no problem bringing them with me on Garth's private plane."

Crystal watched how he checked each one out, making sure there was enough ammunition for each. It was close to one in the morning. "You have some awesome teammates, Bane. I enjoyed reading about them, and they have been here for you. For us. Throughout this ordeal.

I can't wait to meet Coop. You mentioned him a lot in your letters."

She noticed Bane's hands go still, and when she glanced into his face she saw pain etched in his features. "Bane? What is it? What's wrong?"

He looked at her. "You won't get a chance to meet Coop, Crystal. We lost him during one of our covert operations."

"Oh, no!" She fought back tears for a man she'd never met. But in a way she had met him through Bane's letters and knew from what he'd written that he and Coop shared a special bond. "What happened?"

"I can't give you the details but it was a setup. I'm not sure how it was done but he was taken alive. Then a few days later they sent our CO Coop's bloody clothes and military tag to let us know what they did to him."

She wrapped her arms around Bane's waist. "I am so sorry for your loss. After reading your letters I know what a special friendship the two of you shared."

Bane nodded. "Yes, he was a good friend. Like a brother. I'm sorry you didn't get to meet him."

Hearing the sadness in his words, Crystal leaned up on tiptoe and pressed her lips to his. It was a quick kiss, because they didn't have much time and the situation wouldn't allow anything else. She released him, took a step back and glanced at the clock on the wall. "That's strange."

"What is?"

"I'm surprised no one has called. I would think Oakwood would be keeping tabs on us, letting us know what's going on or how close those people are to here." When Bane didn't say anything she studied his features. "You noticed it, too. Didn't you?"

"Yes, I noticed it and I think I know the reason."

"Why?"

"Someone blocked any calls coming in or out of here. Whoever did it assumes they have us cornered, but I was able to text Walker and the Outlaws right after talking with Oakwood to apprise them of what's going on. I have every reason to believe they are on their way if they aren't here already." He looked down at her. "I'm asking you again to go down below, Crystal."

"Only if we're down there together."

She heard his deep breath of frustration before Bane said, "Then take this," and passed her one of the smaller handguns off the table. "Not that you should need to use it," he added. She inserted it into the pocket of her jacket.

At that moment the light in the room flickered a few times before going completely out, throwing the entire house into darkness. "Bane?"

"I'm here," he said, wrapping an arm around her.

She jumped when suddenly there was a hard knock at the door.

"Seriously? Do they think we plan on answering it?" Bane said in an annoyed tone.

"But what if it's Walker or the Outlaws? Or even Oakwood?"

"It's not," he said. "Too soon to be Oakwood. And as far as Walker and the Outlaws, we agreed to communicate by a signal."

"What kind of signal?"

"The sound of a mourning dove's coo. I didn't hear the signal so you know what that means."

She nodded. Yes, she knew what that meant.

Bane wished like hell that Crystal had done what he'd said and gone down below. He needed to concentrate and wasn't sure he could do that for worrying about her.

Suddenly a loud voice that sounded as if it came through a megaphone blared from outside. "Mr. Outlaw. Miss Newsome. We are members of the Department of Homeland Security. We're here to take Miss Newsome to safety."

"Like hell," Bane whispered in a growl. "Those bastards expect us to just open the door and invite them inside in total darkness. They figure we're stupid enough to fall for that?"

"If you don't respond to our request," the voice continued, "we will assume the two of you are in danger and will force our way in."

Your decision, Bane thought. *Bring it on.*

"You think they really will force their way in?" Crystal asked softly.

"That's evidently their plan, so let's get prepared," he said, lowering her to the floor with him. At that moment his cell phone vibrated in his pocket. Someone had gotten past the block. He quickly pulled the phone out and read the text message from Walker. 5 of them.

"Somehow Walker got through the block to let me know there are five men surrounding the cabin. At least that's all they see. There might be others."

"At least Walker and the Outlaws are here."

"Yes, and they know to stay low and not let their presence be known unless something serious goes down. We need to get the ringleader."

"So for now it's five against two."

He frowned. "I want you to stay down, Crystal. They won't do anything that will harm you since you're valuable to them. That means they'll try to get inside to grab you."

Suddenly there was a huge crash. It sounded like the front door caving in. "Shh," Bane whispered. "Someone just got inside."

* * *

Male voices could be heard from another room. "Miss Newsome, let us know where you are. We know you think you're safe here with Cash Outlaw, but we have reason to believe he can't be trusted. We need to get you out of here and get you to safety."

Multiple footsteps could be heard going from room to room, which meant more than one man had gotten inside. Suddenly the lights came back on. "Stay down," Bane ordered her as he moved to get up from the floor.

"Not on your life." The moment she eased up with Bane, who had his gun drawn, two men entered the room with their guns drawn, as well. Bane shoved her behind him.

"Miss Newsome? Are you okay?" one of the men asked. Both were dressed in camouflage. One appeared to be well over six feet and the other was five-nine or so.

"I'm fine," she said, poking her head from around Bane to size up the two men. Both looked to be in their forties, with guns aimed right at Bane. He in turn had his gun aimed right at them.

"Then, tell your friend to put his gun down," the shorter of the two men said.

"Why can't the two of you put yours down?" Crystal retorted. She tried to block from her mind the sudden thought that this was how things had played out in the dream she'd had a few nights ago.

"We can't. Like we told you, Homeland Security has reason to believe he's dangerous."

As far as Crystal was concerned, that wasn't an understatement. She could feel the anger radiating off Bane. "Who are you?" she asked the one doing all the talking.

"We're with Homeland Security," the taller man said.

"I want names."

She could tell from his expression that he was getting annoyed with her. "I'm Gene Sharrod, head of the CLT division, and this is Ron Blackmon, head of DMP."

"You're both heads of your divisions. I'm impressed. Why would the top brass personally come for me?"

"The people after you want you for insalubrious reasons. Reasons that could be a threat to our national security."

"I got the note."

"Yes, and we believe you did the right thing by disappearing like it told you to. But now we're here to handle things and keep you safe."

Crystal lifted her chin. "How did you know what the note said?" She could tell from the look on the man's face that he realized he'd just made a slip.

"Let's cut the BS." Bane spoke up in an angry voice. "Bottom line is she isn't going anywhere."

"You aren't in any position to say anything about it, Mr. Outlaw," the shorter of the two men said with a sneer. "In case you haven't noticed, there are two guns aimed at you so I suggest you drop yours."

"And I suggest the two of you drop yours," Bane responded tersely, looking from one man to the other.

The taller man had the audacity to snicker. "Do you honestly think you can take the both of us down, Outlaw?"

A cocky smile touched Bane's lips. "I know I can. And the name isn't Outlaw. Cash Outlaw is my cousin. I'm Brisbane Westmoreland. Navy SEAL. SE348907. And just so you know, I'm a master sniper. So be forewarned. I can blow both your heads off without splattering any blood on that sofa."

The shorter man seemed taken aback by what Bane had said, but Crystal could tell by the look that appeared in the taller man's eyes that he thought Bane was bluffing.

"Trust me," she said. "He's telling the truth."

The taller man's eyes darkened in anger. "We're not leaving here without you."

"Wanna bet?" Bane snarled. "My wife isn't going anywhere with either of you."

"Wife?" Sharrod asked, shocked.

"Yes, his wife," Crystal confirmed, holding up the finger of her left hand, where her diamond ring shone brilliantly.

"I'm tired of talking," Bane said. "Put your damn guns down now."

Blackmon narrowed his gaze at Bane. "Like Sharrod said. You're in no position to give orders."

Suddenly shots rang out and before Crystal could blink, Bane had shot the guns right out of both men's hands. "I am now," Bane said easily.

The two men bowed over, howling in pain. One of them, Crystal wasn't sure which one, claimed one of his fingers had gotten shot off. Then they heard the mourning dove coo just seconds before Walker, Bailey and Garth stormed into the room with their own guns drawn.

"You guys okay?" Bailey asked, rushing over to them, while Walker and Garth went over to the two men, who were wailing at the top of their lungs, sounding worse than babies. "Sloan and Maverick are outside taking care of the men who came with these two."

"You're going to regret this, Outlaw… Westmoreland, or whatever your name is," Blackmon snarled. "Homeland Security is going to nail your ass. This is treason. You are betraying your country."

"No, I think the two of you are betraying yours," Oakwood said, charging in. "Gene Sharrod and Ron Blackmon, you are both under arrest. Get them out of here," he told his men as they rushed forward.

"We need medical treatment," Blackmon screamed, holding his bloodied hand when agents came to grab him.

Bane frowned. "Better be glad it was just your hands and not your damn heads like I threatened to blow off. So stop whining."

After Oakwood and his agents had taken both men out the door, Bane turned to Crystal and frowned. "I told you to stay down."

She reached up to caress the angry lines around his jaw. "I know, but you forgot what you also said."

"What?"

"That we were in this together."

And then she leaned up to place a chaste kiss on his lips, but he evidently had other ideas and pulled her into his arms and deepened the kiss. She wrapped her arms around him and returned the kiss, not caring that they had an audience.

When one of the men cleared his throat, they broke off the kiss and Bane whispered against her moist lips, "Come on, Mrs. Westmoreland. Let's go home."

Twenty-One

A week later

Crystal hadn't meant to awaken Bane. But when he shifted in bed and slowly opened sleepy eyes that were filled with a heavy dose of desire, she saw he was now wide-awake.

She knew of no other man who could wake up ready to make love after going to bed the night before the same way. But then, hadn't he warned her that as far as the intensity of their lovemaking was concerned, this was just the beginning?

"Good morning," he said in that deep, husky voice that she loved hearing.

She smiled. "And good morning to you, too, Bane."

And as far as she was concerned, it was a good morning, especially after that phone call they had received

yesterday. According to Oakwood, Sharrod had caved
in under pressure and told them everything, including
the location where those other two chemists were being
held. By now the two men had been reunited with their
families.

She glanced around the cabin. Their cabin. Bane had
built it years ago for her as their secret lovers' hideaway.
Now it was her home. Originally it had just one large
room with a bathroom, but last year Bane had instructed
Riley to hire someone to add a kitchen nook and a sitting area and to enlarge the bathroom. His sister Gemma,
who was an interior decorator, had put her signature on it
both before and after the renovations. There was an iron
bed in the bedroom with colorful curtains that matched
the bedspread.

The sitting room was the perfect size, just large
enough for a sofa, a chair and a table. And she loved
the fireplace that provided such great heat on those really cold days and nights. There was also a flat-screen
television on the wall. Bane told her that he had begun
spending his days and nights here whenever he came
home. For that reason, he had installed internet services
and didn't have to worry about missing calls due to his
phone being out of range. Now he could send and receive
phone calls just fine.

Already plans had been made to build the house that
would become their permanent home. It wouldn't be far
from here on Bane's Ponderosa, the name of the spread
he had inherited. They would start looking at house plans
next week. The one thing they did know was that whatever house they built would have to be large enough for
all the kids they planned to have one day.

She had gotten around to reading all his cards and

letters, and if she could have loved him even more than she already did, she would have. He had poured out his heart, his soul and his agony of a life without her in it. She needed no further proof that she was loved deeply by the man who was meant to be hers always, just as she was meant to be his.

Yesterday she and Bane had visited her parents' property. Property that was now hers. The place was deserted and badly in need of repairs. However, they'd decided not to make any decisions about what they would do with it for now.

In a way the five years of separation had done what it was meant to do. It had helped them grow into better people. She definitely saw a change in Bane. He could still be a badass when he needed to be, but there was a calmness about him, a discipline, self-control and purpose that hadn't always been there before. He'd always loved her and his family. And now he loved his country with just as much passion.

And his family was wonderful. She was enjoying getting to know the ladies his brothers and cousins had married. She had always been a loner, and for the first time in her life she was feeling part of the family.

Because Crystal had lost a lot of her things in the fire, Pam had organized a welcome-home party for her and Bane where she had received a lot of gift cards. It just so happened they were all from the ladies' favorite places to shop.

And then there was the Westmoreland family tradition. Every other Friday night, the Westmorelands got together at Dillon's place. The women would do the cooking and the men would arrive hungry. Afterward, the men took part in a poker game and the women did whatever they pleased. Usually they planned a shopping expedition. Tonight would be Crystal's first Westmoreland Family Chow Down, and she was looking forward to it.

Bane shifted his position in bed and Crystal was instantly aware of the erection poking against her backside. Instinctively, she scooted back to bring her body closer to his. All that desire bottled up inside him was beginning to affect her, as well. "What happens when you get tired of me?"

"I won't. You're in my blood, baby. And in my soul. And especially here," he said, taking her hand and placing it on his chest, right against his heart.

His words touched her deeply. And it didn't help matters that he was staring down at her, seducing her with those gorgeous hazel eyes. "Oh, Bane." At that moment she wanted him. "Make love to me."

"It will be my pleasure."

Later that evening Crystal sat beside Bane at the dinner table at Dillon's home, surrounded by Bane's brothers, cousins and their spouses. And then there were the children. A lot of children. Beautiful children who were the joy of their parents' lives. Seeing them, spending time with them, made her anxious to have a child of her own. A baby. Bane's baby.

Dillon had made a toast earlier to her and Bane, officially welcoming her to the family and telling them how proud he and the family were of them, and their strong and unwavering commitment to each other. He also gave them his blessings, just as he'd known his parents would have done, for a long and happy marriage. His words had almost brought tears to her eyes because she felt she was truly a part of this family. The Westmoreland family.

A short while later, when dinner was over and the women were clearing off the table as the men geared up for a card game, Bane's cell phone rang. "It's my CO," he said, quickly pulling his phone out of his jeans pocket. "Excuse me while I take this."

She felt a hard lump in her throat. She knew Bane was on military leave until March. Had something come up where his CO was calling the team together for an assignment? It was three weeks before Christmas. Besides that, it was their first week together without all the drama. Crystal wasn't sure how she would handle it if he had to suddenly leave.

You will handle it the same way any SEAL wife would, an inner voice said. *You will love him, support him and be there with open arms when he returns.* She was suddenly filled with an inner peace, prepared for whatever came next.

"What is it, Bane?" Dillon asked.

Crystal, like everyone else, turned to gaze at Bane when he returned to the dining room. There was a shocked look on his face. Although it had been Dillon who asked the question, Bane met Crystal's gaze and held it.

"That was my CO. He wanted to let me know he got a call from the Pentagon tonight that Coop is alive and is being held prisoner somewhere in Syria."

"Your friend Coop?" Crystal asked, getting up out of her seat and crossing the room to Bane.

"Yes. And the CO is getting our team together to go in and get Coop, and any other hostages they're holding, out of there."

She nodded. "When will you be leaving?" she asked softly.

He placed a hand on her shoulder. "I'm not. The CO just wanted me to know. He's aware of our situation and what we went through last week. He's letting me know he's exempting me from this mission if that's what I want."

Crystal studied Bane's features. And not caring if they had an audience listening to their every word, she said, "But that's not what you really want, is it?"

He rubbed his hand down his face. "Doesn't matter. It's three weeks before Christmas. There's no telling when I might return. I might not make it back until after the holidays, and I wanted to spend every single day with you."

"And I with you. But you *must* go," she said, not believing she was actually encouraging him to do so. "Coop is your best friend."

"And you are my wife."

A smile touched her lips. "I'm also the wife of a SEAL. So things like this are to be expected. I know it and I accept it. I will be fine until you get home, and if you don't make it back by Christmas, I won't be alone. For the first time, Bane, thanks to you I have a family," she said, glancing around the room. "I have a big family."

"Yes, you do," Dillon said, joining the conversation. "And whenever Bane has to go out on covert operations we will be here for you."

"Thanks, Dillon." Crystal returned her gaze to Bane. "So go, Bane, and be the dedicated and fierce SEAL that you are. The one you were trained to be. Be careful and do everything in your power to bring Coop home."

Bane stared at her for a long moment before he reached out and pulled her to him and held her close. And then he leaned down and kissed her with all the love she actually felt. The love she knew was there and had always been there between them. Suddenly she was swept off her feet and into big, strong arms.

"Bane!"

Holding her tight, he headed for the door. "We're going home," Bane said over his shoulder as his whole family watched them. "Crystal and I bid you all a good night."

Twenty-Two

Christmas Eve

"And you're sure you don't want to spend the night at our place, Crystal? You're more than welcome."

Crystal smiled at her brother-in-law when he brought the car to a stop in front of the cabin. "Thanks, Dillon, but I'll be okay."

"I promised Bane I would look out for you."

"And you have. I really do appreciate the invitation, but I'm fine."

She knew she would be a lot better if Bane called, but neither she nor his brothers and cousins had heard from him since he'd left three weeks ago. He had told them that no one knew how long this operation would take. She just hoped he was safe and all was going well.

In the meantime she had tried staying busy. Bane had

wanted her to look at house plans while he was gone, and she had helped Pam at her acting school in town. Jason's wife, Bella, had invited her for tea several times, and there had been a number of shopping trips with the Westmoreland ladies. There had been the annual Westmoreland charity ball. It was her first time attending one and she wished Bane could have been there with her. But it had been good seeing the Outlaws again.

And she had been summoned to the nation's capital last week. Dillon, Canyon and their wives had gone with her. She'd had to give a statement about Sharrod and Blackmon. No one had asked about Bane's whereabouts and she figured they knew it was classified information.

The director of Homeland Security had told her of the value of her research and that someone would be contacting her soon. They wanted her, along with the other two biochemists, to come work for the government to perfect their research while she completed her PhD. She promised she would give it some thought but refused to make any decisions until Bane returned.

"I used to worry about Bane whenever I figured he was out on one of those operations," Dillon said softly to her as he unbuckled his seat belt. "But then I figured it didn't pay to worry. Besides, we're talking about Bane, the one person who can take care of himself. If we should be worried about anyone, it's those who have to come up against him."

Crystal smiled, knowing that was true. She had seen how Bane had handled Sharrod and Blackmon. He had been confident, cool and effective, even when it had seemed the odds had been stacked against him.

"Bane will be okay, Crystal," Dillon said when she didn't respond to what he'd said.

She nodded and absently touched the locket she still wore around her neck. "I hope so, Dillon."

"Don't just hope. Believe."

Her smile spread. "Okay, I believe."

"Good."

He got out of the car and came around to open the door for her. "You will be joining us for Christmas breakfast in the morning and then later a special Westmoreland Holiday Chow Down tomorrow night, right?"

"Yes, I'm looking forward to it."

"The Outlaws will be arriving about noon along with Bailey and Walker and some of the Atlanta Westmorelands."

She had gotten the chance to meet Charm Outlaw before she and Bane had left Alaska. Charm and her father had been returning from their business trip. The woman was as beautiful as she was nice. However, Crystal thought the father of the Outlaws had been reserved, as if he'd rather them not be there. Bane had explained that the old man was having a hard time accepting the fact that his father had been adopted.

"You know the drill," Dillon said, grinning when they reached the door of the cabin.

"Yes, I know it." Because she was living in a secluded area, the men in the family refused to let her drive home alone. They either drove her back home or followed behind her in their car to make sure she got there safely. And then before they would leave, she'd have to give a signal that everything was okay by flashing the window blinds.

"Good night, Dillon."

"Good night. Do you need a ride to my place in the morning?"

"No, thanks. I'll drive."

She opened the door to go inside the house and was glad she'd left the fireplace burning. The cabin felt warm and cozy. She was about to turn and head for the window to flash the blinds when she saw a movement out the corner of her eye. She jerked around.

"Bane!"

She raced across the room and was gobbled up in big, strong arms and kissed by firm and demanding lips. It seemed as though the kiss lasted forever as their tongues tangled and mingled, and they devoured each other's mouths. Finally, he broke off the kiss. "I missed you, baby."

"And I missed you," she said, running her arms all over him to make sure he was all in one piece. His skin was damp, he smelled of aftershave and he was wearing his jeans low on his hips. It was obvious he'd just gotten out of the shower.

"Why didn't you let me know you were coming home tonight?"

A smile touched his lips. "I wanted to surprise you. The mission was a success, although it was damn risky at times. They were keeping Coop and two other American prisoners secluded up in the mountains. Getting up there was one thing and getting them out alive was another. It wasn't easy but we did it, and all returned home safely. No injuries or casualties."

He paused a moment and said, "Coop was glad to see us and they didn't break his spirit, although they tried. He said what kept him going was believing that one day we would come rescue him. And we did. He and the others were taken to Bethesda Hospital in Maryland to get checked out."

Crystal was about to open her mouth to say something when there was a loud pounding at the front door. "Oops. That's Dillon. He brought me home and I forgot to flash the blinds to let him know I was okay," she said, racing across the room to open the door.

"Crystal, are you okay? When you didn't flash the blinds I—" Dillon stopped talking when he glanced over her shoulder and saw his brother. "Bane!"

The two men exchanged bear hugs. "Glad to see you back in one piece," Dillon said, grinning as he looked his baby brother up and down.

Bane pulled Crystal to his side and planted a kiss on her forehead. "And I'm glad to be back, too."

"I'll let the family know you're home. And I guess we won't be seeing you bright and early tomorrow morning for breakfast as planned, Crystal," Dillon said, his grin getting wider.

"No, you won't," Bane answered for her. "My wife and I are sleeping in late. We will try to make it for dinner, however."

Dillon chuckled. "Okay." He then looked at his watch. "It just turned midnight on the East Coast. Merry Christmas, you two."

"And Merry Christmas to you, Dillon," Crystal said, cuddling closer in her husband's strong arms. And in that moment she knew that for her this would be the merriest because she had her Bane. It would be their first Christmas spent together as man and wife.

As soon as the door closed behind Dillon, Bane tightened his embrace and looked down at her. "I like the tree and all the decorations."

She glanced over at the Christmas tree she'd put up a couple of weeks ago. What was special about it was that it had come right off Bane's Ponderosa. Riley had chopped it down for her. She'd had fun decorating the tree and had even trailed Christmas lights and ornaments along the fireplace mantel. "Thanks."

And then Bane pulled her even closer into his arms. "I've already placed your gift under the tree, baby."

She glanced over her shoulder and saw the huge red box with a silver bow. She looked back at him, feeling like a kid on Christmas morning. "Thanks. What's in it?"

He chuckled. "You get to open it in the morning." He leaned down and placed a kiss on her lips. "Merry Christmas, sweetheart."

She reached up and wrapped her arms around his neck. "And merry Christmas to you, Bane."

And then their mouths connected, and she knew this was still just the beginning. They had the rest of their lives.

Epilogue

Valentine's Day

"I would like to propose a toast to the newlyweds," Ramsey Westmoreland said, getting everyone's attention and holding up his champagne glass. "First of all, we didn't ever think you would leave us, Bay, but we know you'll be in good hands living in Alaska with Walker. We're still going to miss you showing up unannounced, letting yourself into our homes and eating our food."

"And getting all into our business," Derringer hollered out.

Ramsey chuckled. "Yes, she did have a knack for getting all in our business. But I think we can safely say we wouldn't have wanted it any other way. I know Mom and Dad are smiling down on us today, happy for their baby girl."

He paused as if to compose himself before he continued, "And, Walker, she's yours now and I'm going to tell you the same thing I told Callum when he married Gemma, and Rico when he married Megan. You can't give her back. You asked for her, flaws and all, so deal with it."

Everyone laughed at that. Ramsey then raised his champagne glass higher. "To Walker and Bailey. May you have a long and wonderful marriage, and watch out for the bears." The attendees laughed again as they clicked their glasses before drinking their champagne.

Dillon then stepped up to stand beside Ramsey. The wedding had been held inside the beautiful garden club in downtown Denver. Riley's wife, Alpha, who was an event planner, had done her magic. The wedding theme had been From This Day Forward, and since it was Valentine's Day the colors had been red and white.

"No, I'm not giving Walker and Bailey another toast," Dillon said, grinning. "With so many members of the family gathered here together, I want to take this time to welcome our cousins, the Outlaws of Alaska. Your last names might be Outlaw but you proved just how much Westmoreland blood ran through your veins when you gave Bane and Crystal your protection when they needed it the most. And all of us thank you for it. Our great-grandfather Raphel would be proud. And that deserves another toast."

Crystal felt Bane's arms tighten around her waist. What Dillon had said was true. The Outlaws had come through for them during a very critical time. Their last names might be Outlaw, but they looked and carried themselves just like Westmorelands.

Later, she saw Dillon and Ramsey talking to Garth

and Sloan and couldn't help but notice how the single women at the wedding were checking them out. With all the Denver Westmoreland males marked off the bachelor list, it seemed that the single ladies were considering the Outlaws as hopefuls. Evidently the thought of moving to Alaska didn't dissuade them one bit.

"What's this I hear about the two of you moving to Washington?" Senator Reggie Westmoreland approached to ask. He had his beautiful wife, Olivia, by his side.

Bane smiled. "It will be just for a little while, after Crystal graduates in May with her PhD. She will be working at that lab in DC for six months and I was offered a position teaching SEAL recruits how to master a firearm."

"That's great! Libby and I will have to invite the two of you over once you get settled."

Jess Outlaw walked up to join them. Because he had been out on the campaign trail when they were in Alaska, the first time Bane and Crystal had met him had been when the Outlaws had joined the Westmorelands for Christmas.

"And I hope to see you soon in Washington, as well," Reggie said to Jess.

Jess smiled. "I hope so. The race is close and has begun getting ugly."

"Been there before," Reggie said. "Hang in there and stick to your principles."

Jess nodded. "Thanks for your advice, and thanks so much for your endorsement."

A smile spread across Reggie's lips. "No thanks needed. We are family. Besides, I reviewed your platform, and it's a good one that could benefit the people of your state. I think in the end they will see that."

"Let's hope so," Jess said.

A few moments later Crystal found herself alone with Bane. Coop was doing fine and had visited them in Westmoreland Country a few times. So had Nick, Flipper and Viper. Flipper had personally delivered to her the items that he and his brother had removed from her house before the fire.

She had gotten to know all of Bane's team members and thought they were swell guys. And she had met their wives, as well. But Flipper, Viper and Coop were single and swearing to stay that way. Since the three were extremely handsome men, she couldn't wait to see just for how long.

"Did I tell you today how much I love you?" Bane leaned down to ask her, whispering close to her ear.

"Yes," she said, smiling up at him. "But you can tell me again."

"Gladly. Crystal Gayle Westmoreland, I love you very much. With all my heart."

She reached up and caressed his cheek as she thought about all they'd endured over the years. A lot had changed, but the one thing that had remained constant had been their love. "And I love you, too, Bane. With all my heart."

And then they kissed, sealing their words and their love. Forever.

* * * * *

Kristi Gold has a fondness for beaches, baseball and bridal reality shows. She firmly believes that love has remarkable healing powers, and she feels very fortunate to be able to weave stories of love and commitment. As a bestselling author, a National Readers' Choice Award winner and a three-time Romance Writers of America RITA® Award finalist, Kristi has learned that although accolades are wonderful, the most cherished rewards come from networking with readers. She can be reached through her website at kristigold.com, or through Facebook.

Books by Kristi Gold

Harlequin Desire

The Return of the Sheikh
One Night with the Sheikh
From Single Mom to Secret Heiress
The Sheikh's Son
One Hot Desert Night
The Sheikh's Secret Heir

Texas Extreme

The Rancher's Marriage Pact
An Heir for the Texan
Expecting the Rancher's Baby?

Visit the Author Profile page at Harlequin.com for more titles.

AN HEIR FOR THE TEXAN

Kristi Gold

To my former farrier and dear friend Stephanie S., and her fantastic mother-in-law, Florence, for all the support they've shown me throughout the years.

Love ya both.

temporary freedom. He passed by the family homestead, where his sister-in-law, Paris, sat on the front porch, hands resting on her pregnant belly. He raised his hand in a wave, and grinned when he noticed his brother, Dallas, struggling to set up the inflatable Santa beneath the massive oak while his blond-haired bride cheered him on. But his smile faded fast when he thought about his own failed marriage, and the loneliness that plagued him during the holidays.

Shaking off the self-pity, Austin picked up speed before someone chased him down, namely one of the two self-proclaimed elves now hanging angels on the manicured hedges. As much as he appreciated Maria, the former nanny who'd become his much loved stepmom after the death of his birth mother, and Jenny, the surprise stepmom they'd only learned about six years ago during the reading of his father's will, he was more than done with the decorating demands.

Once he rounded the corner and reached his own cedar-and-rock house, he pulled into the driveway, shut down the ATV, then slid into the cab of his dual-wheel truck. He backed out and retraced the path he had taken, not bothering to acknowledge the family members standing on the lawn, shooting dagger looks in his direction. He continued toward the safety of the highway as he headed to an atmosphere where he could feel more macho.

A few miles down the road, Austin pulled into the gravel parking lot at the outdoor arena and claimed a spot among all the stock trailers, plagued by past memories of the life he'd left behind. He'd said goodbye to the rodeo circuit several years ago to enter the cutthroat world of car dealerships. Actually, several truck dealerships spanning three states, thanks to the help of his winnings and inheritance. At least he'd succeeded at that endeavor, even if he had failed at his marriage.

Shaking off the regrets, he walked through the entry, nodding at several cowboys, some who had been his competition. He immediately noticed all the young bucks crowded round the catch pens, eyeing him with awe like he was some sort of rodeo god. Those glory days were long gone and only remnants of the memories remained. But at least he'd left some sort of positive legacy to some kids since he'd probably never have any of his own.

He climbed the steps two at a time and slid onto a wooden bench as a spectator, not a participant. That's when he spotted her rounding the arena—a great-looking filly he knew all too well. A literal blast from his past. She was as flighty as a springtime moth, and as stubborn as a rusty gate. She could bring a man down with the swish of her tail. Austin should know. She'd brought him to his knees on more than one occasion. And even though several years had passed since he'd last seen her, he fondly recalled how she'd always given him a damn good ride.

He shifted slightly as he watched her weave in and out of traffic, black mane flowing behind her in the breeze. She hadn't lost her spirit, or her skill, or her ability to completely captivate him.

Austin tensed when he noticed a gelding coming toward her, trying his best to buck off the cowboy on his back. If the filly didn't slow down, move over, an equine wreck was imminent.

No sooner than he'd thought it, it happened. The filly in question went one way, the mare she was riding went the other, and Georgie Romero, his black-maned, flighty, spirited first real girlfriend, ended up on the ground in a heap.

A distant memory from his early childhood shot through Austin's mind in response. The recollection of his own mother falling from her horse when he'd been too young to comprehend the consequences, or the impending loss. When he'd been too little to understand.

That alone sent him on a sprint toward the arena in an effort to come to *this* woman's rescue. He damn sure didn't want to relive that tragedy.

He hoped like hell this time he wasn't too late.

When Georgia May Romero opened her eyes, she sensed a gathering crowd, but a pair of brown boots earned her immediate focus. She then noticed jean-encased legs and two large masculine hands resting casually on bent knees. And next—one very impressive, extremely big… belt buckle.

Clearly she had died and gone to Cowboy Heaven.

Her gaze traveled upward to take in the blue plaid shirt rolled up at the sleeves, revealing arms threaded with masculine veins and, above that, an open collar showing a slight hint of chest hair. She then visually journeyed to a whisker-shaded jaw surrounding a stellar mouth and an average nose with a slight indentation on the bridge. But there was nothing average about the midnight blue eyes. Devilish eyes. Familiar eyes. Surely not.

"You okay, Georgie?"

No, she'd died and gone to Cowgirl Hell.

Shaking off her stupor, Georgie sat up and scrambled to her feet, silently cursing her bad luck and the man standing before her. The only man who could shake her to the core with only a smile. The man who'd changed her life six years ago, and he didn't even know it. "Where's my horse?"

He pointed toward the outside of the arena. "Over there, tied to the rail. She's a little bit shaken but she's physically fine."

Only then did she venture another glance at her walking past, Austin Calloway. "Thanks," she muttered. "She's a two-year-old and still a little green. I brought her out to get used to the crowds. Obviously she's not ready for competition."

He had the gall to grin. "I figured that much when she tossed you on your head. You fell pretty hard."

Oh, but she had…for him. Ancient history, one she didn't dare repeat despite this chance meeting.

Chance.

She did a frantic search for the dark-haired, hazel-eyed boy who'd been the love of her life for the past five years, and thankfully spotted him still seated in the stands, holding cowboy court with a host of familiar men laughing at his antics. Andy Acosta, the middle-aged father of five, and horse trainer extraordinaire, sat at Chance's side. Not only had Andy been a longtime hand on her family's ranch, he happened to be one of the few people she trusted with her son.

"Are you sure you're okay, Georgie? No headache or double vision? Broken bones?"

Just a pain in her keister. "I'm fine," she said as she tore her gaze from her son to Austin and tried to appear calm. Having him learn of her own child's existence, and the risk of prodding questions, was the last thing she needed at the moment. When she'd made the decision to move back to town to establish her veterinarian practice, she'd known she would have to tell him eventually, but she wanted to prolong that revelation until she'd had more time to prepare. Until she could gauge how he might react. Standing in a busy arena wasn't an appropriate venue to deliver that bombshell.

"You don't look fine," he said. "In fact, you look a little out of it."

She swept the dirt from her butt with her palms and frowned. "I assure you I'm okay. It's not the first time I've been bucked off."

He took off his tan felt hat, forked a hand through his golden brown hair, then set it back on his head. "True. I remember that summer you broke your arm when you tried to ride your dad's stallion."

Leave it to him to bring that up. "I remember when you broke your nose getting into a fight with Ralphie Jones over Hannah Alvarez."

He smiled again, throwing her for a mental loop. "Hey, he started it. Besides, I didn't really like her all that much, and I was young and pretty stupid."

She'd been the same way at that time, and the price for her naivety had been high—losing her virginity to him. "Look, it's been nice seeing you again, but I have to go."

He inclined his head and frowned. "How long are you going to be in town?"

She considered lying but realized he would eventually learn the truth. At least one truth. "Indefinitely."

He looked shocked, to say the least. "You're living here now?"

"Yes."

"How long have you been back?"

She wasn't in the mood for a barrage of questions, although she did have one of her own. "A couple of weeks. Dallas didn't tell you?"

He scowled. "No. Dallas doesn't tell me a damn thing. When did you see him?"

"Actually, he called me after he learned I've taken over Doc Gordon's practice. He asked me if I'd be the vet for the D Bar C, and this new venture you have in the works, although he didn't exactly explain what that entails other than it involves livestock."

"We're calling it Texas Extreme," he said. "We're starting a business that caters to people who want the whole cowboy experience. Roping and bull riding and all things rodeo, plus we're considering a good old-fashioned trail ride."

Just what the Calloways needed—another business that would pad their pockets even more. "Interesting. I don't think the ranch house is large enough to accommodate guests and your brothers, so I assume you're going to put them in the bunkhouse."

"We're in the process of building a lodge. And since you've been away awhile, you probably don't know that we've all built our own houses. Or at least Dallas, Houston, Tyler, Worth and me. Fort won't step foot on the place. He basically hates the entire family."

She recalled how upset Austin had been when he'd learned he had twin brothers, Forth and Worth, and a stepmother in Louisiana, thanks to a bigamist father who'd revealed all after his death. She also remembered how Austin had turned to her following the reading of the will, and his distress that had led to her providing comfort. If only she could forget that night, but she'd been left with a constant, precious reminder.

Georgie sent a sideways glance toward her son, who fortunately didn't seem interested in her whereabouts. But if she didn't get away soon, he might notice her and flag her down. Worse still, call her "Mama." Then she'd have to explain everything. Almost everything. She backed up a couple of steps and hooked a thumb over her shoulder. "I guess I better go now."

"You aren't competing in the barrel racing with a more seasoned horse?" he asked.

She shook her head. "Not today."

He favored her with another sexy grin. "Guess I'll be heading out, too."

"But you just got here." And she'd just given herself away.

His smile faded into a confused look. "How do you know that?"

She studied the dirt at her feet before raising her gaze to his. "I saw you take a seat in the stands." The distraction had resulted in her lack of concentration in the arena, and the fact that he'd come to her rescue still stunned her.

He hooked both thumbs in his pockets, causing her to glimpse a place no self-respecting mother should notice, and it wasn't his buckle. "I was only here to escape all the holiday decorating at the ranch," he said. "If I don't get back, my stepmom is bound to send out a posse."

She forced herself to look at his face. "How is Maria?"

"Feisty as ever. How are your folks?"

Georgie didn't care to broach that topic in detail, and preferred to let Austin assume she still lived at home. That would guarantee he wouldn't come calling, considering the long-standing feud between both their families, compliments of their competitive fathers. Only one time had a Calloway son entered their abode. Through her bedroom window. She had given Austin everything that night eighteen years ago, including her heart. "Mom and Papa are doing fine," she said, banishing the bitter-sweet memories from her mind.

"I'm sure they're glad to have you back from school. I bet Old George is strutting around like a rooster over his only kid becoming a veterinarian."

Not so much. Her father was still shamed over having a daughter who'd had a baby out of wedlock, information her family had kept away from the public eye. In fact, she hadn't spoken to her dad to any degree in years. Luckily her mother hadn't passed judgment and still supported her when she'd stayed away from the small town and the prospect of gossip. She purposefully lost touch with friends, and now that she'd returned, she'd fortunately been able to find a remote place of her own, even if it was only a rental. But eventually everyone would know about her son because she couldn't hide out forever, nor did she want to.

When Chance waved, Georgie tried for a third departure. "Well, I better load up and leave before the competition begins."

A slight span of silence passed before Austin spoke again. "You look real good, Georgie girl."

So did he. Too good. Otherwise she might scold him for calling her by his pet name. "Thanks. I'll see you around."

"You most definitely will."

Georgie disregarded the comment, turned away and then walked through the gate to retrieve her mare. She lingered there for a few moments and watched Austin leave the arena before seeking out her son. "Let's go, Chance," she called as she untied the horse and started down the aisle.

Chance scampered down from the bleachers and came

to her side, his face and baseball cap smeared with dirt. "Who was that man, Mama?"

Oh, heavens. She had so hoped he hadn't noticed. "Austin Calloway."

"Who is he?"

She kept right on walking as she considered how she should answer. She settled on a partial truth instead of full disclosure as she walked toward her trailer, her baby boy at her side.

"He's an old friend, sweetie."

An old friend who'd been her first lover. Her first love. Her one and only heartbreak. But most important, the father of her child.

If or when Austin Calloway learned that she'd been withholding that secret, she could only imagine how he would react—and it wouldn't be good.

Austin stormed into the main house to seek out the source of his anger. He found him in the parlor where they'd grown up, his pregnant wife seated in his lap. "I've got a bone to pick with you, Dallas."

Both Dallas and Paris stared at him like he'd grown a third eye, then exchanged a look. "I think I'll go see if Maria and Jenny need help with dinner," Paris said as she came to her feet.

Dallas patted her bottom. "Good idea. I can't feel my legs."

She frowned and pointed down at her belly. "Hush. This is all your fault, so complaining is not allowed."

"You sure didn't complain when I got you that way," Dallas added with a grin as his wife headed toward the kitchen.

Watching his brother and sister-in-law's banter didn't

sit well with Austin. "If you're done mooning over your bride, we need to talk."

Dallas leaned back on the blue floral sofa that Jenny had brought with her, draped an arm over the back and crossed his boots at his ankles. "Have a seat and say what's on your mind."

Austin eyed the brown leather chair but decided he was too restless to claim it. "I don't want to have a seat."

"Then stand, dammit. Just get on with it."

He remained planted in the same spot even though he wanted to pace. "Why the hell didn't you tell me Georgia Romero was back in town?"

"Georgia's back in town?" came from the opening to his right.

Austin turned his attention to Maria, his stepmother, mentor and crusader for the truth, and sometimes intruder into conversations. "So he didn't tell you, either?"

Dallas's jaw tightened and his eyes narrowed. "I'd forgotten I'd talked to her day before yesterday. Besides, it's not that big a deal. A drought is a big deal."

"It's a big deal to your little brother, *mijo*," Maria said as she tightened the band at the end of her long braid. "Austin and Georgia have a special relationship."

Obviously the family was intent on throwing the past up in his face like prairie dirt. "*Had* a relationship. That was a long time ago."

Dallas smirked. "You'd take her back as your girlfriend in a New York minute."

"You have a girlfriend, sugar?"

Enter the blonde, bouncy second stepmom. The woman Austin's dad had married without divorcing Maria. Jenny was a good-hearted gossip and that alone made him want to walk right back out the door. Doing so would only prolong the conversation, unfortunately. "No, Jen, I don't have a girlfriend."

"He used to have a girlfriend," Maria added. "Georgia and Austin were real close in high school."

Jenny laid a dramatic palm on her chest below the string of pearls. "I just love Georgia. Atlanta in the springtime is…"

"Focus, woman," Maria scolded. "We're talkin' about a girl, not a state."

Jenny lifted her chin. "I know that, Maria. You're telling me about Austin being joined at the hip to his high school sweetheart, who happens to be named Georgia."

Dallas chuckled. "You've got that 'joined at the hip' thing right, Jen, but Austin chased her for years before that *joining*."

Austin needed to set this part of the record straight. "I damn sure didn't chase her." Much. "She hung around all of us when we were kids. I never paid her any mind back then."

"Not until she came back from camp that summer after she turned fourteen," Dallas said.

Man, he hadn't thought about that in years. She'd returned with a lot of curves that would make many a hormone-ridden guy stand up and take notice. Every part of him. She still had a body that wouldn't quit, something he'd noticed earlier. Something he wouldn't soon forget. "Yep, she'd definitely blossomed that summer."

"You mean she got her boobies," Jenny chimed in. "Mine came in at twelve. That's when the boys started chasing me like Louisiana mosquitoes."

Maria waved a dismissive hand at Jen. "No one wants to know when you reached puberty and how many times you got a love bite."

Austin didn't want to continue this bizarre conversation. Luckily Paris showed up to end the weird exchange. "Dinner will be ready in about five minutes."

Jenny turned her attention to Austin. "Maybe you should invite your special friend to dinner."

Of all of the stupid ideas—subjecting Georgie to an ongoing conversation about puberty. Then again, he wouldn't mind sitting across a table from her. He wouldn't mind her sitting in his lap, either. "It's late and I'm sure she's busy."

Paris perked up like a hound coming upon a rabbit's scent. "She? So that's what you were discussing in my absence."

Dallas pushed off the sofa. "Yeah, and boobies and mosquitoes."

"Don't ask, Paris," Maria stated. "Now you boys wash up while we put the food on the table."

No way would he subject himself to more talk about his history with Georgie. "I'm not staying for dinner."

"Suit yourself," Dallas said. "But you'll be missing out on Jen's chicken-fried steak."

Any other time he would reconsider, but not today. "I'm sure it'll be great. Before I take off, Dallas, we need to finish our conversation."

His brother shrugged. "I'm listening."

When Austin noticed the women still hovering, he added, "In private. Outside."

Dallas sighed. "Fine. Just make it quick. I'm starving."

He had every intention of making it quick while getting his point across.

After they walked out the door onto the porch, Austin faced his brother. "Look, I would've appreciated you consulting all the brothers before you hired Georgie as the ranch vet."

Dallas streaked a hand over his jaw. "Actually, I did. Houston doesn't have a problem with it, and neither does Tyler. Worth doesn't know about it but he trusts my judgment, unlike you."

Austin's ire returned with the force of a tornado. "You consulted them but you didn't bother to ask me?"

"Majority rules, and I figured you weren't going to be too keen on the idea after the way you two ended it."

"What the hell does it matter what happened when we were in high school?"

"I meant six years ago, after the reading of Dad's will."

"How did you know we hooked up then?"

"Georgie called me a few months later and asked how she could get in touch with you. By that time you'd already married Abby. When I told her about that, she was upset. In other words, you broke her heart. Again."

Yeah, he probably had, and he'd never been proud of it. "It was just one night, Dallas, and I didn't marry Abby until four months later, so I wasn't cheating on either Georgie or Abby. Besides, I married Abby on a whim."

"A whim involving a woman you barely knew."

Only a partial truth. "Not so. I'd known Abby for years. I just didn't date her on a regular basis."

"But you did date Georgie at one time, and she's not the kind of woman to take sex lightly."

He was inclined to agree but decided not to give Dallas the pleasure of knowing he was right. "Georgie and I agreed no promises, no expectations, the last time we were together."

"Maybe you didn't have any expectations, but I suspect she did. She's always loved you, brother. I wouldn't be surprised if she still did, although I don't get why she would after the way you've treated her."

He didn't welcome his brother's counsel or condemnation. "You're a fine one to talk, Dallas. You left a trail of broken hearts all over the country."

"Yeah, but it only took one woman to set me straight."

"A woman you married because you wanted to keep control of the ranch."

Dallas leaned against the porch railing. "In the beginning, that was true. But it didn't take me long to realize Paris could put an end to my wicked ways."

He'd thought that about Abby, too, but his ex-wife hadn't been as sure. In the end, they realized they'd had no choice but to go their separate ways after rushing into a marriage that should never have taken place. "I'm glad for your good fortune, Dallas. But I don't think that woman exists for me."

Dallas's expression turned suddenly serious. "If you open your eyes, you might just see you've already found her. In fact, you ran into her today."

With that, Dallas went back inside, leaving Austin to ponder his words. True, he'd always had a thing for Georgie, but he'd chalked that up to chemistry. And she'd always been a beautiful woman, even during her tomboy phase. But he couldn't see himself with her permanently. See himself with anyone for that matter.

He'd already wrecked one marriage and he wasn't going to wreck another. He refused to fail again.

That said, if he and Georgie decided to mutually enjoy each other's company down the road, he wouldn't hate it. As long as she understood that he wasn't in the market for a future.

When it came to Georgia May Romero—and his ever-present attraction to her—keeping his hands to himself would be easier said than done.

"How's your first day as the Calloway vet going, Georgie girl?"

Fine…until he'd walked into the main barn dressed in chambray and denim, looking like every gullible girl's dream. Yet when she decided to accept Dallas's job offer, she'd known seeing Austin would be a strong possibility. In fact, that had been part of her reasoning to sign on as the resident veterinarian—to size him up, but only when it came to his life, not his looks. However, she was still a bit shaken over their encounter yesterday, and she was bent on ignoring him today.

For that reason, and many more, she continued putting away her equipment in the duffel without looking at him. "I was just vaccinating the pregnant mares."

"At least we only have four this year, not ten like in years past."

"True." Georgie straightened and patted the bay's muzzle protruding through the rail. "I remember when this one was born, and that had to be fifteen years ago. We're both getting on up there in age, aren't we, Rosie? They should really give you a break from the babies."

Georgie sensed Austin moving toward her before he said, "She keeps churning out prime cattle horses, but hopefully Dallas will decide to retire her from the breeding program after this year."

"Good, although I'm sure she'll have no trouble foaling this year. Dallas did ask me to be here when Sunny foals since she's a maiden mare. I told him I'd try, although horses have given birth without help for centuries. Of course, I expect to have to pull a few calves in the future."

When he didn't respond to her rambling, she faced him and met his grin. "Do you find some sort of warped humor in that?"

He braced his hand on the wooden frame and leaned into it, leaving little distance between them. "No. It's just strange to see you doing your animal doctor thing."

Boy, did he smell good, like manly soap, as if he'd just walked out of the shower. She imagined him in the shower...with her. Slick, wet bodies and roving hands and... Good grief. "Are you worried I'm not qualified?"

His come-hither expression melted into a frown. "I have no reason to believe you're not qualified since you went to the best vet college in the country. I guess I'm just used to you riding horses, not giving them shots. It's going to take a while to adjust to the new you."

"I'm the same old me, Austin." And that had never been more apparent than when she continued to react to him on a very carnal level. "Only now I have a career that I've talked about since we were climbing trees together."

He reached out and tucked one side of her hair behind her ear. "Do you remember that one time we were in the tree near the pond on your property? You were twelve at the time, I believe."

What girl didn't remember her first kiss, even if it had been innocent and brief? "If you're referring to that day when you tried to put me in a lip-lock, I definitely recall what happened next."

His grin returned. "You slugged me."

"I barely patted your cheek."

"I almost toppled out of the tree. You didn't know your own strength."

He hadn't known how much she had wanted him to kiss her, or how scared she had been to let him. "That kind of thing was not at the top of my to-do list at that time."

"Maybe, but I found out kissing had moved to number one on the list that summer after you came back from camp."

She felt her face flush. "I was fourteen and you were fifteen and a walking case of hormones."

He inched a little closer. "You had hormones, too. They were in high gear that first night we made out behind the gym after the football game."

She shivered over the recollection. "Big deal. So you managed to get to first base."

His blue eyes seemed to darken to a color this side of midnight. "Darlin', I got to second base."

"Your fumbling attempts weren't exactly newsworthy."

Oddly, he didn't seem at all offended. "Maybe I was a little green that first time, but I got better as time went on."

Her mind whirled back to that evening full of out-of-control chemistry. She didn't want to acknowledge how vulnerable she'd been that particular night, and many nights after that when they'd met in secret. How completely lost she had been for three whole years, and she hadn't been able to tell one solitary soul. "We were so reckless and stupid and darn lucky. If my father would have ever found out I was with a Calloway boy—"

"He would've shot first and asked questions later. He'd probably do that now."

Time to turn the subject in a different direction. "I'd hoped that after J.D. died, my father would've buried the hatchet and been more neighborly to you and the brothers."

"Ain't gonna happen," Austin said. "Last month he called the sheriff when one of our heifers ended up on his property. He blamed us for not maintaining the shared fence line when it's his responsibility, too."

"That doesn't surprise me."

"I'm surprised he approves of you working for the enemy."

"Actually, he doesn't know because I haven't told him." Just one more secret in her arsenal.

Austin pushed away from the wall, giving her a little more room to breathe. "That's probably wise. It's not fun to suffer the wrath of George Romero. But he's bound to find out eventually."

She shrugged. "Yes, but it really doesn't matter. I'm all grown up now and I make my own decisions, not him."

He winked. "Yep, you're all grown up for sure."

Her heart executed a little-pitter patter in her chest. "I need to get back to work now."

"Me, too. If I don't get busy soon, I'm going to suffer the wrath of Dallas."

If she didn't leave soon, she might be subjected to another journey into their shared past, including their sex life. *Former* sex life. "I've got a very busy day ahead of me, so I'll see you later."

He moved closer, as if he didn't want her to leave. "Then business is good?"

"So far." Yet she wouldn't be tending to livestock for the remaining hours. She would be sending her son off on a trip without her for the first time since his birth.

"I'm glad you've returned, Georgie," he said as he finally stepped back. "And by the way, if you're not busy this evening, Maria wants you to have dinner with us. All the usual suspects will be there. Have you met Worth or his mom, Jenny?"

"No. I haven't had the opportunity yet."

"All the more reason for you to come."

But being close to Austin was the best reason to decline. "I'm not sure I'll be finished with everything before dinnertime."

"We don't usually eat until around seven. If you decide to join us, and we really hope you will, just show up. We'll set a place for you."

If she agreed, she would have to spend even more time with him, all the while trying to conceal her true feelings. If she didn't, she would insult Maria. "I'll think about it."

He grinned, started away then said without turning around, "I'll see you tonight."

His confidence drove her crazy. *He* drove her crazy. But right then she had only one immediate concern… Her son's impending departure.

Two

Georgie climbed into her truck and headed home to face what would probably prove to be one of the most difficult times of her life. After she pulled into the drive and slid from the cab, Chance rushed out of the door and ran to her as fast as his little legs would let him. He wrapped his arms around her waist and stared up at her, his grin showing the space where he'd just lost his first tooth. "Mama, did you see the rolling house?"

Georgie glanced to her right to find the massive RV parked on the dirt road leading to the barn. "I see that, baby. It's huge."

Chance let her go and rocked back and forth on his heels, as if he was too excited to stand still. "Aunt Debbie said I could ride up front with Uncle Ben and she could stay in the back and play cards with Grandma."

No doubt the wily pair would be engaging in poker. "That sounds like a plan. Are you packed?"

He nodded vigorously. "Uh-huh. I gotta get some toys." He grabbed her by the hand and jerked her forward with his usual exuberance. "Come on, Mama."

"All right, already. Just hold your horses."

Chance released his grasp on her and threw open the front screen door. Georgie followed him inside to find her mother's sister, Debbie, decked out in a blue floral sundress and an inordinate amount of jewelry, and her Uncle Ben wearing a yellow polo and white shorts that revealed his usual golf tan that ran from the top of his bald head to his beefy legs. Not exactly December attire, but luckily the region had yet to experience any significant cold weather. But that was all about to change in the next two days, according to the forecast.

"Georgia May!" Debbie said as she crossed the room and drew Georgie into a hug. "You are still as pretty as ever."

Georgie stepped back and smiled. "You look great, too, Aunt Debbie. I love the blond hair."

Debbie patted her neatly coifed bob. "Glad you like it. I just wish I could say the same for my husband. When I got it done, he didn't say a word. I don't think he's even noticed."

"I noticed, woman." Uncle Ben crossed the room, picked Georgie up off her feet, hugged her hard and then put her back down. "You're still no bigger than a peanut, Georgie. And don't listen to Deb. She knows I'm jealous because she still has all her hair."

"So how are you enjoying retirement?" Georgie asked.

"Love it," Ben said. "We just drove all the way from California."

Debbie smiled. "Los Angeles was so wonderful and warm, but the traffic was horrible."

Chance tugged on Georgie's hand to garner her attention. "Can we go now, Mama?"

Georgie swallowed around an annoying lump in her throat when she thought about watching him leave without her. "Don't you need to pick out some toys?"

"Oh, yeah."

"Don't bring too many things, Chance." Her directive was lost on her child as he sprinted out of the room.

"Your place is really precious, Georgie," Debbie said as she surveyed the area. "And it's been so well done."

Quite the change from when Georgie had first seen it—a basic two-bedroom, one-bath rental with outdated everything. But the appeal had been in the ten surrounding acres, complete privacy and the four-stall red barn. "You can thank Mom for the restoration. She had the hardwoods refinished, put new carpet in the bedrooms, remodeled the kitchen, including appliances, and redid the entire bathroom before I moved in. As much as I appreciated the effort, I do think it was overkill for a house I don't own."

Right on cue, Lila Romero breezed into the room, her silver hair pulled back in a low bun, her peach slacks and white blouse heralding her classic taste in clothing. "I couldn't let you live in squalor, dear daughter."

Leave it to Lila to overexaggerate. "It wasn't that bad, Mom."

"It wasn't that good, either." Lila turned to her sister and sighed. "Georgie is such a nervous Nellie, I'm surprised she's actually allowing my grandson to go with us to Florida."

Ben turned to Georgie. "He'll be fine, pumpkin. I used to fly big jets holding hundreds of passengers, so rest assured, I can handle a forty-five-foot motor home."

Georgie took some comfort in knowing her son would be on the ground in good hands, not in midair. "I trust you, Uncle Ben. I'm more worried that Chance will drive you insane with all his energy."

Aunt Debbie patted her cheek. "Honey, we have eight grandchildren. We're used to high energy. We'll be stopping along the way and—"

"If he acts up, we'll lock him in the toilet." Uncle Ben topped off the comment with a teasing grin.

Chance ran back into the room, his arms full of stuffed animals, miniature trucks and his special blue pillow. "I'm ready. Can we go now?"

Georgie fought back the surge of panic. "Can I at least have a hug, baby boy?"

As if she sensed her daughter's distress, Lila took the toys from her grandson's grasp. "I'll put these in the RV while you tell your mama goodbye."

In that moment, Georgie appreciated her mother more than she could express. "Thanks, Mom."

"You're welcome, honey. Take your time."

After her family filed out the exit, Georgie knelt down on Chance's level and brushed a dark lock from his forehead. "You'll be a good boy, right?"

"I'll be good. I'll brush my teeth and go to bed on time. And I'll mind Grandma."

"Are you going to miss me?"

He rolled his eyes. "Yeah, Mama."

She drew him into her arms. "I'm going to miss you something awful, too. I love you, sweetie."

"I love you, Mama."

Georgie held him tightly until he began to wriggle away. "I gotta go now, okay?" he said, his hazel eyes flashing with excitement.

"Okay." She kissed his cheek and straightened. "Eat some vegetables while you're gone."

He wrinkled his nose. "Do I hafta?"

"Just a little. That's better than nothing."

After taking him by the hand, Georgie led her son to the RV where she earned one more hug, one more kiss and an understanding smile from her aunt. Chance scurried up the stairs with Debbie following behind him, and once he had disappeared, Georgie turned to her mother. "You'll call me later, right?"

Lila raised her hand as if taking an oath. "I swear I will report back to you on a regular basis. And I also swear I will not sell my grandson for gas money."

Georgie felt a little foolish. "I'm sorry, Mom, but this is the first time we've been away from each other for any length of time. He'll be gone for two weeks."

"Two weeks' worth of amusement parks that he'll dearly love." She laid a palm on Georgie's cheek. "I know it's hard, honey, yet there comes a time when you have to let go a little. I learned that the hard way with you."

"I know, Mom. It's just so difficult."

"It is for both myself and your father, even if he doesn't show it."

"I wouldn't know since he's clearly still refusing to speak to me, much less see me or Chance."

"He'll come around, and that reminds me…" Her mother hesitated a moment, which gave Georgie pause. "Speaking of fathers and their children, have you given any more consideration to telling Chance's father about him?"

She'd been considering it nonstop. "I'm still on the fence about that. The hows and the whens and whether or not it would serve any purpose at this point in time."

"Honey, it would serve a major purpose. It would give your son the opportunity to know his dad. They deserve to know each other."

With that, Lila climbed on board and closed the door without awaiting her daughter's response.

As Georgie watched the RV drive away in a cloud of dust, she felt more alone than she had since she'd realized she would be raising a child on her own.

She could stay at home this evening, missing her baby boy. Or she could go to the Calloways for dinner. Then again, that would mean facing Austin while reuniting with his family. Several years had passed since she had seen Maria and the boys, and the thought of eating a frozen dinner held little appeal.

Decision made. Wise or not, she would go.

"She's not coming." That reality had become apparent to Austin with every passing moment.

Dallas stopped rocking the back porch glider and shot him a hard look in response to the comment. "You don't know that, Austin. Dinner isn't even on the table yet."

Austin pushed off the wooden chair and stared out at the fence row lined with mesquites. "Georgie is never late. If she'd decided to be here, she would've already shown up."

"For a man who claimed five minutes ago, twice, that he didn't care if she stepped foot through the door, you sure seem concerned."

He spun on his brother and glared at him. "I just don't like people to go back on their word."

Dallas leaned forward and rested his arms on his knees. "So she told you she'd be here for sure?"

He had him there. "Maybe not in so many words, but she did seem open to the idea."

"That's a stretch from saying yes."

Austin muttered a few curses as he collapsed back into the chair. "Doesn't matter one way or the other. I was just being nice when I asked her."

"You were wishful thinking, Austin. You can protest all you want but you've always had a thing for her. You still do."

Time for a subject change. "Tyler mentioned that Fort called you earlier today. What did he want?"

Dallas sighed. "A part of the proceeds from Texas Extreme."

Austin couldn't believe his stepbrother's nerve. "He's never even stepped foot on this place. Why the hell does he think he's entitled to any profit aside from what the will stated?"

"Because he's a greedy jackass, and that's what I pretty much told him."

"I just hope he doesn't make this into some legal issue."

"That's why we have attorneys on retainer." Dallas checked his watch. "Looks like it's dinnertime, and that means your girlfriend probably isn't coming."

"No big deal."

Dallas smirked. "Yeah, right. That's why you look so damn disappointed."

He'd obviously been too transparent. "You're full of it, Dallas."

"You're foolin' yourself, baby brother."

"Am not."

"Are, too."

His frustration began to build. "I really don't care if she shows up or not."

When the bell rang, Austin shot off the chair, strode through the hallway leading to the den, then stopped short before going any farther. Truth was, he had no idea who might be at the door. Probably one of the hands. Maybe even a neighbor. Or a brother.

"Georgia, it's so good to see you!"

Okay, so Maria confirmed it was her. No need for him to rush into the room and have her thinking he was anxious to see her again. Even if he was.

On that thought, he took his time as he headed toward the front of the house to the sounds of excited voices. He stopped off in the kitchen, grabbed and uncapped a beer from the fridge, then continued on through the dining room where the food had been laid out like a banquet. He paused at the arched opening to take a drink and watch the women circling Georgie, bombarding her with compliments and questions. He wouldn't blame her if she backed out the door and left for the sake of her sanity.

Jenny glanced over her shoulder and smiled at him. "Oh, Austin, sugar, she is just precious," she said, like she'd been presented a puppy.

Then the feminine wall parted, revealing a full view of the revered guest dressed in a pale blue sweater and jeans tucked into knee-high boots. Her long, black hair, gathered up on top and secured in a clip, fell around her shoulders in soft curls.

Precious wasn't the description that came to Austin's mind. *Sexy* was much more like it. She might be small in stature, but she had an abundance of curves that would kill a lesser man. He'd had the good fortune to explore that territory on more than one occasion. He'd like to do a little exploring tonight. Slowly. With his mouth.

He felt the stirrings down south, thanks to his sinful thoughts, and realized if he didn't get a grip, he'd have to step outside.

Austin took another swig of beer and moved forward. "Glad you could come."

She sent him an overly sweet smile. "I wouldn't have missed good home cooking for the world."

Maria hooked an arm through Georgie's. "*Mija*, you are welcome anytime. Now let's go have a seat."

"Let's," Jenny said. "We don't want the food to get cold."

Austin didn't want to sit through the upcoming interrogation, but it was too late to turn back now. After all, Georgie might need a protector. Nah. She could hold her own better than most.

"I'll go get Dallas," Paris said as they wandered toward the dining room.

Austin trailed behind the threesome, all the while watching the sway of Georgie's hips. She had a butt that wouldn't quit, and he better quit thinking about that butt or he'd have to stay at the table long after dinner was done.

Jenny gestured toward the place at the head of the table. "Georgie, you sit here since you're the guest of honor."

Georgie looked a little flustered. "That's not necessary. I've sat at this table many times before."

Maria pulled out the chair. "Tonight it's necessary, *mija*. Like Jenny said, you're a special guest, even if you are practically family. We're all about hospitality around here."

"So true," Jenny said. "I came here for a weekend to let Fort meet his brothers, and I haven't gone back to Louisiana since."

"No matter how many times I've asked her to go," Maria muttered.

Jenny frowned. "Hush up, Maria. You know you like me being here to help out with the place."

"She likes your mint juleps," Austin added.

Maria hinted at a smile. "Bad as I hate to admit it, those would be hard to give up."

Following a spattering of laughter, Georgie took a seat while Maria and Jenny claimed the chairs on either side of her. Austin held back until Paris and Dallas came in and chose the two of the three remaining spots, leaving him the space at the opposite end of the table from Georgie.

He settled in, set his beer aside and eventually passed his plate to Jenny, who took great pleasure in serving the masses every night. She heaped enough food on it to feed the entire town and handed it back to him. "Do you need another beer, sugar?"

"No, thanks. I'm fine." Actually, he wouldn't be fine unless he downed a bottle of whiskey, or poured a bucket of ice down his jeans.

Georgie took a bite and just watching that ordinary gesture sparked Austin's imagination. After she dabbed at her mouth with a napkin, she asked, "I'm sorry Houston and Tyler aren't here tonight."

"They're at a rodeo in Waco," Dallas said. "Houston's determined to get one more national championship, and Tyler's there to pick up the pieces."

"Hush, *mijo*," Maria cautioned. "You'll curse your brother with such talk."

"He's already cursed," Austin added. "And if he gets one more concussion—"

"Boys," Jenny began, "you're upsetting your mothers. Now let's talk about something more pleasant." She turned her smile on Georgie. "I heard at the beauty salon that you're living at the McGregor place."

She glanced at Austin before returning her attention to Jenny. "Yes, I am. The family was nice enough to lease it to me after Liam went into the nursing home. They're not quite ready to sell the place."

Austin had a hard time believing she hadn't moved back into the Romero homestead. He figured there had to be a story behind it. "Did your mom and dad turn your room into a gym while you were gone?"

She took a drink of iced tea and set the glass down a little harder than necessary. "No. I'm an adult and I prefer to be on my own."

Jenny reached over and touched her hand. "Of course you do, but it's good to keep family close."

"As long as it's not too close," Dallas muttered, earning him a dirty look from his wife. "Speaking of family, where is Worthless?"

Jenny scowled at Dallas. "He's heading back from South Padre Island so he's running a little late. And would you please stop calling him that?" She smiled at Georgie. "You would just love Worth, sugar. How old are you?"

"Did you leave your filter in the kitchen, Jenny?" Maria asked.

"It's okay," Georgie said. "I'm thirty-four."

"Worth is twenty-nine, but five year's difference isn't bad," Jenny added. "I think it's okay for you two to date."

"It's not okay with me," Austin blurted without

thought. When everyone stared at him, he had to dig himself out of the hole he'd created. "I mean, Georgie's a nice woman. Worth likes to chase nice women, but he's not the settling down kind."

Georgie lifted her chin. "Just to clarify, I'm not in the market for marriage at this point in time. Actually, I'm really too busy to date. But thanks for the offer, Jenny. I still look forward to meeting him."

"You might want to wear full-body armor," Austin muttered.

Maria stood, plate in hand. "Who wants peach cobbler?"

"I definitely do," Georgie said as she came to her feet. "I'll help you bring it in."

The pair left the kitchen and when they returned, Georgie approached Austin and set the dessert in front of him, inadvertently brushing his arm in the process. That simple touch made him shift in his seat, especially when he got a whiff of her subtle perfume. He remembered that lavender scent well. He also remembered how her hair felt brushing across his chest and lower…

Damn, damn, damn.

After everyone was served, the conversation turned casual, while Austin kept his focus on Georgie and the way her mouth caressed the fork.

Caressed the fork?

Man, he needed to get a grip. He needed some kind of distraction. Something to take his mind off Georgie.

"Hey, folks, what did I miss?"

Worth showing up was not what Austin had in mind. He glanced at Georgie, who stared at him, midbite. He could imagine what she was thinking—where did this overly buff, tanned blond guy fit into the family tree?"

"You missed dinner, Surfer Worth," Paris said. "How's the yacht?"

He walked behind Jenny's chair, leaned over and kissed her cheek. "The *Jenny Belle* is fine. How is baby Calloway?"

Paris patted her belly. "Growing like a pasture weed."

"I see that." Worth slapped Dallas on the back. "Looks like the lodge is almost finished. I'm champing at the bit to see it in its finished state."

"We still have a couple of months before that happens," Paris said.

Austin held his breath while hoping Worth made a hasty exit before he noticed Georgie.

Jenny scooted back from the table and stood. "Sugar, we have someone we'd like you to meet," she said, shattering Austin's hopes. "This is Georgie, a longtime family friend."

Worth leveled his gaze on Georgie, grinned and eyed her like she was a prize heifer. "Where have you been hiding out?"

"College Station," Georgie answered. "Going to college."

"Veterinarian school," Dallas added. "She's going to be taking care of our livestock."

Worth moved closer to Georgie. Too close for Austin's comfort. "Then I guess I'll be seeing a lot more of you."

The veiled innuendo sent Austin from his seat. "Cut it out, Worth."

The man had the nerve to look shocked. "Cut what out?"

"Treating Georgie like she's one of your conquests."

Worth streaked a hand over his jaw. "Relax, brother. I'm just being hospitable."

Jenny patted his cheek. "Just like his mama taught him."

Maria rose and began gathering the empty plates. "Before the brawl starts, I need to clear out your Grandma Calloway's good china."

Dallas and Paris stood at the same time. "There won't be any brawl," Dallas said. "We're going to go outside and act like civil humans, not animals."

Georgie pushed back from the table and grabbed her glass. "I'll clean up."

"Or the boys could clean up," Paris began, "and we'll go out on the porch."

Maria shook her head. "We tried that one time. Their idea of a clean kitchen leaves a lot to be desired. It took me a good hour to get the grease off the stove and rewash the pots and pans. If we all help, we'll get it done faster."

"You two mothers should join the boys," Paris said. "Georgie and I will take care of this. That gives us a chance to get to know each other better."

"I don't believe the boys need a chaperone," Jenny added.

"They might need a referee." Maria rounded the table and came to Austin's side. "Come on, Jenny. We could use the break and we also need to discuss some ranch business."

Austin wasn't in the mood to discuss business with his brothers and mothers. That would mean leaving Georgie alone with his sister-in-law to most likely discuss him. But if he protested, he would wind up catching hell from everyone over his presumed *attraction* to Georgie. Okay, real attraction to Georgie. He'd go along with the plan for now, but later, he had other plans for the lady…provided she was game.

Who the hell was he trying to fool? If he laid one hand on her, she'd probably throw a right hook. Not that the prospect of getting punched would keep him from trying. First, he had to get this little family meeting over with, and then he would put the Georgie plan into action.

"Do you have plans for the upcoming weekend, Georgie?"

She took the last plate from Paris and put it in the dishwasher. "Maybe I'll unpack a box or two." Or maybe she'd just sit around with a glass of wine and mope.

Paris wiped her hands on the dish towel, hung it on the rack near the sink, then leaned back against the marble countertop. "You should come here for the festival."

"Festival?"

"I'm surprised Austin didn't mention it."

He hadn't mentioned anything other than old memories. "We haven't been together that long." And that sounded suspect. "*Together* as in the same room, not *together* together."

Paris smiled. "No need to explain. I already know you and Austin were an item in high school."

More like idiots. "Yes, we were. Now what about this festival?"

"Well, Jenny came up with the concept when she decided to leave Louisiana behind and move here. We decorate the entire place and open the ranch to the public from the second to the last week in December. It's family entertainment and it's affordable."

"How much?"

"Free."

Very surprising. The Calloways she'd always known

were in the business of making money, not giving the goods away. "Seriously?"

"Seriously. Admission is the price of a toy, but that's voluntary. No one is turned away."

"That's very generous. And it includes a festival?"

"Actually, the festival is invitation-only and all the proceeds from ticket sales go to shelters in the region. We have a lot of the local ranchers attending, and several rodeo champions, along with a few San Antonio VIPs with big bucks. The food is complimentary, but we have a cash bar for safety reasons."

"Good idea. Free booze and rowdy cowboys is a sure-fire recipe for disaster."

"Hunky cowboys," Paris said with a smile. "I'd like to claim I haven't noticed a few in town, but I've discovered pregnancy does not render you blind. It does mess with your hormones. Just ask my husband. He told me the other night I was wearing him out."

Georgie did recall the hormone rush, and no place to go to take care of them. "I suppose you could say the D Bar C has its share of hunks."

"True, and I suspect we'll see several other sexy men this weekend from all walks of life. So if you're available, please come. And you don't have to worry about buying the ticket. It's my treat. I could use all the support I can get."

Georgie could use a night out, and since her son wouldn't be returning until three days before Christmas, she had no prior engagements. Yet she had to consider the Austin element… "I'll definitely think about attending, as long as something work-related doesn't come up."

"I'll send good thoughts that no emergencies arise." Paris laid her palm on her abdomen. "However, if I get any bigger between now and then, I'm going to need a wide-load sign to wear with my maternity cocktail dress."

Georgie smiled, remembering how she had felt that same way during her own pregnancy. "Stop it. You look great. When are you due?"

"Mid-January, as best we can tell from the ultrasound. I'm not exactly sure when I got pregnant. I found out the morning Dallas and I married the second time."

"Second time?"

Paris laughed. "It's a rather strange tale. The first time we married for all the wrong reasons. I needed a job and Dallas needed a wife before his birthday to keep control of the ranch, thanks to J.D.'s stipulation in the will. As it turned out, my ex-husband lied to me about my divorce being finalized. Dallas threatened him, I quit my position as designer for the new lodge and then he realized he couldn't live without me, so we married in earnest. End of story."

And quite a story it was. "I'm glad it worked out for you both."

"So am I." Paris flinched. "I swear, Junior here is playing soccer with my rib cage. Dallas is always asking me if the baby's kicking so he can feel it."

"Do you mind if I do?"

"Not at all, and thanks for asking. I've had complete strangers coming up to me in the store and patting my belly like a pet without my permission."

Georgie laid her palm over the place Paris had indicated, and received a tap as a reward. "Wow," she said after she moved her hand away. "Definitely a strong little guy. Or girl. Do you know the gender yet?"

Paris shook her head. "We've decided to be surprised."

"Any names picked out?"

"If it's a girl, Carlie. And if it's a boy, Luke."

"Please tell me that Luke isn't the short version of Luckenbach to carry on the tradition of naming the kids after Texas cities."

Paris grinned. "Funny you should mention that. Dallas thought it would be clever to name him Luckenbach, which I immediately nixed since it would be difficult for a child to spell it. Of course, he then came up with a whole alternate list, including Midland, Odessa, Arlington and the crowning glory, Texarkana."

"Glad you decided on Luke and Carlie."

They exchanged a laugh followed by Paris pressing her palms in her lower back. "These spasms are not fun."

"I remember that pain and pressure. It makes it very hard to sleep, especially when it's coupled with having to go to the bathroom five times a..." Her words trailed off when she realized she'd completely given herself away.

Paris raised a brow. "Sounds to me like you've had some experience with pregnancy."

She saw no reason to lie to Paris at this point, at least about her child's existence. "Actually, I have a five-year-old son."

Paris's eyes went wide. "I didn't know that."

"Aside from my mother and father, no one around here knows."

"Not even the Calloways?"

"Not yet." But if all went as planned, they would eventually know... As soon as she figured out how to tell the father.

"What about your son's dad?" Paris lowered her gaze. "I'm sorry. I'm being too nosy."

"It's okay. I appreciate having someone to talk to. He hasn't been in the picture."

"I'm so sorry, Georgie. I hate it when a man doesn't take responsibility for his child."

"He doesn't know."

Once more, Paris looked stunned. "Why?"

"It's complicated." More than anyone would ever know.

Paris sent her a sympathetic look. "I can do complicated, but only if you want to talk about it."

Although she'd only known Paris for an hour, Georgie sensed she could be objective, and nonjudgmental. Not to mention she'd kept the truth bottled up far too long. "When I found out I was pregnant, I tried to contact him and discovered he'd recently married. I didn't want to rock that boat."

"Is he someone you met in college?"

"No. He's from around here. That's one of the reasons I decided to return here to set up my practice. I needed to be close to my family, as well."

"Then you plan to involve him in your son's life."

She hadn't even planned how she would tell him. "Whether or not that's an option would solely be dependent on his attitude. He's not going to be thrilled that I've kept him in the dark for so long."

Paris remained silent for a few seconds, as if she needed time to digest the information. "Georgie," she began, "do the Calloways know this mystery man?"

She hesitated a moment to mull over how she would answer, and how much she would reveal. "Everyone knows everybody around here."

Paris turned and began to fold a dish towel. "Okay. It's not Dallas, is it?"

"Heavens no." Georgie realized the comment was borderline rude. "Don't get me wrong, Dallas is an attractive man, but he's always treated me like a kid sister."

Paris laid a palm on Georgie's arm. "I wasn't exactly serious. I can tell there's nothing between you two. Which leads me to another question. It's your decision whether to answer or not."

Georgie braced for the query. "Ask away."

Paris leaned back against the counter and studied her straight on. "Is it Austin?"

Georgie studied the toe of her boot. "Well...uh... I..."

"I know you two have been involved before," Paris continued. "And I can tell you still care about him by the way you look at him."

If Paris had noticed, what about the rest of the Calloways? What about Austin? Had she really been that obvious? "Yes, I cared about him a lot a long time ago, and in some ways I still do. Unfortunately I made the fatal mistake of letting those feelings get in the way of logic six years ago."

"Then if you do still care about him, Georgie, you should tell him you have a child together."

"I never actually said he's the father."

"You haven't denied it, either."

Georgie resigned herself to the fact that she couldn't get out of this predicament without digging a deeper deception hole. "All right. Austin is Chance's father. We got together the night after the reading of his father's will. He was upset when he learned about J.D.'s double life, and I wanted so badly to comfort him. That's how we conceived our son."

Paris sent her a sympathetic look. "Austin is a good man. He'll understand why you felt you couldn't tell him at that point in time."

If only she could believe that theory. "I had every intention of telling him, but when I found out he was married, I didn't have the heart to mess up his life. At the time it seemed like the right thing to do. But when I learned he was divorced right before I finished vet school, I realized maybe I'd been wrong. Now he's going to hate me for not telling him sooner."

"He's going to be angry, but I doubt he'll hate you. And I know he won't hate having a son. That's why I believe you should let him know, unless you plan to keep your son hidden until he's an adult."

She needed more time to think. She needed to get home before her mom called.

With that in mind, Georgie turned to Paris and attempted a small smile. "I'm going to take everything you've said into serious consideration. In the meantime, if you don't mind—"

"Not saying anything to anyone?" Paris returned her smile. "I promise I won't mention it, and after you've told Austin, I'll pretend to be as surprised as everyone else."

"After you've told me what, Georgie?"

Three

Georgie startled at the sound of Austin's voice, so much so she physically jumped. "We were talking about…uh… We were playing a game."

He tossed the beer can in the recycle bin and frowned. "What kind of game?"

"A guessing game," Paris said. "Georgie tells me a story from your childhood, and I have to guess which brother did what."

Georgie thanked her lucky stars Paris had such a sharp mind. "That's right. I just mentioned the time someone was doing donuts in the Parkers' pasture. I told her everyone thought it was Dallas, when it was really you, and she thought I should tell you to confess to Dallas to clear the air." And that had to be the lamest fabrication ever to leave her mouth.

He strolled farther into the kitchen and frowned. "Yep,

that was me doing the donuts on the night after I found out I got accepted into college. And FYI, Dallas already knows. He took the blame because he knew Dad would come down harder on me."

Georgie recalled that fateful day when Austin had informed her about his college acceptance, and she had assumed he would be out of her life forever. Now just the opposite would be true, if she told him about Chance.

She did a quick check of her watch and saw an excuse to escape both Austin's and Paris's questions. "It's time for me to go. I have to be up very early in the morning to make my rounds."

"I'll walk you out," Austin said.

"Thanks, but I can make it to the truck on my own. Finish your visit with the family."

"I see the family almost every day and Mom would skin me alive if I wasn't gentlemanly." Austin turned around and headed away. "I'll wait for you on the porch."

Great. Just great. The man was as persistent as a gnat on a banana.

Paris drew Georgie into a brief hug. "I've enjoyed our talk. Let's do it again very soon."

Georgie didn't have to ask what they would be discussing. "That sounds like a plan. Maybe we can have lunch."

"Lunch would be great. And I know you're going to do the right thing and eventually clear the air, once and for all."

That's exactly what Georgie intended to do. She simply wasn't sure when, where or, most important, how.

Now was not the time. Georgie recognized that reality the moment she stepped onto the porch and met a swarm of Calloways bombarding her with goodbyes.

Jenny gave her the first hug. "Please come again soon, sugar. I'll make my juleps."

"You'll make her drunk," Maria said as she gave Georgie a quick embrace, as well. "It's been good to see you, *mija*."

"Don't be a stranger," Dallas added as he patted her back like the brother he'd always been to her.

Worth stepped forward, kissed her hand and grinned. "Call me sometime and we'll hang out."

"When he's not hanging ten on a surfboard," Jenny said.

"Or hanging out in town, trying to pick up women," Dallas remarked.

"Yeah, all three of them," Worth said.

The comment earned some laughter from everyone but the man leaning back against the railing, arms folded across his chest, his blue eyes boring into Georgie. She waited until the crowd reentered the house before she moved forward, seeking a quick getaway.

Unfortunately Austin had other ideas, she realized when he clasped her arm before she made it down the first step. "Where are you going so fast?"

She turned a serious gaze on him and he relinquished his grasp on her. "I'm heading home. It's getting late."

"Are you sure you don't want to hang around a little longer and tell me what's going on with you?"

Hey, I had a baby over five years ago and he happens to be yours. Just thought you might like to know. "Nothing's going on, Austin, other than I'm tired. As I said earlier, I have to be up at dawn."

He pushed off the rail and moved close enough to almost shatter her composure. "You're as nervous as a colt in a corral full of cows. I can't help but think it has something to do with me."

He would be right. "Check your ego at the door, Austin. Not everything has to do with you. Now if you don't mind, I'm leaving."

She sprinted down the remaining steps and quickened her pace as she headed down the walkway without looking back. When she reached her silver truck, she grasped the handle only to have a large hand prevent her from opening the door.

Frustrated, she turned around and practically bumped into Austin's chest. "What is it now?"

"Before you run off, I wanted to ask you something."

"Okay, but make it quick."

"We're having a party here this weekend and—"

"Paris invited me."

"Are you going to come?"

With the cowboy in such close proximity, his palm planted above her head on the door, she could barely think, much less make a decision. "I'm not sure. It depends on my schedule."

His grin arrived as slow as honey and just as sweet, with a hint of deviousness. "It's been a long time since we've danced together."

"True, and I've probably forgotten how."

He took a lock of her hair and began to slowly twist it around his finger, as he had done so many times before. "Do you remember that barn dance back when we were in high school? Specifically, what happened afterward?"

Here we go again… "I recall several dances back in the day."

"The one right before my graduation, when we fogged up all the windows in my truck while we were parked down by the creek."

He seemed determined to yank her back down memory mile. "It wasn't all that monumental, Austin. Only some minor teenage petting."

"Minor? You were so hot you took my hand and put it right between your legs."

"I don't exactly remember it that way." One whopper of a lie.

"Do you remember that you didn't stop me from undoing your pants and slipping my hand inside? I sure as hell haven't forgotten, even if you have."

A woman never forgot her first climax. "Your point?"

"I definitely had a *point* below my belt buckle," he said, his voice low and grainy. "I went home with it that night, and several times after that until the night before I left for college."

Ah, yes, another enchanted evening…and one colossal mistake. "That should never have happened, Austin. I didn't plan to give you my virginity as a high school graduation gift."

"But what a gift it was." He leaned over and brushed a kiss across her cheek. "I liked the sports socks, but not as much."

"Not funny," she said as she unsuccessfully tried to repress a smile.

"Seriously, Georgie girl, don't you ever believe I didn't appreciate what that night meant to you, and me. I've never wanted you to think I took it for granted."

Over the past few years, she'd managed to suppress those particular recollections. But now, they came rushing back on a tide of unforgettable moments. "I know you didn't, Austin. You apologized to me a million times, not to mention you were so gentle. When it comes right down to it, I'm glad it was you, and not some jerk bent on bragging to all his friends that he nailed the school wallflower."

"Wallflower?" He released a low, rough laugh. "Georgie, you were anything but a wallflower. Every girl wanted to be just like you, every guy in high school lusted after you and because you wouldn't give those guys the time of day, that made you all the more attractive."

Like she really believed that. "I highly doubt anyone was lusting after me, and even if they did, I was too busy maintaining a secret relationship with you."

"We still had some good times, didn't we?"

"Yes, we did." Something suddenly occurred to her. "Did you ever tell anyone about us?"

He glanced away before returning his gaze to her. "Dallas knew. He told me several times we were playing with fire and we were going to get burned if either of our dads found out. Did you tell anyone?"

She shook her head. "No." Not until she'd found out she was pregnant, and then she'd only revealed the secret to her mother. "I didn't dare."

Georgie's cell phone began to vibrate and after she fished it from her pocket, she discovered Lila on the line, as if she'd channeled her mom. "I need to take this, so I better go."

Austin pushed away from the truck but didn't budge. "I'll wait."

She couldn't have a conversation with her son while Austin stood by, staring at her. That became a moot point when she noticed the call had already ended. "It's just my mom checking in from Florida. I'll get back to her when I'm home."

"Good. I've enjoyed talking to you again, just like old times."

Fortunately talking hadn't turned into something more, just like old times. "I've enjoyed it, too, but I really do need to go."

"Before you go, there's something I just have to do."

She pointed at him. "Don't even think about it."

He had the nerve to look innocent. "Think about what?"

"You know what."

"No, I don't. I was going to give you my cell number, in case you need anything."

Feeling a little foolish, she opened the contacts list and handed him her phone. "Fine. Plug it in there. But hurry."

He typed in his number, then handed the cell back. She laughed when she noticed he'd labeled himself "Studly," the name she jokingly used to call him. "Very clever."

"Can I have your number?"

"I'll text it to you."

"Can I have one more thing?"

She released a weary sigh. "What now?"

"This."

He framed her face in his palms and covered her mouth with his before she had time to issue a protest. She knew she should pull away, but as it had always been, she was completely captive to the softness of his lips, the gentle stroke of his tongue, his absolute skill. No one had ever measured up to him when it came to kissing. She suspected no one ever would.

Once they parted, Austin tipped his forehead against hers. "Man, I've missed this."

Sadly so had she. "We're not children anymore, Austin. We can't go back to the way it was."

He took an abrupt step back. "I'm not suggesting we do that. But we can go forward, see where it goes."

"It won't go anywhere because you'll never be able to give me what I want."

"What do you want, Georgie?"

"More."

"How much more?"

"I want it all. Marriage, a home and family."

"I've gone the marriage route, and I blew it. I don't want to travel that path again."

She turned and opened her truck door. "Then it's probably best that we stay away from each other."

"Is that what you really want?"

Her head said yes, while her heart said no. "Right now I want to go to bed."

He grinned like the cad he could be. "Mine's just down the road a bit. A big king-size bed with a top-grade mattress made of memory foam. A good place to make a few more memories."

She tossed her phone on the passenger seat, withdrew the key from her pocket and started the truck. "Good night, Austin."

"Night, Georgie. And if you change your mind about us exploring our options, just let me know."

"Don't count on it."

When she tried to close the door, he stopped her again. "Just one more question. Are you still worried about what your folks would think if they knew we were together?"

In many ways, she was. "If we started seeing each other again, and I'm not saying that will happen, I'm sure my father would go ballistic. I'm fairly certain my mother wouldn't care what we do together."

"Georgia May, have you taken leave of your senses?"

Georgie collapsed onto the bed and sighed. "I went

there to see the family, Mom. Just because you've never cared for the Calloways because of that stupid dispute between J.D. and Dad, doesn't mean I don't like them. They've always been nice to me."

"I assume Austin was there."

"Yes, he was."

"You didn't tell him about Chance, did you?"

The panic in her mother's voice wasn't lost on Georgie. "No, not yet."

"I don't think you should tell him."

Georgie couldn't be more confused. "But you told me right before the trip that you thought I should tell him."

"I've changed my mind. Your father agrees with me."

A strong sense of trepidation passed through her. "Dad knows Austin is Chance's father?"

"Not exactly, but he has his suspicions. Regardless, we think it's better if you remain silent to avoid any disappointment for both you and Chance."

They'd been having this back-and-forth conversation since she'd told her mother about the baby. "Mom, we've been through this a thousand times. I'm going to do what's best for my child, not to mention Dad has no say-so in the decision. He refuses to even acknowledge he has a grandson. He's barely spoken to me for the past six years."

"I know, sweetie, but—"

"Where are you now?" she said in an effort to move off the subject.

"Alabama for the night. We'll be in Florida tomorrow afternoon."

"Is Chance doing okay?"

"He's been an angel. Right now he's outside with Ben and Deb hooking up the RV. He's so inquisitive."

Georgie wouldn't debate that, and her son's curiosity about his father had begun to increase by leaps and bounds with every passing year. "Do you mind putting him on the phone? It's getting late."

"All right. Hold on a minute."

"Mom, before you go, I just wanted to say how much I've appreciated your support. I couldn't have raised my baby boy without your guidance. I love you for it."

"I love you, too, dear, and I only want what's best for you and Chance. If that means you decide that telling Austin he's a father is best, then so be it."

She was simply too befuddled to make any serious decisions right now.

A few moments later, she heard the muffled patter of footsteps, followed by, "Hi, Mom. I have my own bed and we have a kitchen. Uncle Ben showed me how to plug in the 'lectricity and roll down that big thing over the door so we don't get sunburned. It's so cool."

She could imagine her son rocking back and forth on his heels, his hazel eyes wide with wonderment. "It sounds great, baby. It's way past your bedtime. You must be tired."

"Nope. We're gonna roast marshmallows."

Lovely. Her child was being exposed to electricity and fire. "Be very careful, Chance. I don't want you to hurt yourself."

"Aw, Mom, I'm not a baby."

No, he wasn't. "You're still my baby. I love you, ya know."

"Love ya, too, you know. Gotta go now."

"Don't stay up too late and—"

When the call cut off, Georgie's heart sank. How would she survive the next two weeks without him? By keeping herself occupied with work. By having lunch with Paris. Maybe she would even attend the Calloways' party.

And perhaps she would finally get off the fence and tell Austin he had a son. She worried he already suspected something was up.

As sure as the sun would rise in the east, Austin sensed Georgie was hiding something. Then again, she'd always been one to hold back.

He strode into the den, grabbed the remote and started to watch a replay of his last national championship roping. But the thought of revisiting that part of his past didn't seem all that appealing. He'd rather relive another part.

On that thought, he pulled down the yearbook, dropped into the brown leather chair by the fireplace and flipped through the pages until he reached the class photo of Georgie. She'd been a junior, he'd been a senior, and they'd been secretly hot and heavy that whole year.

Funny, she hadn't changed all that much. Her hair was still as long, her face still as beautiful, her brown eyes still as enticing. She could never see what everyone had seen in her—a perfect blend of her Spanish/Scottish heritage.

She hadn't been a cheerleader or a drill team member. She'd been a rodeo girl through and through, friends with many, and more popular than she'd realized until she'd been elected homecoming queen her senior year. And class president. And eventually, prom queen. During all those milestone moments, he'd been away at college, never serving as her escort, never revealing they had been an item in high school. He should've been horsewhipped for not standing and shouting it from the rooftop when he'd had the chance, their fathers and distance be damned. He should have been there for her.

Too late now, he thought as he closed the book and set it aside on the mahogany end table. He couldn't help but think his life might have been different if he'd stayed home six years ago instead of moving back to Vegas.

He recalled that last night with Georgie, when her touch had temporarily eased his anger over learning about his father's deceit. They'd made love until dawn, then parted ways. And then he'd met Abby, married in a matter of months and ended it without much thought. Not that it could have been any other way. Not when Georgia May Romero still weighed on his mind on a regular basis. Abby hadn't known about her, but she'd always claimed she'd never had all of his heart. She would have been right.

Now he found himself reunited with Georgie. Together again, to quote an old country song. Nope, not exactly together. If Georgie had her way, he'd fall off the face of the earth, or go back to Nevada. But damn, she had kissed him back. And damn, he wanted to kiss her again. Maybe that wouldn't be fair in light of their opposing goals—he wanted to stay single, she wanted to be a wife.

If he had any sense, he'd grow up, get with the program and open himself to all the possibilities. But the thought of failing Georgie, not being the man she needed, battered him with doubts.

But the thought of having her so close, and not being with her again, didn't sit well with him. He would just keep his options open whenever he saw her again. And he damn sure planned to see her again.

Four

When she maneuvered through the D Bar C's iron gate, Georgie pulled behind several slow-moving, white limos as they traveled down the lane leading to the party site. She marveled at the complete transformation of the Calloway ranch.

The lawn of the main house to her left had been laden with various decorations depicting holidays from around the world. Every tree and hedgerow had been draped with twinkling lights, and laser beams in rotating colors sparkled across its facade. Several cartoon characters and giant candy canes lined the curbs on either side of the street, enhancing the fairy-tale quality.

Georgie passed by three more massive houses set back from the road, all adorned like the first, and she wondered if one of the cedar-and-rock houses belonged to Austin. She hadn't bothered to ask him the other night for fear he might get the wrong idea, but she couldn't deny her curiosity.

She also couldn't deny her building excitement as the caravan turned to the right to reveal a large silvery tent set out at the end of the road, a two-story residence, bigger than any she'd seen to this point, serving as its backdrop.

Georgie came to a complete stop when a parking attendant, dressed in a tuxedo and cowboy hat, approached her. She shut off the ignition, grabbed her silver clutch that complemented her sleeveless black dress, draped her silk wrap around her shoulders and slid out of the cab.

The valet offered her a long once-over and a somewhat lecherous grin. "What's a beautiful little thing like you driving a big ol' truck like this? You belong in a limo."

You belong back at college, frat boy. "My big ol' boyfriend owns this big ol' truck."

He looked unfazed by the threatening lie. "He's an idiot for letting you attend this little get-together all by your lonesome."

"He had to work."

"Oh, yeah? What does he do?"

She handed him her keys, a ten-dollar tip and another tall tale. "He's a professional wrestler. Take good care of his truck."

With that, she turned on her spiky black heels and carefully made her way to the party. Once inside the tent, she navigated the milling crowd, past tables filled with sophisticated finger foods and prissy desserts, searching for a familiar face among the strangers. Luckily she spotted two familiar faces positioned near the makeshift dance floor. With Paris wearing a flowing green empire-waist dress barely showing her belly, her blond hair cascading in soft curls around her bare shoulders, and Dallas decked out in a black suit, complete with red tie and dark cowboy hat, they looked as if they belonged on the cover of a trendy fashion magazine…or a bridal cake. A forty-something man with a hint of gray at his temples stood across from the couple. Most women would label him debonair. From the looks of the expensive suit and high-dollar watch, Georgie would label him wealthy.

After Paris waved her over, Georgie wandered toward them, hoping she hadn't inadvertently interrupted some sort of business deal.

Paris immediately left her husband's side and greeted Georgie with a hug. "You look beautiful, Georgie."

She nervously tugged at the dress's crisscross halter neck that felt a bit like a noose. "Thanks. I haven't worn anything like this since my college senior spring formal a dozen years ago."

Paris looked surprised. "You're thirty-three?"

"Actually, thirty-four."

"I swear you could go to a high school dance right now and blend right in. And that is not a bad thing."

Unless I tried to purchase a glass of wine without being asked for my ID. "That's nice of you to say, but the only thing that might help me pass for a student happens to be my height. My dad used to call me 'Peanut.'" And now he wouldn't even acknowledge her as his daughter. The thought dampened her mood.

"Don't discount your beauty," Paris said. "Every man in the room, from twenty-one to eighty-one, would like to take you home."

Yeah, sure. "I'm flattered, but I don't believe it."

"Hello. I'm Rich Adler. Who are you?"

Georgie turned her attention to the man behind the

introduction. The same man who'd been conversing with
Dallas. She found his name both ironic and appropriate.
"Georgia Romero," she said as she took his offered hand
for a brief shake.

Dallas moved forward as if running interference.
"Rich is an attorney. He also owns a quarter horse operation outside San Antonio."

The lawyer sent her a somewhat seedy smile. "I'm
into breeding."

She resisted rolling her eyes. "I'm sure that keeps you
busy."

"Not as busy as I'd like," he said. "Dallas tells me
you're a veterinarian."

"Yes, I am."

He winked. "I could use a good vet."

She could use a quick exit. "I'm sure you have several
options in the city."

"Not any who look as good as you. Have you ever
been to Italy?"

She sent him an overly sweet and somewhat sarcastic
smile. "Oh, yes. That nice little town right outside Hills-
boro. I passed by it once on the interstate on my way
to Oklahoma."

Now he looked perplexed. "I'm referring to the country, not the town in Texas."

She started to mention she was kidding, but she suspected his arrogance trumped any true sense of humor.
"'Fraid not."

He had the gall to move closer. "You would enjoy
it there. Extraordinary cuisine and superior wine. The
Amalfi coast is a great place to don your bikini and sun-
bathe. Do you have a passport?"

She had a strong urge to back up and run. "Passport,

yes. Bikini, no. I do have a very busy practice to run. No time for vacations." Even if she did, she had no desire to travel with him.

Dallas cleared his throat and slapped randy Rich on the back. "Let me buy you a drink, Adler, and we'll leave the ladies to talk about us."

Georgie planned to do just that, and she would have nothing flattering to say about the lecherous lawyer. "Nice to meet you, Mr. Adler." Not.

"It's Rich." He pulled a card and pen from his inside pocket, jotted something down, then handed it to her. "If you need a job, here's my info."

She wouldn't work for him if he happened to be the last employer on earth. "Have a good night."

He leaned over and murmured, "Call me. For business or pleasure."

Oh, she'd like to call him…several names that wouldn't be fit to utter in this atmosphere.

As soon as the men left the area, Paris turned to Georgie. "I'm so, so sorry. That guy is a first-class jerk."

As far as Georgie was concerned, that was a colossal understatement. "A jerk and a creep."

"A married, creepy jerk."

Georgie wadded up the card and tossed it into a nearby waste bin. "Figures."

"He's on his fourth wife."

"What a shocker. I could have gone all night without meeting the likes of him."

When a roving waiter passed by, Paris snatched a crystal tumbler from his tray and offered it to Georgie. "Drink this. It might help erase the memory."

Georgie took the glass and held it up. "What is this?"

"It's Jenny's infamous mint julep. She made several gallons' worth to go with the champagne."

She eyed the dark gold liquid for a moment. "Does she use a lot of bourbon?"

"Yes, and a splash of rum and she adds tequila for a little extra kick."

"Interesting." Georgie took a sip and found it to be surprisingly palatable, albeit extremely strong. "Wow. This will wake you up today and give you a headache tomorrow."

Paris leaned over, lowered her voice and said, "Take some advice. Sip it slowly, and don't have more than one, unless you have a designated driver."

"Believe me, I won't."

For the first time since her arrival, Georgie scanned the room to study the attendees…and spotted Austin standing nearby, dressed in a navy jacket, white shirt and dark jeans with a dark cowboy hat to complete the look. He had a bevy of woman hanging on his every word and wore a grin that could melt the icing off the red velvet cupcakes lined up on the stand behind him.

As bad luck would have it, he caught her looking, and when he winked, Georgie downed a little more of the julep than she should. "Still the cowboy cad," she muttered, the taste of tequila and jealousy on her tongue.

Paris frowned. "Who are you referring to?"

"Your brother-in-law. The one who's named after the capital of Texas." She nodded to her left. "He's over there, draped in women."

She followed Georgie's gaze to where Austin was surrounded by several young females who were probably quite willing to be at his beck and call. "He came here alone," Paris said. "In fact, I haven't known him to date anyone since we met."

Georgie took another ill-advised gulp. "Austin doesn't date. He passes through a girl's life, shows her a good time, then blows away like a tumbleweed."

"He dated you, didn't he?"

"Using today's teenage vernacular, we basically hooked up."

Paris remained silent for a moment before she spoke again. "Have you talked to him yet about...the issue?"

Issue as in their child. "I've been busy, and I'm waiting for the right time."

"Maybe you'll have the opportunity to speak to him tonight."

She glanced Austin's way to find his admirers had disappeared and he was now leaning back against the bar, his gaze trained on her. "Maybe I will." Maybe not.

Paris hooked her arm through Georgie's. "You'll know when the time is right. And by the way, I have a doctor's appointment Tuesday morning. After that, I'm free for the day. Why don't you and I have lunch in San Antonio?"

Georgie could use the break and the camaraderie. "Most of my appointments are in the morning. I can probably rearrange my schedule and clear the afternoon."

"Good." Paris looked a bit distracted before she returned her attention to Georgie. "I need to go rescue my husband from the creepy jerk. I'd invite you over but—"

"No offense, but no thanks. I've had enough exposure to Rich. I'll just mingle a bit and we can catch up later."

"Sounds like a plan." Paris started away then turned around again. "Be careful with that drink."

What was left of the drink. "I will."

After her friend departed, Georgie milled around the

tent, greeting a few people she'd known a while back and nodding at several strangers. She could see Austin from the corner of her eye, basically tracking her path like a cougar stalking his prey, yet keeping his distance. She felt like a walking bundle of nervous energy, and that led her to finish the drink and take another from the waiter as he walked by. She planned to only hold this one, not drink it. But when the cat-and-mouse game with Austin continued and he smiled at her, she took another sip. And then another, even with Paris's warning going off in her head like a fire alarm.

After she noticed Austin approaching her, she began to survey the silent auction offerings laid out on a lengthy table. If she ignored him, maybe he'd just go away—and that was like believing the temperature wouldn't reach one hundred degrees in South Texas next summer.

"Georgie girl, I'm going to bid on that six-horse trailer with the sleeping quarters."

The feel of his warm breath playing over her neck and the sultry sound of his voice caused her to tighten the wrap around her arms against the pleasant chills. If she turned around, she would be much too close to him, so she continued to peruse the items until she regained some composure. "The spa day looks intriguing."

"I've never had a massage for two. I'm game if you are."

She disregarded the comment and sidestepped to the next offering displayed beneath a small glass case—an exquisite oval diamond ring encircled by a multitude of sparkling rubies. "Now this is quite nice." She then noted the shocking top bid on the sheet. "Surely I'm not read-ing this right."

Austin leaned over her shoulder, causing her to shiver

slightly and take another sip of the drink. "Yep, you are. It's twenty-thousand dollars' worth of nice. You should go for it."

She regarded him over one shoulder. "I don't believe wearing this while inoculating cattle would be practical."

"All work and no play makes for a boring life."

"As beautiful as it is, it's not me." She noticed another, less gaudy ring to her left. A simple silver setting with a round sapphire surrounded by petite diamonds. "Now that's more me, but ten thousand dollars still isn't in my budget."

"Maybe Santa will bring it to you."

Against better judgment, she pivoted around and confronted Austin head-on. "If Santa Claus, Mrs. Claus, the elves and the tooth fairy pooled their funds, I still doubt they can afford this ring."

"Then let me bid on it for you."

He'd clearly lost his mind. "Don't you dare."

He sent her a sexy, sultry grin. "I have something better to give you."

She could only guess what that entailed. "We're not going there, either, Austin."

He frowned. "Get your mind out of the gutter, Georgie. I want to give you a dance."

That took her aback. "What?"

"The band's playing a slow song. Dance with me."

"As I told you recently, I highly doubt I remember how."

"I highly doubt you could ever forget. Now put down that drink and that bag you've been hanging on to like a lifeline, and follow me onto the floor."

She scraped her mind for some excuse to prevent her

from falling into his sensual trap. "I can't just leave my purse unattended."

"What's in it?"

"My phone, driver's license, a five-dollar bill and lipstick."

"Credit cards?"

"No, but—"

"I guarantee no one in this crowd is going to steal that dinky bag, and if someone does, I'll replace your phone and the cash. You're on your own when it comes to the lipstick and driver's license."

Against better judgment, she finished off the last of the julep. "I'm holding you responsible if my *dinky* bag turns up missing."

Austin took the purse from her grasp and handed the glass off to a waiter. He then set the clutch on a table and used her wrap to cover it. "No one will even know it's there."

No one would know how needy she felt at the moment when Austin clasped her hand, either.

Unable to fight his persistence, Georgie allowed Austin to lead her onto the floor and, once there, he took her right hand into his left, wrapped his arm around her waist and pulled her close.

The slow country song spoke of lost love and long-ago memories, a fitting tribute to their past. Georgie felt a bit light-headed, and she wasn't sure if it was because of the booze, or her partner. She pressed her cheek against his chest, closed her eyes and relaxed against him. She relished the feel of his palm roving over her back, his quiet strength, his skill. The first song gave way to another, then another, and still they continued to move to the music, as if they didn't have a care in the world.

When Austin tipped her chin up, forcing her to look into those magnetic cobalt eyes, she sensed he wanted to say something. Instead, he kissed her softly, deeply, taking her breath and composure. After they parted, Georgie could only imagine what the attendees were thinking, particularly Paris and Dallas, who were standing not far away, staring at them. She also noticed the couple had been joined by a crowd of Calloways. Mothers Jenny and Maria seemed pleased, the two dark-haired brothers, Houston and Tyler, looked annoyed, and the only blond sibling, Worth, evidently found the whole scene amusing, considering his grin.

Georgie tipped her forehead against his chest. "We're going to be the talk of the town."

"So?"

She looked up at him. "So if my father finds out I was canoodling with a man in public, and that man happens to be a Calloway, it won't be good for either of us."

Austin stopped and escorted her into a secluded corner. "Georgie, it's high time you stop caring what your dad thinks. And when it comes down to it, we weren't making out on the dance floor. I just gave you a simple kiss."

A kiss that curled her toes in her stilettos. "Some would deem it inappropriate."

"*Some* can kiss my ass."

Georgie suddenly felt very warm and a tad bit dizzy. "I need some air."

Taking her by the arm, Austin guided Georgie outside the tent and set her on a wooden bench. "Better?" he asked.

She pinched the bridge of her nose and closed her eyes. "It's the drinks."

"Drinks? You had more than one of those mint juleps?"

"I know. Paris warned me, but I was...thirsty."

"You could've gotten water or a soda at the bar."

She frowned up at him. "I don't need a lecture. I need to go home."

"You're not fit to drive, Georgie."

She wouldn't debate that. "I know. Do you mind driving me home?"

"You can stay at my house."

She wasn't *that* tipsy. "Not a good idea."

"I have four bedrooms and four bathrooms. You can take your pick."

She found that odd. "Why so many?"

He shrugged. "The builder told me it was better for resale, not that anyone would buy a house in the Cowboy Commune."

Georgie giggled like a schoolgirl. "Is that what you're calling it these days?"

"That's what people around these parts have labeled it."

"I suppose it does fit."

He took both her hands and pulled her up. "Let's get your things and get you to bed."

She gave him a quelling look. "Austin Calloway—"

"A bed in a guestroom." He wrapped his arm around her waist and traveled toward the tent. "Of course, my bed is probably the best."

"Hush."

He favored her with a grin. "Okay. I'll be good."

Georgie knew how good he could be when he was being bad. For that reason, she should demand he drive her home. But all her wisdom went the way of the cool wind when he paused and gave her another kiss, and this one wasn't simple at all.

She wasn't too mentally fuzzy to know that if she didn't keep her wits about her, she would end up in Austin Calloway's bed.

"Here's the bedroom." Austin opened the door and stepped aside to allow Georgie some space to move past him. When she brushed against his belly, he realized he should've stood at the end of the hall. Or outside on the front porch.

He could hear his stepmom telling him to be a man about it and leave her be. Unfortunately, that seemed to be his problem. What man wouldn't want to sweep this woman up and make love to her until dawn?

Don't even think about it, Calloway.

But that was all he could think about when Georgie wandered into the room, perched on the edge of the bed and ran her palm over the teal-colored comforter like she was stroking a pet. "This is a really nice room. Has anyone stayed in here before me?"

He moved into the doorway but didn't dare go farther. "Nope. You're the first. Jenny's the one who decorated the place. That's why it's so frilly."

"It's pretty. I like peacock colors." She hid a yawn behind her hand. "I want to apologize for my behavior. I didn't plan to get drunk."

"I wouldn't qualify you as drunk. In fact, in all the time I've known you, I've never even seen you have a beer."

She crossed her legs, causing the dress to shift higher, revealing some mighty nice thighs. "I've only done it once. On my twenty-first birthday, a group of my college girlfriends and I hired a limo and went bar hopping. I had several cosmopolitans and a hangover to beat all hangovers the next day. It was awful."

"We've all been there before."

She leaned back and braced herself on her elbows. "I prefer not to go there again. Do you have a spare toothbrush?"

"Yep." He pointed at the sliding door across the room. "In the bathroom. That's Jenny's doing, too. She stocked the place with everything any guest would need, male or female."

"She didn't happen to put a gown in there, did she?"

"I don't think so."

"Then can I borrow one of your T-shirts? Otherwise I won't have a thing to wear."

Damn. Just when he'd gotten his mind off seeing her naked. "Sure. I'll be right back."

He took off down the hall at a fast clip and, when he reached his bedroom closet, tugged a faded blue rodeo T-shirt off the hanger. On the way back, he gave himself a mental pep talk on the virtues of keeping his hands to himself and his mind on honor.

Georgie sent him a sleepy smile when he reentered the guestroom. "That was fast. Hand it here."

Austin almost froze in his tracks when Georgie began to fiddle with the collar at the back of her neck. Honor and virtue went down the drain when he imagined the front of the dress dropping to her waist. Maria's cautions went unheeded when he fantasized about putting his hands on her. And to make matters worse, she came to her feet and turned around, giving him a bird's-eye view of her butt. "Can you help me with this?"

Man, he'd love to, but probably not in the way she'd meant. "Help you with what?"

She held her hair up with one hand. "This bow thingie. It's in a knot."

His *gut* was in a knot, and that would be the least of his problems if he came anywhere near her.

He could do this. He could help her with the kink in her collar and ignore the one building below his belt buckle. Good thing she didn't have eyes in the back of her head.

After tossing the T-shirt on the bed, he studied the twisted bow and worried over what would happen if he managed to get it untied. "Just hang on to the dress."

"Of course I will," she said, her tone hinting at irritation.

He'd been known for his steady hands, but he actually fumbled with the tie for a time before he had it undone. "There you go. All set."

Without warning, Georgie spun around and somehow managed to whack him in the jaw with her elbow. He hadn't been at all prepared for the accidental blow, nor had he expected his inadvertent attacker to frame his face in her palms. "I'm so sorry, Austin. Did I hurt you?"

Oh, yeah, he was hurting, but it wasn't from getting smacked. Right there, in his field of vision, a man's biggest fantasy, and in his case, worst nightmare—a pair of bare breasts. Tempting, round breasts close enough to touch. He'd seen breasts before. He'd seen hers before, several times, although they looked a bit fuller than he recalled. He'd touched them before, with his hands and his mouth. Damn if he didn't want to do that now.

"Austin?"

He forced his gaze back to her face. "You forgot something."

She glanced down, then back up and her eyes went wide. "Oops."

The next oops came when he noticed *that* look, the one she'd always given him when she'd wanted a kiss. But maybe that's only what he wanted to see. Regardless, he had to maintain some control. Be a true gentleman. Hang tight to his honor.

And that plan went right out the window when she pulled him down to her lips. That's when caution gave way to chemistry. She started walking backward, taking him with her. and before he knew it, they were on the bed, facing each other with their legs twined together. He managed to remove his jacket while they continued to kiss like there was no tomorrow. She worked the buttons on his shirt and slipped her hand inside. He slid his palm slowly up the back of her thigh and continued on until he contacted a skimpy pair of silk panties.

Completely caught up in his need, Austin planted kisses down Georgie's neck and traveled to her breasts. He circled his tongue around one nipple before taking it into his mouth, using the pull of his lips to tempt her. She answered by running her hands though his hair and moving restlessly against him.

He wanted more from her. He wanted it all. But he couldn't have it unless he knew she wanted the same. On that thought, he raised his head and sought her eyes. "Before this goes any further, convince me you know what you're doing."

Unfortunately the interlude ended as quickly as it started when Georgie broke away, scrambled to her feet and pulled the top of her dress back into place. "Apparently I don't know what I'm doing since I swore this wouldn't happen again," she said, clear frustration in her voice.

Austin rolled to his back, draped an arm over his closed eyes and tried to catch his breath. "You started it."

"You didn't seem to be complaining."

"I couldn't complain with our tongues in each other's mouths."

When he heard the sound of a slamming door, Austin opened his eyes, expecting to discover Georgie had left the premises, if not the house. Instead, he noticed the bedroom door was still open, but the one leading into the bathroom had been closed.

Austin sat up and rubbed both hands over his face in a futile effort to erase the memories of their encounter. He figured he might as well leave now since he doubted she'd come out unless he made a quick exit. Obviously he'd been wrong, he realized when she walked back into the room wearing only his T-shirt and no smile.

She folded her arms around her middle and leaned back against the wall next to the door. "I'm sorry. You're not to blame for my behavior."

Regardless of blame, the damage to his libido had already been done. "I need to apologize to you. After two of Jenny's drinks, I should've realized you're not in charge of your faculties."

She crossed her arms around her middle and raised her chin. "I wasn't drunk."

"Okay. Tipsy."

"Maybe, but I'm quite sober now."

And he was still so jacked up he could pull that too-big shirt up over her ruffled hair and take her up against the wall. "And I'm betting you're tired. Have a good night. See you in the morning."

He turned on his heels and almost made it to the door before she asked, "Where are you going?"

Straight to hell if he faced her again. "To bed."

"I thought we could talk awhile."

He didn't want to talk. He wanted to get back down to business. "I'm pretty worn out," he said without moving.

"Come on, Austin. You're a night owl just like me."

He'd be hooting up a storm—or howling like a coyote—if he got anywhere near her again. "Georgie, I'm fairly sure if I stay, I wouldn't want to use my mouth to talk, especially since you're half-dressed."

She laughed. "You've seen me in a bikini. Actually, you've seen me wearing nothing."

If she kept talking that way, she'd see the evidence of what those memories did to him. What she'd done to him a few minutes ago. He had one hell of an erection and no place to go. "I think it might be better if I go to my own room."

"Man up, Calloway. You're not a teenager anymore. You can have an adult conversation with a woman without any other expectations."

Under normal circumstance, that was a given. But with her...

Dammit, he was up for the challenge, *up* being the operative word. Still, he vowed to prove to her he could be mature in spite of the noticeable bulge below his belt buckle. In an effort to calm down, he ran through a mental laundry list of a few times he'd been in pain. His first broken rib during one rodeo. When Maria made him eat spinach. The day Abby had him served with divorce papers.

That did it, or so he thought until he faced Georgie again. The T-shirt hit her well above the knee and hung off one shoulder. He could see the outline of her breasts and that's exactly where his gaze landed again, and his imagination kicked into overdrive.

"Austin."

He finally tore his attention away from her attributes and came in contact with her scowl. "What?"

She pointed two fingers at her eyes. "Up here."

"Sorry," he muttered, although in some ways he wasn't.

Georgie dropped down onto the bed and patted the space beside her. "Sit for a few minutes."

She really expected him to remain upright after their recent make-out session? Yeah, she did, and so would his stepmothers. With that in mind, he perched on the edge of the mattress, keeping a decent berth between them. "So what's on your mind?"

"Us," she said as she stretched the hem of the shirt to her knees. "Everything we've been through over the years."

He smiled. "We have been through quite a bit."

"And during all that time," she continued, "our friendship always meant the most to me."

Now he got it. She was about to deliver the "let's be friends" speech. "Yeah, we've always had a good friendship, and some really friendly foreplay in the bed of my truck."

She playfully slapped at his arm. "You know what I mean. I'm referring to all those instances when we were there for each other, like the time I made an A minus in Mr. Haverty's class."

"Oh, yeah. You nearly had a nervous breakdown over

that one. What about the time you helped me pass calculus?"

"And biology and world geography and, I believe, algebra one."

"You never had to help me with athletics."

"True enough."

They paused to share a smile before Austin said, "Now that we've established we've been friends for a long, long time, is there another point to this conversation?"

She studied her hands and twisted the silver ring round and round her little finger. "That's what I want from you right now, Austin. That's what I need from you."

Damn. "Fine. You've got it."

She leveled her gaze on his. "Problem is, I'm not sure you're capable of being only my friend."

Anger sent him off the bed to face her. "You're being freakin' unfair, Georgie. We were friends long before we were lovers."

"I just don't know if you're willing to go back to that. I'm not sure you can."

He might be willing, but that didn't take away the wanting. "I damn sure could be only your friend, and I'll prove it."

"How do you propose to do that?"

Hell if he knew. "From now on, when I see you, I'll only shake your hand."

That earned him her smirk. "If you say so."

"I say so." Starting now. He stuck out his hand. "Hope you sleep well."

Ignoring the gesture, she rose from the bed and damned if she didn't draw him into a hug. She then stepped back and smiled. "See there? You managed to accept a friendly show of affection and you didn't even try to cop a feel. Maybe I've underestimated you."

Yeah, she had, because it had taken all his fortitude not to grab her up and toss her back onto the bed. "I'm a lot stronger than you think, Georgie."

"Only time will tell, Austin. And I hope you get a good night's sleep, too."

"Not hardly," he muttered as he headed out the door and down the hall.

Being only friends with Georgia May Romero could be the biggest mountain he'd ever had to climb, but he was determined to do it. He would find some way to show her he could be the man she wanted him to be, even if it might do him in during the process.

To postpone the inevitable test of his mettle, he hoped that when he woke up in the morning, he'd find her gone.

Five

Before she went home, Georgie sought out an energy boost and the means to wake up after a restless night. She padded into the deserted upscale kitchen on bare feet, wearing Austin's oversize T-shirt and suffering from a mild hangover. She retrieved a cup from the gray cabinet and located the canister of dark roast on the white-quartz countertop, right next to the fancy coffeemaker that looked as if it might require a barista degree to operate it.

After two attempts, she finally figured out the formula and waited for the stainless carafe to fill before she poured the brew into the mug. Normally she preferred cream and sugar, but black coffee seemed more appropriate under the circumstance.

She leaned back against the center island, clutching the cup and worrying over her behavior after stupidly finishing off two high-powered cocktails the night before. But she couldn't blame her complete lack of control on the booze. Not when the situation involved a sexy cowboy.

How could Austin still affect her so strongly? How could she forget how he'd flitted in and out of her life without a second thought? More important, how could she disregard that he'd fathered her child and still didn't know it?

She had to tell him soon. When and where remained a mystery yet to be solved.

"Mornin'."

Georgie glanced to her right to see Austin trudging into the room, his hair slightly damp and his jaw blanketed with whiskers. He hadn't bothered to put on a shirt, but at least he'd had the wherewithal to put on a pair of faded jeans that rested a little too low on his hips to be deemed decent. She didn't need to see the slight shading of hair centered into his broad chest or the flat plane of his belly or that other stream of hair that disappeared into his waistband. She definitely didn't need to look any longer, but she did.

Bad Georgie. Bad, bad Georgie.

Austin seemed oblivious to her blatant perusal of his body and continued toward the coffeemaker to pour a cup. He briefly brushed against her shoulder and gave her a good whiff of manly soap as he turned to face her. "I thought you'd be gone by now, or at least dressed." He topped off the comment by raking his gaze down her body and back up again, slowly.

She experienced a sensual electric shock down to the bottom of her soles. "I just needed to wake up a bit before I drove. I'll be leaving very soon."

He sent her a sleepy grin. "Don't go on my account, unless you have appointments."

She took a sip of coffee before setting the cup on the counter. "Only emergencies on Saturday and so far I haven't had any."

"I could always put you to work in the barn."

He could do a lot to her in the barn that had more to do with pleasure. He already had. "I still have some boxes I need to unpack and some things to put away. I didn't have a lot of time to do that in the past two weeks since I dove right into work."

"Do you need help?"

If he stepped through her doorway, she'd be too distracted to get anything done. Not to mention he would notice all the signs pointing to a child in residence. "I'll manage, and I really need to get out of here."

Austin leaned a hip against the counter. "Before you leave, I have a proposition."

Oh, brother. "I believe we established there would be no more of that last night."

He looked highly incensed. "It's not *that* kind of proposition. I'm talking about my second favorite pastime—a trail ride on open land. Just you and me and total freedom."

She didn't dare ask about his first favorite pastime, although she suspected it was a toss-up between calf-roping and carnal endeavors. "Does that include prancing naked on the prairie?"

He released a low, sexy laugh. "No prancing on my end, and since it's going to be in the forties, naked won't be happening for the sake of my dignity."

Georgie suddenly longed for summer. "It's been a while since I've ridden for pleasure." When he smirked and opened his mouth to speak, she pointed at him. "Before you make some suggestive comment, I'm referring to horseback riding."

"I didn't have one dirty thought rolling around in my brain."

"Yeah, sure."

He winked and smiled. "Just so you know, it's been a while since I've ridden just for the heck of it. We could have a good time. As friends."

The friend part still concerned her. "When do you propose we take this ride?"

He forked a hand through his dark hair. "We'd leave out this afternoon and come back tomorrow."

She raised both hands, palms forward. "Wait a minute. You're talking about an overnight trip?"

"Yeah. We're gearing up for the opening of Texas Extreme, so I thought I'd map out the best course for the trail ride for beginners."

"You can't do that in an afternoon?"

"We're going to be taking the guests on an old-fashioned campout, complete with a chuck wagon. We might even herd a few cows."

As much as Georgie would enjoy the getaway, warning bells rang out in her head. "Couldn't you ask Dallas to go with you?"

"Nope. Dallas is freaking out over the baby coming in less than a month. He barely leaves Paris's side."

That made sense, but still… "What about Houston or Worth?"

"Houston's busy chasing the dream and Worth, well, he's busy chasing women."

She was down to her last option. "That still leaves Tyler."

"He left this morning to check out a couple more pack mules for the trail ride and I'm not sure when he'll be back."

Georgie narrowed her eyes. "If you expect me to ride a mule, my answer is definitely no."

His grin arrived, slow as sunrise. "Do you have a problem with my ass?"

She slapped at his arm. "You're so comical this morning."

"Thanks, and for the record, I don't expect you to board a mule."

"Good to know, but my mare isn't ready for a trail ride. She's still pretty skittish."

"I know," he said. "I saw her dump you on your butt last week, remember?"

She wished she could forget. "I guess that settles it then. I don't have an adequate ride, so you're on your own."

"I still have the dynamic duo."

She was blasted back into the past to a wonderful time when they'd set out on horseback in secret. "You mean Junior and Bubba?"

"Yep. They're still going strong at the ripe old age of fifteen."

"I loved Junior."

"He probably feels the same about you. Only one way to find out. Come with me on the ride."

She turned the idea over and over and couldn't quite pull the trigger on a definitive decision. "I'm still not too keen on the overnight idea."

He rubbed a hand over his jaw. "Tell you what. If you agree to go, and you decide you don't want to spend the night with me, we'll ride back."

That she could live with, but she still had responsibilities. "I'll see what I can get done before noon and I'll let you know."

"Fair enough," he said. "But don't take too long. I want to get started right after lunch."

"If I do agree, what do you propose we have for dinner? Or do you plan to play hunter and gatherer and catch our meal in the creek?"

He winked. "Leave that up to me. I promise you won't be disappointed."

He'd never disappointed her when it had come to showing her a good time. He *had* let her down during those two mornings when he'd disappeared out of her life to pursue his interests. Yet Chance had become the most important person in her life, and maybe this journey would present a prime opportunity to have a heart-to-heart with Austin.

On that thought, Georgie walked to the sink, rinsed out her cup then turned to find Austin staring at her. "Where and when do you want me to meet you?"

He looked mildly surprised. "Around one p.m., at the main barn. Be sure to bring a coat. The temperature's going to be dropping this afternoon when the cold front comes in."

She might be better served by wearing several layers of clothing for protection, both from the elements and her escort. "Okay. Right now I better get dressed and retrieve my truck."

He hooked a thumb behind him. "Your truck's in the driveway. Feel free to wear my T-shirt home."

Oh, sure. "With my high heels?"

He streaked a palm over his face. "Get out of here, Georgie, before I…"

She couldn't hold back a smile. "Before what?"

"Before I forget we're just friends."

Georgie needed to remember the friend pact, too, no matter what Austin Calloway might throw at her. But if their past behavior predicted future deeds, that would darn sure prove to be difficult.

"Where in the hell are you going?"

Austin ignored Dallas's question and continued to secure the bedrolls to Bubba's saddle. "I'm going to chart out the trail ride for Extreme."

Worth wandered into the barn and eyed the bay gelding. "Seems a little early to be worrying about that. The lodge isn't going to be finished for a couple of months and we haven't even started building the new catch pens yet."

Austin moved across the aisle to Junior and tightened the jet-black gelding's girth strap. "I'll be busy with the dealerships after the first of the year. I figure now's as good a time as any."

Tyler suddenly made an appearance to add to the unwelcome audience. "Since you have two horses saddled, I'm guessing you want one of us to go with you."

He began to shorten the stirrups without looking back. "Nope."

"You're going to take both horses?" Dallas asked.

Austin finished and finally turned around. "Yep."

Worth pulled a piece of straw from his pocket and started chewing on it. "You must be planning to cross the border if you're taking both horses."

He really wished they'd all leave before Georgie arrived. The odds of that happening were slim to none, he realized, after he heard the sound of approaching footsteps. Austin braced for the fallout until Jenny—not

Georgie—breezed into the barn, wearing a crazy red Christmas sweater and matching slacks.

She strode over and offered him a small square blue cooler and a plastic sack. "Here you go, sugar."

Austin took the containers, strode to Bubba and draped the straps over the saddle horn. "I appreciate it, Jen. Hope you didn't go to too much trouble."

When he faced Jenny again, she patted his cheek. "No trouble at all. Oh, and I just talked to Georgie. She said she had to make a phone call and then she'll be heading this way. Ten minutes tops."

Damn. The companion cat was out of the bag, and no doubt he'd have hell to pay. "Thanks for letting me know."

The look Dallas sent him wasn't lost on Austin. "Georgie, huh?"

He figured he should just fake indifference and hope for the best. "Yeah, Georgie. She wasn't busy this afternoon so we decided to do it together."

Worth chuckled. "Doing it together is a lot more fun than doing it alone."

Jenny sent her son a frown. "Hush, Worth Calloway. A man can go for a ride with a woman without anything disreputable going on." She turned her attention back to Austin. "Your supper should be set. I put in all the fixings for a wiener roast."

When the boys began to chuckle, Austin balled his fists at his sides, itching to throw a punch. Jenny's weapon of choice involved a stern look aimed at the brothers before she turned to him again. "I added marshmallows and I wasn't sure what Georgie liked on her hot dog, so just to be safe, I included several condiments."

"If you're really worried about safety, Mom," Worth

began, "you might want to pack some condoms with the condiments."

Jenny laid a dramatic hand over her heart. "My dear, sweet child, don't be so crass. You're acting like an over-sexed heathen."

Like a bunch of junior high jocks, the brothers' chuckles turned into full-fledged laughter. "Come on, guys," Austin said. "Get your minds out of the sewer and have some respect for Jen."

Jenny propped her hands on her hips. "Austin is absolutely right. You boys have apparently forgotten your raising."

"Sorry, Mom," Worth muttered, followed by Dallas's and Tyler's apologies.

Jenny gave Austin a quick hug. "I'll see you tomorrow, and, you two, be careful."

"We will," Austin said. "And thanks again for everything."

After Jen strode out of the barn, Tyler said, "I personally think Worth had a good idea about the condoms. Do you have one in your wallet that's not from your high school years?"

Austin had about enough. "Look, Georgie is just a friend. That's all. We're not doing anything we haven't been doing for years."

Dallas took on a serious expression. "That's what worries me. I've already warned you about—"

"Dammit, I know, Dallas." Austin drew in a calming breath and let it out slowly. "You're just going to have to trust me on this one. We're not the same stupid kids we used to be."

Tyler came up and slapped Austin on the back. "Good luck, bud. Wide-open spaces and a beautiful woman can equal a lack of control. If you can resist her, you're a better man than me."

"Or crazy," Worth added. "But if you only want to be friends with her, I'll be glad to pick up where you leave off."

Austin sent him a menacing glare. "Not every woman is interested in you, Worth."

Dallas stepped forward. "We're not trying to get into your business. We just don't want you leading Georgie on."

Same song, fiftieth verse. Austin understood where his brothers were coming from, but he was up for the challenge. He could have a platonic relationship with a woman, even one he'd slept with before. Even one he'd wanted to sleep with last night, minus the sleeping...

"Sorry I'm late."

His focus went straight to Georgie strolling down the aisle, her hair pulled up high into a ponytail. She wore a heavy flannel shirt over a white T-shirt, a pair of faded jeans and worn brown boots. With every move she made, every smile she gave the boys who now stood, hats in hands, staring at her, Austin's confidence began to slide.

He cleared the uncomfortable hitch from his throat. "No problem. I'm just now finishing up with the supplies."

She held up the small nylon duffel. "Do you have room for this?"

"What's in it?"

She glanced over her shoulder at the brothers, who continued to stand there like statues, eavesdropping. "Just a few essentials in case we lay over. Toothbrush, toothpaste, that sort of thing."

Too bad she hadn't said a sexy nightgown, but he supposed that wouldn't be practical. Fantastic, yeah, practical, no. "Hang it over the saddle horn."

"Good idea." After she complied, she brought her attention to the brothers. "Are you guys going, too?"

Dallas shook his head. "Nope. I'm hanging out with the wife."

Tyler scowled. "I'm hanging out with the mothers."

"I'm hanging out at the local dance hall," Worth began, "but I'd be glad to change my plans and accompany you."

Georgie smiled at him sweetly. "I wouldn't feel right leaving all those local women without a dance partner."

Worth returned her smile. "You and me, we could take a stroll in the moonlight while Austin roasts a few marshmallows."

Austin pointed at the door. "Out. Now. All of you."

While the crew trudged away, Tyler muttered, "Fifty dollars says he'll need the condiments."

"I'll see your bet and raise you fifty," Worth added as they walked out the barn, laughing all the way.

Georgie frowned. "What was that all about?"

He checked to see if both bedrolls were secure beneath the saddles' cantles. "Nothing. They're just mouthing off like usual."

"It sounded like they were making some kind of bet on me."

Austin ventured at glance at Georgie to find she looked a little put out. "It has more to do with me. I told them this was a friendly trip, and they don't believe I can be only friends with you without getting too friendly."

"Can you?"

He was going to do his best. "Sure. Are you ready to roll?"

"I guess so."

He sensed her hesitation, and felt the need to reassure her. "Georgie, I promise to be a gentleman, just like Maria taught me to be. And if I slip up, Junior knows his way back to the barn."

She patted the black gelding's neck and received a nuzzle in return. "Yes, he does, and he's still as gorgeous as ever."

So was she. "Yep, he's in good shape. He also recognizes you."

She pulled the headstall from the hanger and began to remove the horse's halter. "We all had some unforgettable times."

Austin recalled one great time that had occurred not so far away in the tack room. Some hot and heavy kisses, taboo touches and a moment when they'd almost gone all the way. His focus went straight to her body and it took all his strength not to grab her up and carry her back in the cramped room to refresh her memory. "Are you ready to go?"

She sent him a look over her shoulder. "Do you plan to ride Bubba without a bit?"

Keep your mind on your business and not her butt, Calloway. "I probably could, but I guess it's best I don't."

After they were all tacked up, Georgie mounted Junior with ease and Austin followed suit on Bubba. "Let's get this adventure started," he said as he guided the gelding down the aisle with Georgie and Junior tagging along behind them.

Once they emerged into daylight, they rode through the gate, side by side, and into open pastureland. A strong gust of wind kicked up some dust, and Austin wondered if Georgie had on enough clothes to keep warm. He could keep her warm. Give her his heat in ways she wouldn't forget…

"I've forgotten how wonderful this feels," she said, interrupting his suspect train of thought.

"Yeah. Nothing better than wide-open spaces." *Wide-open spaces and a beautiful woman can equal a lack of control.* Austin erased Tyler's warnings from his mind as they continued down the path leading to the creek.

They rode in silence for a long time before Georgie spoke again. "Any ideas on your route?"

He had some ideas, but none having to do with routes. "I thought I'd follow along the fence line for a couple of miles."

She sent him a fast glance. "That means you'll be bordering the road leading to my dad's ranch. Nothing will ruin an Old West fantasy more than a delivery truck."

He couldn't argue that point. "Hadn't thought about that. Then I guess we'll head south and ride toward the far end of the creek."

She looked straight ahead and smiled. "Ah, the creek. I can remember spending a lot of summers at the place."

So could he. "The rope is still there, but the water isn't as deep as it used to be. I wouldn't suggest using it."

That earned him a sour look. "It's a little too cool to be swimming today, don't you think?"

He adjusted his hat on his head with one hand. "Probably so."

She favored him with a smile right out of a dirty dream. "Wanna race?"

He wanted to pull her off the horse and into his arms. He wanted her. Real bad. "No need to ask me twice."

He cued Bubba into a lope and Georgie didn't miss a beat. When he picked up speed, so did she, smiling all the way. And she became that girl again, the one who'd spurred his adolescent fantasies. A more mature version, but still as pretty. Still as spirited.

They ran headlong past the places where they used to meet in secret, sometimes at midnight, sometimes in broad daylight if they were feeling more daring, avoiding detection by their fathers and caught up in the thrill of trying not to get caught. They'd engaged in long conversations, when they hadn't been engaging in experimentation.

So many ghosts on this land. Good times mixed with the not so good. Most had been good, except for one in particular, the old windmill on the horizon serving as a reminder. The place where he'd planned to tell her goodbye before he'd left for college, but she hadn't shown up.

As they slowed their pace, Georgie's laughter echoed over the plains and, in that moment, he couldn't want her more. But he had to remember the friendship pact, and adhere to it. He had to take hold of some serious honor and not act on his desires.

If he could manage that accomplishment, then he expected to encounter a few flying pigs before the end of the day.

Six

Before the end of this trip, Georgie planned to fully disclose her secret to Austin. If only she could find the appropriate place, appropriate time and, most important, the appropriate words. Right then those words escaped her.

As they neared the familiar creek, she noticed gray clouds gathering on the horizon, completely concealing the sun. They'd been riding for a little over two hours when she sensed now would be a good time to take a break and assess the weather.

"Let's stop for a while," Austin said before she could get the suggestion out of her mouth.

They trotted to the tree line and, after they dismounted, led the horses to the shallow brook for a drink. Austin then took the reins from her hands and guided the geldings to the pasture to turn them loose.

"Shouldn't we tie them up?" she asked as soon as he returned to her side.

"Nah. They'll hang around here and if they don't, they'll find their way back to the barn."

Great. "And that would leave us stranded in the middle of nowhere on foot."

Without responding, Austin put both pinkies in his mouth and blew out a loud whistle, bringing the equine boys back in record time. He grinned at Georgie as he patted the geldings' necks. "They don't have any intention of going anywhere without me."

Georgie had felt the same way about him at one point in time. "They've always been well trained."

Austin rummaged around one of the saddlebags, withdrew two carrot chunks, laid them in his flattened palms and offered them to Junior and Bubba. "They know who feeds them." He waved them away. "Now you two go back to the grass for a bit."

As if they understood every word, the geldings turned around and hurried back to the pasture to graze. "You missed your calling, Austin. You should've been a lion tamer in the circus."

"Maybe so. I pretty much grew up in a circus." He wandered over to the bank and sat down on a rock. "Come over here and take a load off."

"I've been sitting for almost two hours."

"Then suit yourself and stand."

In reality, her legs felt a little shaky from the long ride, but the thought of sitting next to him didn't help matters. Still, this could be an opportunity to open up the lines of communication before she lowered the baby boom.

Georgie strolled over to Austin, lowered down onto the dirt slope and hugged her knees to her chest. "Looks like it might rain."

"The forecast says tomorrow midday."

She sent him a sideways glance. "This is Texas and when Mother Nature comes for a visit, she doesn't always listen to meteorologists."

"True."

A brief span of silence passed before Georgie spoke again. "I'm still amazed at Bubba's and Junior's obedience. Way back when, they were both pretty wild, especially Junior."

"But he pretty much taught you how to rope."

"With a little assistance from you."

He sighed. "Yeah. It's hard to believe how long they've been in my life. But so have you."

Yes, she had. A very long time full of happiness and heartache. She snatched up a stick and began tracing random circles in the soil. "How long did you know your wife?"

"For a while," he said. "We ran into each other on the circuit on a regular basis during my rodeo years before we got hitched."

A possibility burned into Georgie's mind, and it wasn't good. She shifted slightly to gauge his reaction to the impending question. "Were you dating her when your dad passed away?"

He studied her for a moment before reality dawned in his expression. "If you're asking if we were together when I was with you, the answer is not only no, but hell no. I can't believe you'd even think such a thing."

"What did you expect, Austin? I found out you'd married her four months after that night."

He lowered his gaze to the ground. "I guess that's a reasonable assumption under normal circumstances, but it shouldn't be with us. Not with our history."

A lot of their history hadn't exactly been hearts and

flowers, or complete honesty. "When I didn't hear from you after that last night we spent together, I assumed you'd moved on again. I just didn't know you'd moved on into a marriage."

"More like a huge mistake."

For some reason the declaration pleased her. "Surely it wasn't all bad."

He ventured a quick glance in her direction. "Not all of it. Not in the beginning. But sex alone can't sustain a relationship."

She cringed at the thought of him with another woman, even though she'd never had any real claim on him. "Did it ever occur to you that maybe you two should have tried living together before tying the knot?"

Austin sent her a cynical grin. "The whole wedding was spontaneous, and stupid. Too much beer and too much time on our hands and a Vegas chapel at our disposal."

At least that explained the hasty nuptials. "Never in a million years would I have believed you'd be a drunken Vegas wedding cliché, Austin."

"Well, believe it. I tried to make it work but Abby wasn't willing. In fact, to this day, I'm still not sure what I did."

"Maybe it wasn't what you did, but what you didn't do."

He frowned. "What do you mean?"

He was such a guy. "Were you attentive? Romantic? Did you tell her you loved her more than once in a blue moon?"

He almost looked ashamed. "None of the above, and I'm not sure we were in love. I mean, I cared about her, but I knew the marriage idea was wrong when I finally signed the divorce papers and I didn't feel anything but relief."

"Yet you hung in there for quite some time, right?"

"Three years, but it was pretty much over in the first six months."

"Wow. I'm surprised you didn't end it sooner."

"I didn't want to admit to the failure."

Nothing new there. "You can't shoulder that burden alone. It takes two to make or break a solid marriage."

"Maybe you're right, but there was one thing she wanted that I wasn't willing to give her."

"What was that?"

"A kid. I told her several times I didn't want any, but she started making noise about two months into the marriage. I reminded her that wasn't in my immediate future."

His assertions gave Georgie pause. "Then you're not completely ruling it out."

He shrugged. "I'm not sure. I only know I'm not going to be ready for that responsibility for a long, long time."

Georgie swallowed hard around the swell of disappointment mixed with panic. She had to acknowledge one serious reality—Austin might never accept their son. "I guess I always saw you as the fatherly type. You did a good job keeping your younger brothers on the straight and narrow."

He picked up a pebble and tossed it into the creek. "But if they screwed up, it was ultimately my folks' responsibility. And maybe I got my belly full keeping them in line while my dad was off doing whatever he was doing aside from work."

Meaning marrying another woman and birthing two more boys without telling anyone. Essentially she had done something similar by not telling him about their child, although her reasoning had seemed honorable at the time. "Did his deception influence your attitude about having children at all?"

"Nah. That would be Dallas, although he obviously changed his mind." He stared off into space for a moment before presenting a surprising smile. "Do you think it's still here?"

He'd always been a master at changing the subject when it got too hot in the emotion kitchen. Admittedly she could use a break, too. "What is still here?"

"The tree."

She'd known it was still around from the moment they'd ridden up to the creek. "To my right, about three oaks down."

He slapped his palms on his thighs and stood. "Let's go look at it before we head out."

"Why?"

He took her hand and pulled her to her feet. "I could use a good memory about now."

Georgie had to admit that secret meeting site did hold more than a few fond recollections. "Oh, all right. Lead the way."

She followed behind Austin along the bank, weaving in and out of foliage, until they reached the memorial tree sporting a pair of initials. She ran her palm over the carvings. "I wonder if anyone ever saw this."

Austin came to her side and grinned. "If they did, I'm sure they're still trying to figure out the identity of R and J."

She returned his smile. "Randy and Jill?"

"Ralph and Julie."

"Ronald and Jessie."

"Wasn't that a real couple from high school?" he asked.

"Possibly, but I guarantee we didn't know any Romeos or Juliets." And that had been the inside joke—star-crossed lovers caught between feuding fathers. She turned and leaned back against the trunk. "At least no one packed any daggers or poison."

He braced his palm on the tree, right above her head. "But the first time I kissed you here, that really packed a punch."

A kiss that had almost sent her to her knees. "I suppose."

"Suppose?" He leaned forward and ran a fingertip along her jaw. "Maybe I should refresh your memory."

As he leaned forward and rested his other hand on her waist, Georgie fought that same old magnetic pull. She decided to verbally push back. "Why do you continue to do this?"

"Do what?"

"Test my strength."

He traced her lips with a fingertip. "Maybe I'm testing mine."

"Friends, Austin," she muttered without much conviction.

"Good friends, Georgie girl."

When Austin traced the shell of her ear with his tongue, Georgie released a ragged breath and shivered. And when he centered his gaze on her eyes, she tried to prepare for what would predictably come next…a kiss that she couldn't resist.

Then he stepped back and winked. "Guess I'm stronger than we both thought."

Georgie gritted her teeth and spoke through them. "You're a tease."

To the sound of Austin's laughter, she stormed away through the trees, half tempted to ride back in the direction of the ranch. She then realized she had no horse, and whistled at the geldings the way Austin had. They didn't budge, at least not for her. After Austin summoned them, they came running back, looking for a handout from their master.

Georgie didn't afford Austin a glance, didn't say a word, as they mounted their respective horses. Frustration kept her and Junior in the same spot as Austin headed away, leaving her behind. Frustration over his actions, and her typical feminine response.

A few moments passed before he glanced back and pulled Bubba to a stop, then turned the gelding to face her. "Do you have a problem?"

"Yes. You."

He released a low, grainy laugh. "Obviously you traded in your sense of humor to get that vet degree."

"I don't exactly find your determination to play with me very funny."

"Sweetheart, if I'd seriously played with you, you'd be moaning, not complaining."

Now why did that make her want to twitch in the saddle? "Look, before I agree to continue this little trip, you have to promise you won't tease me again."

He narrowed his eyes and studied her straight on. "Best I recall, you used to like to be teased, especially when I had my hand in your—"

"Austin," she cautioned, despite the damp heat gathering between her thighs.

He raised both hands, as if surrendering. "Okay. I'm sorry. Old habits die hard."

Old memories clearly never died. "Apology accepted, as long as you don't pull anything like that again."

"Okay. But keeping my hands off you isn't going to be easy. Keeping my mouth off you is going to be really tough."

A very detailed sexual image filtered into Georgie's mind, bringing about a blanket of goose bumps. The girl she'd once been might have begged him to end her misery, but she wasn't that girl anymore. She was a woman. A vital woman who hadn't been with a man in six years. A woman who desperately needed his touch, his kisses, but recognized that the cost of intimacy with this man could be too high. "Where are we heading now?"

"The old cabin."

Just one more monument to the past, she thought as she cued Junior forward. She'd been at the ramshackle cabin before, but not to fool around with Austin. She'd met him there on his late mother's birthday at his request, an unusual appeal, but he'd been uncharacteristically sentimental. Those moments hadn't been about teenage hormones and unbridled lust. They'd been about comfort and communication. Buried regrets and obvious pain. Emotional exposure. Friendship at its finest.

Yes, she had been at that cabin, and during that fateful encounter, Georgie had quietly, completely fallen in love with Austin Calloway. Sadly, she still was, proving some things never changed.

The place hadn't changed a bit. Austin realized that when they arrived at the rickety structure that had somehow weathered at least a hundred years' worth of Texas heat. The windows were still boarded up, and he found that funny considering anyone could probably knock the door open with the swing of a rope. But his dad had always been a stickler when it came to security, even if it involved a one-room house that was barely hanging on. At least the front porch still appeared to be intact, and that might be a good thing if it rained.

He looked to his left to find Georgie staring at the cabin like she'd never seen it before. "It's exactly how I remembered it," she finally said. "Old and probably moldy."

Austin climbed off the saddle and guided Bubba to the pole barn adjacent to the cabin. "I imagine it's pretty dusty inside. Maybe even a critter or two hanging out."

Georgie dismounted and joined him. "Lovely. Nothing like stumbling upon a skunk."

"Skunks come out in the spring. Same with snakes. In fact, most of the animals are hibernating. Come to think of it, the last time I was here, I didn't see one living creature except maybe a spider or two."

"Bugs don't hibernate."

"That's true, but I don't see any reason why we'd have to go inside."

She studied the dreary sky. "A storm comes to mind."

"We'll worry about that if it happens." He needed to ask a question before they settled in for dinner. "Do you want to go back to the ranch?"

She sighed. "After sitting for the better part of six hours, I'd rather just relax for a while. We'll play the overnight plan by ear."

He couldn't deny his disappointment if she didn't spend the night with him, not that he expected anything to come of it aside from companionship. But that was okay. It was high time he relearned how to be her friend, although he figured he'd be fumbling his way through it.

He also envisioned sitting on his hands and keeping his mouth shut when he wasn't talking. "All right then," he said. "Let's get these guys unsaddled. I'll turn them out with some hay, then I'll build a fire for dinner."

After they'd accomplished that goal, Austin retrieved the supplies, tossed them onto the porch and searched the yard for a few rocks to fashion a makeshift fire ring. He placed them in a circle in front of the house then went about gathering kindling from fallen limbs on the side of the house. He returned to find Georgie sitting on the top porch step, elbows resting on her knees, palms supporting her jaw, a smile on her pretty face.

He dropped the wood into the middle of the circle and faced her. "You look amused."

"You look cute, all dressed in your red flannel shirt, getting ready to cook dinner. A cross between Paul Bunyan and Betty Crocker."

"I'm not sure how I feel about that description."

She straightened and pushed her hair back from her shoulders. "I didn't mean to insult your manhood. Actually, I'm impressed you're going to be playing chef tonight."

"Don't be too impressed." He leaned over and pulled two of the straightest limbs from the pile. "Here's our utensils."

She laughed. "We're having hot dogs?"

"Yep."

"Darn. I was hoping for filet mignon."

"Sorry to disappoint you."

"I'm not disappointed at all, Austin. I'm looking forward to it because I'm starving. So come on, baby, light that fire."

He'd like to have his fire lit by her. Ignoring the dirty

thoughts, Austin pulled an old book of matches from his back pocket. "Keep your fingers crossed this doesn't take more than a few tries. I don't have too many of these things."

Georgie came to her feet and brushed off her bottom. "We can always rub two sticks together."

Why the hell did hearing the word *rub* suddenly threaten his dignity? "Yeah, sure. You get going on that."

Turning his attention back to the fire pit, Austin struck the first match and watched it fizzle out. The second try didn't turn out any better. Now down to his last two, he wondered if they might have to return to the ranch for a decent meal. If that happened, he'd be sorely disappointed.

"Look what I found, Calloway."

Austin turned toward the porch where Georgie stood, holding a red-and-black barbecue lighter. "Where did you find that?"

She hooked a thumb over her shoulder. "In the sack back there. I also found marshmallows and a lot of little packets of condiments."

That reminded him of the previous condiment and condom conversation with the brothers. Funny thing was, he always carried a condom with him. Not that he had a snowball's chance in the desert to use it this trip. "That's Jenny for you. She hoards those things."

"They do come in handy."

After Georgie sprinted down the steps and gave him the lighter, Austin had little trouble getting the fire going, in spite of the steady breeze. Seated on the ground, they ate their hot dogs, roasted marshmallows, reminisced and laughed a lot. The whole time Austin kept his attention on Georgie's mouth, imagining another kiss. Imagining was all he could do, unless she gave him some sign she wanted it, too. Not a whole lot of chance that would happen.

By the time they were done with dinner, the only light that illuminated the area came from the dwindling fire. Austin found more wood to stoke the blaze, then returned to the porch to retrieve the one thing that would give him an excuse to have her in his arms. He set the radio on the wooden slats and tuned in to a country music station.

"Oh, my gosh," Georgie said from behind him. "You still have that relic?"

He turned to find she was real close. "Yeah, and it still works."

"If I'd known you wanted music, I would've brought my MP3 player and speakers."

He reached over and tucked one side of her hair behind her ear, revealing a pair of diamond heart studs. They looked a lot like the same earrings he'd given her for her sixteenth birthday. He'd worked overtime at the feed store to earn enough money to buy them for her, and it had been worth it when she'd been so damned pleased. "I enjoy having the past around now and then."

She smiled. "So do I."

On cue, the radio went from a commercial break to a country ballad. "Care to dance with me again?"

"Twice in one week? That's so daring."

And kind of dangerous if he didn't control his hands and mouth. "You've never shied away from risky behavior."

"That was before..." Both her gaze and words trailed off.

"Before what?"

"Before I became an adult with adult responsibilities.

However, I wouldn't refuse a dance with the consummate cowboy."

"Good to know."

After taking Georgie's hand, he led her down the steps and close to the fire where he put his arms around her. She laid her head on his shoulder and he placed his palm lightly against her back. As the song continued, he found his hand drifting lower, like he didn't have control of his appendages. He managed to stop the progress before he lost the wager that he could ignore his libido. But if she made one encouraging move, all bets were off.

They remained that way for a time as the wind picked up steam, and then came the deluge. Georgie pulled back and did something Austin would have never predicted. She laughed. Just the sound of it caused him to laugh, too. They continued to stand there, drenched to the bone and behaving like preschoolers who didn't have the good sense to come out of the rain.

When he noticed she was shivering, he led her to the porch, drew her against him and held her close. Then she did something else he didn't expect—brushed her lips across his neck.

He bent his head and took her mouth with a vengeance, sliding his tongue against hers slowly, deliberately, and she responded with a little action of her own. They stayed that way through one more song, making out like they had as kids. But the man in him backed her against the wooden wall, grabbed her butt and pressed against her, seeking relief but finding none. And what he was about to do wouldn't help a damn bit, but he wanted to do it. Had to do it.

He shoved her shirt off one shoulder then slid the strap to the tank she wore underneath down her arm partway.

Now that he'd gained access, he broke away and took her breast into his mouth, circling her nipple with the tip of his tongue. She answered by undressing enough to reveal her other breast and framed his head in her hands. The small sexual sound she made drove him to the brink of insanity, pushed him toward forbidden territory. Right then, right there, he could take her down to the ground just to be inside her. Instead, he decided he would make this about her, but only if she agreed.

With that goal in mind, Austin released the button on her jeans and paused for a protest. When that didn't happen, he slid the zipper down and whispered, "Do you want me to stop?"

"I…" She let out a long, broken breath. "No. Don't stop."

That was all he needed to hear. He worked his hand into her jeans, where he rimmed the edge of her panties. She gave no indication she'd changed her mind, which drove him to keep going, keep searching beneath the silk for that very sweet spot. She was warm and wet and definitely ready for the attention. He gave it to her with slow strokes before he quickened the pace. She gripped his shoulders tightly, moved her hips rhythmically in time with his touch.

After she tensed, he raised his head from her breasts and brought his mouth to her ear. "It's okay, babe. Just let go."

And she did, with a rush of dampness and a low, ragged moan. He didn't let up until he knew he had milked every last pulse of her climax and she collapsed against him. He kissed her again, softly this time, as he pulled her clothes back into place. He turned away and rested his palms on the railing to regain some scrap of composure.

Seven

Georgie truly wanted to scold him, but this wasn't all his fault. He had asked if she wanted to stop, and she'd told him no. She wasn't some weak wilting flower with no free will. Truth was, she had wanted him so much she hadn't been able to control the familiar underlying chemistry. They were combustible together. They always had been. She'd known that when she'd agreed to come with him. Deep down she knew this would likely happen. And in all honesty, she didn't care, even if she should.

She stood there, shivering, her damp shirt and jeans only adding to her overall discomfort. "I'm freezing."

He pushed away from the banister and faced her. "Understandable. You're soaked to the skin."

"So are you."

"Sweetheart, that's the least of my concerns at the moment."

She sent a pointed look at his distended fly, somewhat surprised that he didn't invite her to finish what they'd started.

"Take your clothes off, Georgie."

Apparently she'd been mistaken. "Excuse me?"

He bent over, snatched one of the blankets from the floor and tossed it to her. "Don't look so worried. I'm not going to ravish you."

"You just did."

His patent slow grin came out of hiding. "Yeah, I did, and I don't regret it because obviously you really needed it."

Boy, had she. "It's been a while."

"Same here."

She had a hard time believing that. "Try six years."

Shock passed over his expression. "You mean—"

"The last time you and I were together was the last time for me. Now turn around so I can get these clothes off."

He started unbuttoning his shirt. "I've seen you naked before."

"Maybe, but I'd rather that not happen now."

"Fine, but if I turn around, you're going to see my bare ass."

"Not if I don't look." Maybe she'd take just a little peek. Or a long gander.

"Alrighty then."

Georgie made quick work of shedding her clothes, socks and boots, while Austin took his sweet time. She was already wrapped securely in the blanket by the time he shoved down his pants. She remained glued in place, holding the blanket closed with one hand and her wet clothes in the other. She studied all the planes in his broad back, the buns of steel, the strong thighs and calves dusted with hair, and decided she couldn't speak if her life depended on it. Then he did something completely off-the-wall—laced his hands behind his neck and flexed his muscles, then did some crazy thrust reminiscent of a male-stripper movie she'd seen a while back.

A chuckle bubbled up in her throat and came out in a full-fledged laugh when he looked over one shoulder and grinned. "Stop it," she said when she'd recovered her voice. "And cover up."

"You didn't like my moves?"

Oh, yeah. "Please put something on before you catch a good case of pneumonia."

"Fine, but just let me know if you want some more cheap entertainment."

She averted her gaze when he leaned over and snatched the blanket from the porch slats. When she ventured another look, fortunately she found him covered from the waist down. Of course, that left his stellar chest in full view.

In order to distract herself, Georgie draped her shirt, jeans and pink panties over the railing while he came to her side to do the same. Once that was done, she faced him with a frown. "What now?"

"I guess we could go to bed."

"We don't have a bed."

"We have a couple more blankets and a dry floor in the cabin, unless you want to sleep out here."

A sudden clap of thunder and subsequent bolt of lightning told her that wouldn't be wise. "The cabin it is. Did you bring a flashlight?"

"Yep. It's in that bag behind you."

"Then get it."

"You're closer."

She muttered a few mild oaths as she bent down, opened the canvas duffel and rifled through the contents. "You brought clothes."

"An old shirt and a few rags. Keep going."

Of course the flashlight happened to be on the bottom. She straightened and handed it to him. "You're going in first."

"I wouldn't have it any other way."

Austin opened the door and shone the beam into the vacant cabin. Georgie followed him inside and couldn't see much of anything aside from the pine floor and barren walls, but she didn't spot any wildlife, either. Then suddenly he spun around and headed out the open door, leaving her all alone, in the dark.

"Austin Calloway, where are you going?"

"Don't panic," he said as he returned with the light. "I just grabbed the rest of the bedding so we can tolerate the bare floor."

"I'm not sure I'll get much sleep with the threat of vermin hanging over me."

"I'll protect you," he said. "Here, hold this so I can see what I'm doing."

She aimed the beam on her half-naked bed buddy while he spread out two more blankets, one on top of the other. Once that was done, he rolled what appeared to be the aged shirt and the aforementioned rags into two pillows.

"Your accommodations are ready, ma'am," he said.

"Not exactly a five-star hotel, but it will do."

Austin dropped down onto the pallet and patted the blanket. "Soft as a mattress."

"Maybe a concrete mattress." Georgie lowered herself beside him and scanned the room with the narrow beam, thankful she didn't see any animal eyes staring back at her.

"Hand it over, Georgie."

"Why?"

He stretched out on the pallet, easy as you please, not leaving a lot of space between them. "I don't want to wake up with a light shining in my eyes because you heard a noise. Worse still, I don't want you whacking me with it when you mistake me for a raccoon."

She reluctantly relinquished the flashlight and laid back, making sure the blanket was secure around her. Still, she didn't find much comfort in the limited covers, the floor beneath her or his close proximity. "I wonder how long this storm is going to last. If it doesn't end soon, our clothes won't be dry."

"You brought an extra pair of panties."

She paused until the shock subsided. "How do you know that?"

"I peeked inside your bag."

"That makes you a snoop, don't you think?"

"Yeah, you're right. Sorry. Sometimes I'm just a little curious."

A little too familiar with her, she decided, as she rolled to face him. "Extra panties or not, they're not going to do me much good when we head back to the ranch."

"You wouldn't be the first woman to ride naked as a jaybird through town on a horse."

"Very funny."

He turned the light on her. "I'd buy tickets to that, and so would every man in a thirty-mile radius."

She refused to honor him with a response. "Turn that thing off, please. I'm half-blind."

"You got it."

After he snapped off the flashlight, silence hung over them for a few moments before he spoke again. "How many boyfriends have you had in the past six years?"

None. Zero. Nada. "There you go again, being intrusive."

"Hey, I told you about my marriage. Turnabout is fair play, right?"

He did have a point. "If you must know, I was too busy to date."

"You're saying you didn't have one man in your life?"

Only her little man. "No, I did not, and I assumed you would figure that out when I told you how long it's been since I've had sex. And for your information, women don't have to have a man to be happy. I had school and now I have my career, and that's all I need."

"All signs pointed to the contrary on the porch a little while ago."

Darn his insistence on reminding her of her vulnerability. "I had a moment of weakness."

"You had one hell of an orgasm. Do you want another one?"

Oh, yes… "No, thanks. That should last me another six years."

He chuckled. "Sweetheart, I don't believe for a minute that's true. And if it is, you're a lot stronger than me."

"I don't know about that. You didn't ask for a thing in return after our interlude."

"Interlude? Is that sophisticated talk for foreplay?"

"Go to sleep, Austin."

"Whatever you say, Georgie girl. And FYI, I apologize in advance for the tent I'll be pitching in the morning underneath this blanket."

That sent all sorts of naughty visions running amok in Georgie's mind. But the heat those fantasies generated did little to rid her of the sudden cold when a breeze blew through the ancient cabin. She pulled the blanket closer and tried hard to control her shivering body and chattering teeth, to no avail.

"Roll over, Georgie."

"I beg your pardon?"

"I'm going to put my arms around you because you're cold."

"We're also naked."

"All the better."

"No way."

"We'll keep the blankets between us."

She wanted to rebuff his request, but her chilled state wouldn't let her.

After Georgie shifted to her side, away from him, he scooted flush against her and wrapped her up in his strong arms. She had the strongest urge to rub her hands over that masculine terrain but realized it would be in her best interest to remain cocooned in the blanket, maintaining some semblance of separation. "Try to make sure we don't have any skin-to-skin contact."

"Darlin', we already have several times in the past."

"But this is the present. We don't need to stir up something again."

"Too late."

Infuriatingly sexy man. "Good night, Austin."

"Good night, sweetheart."

Georgie closed her eyes, but sleep wouldn't come. She thought about her schedule for the following week, a spattering of Monday appointments, lunch with Paris on Tuesday, her son's arrival home on Thursday.

Her son. *Their son.* She had very few hours to tell Austin the truth if she stuck to her original plan. She had so many qualms about doing that very thing after his previous statement about not wanting to be a father for a long time.

He *was* a father. But could he transition into being a dad to a little boy who needed one so desperately?

As soon as she finally confessed, only then would she know for sure. And that confession would need to come in twenty-four hours or less.

Austin woke up with an erection as hard as a hammer and a sexy woman beside him. He rolled to his side, bent his elbow and supported his jaw with his palm to do a little studying of that woman.

At some point during the night, Georgie had flipped onto her belly, the blanket draped low to expose her dark hair trailing down her back, her eyes closed tightly against the morning light. He took a visual trip down what he could see of her body and paused where he glimpsed the curve of her bottom.

He wanted to uncover her completely, make love to her until noon. Maybe even later. Then suddenly she caught him off guard when she shifted to her side and draped her arm over his bare hip underneath the covers. Worse still, she buried her face into his chest, right below his sternum, and he could feel the warmth of her lips pressed against his skin.

Oh, man, what was he going to do now? He knew what he'd like to do, but since he saw no real signs she was fully awake, he remained in the same position, rigid as an anvil. All of him.

Refusing to take advantage of a woman in a sleep-induced coma, Austin considered all the ways he could bring her around and a kiss came to mind. Or a touch. Or the sound of a honking horn outside the cabin.

Startled, Georgie popped up and looked around like she needed to gain her bearings. "What was that?"

Unfortunately for Austin, those thick locks of hair concealed her breasts. "I think someone's here."

"Who?"

"I'm not sure, but I'll find out." And he planned to give them a piece of what was left of his mind.

He came to his bare feet, taking the blanket with him and tucking it around his waist to hide the result of his sinful thoughts. He then strode to the window and swiped the dust from the panes to discover one familiar black truck and two equally familiar men leaned back against it. "It's Dallas and Houston."

"Oh, no. What are they doing here?"

"I have no idea, but I'm damn sure going to find out."

Austin swept open the door and closed it behind him after he stepped onto the porch. He immediately noticed his brothers eyeing the discarded clothes draped over the rail.

"Nice panties," Houston said. "I wouldn't have pegged you for a pink kind of guy."

He'd just stepped on his last nerve. "What in the hell do you two want?"

Dallas held up his hands. "Simmer down, Austin. We thought you might be needing a ride."

Likely story. "We've got two perfectly good geldings as transportation, so thanks but no thanks."

"Two geldings that showed up at the barn this morning," Houston added. "They must not have taken too kindly to the storm."

Damn. "Maybe we'll just walk back."

Dallas smirked. "You might want to ask Georgie if she's up for a six-mile hike."

Houston rubbed his stubbled chin. "Georgie, huh? Glad that explains the panties on the porch. I was worried about you, bro."

He didn't appreciate their kidding, or their laughter or the fact that they'd just shown up, unannounced. "You guys could've called. I have my cell with me."

Dallas exchanged a look with Houston before regarding Austin again. "Actually, Jen called and when she didn't get a hold of you, she called me to check on you two."

Austin realized he hadn't taken the phone from the bag, and he hadn't checked the battery. "Fine. Give us a few minutes and we'll head back with the two of you. And you better be on your best behavior around Georgie."

"Before you go inside," Houston said, "I have a question."

That was the last thing he needed, more stupid questions. "Make it quick."

"Could you not have waited until you got in the house before you started taking off your clothes?"

He'd had too little sleep and not enough sex to deal with this. "Not that it's any of your concern, but we both got wet."

Dallas chuckled. "I just bet you did."

Austin pointed at the truck. "Go start up the rig and we'll be out as soon as we're finished."

"Finished with what?" Houston asked, looking way too amused.

Austin ignored the question, grabbed all the clothes, both pairs of boots and headed into the cabin without looking back. "Get dressed," he said as he tossed Georgie her things. "The horses went back to the barn so Dallas and Houston are taking us back."

She shimmied her panties into place beneath the blanket, sparking Austin's fantasies. "I can only imagine how this looks to them," she said as she worked the tank top over her head, giving him a glimpse of her nipple. "I'm sure they think something wicked happened between us last night."

He'd like to try out a little wicked right now, to hell with his brothers. "They do think something happened, and actually, it did."

She sent him a harsh look as she put on both her shirts and then tossed the blanket back to wriggle into her jeans. "I prefer not to be reminded of my few moments of weakness."

He dropped the blanket without regard to his naked state. "Darlin', if it was that forgettable, then I'm not doing my job."

She stared below where his belt would be, then brought her gaze up to his eyes. "If you decide to return to the ranch like that, then we'll definitely be the talk of the D Bar C, if not the nearest town."

He grinned when he noticed her attention drifting downward again. "As soon as you're done looking, I'll put my pants on."

"I'm not looking," she said as she scrambled to her feet. "Now please get dressed."

"Yes, ma'am."

While Georgie pulled on her boots, Austin managed to get into his clothes in record time. He helped her gather the bedding and walked out the door to meet the verbal firing squad, thankful to find they were both seated in the truck's cab. After tossing the supplies into the bed of the truck, Austin opened the back door for Georgie and they climbed inside.

"Good to see you, Houston," she said in a meek voice. "How's it going on the circuit?"

"Good to see you, too, Georgie," he replied. "I'm doing fairly well so far this year."

When Austin draped his arm over the back of the seat, Georgie shifted closer to the door and asked, "How's Paris, Dallas?"

"She's cranky," he answered. "She told me to tell you she's looking forward to your lunch together in San Antonio on Tuesday."

Austin wouldn't be surprised if he ended up being the primary topic of conversation during that meeting. "You're off on Tuesday?"

She clutched her shirt closed, like she thought he might actually make a pass at her in the backseat. If they were alone, he would. "I don't have any appointments that afternoon, although everything is slowing down with the holidays fast approaching."

Austin hadn't experienced much of the Christmas spirit in spite of the fact that he'd been surrounded by excessive decorations for the past few weeks. He hadn't bought any gifts, except for one, and he'd been saving that for the right time. That right time might not come until spring, at this rate.

All conversation died during the ride back, and after Dallas dropped them off in the driveway of his house, Austin turned to Georgie before she had a chance to climb into her truck and escape. "Do you want to come in and take a shower?"

After fishing the keys from her pocket, she tossed her

bag into the passenger seat, closed the door and faced him. "First of all, I don't have any extra clothes aside from the damp ones I'm wearing. Second, I live only five minutes away. And lastly, I prefer to shower alone."

Not what he wanted to hear. He began his own countdown to counter hers. "First, I have a pair of sweats and a T-shirt you could wear. Second, you look cold and miserable and even five minutes will feel like five hours in those wet jeans. Third, I didn't say you had to shower with me, although I'm never opposed to saving water." When she just stood there, arms folded beneath her breasts, he decided to sweeten the deal. "I'll even cook you breakfast."

"You don't cook, Austin."

True that. "I can make scrambled eggs and bacon. I can have a pot of coffee on in a few minutes."

"Maybe some other time."

He really didn't have a clue as to why he was so desperate to keep her there. Why he couldn't just let her go and get on with his day? "Tell you what. Why don't you come here for lunch? It's Maria's turn to cook and she's most likely going to make her famous enchiladas."

She hesitated a moment before asking, "What time?"

"Usually around one."

"Okay."

That was way too easy. "You're going to accept, just like that."

"Yes. And afterward, we need to talk."

"About?"

"I'll see you at one, Austin."

He followed her as she rounded the hood and slid into the driver's side. "Can you give me a hint?" he asked before she closed the door on him.

"Sorry. You'll just have to wait until I'm clean and coherent."

Austin watched her drive away, wondering what he'd done this time that would warrant a serious conversation. He suspected it had to do with his continual pursuit of her affections. Maybe she'd decided she didn't want to be friends. Maybe she wanted nothing else to do with him.

He could drive himself crazy trying to figure it out, or he could go inside, shower and grab some coffee. After that, he'd distract himself with chores, and prepare for anything that might come out of Georgia May Romero's sweet mouth.

"Hello, baby boy."

"Hi, Mama."

Georgie held the phone tightly, wishing she was holding her son. "Are you having fun?"

"Uh-huh. We rode the rides and played some little golf and we even saw Santa and I got to ask him for presents!"

Georgie chuckled over the usage of "little" instead of "miniature" golf comment, but she didn't dare correct him. "That's great, sweetie. What did you tell him you wanted?"

"A fire truck and some games and a pony."

She'd been working on the last wish. "That's some list, Chance."

"I asked him for one more thing."

"What?"

"My daddy, but I don't think he can bring me him."

Her heart broke over the sadness in his voice, and cemented her goal to work on that, too, though she feared the outcome. "Tell you what, sweetie. When you get home, we're going to make cookies together and go pick out a real Christmas tree. How does that sound?"

"Okay, I guess. I gotta go. We're going to go see some sharks."

"That sounds wonderful, Chance. Now put your grandmother…"

The line went dead before her son could answer her request. She would call her mother later, when she returned from Austin's house, because that might be the time when she'd need her most.

On that thought, Georgie postponed the shower and opted to take care of the horses, all the while rehearsing what she would say to the father of her child.

Hey, Austin, guess what? You have a kid. Hey, Austin, a funny thing happened the last time we were together. I gave you comfort and you gave me a child. Hey, Austin, this little boy needs you, and so do I.

She truly didn't want to need him, but she did, and so did Chance.

After tending to the livestock, she returned to the house, bathed and laid across the bed to take a brief nap before the moment of truth arrived. She decided to be positive, let herself imagine they could live as one big, happy family. Let herself dream that Austin loved her, too, and he would love their son equally. That he would forgive her for waiting so long to tell him. Yet deep in her soul, she knew that would probably prove to be only a pipe dream.

Georgie soon drifted off into fitful sleep, and woke with a start when she realized she hadn't set an alarm. She glanced at the clock to discover the digital number displaying five past noon and shot out of the bed to get ready. She dried her hair, put on a little makeup, tried on three different outfits before settling on black slacks and a red silk button-down blouse covered by a black cardigan. She even chose to wear real shoes—a pair of simple black flats.

After putting on a pair of simple silver hoops, she ran a brush through her hair, took one last look in the mirror as well as a few deep breaths, then grabbed her keys, sent a text to Austin letting him know she was on her way and dropped the phone into her black purse.

On the way to the D Bar C, she said a little prayer, recited a few wishes, hoped for a miracle and grew more anxious as she approached the ranch's entrance. By the time she pulled into Austin's driveway, she was a twisted bundle of nerves.

She exited the truck, silently chanting, *It's time, it's time*, all the way to the front door. But when Austin greeted her wearing a black shirt and hat, crisp jeans and a winning smile, she wondered if she would be strong enough to say what she needed to say. He gestured her inside, then closed the door behind them, and as they stood there in silence, studying each other, the tension was palpable.

"Is something wrong?" she asked when he continued to stare.

"Lunch won't be ready for another hour. Something about Jen burning the tortillas."

"Oh. It happens. I guess we could go to the house and visit with everyone."

"Or we could stay here." Austin moved closer, searched her eyes and touched her cheek. "You are so damn beautiful."

She began to feel light-headed, vulnerable, fearful

that she might not be strong enough to resist him. "You know what they say about beauty, Austin."

"It's in the eye of the beer holder?"

Did he have to be so darn cute? "Something like that."

"I'm not holding any beer. Besides, you're also smart, honest and sexy as hell."

She could certainly debate the honesty, considering what she'd been holding back. She also knew what would happen next if she didn't keep her wits about her. But common sense was no match for that continuous spark, or the sensual words the irresistible cowboy whispered in her ear, followed by a deep, provocative kiss.

"I need you, Georgie. I swear you've been all I've thought about since we met up again in the arena."

He'd never been far from her thoughts for years. "I need you, too, Austin, but if we keep giving in, where does that leave us?"

"As far as I'm concerned, we're two consenting adults who enjoy each other's company. We always have. I don't want to be only your friend, Georgie."

"What does that mean?"

"I want to spend time with you, out in the open, without worrying about what anyone thinks."

For years Georgie had longed to hear him say that, but she also recognized he might change his mind once he learned the truth. "Austin, there's something I need to say."

He pressed a fingertip against her lips to silence her. "We can talk later. Right now, I just want to be with you. I want *all* of you."

That *It's time* chant that had been running through Georgie's mind suddenly became *Later. Much later.* Maybe she was simply stalling. Maybe she'd grown weary of fighting the attraction. Maybe she just needed to be with the man she had always loved, perhaps for one final time. "Then, cowboy, take me away."

When Austin literally swept her off her feet and into his arms, Georgie surrendered to her needs, to this strong, handsome man, as she had so many times in the past. As she had last night, when he'd required nothing more than giving her pleasure. Now it was her turn to reciprocate.

Lunch, and the all-important talk, would simply have to wait.

Eight

Georgie closed her eyes as Austin carried her into his room and laid her across the bed. When she opened them, he pulled her up, removed her cardigan and paused with his hand on the top button of her blouse, indecision in his blue eyes.

"I want to make love to you, sweetheart, but only if you want it, too."

She swept one hand through her hair. "I do want it, even if I probably shouldn't."

"But—"

"Let's not talk it to death, okay?"

"That's all I needed to hear."

Everything happened in a rush then. She kicked off her shoes, he toed out of his boots. He unbuttoned her blouse, she undid his shirt. Together they pulled off their pants, leaving them clad in only their underwear. Austin slowed down the pace when he removed her bra, then stood by the bed and shoved down his boxer briefs, leaving no doubt he was primed and ready. After he leaned over and slid her panties away, she expected him to join her, yet he surprised her by sending soft kisses down her torso.

Georgie knew where he was heading, and the thought made her hot as blazes and damp with anticipation.

He stopped below her navel and smiled up at her. "Remember the first time I did this?"

As if it had happened yesterday. "In my bedroom, right before you left for college."

He rubbed his knuckles along the inside of her legs, coaxing them apart. "I wasn't sure you trusted me enough, but you proved me wrong."

Funny, she'd trusted him enough to allow him to do anything, even when they were teens. "I admit I was a little scared, but it turned out to be one of the most memorable experiences I've ever had."

"One you want to repeat?"

"Yes," came out of her mouth in a breathy sigh.

After Austin bent her knees and moved between her legs, Georgie understood the futility in trying to talk. She struggled to stay still when he feathered kisses down the insides of both her thighs. She stifled a moan as he worked his way up and his mouth hit home. She involuntarily lifted her hips toward him, demonstrating how much she needed his attention, and where.

He knew exactly how to use his tongue in slow, deliberate strokes, driving her to the brink. He knew how to let up before she let go, then start again until the pressure began to build. He kept the pace for a few more moments, a sensual tug-of-war until she was prepared to lose the battle. And then he used the pull of his lips to completely shoot her over the edge into an orgasm so intense, she literally cried out.

Georgie clutched the sheet in her fists as she continued to ride the waves of the climax, only remotely aware that Austin had left the bed, and extremely aware when he returned, condom in hand. "Are we ready for this?" he asked as he held up the silver packet.

She glanced at his impressive erection. "You definitely are."

He tore into the package like a dog with a ham bone. "That I am."

Feeling a bit daring, and somewhat impatient, Georgie held out her hand. "Let me do it."

He favored her with a grin as he answered her request. "My pleasure."

"It will be."

And she made sure to focus on that pleasure when he fell back onto the bed. After tossing the condom aside, she swept her hair back with one hand and kissed her way down his belly, the same as he had done to her. She had a few tricks of her own, lessons learned from him, and put them in play, sliding her tongue down the length of him, then back up again.

"Damn, sweetheart," he muttered. "If you keep doing that, this is going to be one short ride."

"We can't have that," she said as she sat up, retrieved the condom and rolled it in place.

He clasped her arm and pulled her atop his chest. "Do we go traditional or your favorite position?"

She was both pleased and surprised he remembered. "What do you think?"

"Your favorite it is. Turn to your side."

Georgie rolled away from him and waited for that first

sensation, that sense of completion. Luckily she didn't have to wait long as Austin draped her leg over his, then eased inside her. The last time she'd been in this position, little had she known they'd made a baby. He still didn't know, but he would in the near future.

All thoughts of sins and secrets faded away as Austin kissed her neck and placed his hand between her legs to again tenderly manipulate her.

"Austin, I don't think I can."

"You can. You will. I promise."

He made good on that vow in a matter of seconds with deep thrusts and deliberate caresses. She wanted so badly to see his face so she'd know when he reached his own climax, but her choice dictated that wasn't to be. She simply relied on the unsteady cadence of his breathing, the strength of his thrusts, the tension in his entire body and the one crude word that slipped out of his mouth.

Austin held her tightly then, his face buried in the back of her neck. She wanted to remain this way indefinitely. She wanted to shut out the world and the burden of truth, but that wasn't logical.

After Austin slid out of her body, Georgie shifted to face him. "It's probably past time for lunch."

He pressed his lips against her forehead. "I'm not that hungry right now."

She released a laugh. "Oh, come on, Austin. You're always starving after sex."

He gave her a slow grin. "Only when I'm finished having sex."

"You're kidding, right?"

"Nope. I have to have some time to recover, so I'm thinking we should put my big ol' shower to good use."

She liked that idea, but... "What about Maria and

Jenny? They're not going to be happy if we don't make an appearance."

"I'll call them and tell them we got tied up." He gave her a quick kiss. "Better still, I'll send a text. That way, I won't have to explain anything in detail."

Thank goodness for small favors, and modern technology. "Good plan."

Austin grabbed his phone from the nightstand, typed in the message, then smiled. "First one in the shower gets to set the temperature."

Georgie was in the bathroom and standing at the shower before Austin even made it to the door. Unfortunately she could only stare at a panel of illuminated blue lights, completely perplexed. "How do you work this?"

Austin reached around her and pushed a button, then keyed in a number, sending several spray heads into action. "It's not rocket science."

She glanced back at him. "It's a little too high-tech for me. What happened to just turning a knob?"

He leaned over and kissed her neck. "If you really want to turn one—"

"I already have."

His rough, sexy laugh gave her more than a few pleasant chills. "Yes, ma'am, you sure did. And it was mighty fine."

Georgie yanked open the glass door and stepped inside the spa-like shower, decorated in brown stone and trimmed in copper mosaic, then attempted to avoid the overhead spray. "I don't want to get my hair wet," she said when Austin joined her.

Without regard to her wishes, Austin pulled her beneath the jet, soaking every inch of her.

She gave him a mock frown. "Not fair."

He kissed her softly, touched her gently, stoking the fire again. "Everything's fair in love and water wars."

"Clever," she said as she reached for the shower gel clearly made for men. "Turn around and I'll wash your back."

"If I don't turn around, what will you wash?"

Cowboy cad. "Hold your horses, Calloway. I'll get to that."

"Lookin' forward to it."

Austin finally turned around, leaving Georgie with an up close view of his broad back and undeniably tight butt. She lathered her hands, then set out to search the terrain with her palms, taking her time investigating every plane, angle and dip at her disposal. Yet Austin disturbed her exploration when he turned around and grabbed the gel from the built-in soap dish.

"Wait a minute," she protested. "I'm not done yet."

He squeezed a few drops into his palm. "Yeah, you are, and I don't want you turning around."

"Interesting. I am going to smell like a guy."

His hands immediately went to her breasts. "You sure as hell don't look like one, and you don't feel like one, either."

No, she felt like a truly desirable woman. A naughty nymph. A needy female when the water play turned into more foreplay. The kisses were hot, the touches deliberate—both his and hers—and in a matter of moments, he had her in the throes of another strong climax. Then, before Georgie realized what was happening, Austin backed her against the tile, dangerously close to throwing caution out the window.

She braced her hands on his face to garner his attention. "Austin, we can't. We don't have any birth control."

He stepped back, went to her side and braced both

hands on the wall. "Damn. I know better. Not once have I ever forgotten a condom."

"Yes, you did." And he was still ignorant of the outcome of that mistake.

He straightened and gave her a confused look before reality showed in his expression. "The last night we were together. We were damn lucky."

Oh, but they hadn't been, although despite the consequences, she wouldn't take anything for the time she'd spent with their child. Now would be the perfect time to tell him, she decided, until he wrapped her in a huge towel, picked her up and returned to the bedroom to lay her across the tangled sheets. When Georgie opened her mouth to speak, he kissed her again. Passion precluded any admissions and, after Austin had the condom in place, the lovemaking began again.

This time Austin moved atop her, guided himself inside her and moved in a tempered rhythm. Georgie ran her hands over his damp back, held on close and listened to the sound of his labored breaths.

Oh, how she cherished the moments right before he climaxed. Oh, how much she cherished him. And when he tensed with his release, the words clamored out of her mouth. "I love you, Austin."

He stilled against her for a moment, then rolled onto his back. She waited for a response, and the one she received was extremely unexpected.

"It was always you, Georgie."

She shifted to her side. "Meaning?"

"The demise of my marriage. Abby never measured up to you. No woman ever has. I've known that for a long time, but I didn't want to admit that you have that much control over me. Call it stupid pride or male ego or however you want to label it. I'm over it now."

Georgie couldn't recall a time when she'd felt so optimistic, yet so fearful when she considered the impending declaration. "You've always been the only man for me. Actually, you've been the only man I've made love with."

He lifted his head and frowned. "Seriously?"

"Seriously."

He slid his arm beneath her and brought her against his chest. "I'm honored, Georgie. And dammit, I love you, too."

She laid a palm over his beating heart, the first hint of tears welling in her eyes. "Seriously?"

"More than my best roping horse. More than my money or all my material wealth. More than I realized until now."

Georgie began to silently rehearse how she would tell him about Chance and her explanation as to why she had withheld the truth for so long. Feeling as ready as she would ever be, she lifted to her head and whispered, "Austin."

He didn't open his eyes, didn't stir a bit. From the rise and fall of his chest, she determined he'd fallen asleep.

Georgie laid her cheek back on his chest, her emotions a blend of relief and regret that she hadn't spoken when she'd had the chance. But she would still have the opportunity once he finally awoke. In the meantime, she would join him in a nap and hope that when the revelations finally came, he would find it in his heart to forgive her, and embrace fathering their son.

An annoying sound jarred Austin out of sleep for the second time in twenty-four hours, only this time it was a buzzer, not a horn. He worked his arm from beneath Georgie, kissed her cheek then went into the bathroom to clean up. He grabbed a T-shirt and jeans from the closet, got dressed quickly and entered the bedroom where Georgie was sitting up against the leather headboard, clutching the sheet to her chin.

"Where are you going?" she asked as he headed toward the door.

The bell rang again, letting him know that the unknown intruder hadn't left. "I'm going to see who's at the door and send them on their way."

"Okay. Hurry back."

Exactly what he planned to do. He strode through the great room and once he reached the entry, he peered out the peephole. Jenny stood on the porch with a paper sack in hand, looking determined as ever. He doubted she would leave anytime soon, which drove him to yank open the door and scowl. "What's up?"

She patted her big blond hair and smiled. "Well, sugar, since you and Georgie didn't come for lunch, lunch is coming to you."

He felt the need to preserve Georgie's reputation. "What makes you think I'm not alone?"

She nodded toward the driveway. "Because that's her truck, sweetie. And don't worry. I'll just hand this over and be on my way."

Austin took the bag and worked up some gratitude. "Thanks. I appreciate the hospitality."

Jenny centered her gaze on his bare feet before focusing on his face. "And I'm sure Georgie appreciates your hospitality, as well. You two enjoy the rest of your afternoon. If you're in the mood for a drink, you know where to find me."

After Jen spun on her heels and stepped off the porch, Austin waited until she'd climbed onto the golf cart and drove away toward the main house. He shut and locked the door, then walked toward the kitchen to drop off the care package before returning to the bedroom. He discovered Georgie seated at the island, dressed in the only robe he owned—a heavy blue flannel that hung off her like a scarecrow.

He set the sack down at the end of the quartz counter and claimed the stool beside her. "Guess you figured out the identity of our guests."

She tightened the sash at her waist. "I kind of heard Jen's voice."

No shock there. "She brought food. Are you hungry?"

She ran a fingertip along the edge of the island. "Not at the moment, but feel free to go ahead."

He sensed something was bugging her. Maybe he'd said too much in the moment. "Are you okay, Georgie?"

When she lifted her gaze to his, he saw a few tears welling in her eyes. "Actually, I'm not okay. I have something I need to tell you. Something I should have told you long before now."

A laundry list of possibilities bombarded his brain. One horrible conclusion came home to roost. "Are you sick?"

She shook her head. "No, that's not it. Not even close."

"Then what is it?"

"Just promise me you won't be too angry."

"I'll try, but that depends on what you're about to tell me."

She fidgeted in the seat, a sure sign of her nervousness. After a deep breath, she said, "Okay. Here goes. I have a five-year-old son."

Austin didn't know what to say or how to react. He did recall with absolute clarity what she'd said to him earlier.

...you've been the only man I've made love with...

The mental impact hit Austin like a grenade, sending him off the stool to pace. Shock gave way to confusion then melted into blinding anger. He turned around to confront her head-on, grasping the last shred of his composure. He had a burning question to ask, although he suspected he already knew the answer. "Who's his father, Georgie?"

Her tears flowed freely now, and she looked away before returning her attention to him. "You are, Austin."

Georgie held her breath and waited, wanting so badly to plead with him to give her a chance to explain. Instead, she remained silent and watchful as he braced his elbows on the table, lowered his eyes and forked both hands through his hair.

"Why the hell didn't you tell me sooner?" he asked without looking up.

"I tried, Austin."

"Obviously not too damn hard, Georgie."

She deserved his scorn, but she wouldn't stop attempting to make him understand. "When I found out I was pregnant, I was pretty much in denial for a couple of months until I finally confirmed it. Then I called your cell phone and some woman answered. I thought I had the wrong number, so I got in touch with Dallas. He told me you'd just married. I was so in shock over the baby, and learning you'd found someone else, I didn't know what to do."

He straightened and leveled a stern stare on her. "You should've called back. You should've told me immediately."

"I considered that, but when I decided not to give Chance up for adoption, I realized that if I told you, I might ruin your relationship."

"And you thought it was okay just to leave me in the dark?"

"Believe me, I've questioned my actions since the day he was born."

"You damn sure should have," he said, barely concealed venom in his tone. "And no matter what excuse you try to hand me, you had no right to keep this a secret."

"I know." She paused a moment to gather her thoughts. "He's an incredible little boy, and so much like you. He loves the horses and he's so smart. If you'll get to know him, I'm sure—"

"You need to leave, Georgie."

So much for that strategy. "I'm not leaving until we discuss this further."

"I don't want to discuss anything right now. I'm too damned angry. Just put on your clothes and go home."

She would grant him this latitude for the time being. "Fine," she said as she came to her feet. "I'll go for now, and I'll wait to hear from you. And if I don't, have a nice life. Chance and I have done fine without you. We'll continue to do the same."

Georgie rushed past him and into the bedroom, holding fast to her sadness until she returned to the safety of her home. After she dressed, she returned to the kitchen, but Austin was nowhere to be found. She didn't bother to seek him out, or attempt to convince him that his little boy needed him. He would have to come to that conclusion on his own.

She would give Austin more time, pray he came around and learn to accept that he might not. She only hoped that she could grant her son's wish, and he'd finally have a daddy for Christmas. If not, she would continue to love him enough for the both of them.

Nine

"I'm so sorry I'm late."

Georgie looked up from the menu at Paris, who was struggling to be seated in the booth of the small San Antonio bistro. "That's okay. How did the appointment go?"

Paris set her bag aside and tightened the band securing her low ponytail. "That's why I'm late. The doctor decided to do a last-minute ultrasound."

"Is everything all right?"

"Yes, aside from the fact that if I reach my due date, the baby will weigh at least eight pounds. No wonder I'm so huge."

"You look great, especially in that dress. Green is definitely your color."

"I look like a giant jalapeno pepper." Paris leaned over and studied her. "You look like you're exhausted."

She was, mentally and physically. "I haven't been sleeping."

"But you have been crying. A lot."

Clearly her reddened eyes had given her away. "I didn't know it was that obvious."

Paris leaned over and touched her arm. "Tell me what's wrong."

Georgie didn't want to burden a very pregnant woman, but she could certainly use a friend. "It's Austin."

"You told him."

"I did, and it didn't go well." She hadn't heard a word from him since.

Leaning back, Paris rested her arm across her rounded belly. "That explains it."

"Explains what?"

"Austin took off yesterday morning for heaven knows where and he didn't come back last night. When Dallas sent him a text, he replied that he was okay, and that's it. And you haven't heard from him, either?"

"I sent him a text to ask if he was okay," Georgie said. "He responded 'no,' and I decided to leave him alone."

Paris seemed surprised. "You didn't try calling him?"

She'd thought about it, several times. "In all the years I've known Austin, I've learned you don't back him into a corner. Usually after he thinks things over, he comes around."

"That's good," Paris stated. "I'm sure he'll be back in touch soon."

If only Georgie could believe that. "He might not this time. He's angry and he's hurt and I have to accept that he could reject the prospect of being a father to Chance."

"Austin is a good man, Georgie. I can't imagine him abandoning his own flesh and blood."

"I hope that's true, but you didn't see the look on his face when I told him. He was furious, understandably so."

"You honestly don't believe he'll get over it?"

She thought back through the years and couldn't recall a time when he'd been so irate. "When we were kids, and he got mad at me for some reason, he wouldn't leave until we worked it out. He'd make self-deprecating comments about his ignorance and a few bad jokes, and before I knew it, I was laughing and all was forgiven."

"The Calloway brothers must share the brooding gene," Paris said. "That's exactly what Dallas did when he learned, as did I, that I wasn't officially divorced and he stood to lose control of the ranch to Fort because our marriage wasn't real. Fortunately, Jenny saved the day on that count."

Her interest piqued, Georgie rested her elbow on the table and supported her cheek on her palm. "So how did you manage to convince Dallas to come back to you?"

Paris laughed. "It wasn't me. The family gave him a swift kick in the jeans and booted him to right here, in San Antonio, to beg my forgiveness. The rest, as they say, is history. Now I'm happily married to the love of my life, for the second time, and about to give birth to a baby apparently the size of a moose."

Georgie smiled for the first time in two days. "Hopefully the doctor is wrong about the baby's weight."

"And hopefully you're wrong about Austin. I wouldn't be surprised if he reaches out to you soon."

Georgie sat back and sighed. "I would love it if that happens before Sunday."

"Then you could all be a family on Christmas," Paris said in a wistful tone.

"And I could answer a little boy's wish. Chance asked Santa if he would bring him a daddy."

Paris's expression turned somber. "Oh, Georgie. That

must have broken your heart. How much does he know about Austin?"

Georgie shrugged. "Very little. He didn't ask a whole lot until about a year ago, and I attribute that to being in preschool and noticing everyone else has a father. I've only mentioned that his dad lives far away, which I thought he did at the time, and that he travels a lot because he's a cowboy."

"Does he know his name?"

"He asked right before he left for Florida, and then he became distracted by something on TV. I'm sure he'll ask again when he gets home." Georgie had given Lila specific instructions to direct Chance to her with any queries, and she had no reason to believe her mother wouldn't comply.

"And you'll know what to do if and when that happens." Paris began to scan the menu. "I'm starving. What are you having?"

A strong urge to call her mom and check on her baby boy. "Probably just a Cobb salad. I'm not very hungry."

Paris closed the menu and set it aside. "I'm going to have the spinach enchilada plate and eat every last bite. And after that, I might even eat dessert. Gotta feed the moose."

They joined in a laugh before the waiter arrived to take their orders. Once he left, Georgie regarded Paris. "As soon as we're finished with lunch, I'm going to go shopping. I haven't bought a thing for Chance, aside from a pony, and I can't put her under the tree."

Paris sipped at her glass of water. "Where did you get a pony?"

"The Carter ranch right outside Cotulla. She's fifteen years old and her name is Butterball, which fits her well. She'll be a good teaching horse for Chance, although I'm sure he'll want to graduate to something bigger very soon."

"That's great, and I could pick up a few more holiday gifts. I could also use a stroll on the River Walk to burn a few calories."

"Great. We'll make an afternoon of it."

Paris sent her a soft smile. "And with your permission, I'll see what I can do about Austin on my end."

Georgie saw more than a few problems with that scenario. "He'll be furious if he knows I told you about Chance before I told him."

"That's too bad. Besides, I'll let him assume you told me today. If he's going to pout like a child, then I'll just sic Dallas on him. Better still, I'll involve Maria, as long as you're okay with it."

She wasn't sure she was, but then again, what other options did she have? If the Calloways could convince Austin to step up to the plate, then maybe that would be best for the sake of her son. No amount of cajoling on their part would change Austin's mind about what she'd done. "I assume you're referring to a family meeting."

"Exactly. Power in numbers."

Georgie imagined Austin encountering his stepmothers and brothers in a showdown. She would definitely buy tickets to that.

Austin walked through his front door to find Paris, Dallas, Jenny and Maria seated on his leather sectional in the great room. He should never have told them he was heading home. He should never have given out spare keys.

After tossing his duffel onto the floor, he gave them all a good glare. "Mind telling me what you're doing here?"

Maria patted the space between her and Jenny. "Come have a seat, *mijo*."

No way would he suffer maternal advice in stereo. "I'll stand, thank you."

Dallas rose from the sofa where he'd been positioned next to his wife. "Makes no difference to any of us whether you sit or stand. We're more concerned with your total lack of responsibility to your family."

His foul mood grew even fouler. "I didn't know building a house on our land came with a clause that states I can't come and go as I please."

"We were worried about you, sugar," Jenny said. "You've been gone four days with almost no communication. That's not like you."

And to think he'd worried someone had found out about his and Georgie's kid. "I wasn't intentionally ignoring you all. I just have another business to run. Several, in fact."

"We're referring to your responsibility to your son."

Damn if he hadn't had cause to worry and wonder exactly how this all went down. "Did Georgie also tell you that she hid him from me for five years?"

"Georgie didn't talk to them," Paris piped up. "She talked to me, and I told Dallas. Dallas told everyone else."

His shortened fuse was about to blow. "When it comes right down to it, this isn't anyone's business."

Maria looked fit to be tied. "It is our business, Austin Calloway. Maybe I'm not your birth mother, son, but I'm the only mother you've had for thirty-two years. That means I consider that little boy my grandchild."

"Mine, too," Jenny said. "At least that's how I see him, even if we're not blood relatives, either. But I'd like to borrow him until Worth and Fort have children."

Maria sent her an acid glare. "As long as you give him back."

Jenny ignored the dig. "Regardless, that little boy deserves to know our family, sugar."

Austin had agonized over that since Georgie spilled the baby beans. He'd been torn between a permanent escape and meeting the child who didn't know him at all. "Look, I've got a lot to think about before we plan a family reunion."

"Georgie's a wreck, Austin," Paris added. "She's beginning to believe you don't want to have anything to do with Chance."

Just one more blow to his and Georgie's relationship. "I'll be sure to thank her for nominating me for jerk of the year."

Maria suddenly rose from the sofa. "Everyone, go about your business. I want to talk to Austin alone."

What Maria wanted, Maria got, and that was apparent by the way everyone stood and started milling toward the door. Everyone but Jenny.

His stepmom stared at the other stepmother for a moment. "That means everyone."

Jenny lifted her chin. "I'm not going anywhere until Austin asks me to leave."

He didn't care if the Pope made an appearance. "Fine by me if you stay. In fact, you can all hang around and crucify me."

Dallas pressed a palm against his wife's back. "We're going home to spend some alone time together. The phones will be turned off."

Paris blushed. "A little too much information, Dallas."

"Who cares?" Dallas said. "It's pretty obvious by looking at you, we've done it before."

Dallas and Paris rushed out the door, leaving Austin alone to face the mothers—Maria wearing her trademark braid and a long green flannel shirt over her jeans, and Jen sporting a red-checkered dress and a matching bow in her big blond hair. Nothing like a verbal beating from a hardscrabble rancher's wife and a throwback from a fifties sitcom. He'd rather eat Nueces River mud.

Austin claimed the cowhide chair across from the sofa, determined to make this little soiree short and sweet. "Speak your mind, then give me some peace."

Jenny sent him a sympathetic look. "I know you're torn up about this, sugar."

"I also know you're mad as hell at Georgie, too," Maria began, "and I don't think anyone blames you for that. But she's always been a good girl and from what I hear, a good mother. If I were you, I'd march to her house right now, meet your son and make amends with Georgie."

If only it was that easy. "Neither of you know what I've been going through since she told me. I kept thinking about the things I've missed, like his first steps and his first words. I could've already taught him how to ride. How to throw a rope. Georgie robbed me of those experiences."

"It's not too late to make memories now, Austin," Jenny said. "I don't care how good of a job Georgie's done raising him as a single mother, that little boy needs his daddy. And you need him and his mother, too."

Austin leaned forward and streaked both palms over his face. "I know you're both right, and I plan to be involved in his life, pay child support, that kind of thing. But I don't know if I can ever forgive Georgie."

Maria frowned. "Why not? She's forgiven you."

They seemed determined to make this all his fault. "What did I do?"

"It's not what you did, sugar," Jenny added. "It's what you didn't do."

He recalled Georgie saying the same thing. "I'm not following you, Jen."

"After playing slap and tickle with her all during high school, did you stay in touch with Georgie, sugar?"

"No, but—"

"After you made a baby while passing through town, did you ever call her?" Maria asked.

He recognized where this was going. "Georgie knew we weren't exclusive, and besides, I met Abby right after that."

"And married a woman you barely knew, totally ignoring the other woman who's loved you since you pulled her ponytail the first time," Maria said. "We all know how that turned out."

He'd always appreciated Maria's brutal honesty, until tonight. Being on the hot seat with all his faults laid bare wasn't his idea of a good time.

Jenny smoothed a palm over her skirt. "I truly believe we only have one love in our lives, and your father was mine and, I assume, Maria's. However, J.D.'s one true love happened to be your mother."

"She's right," Maria added, much to Austin's surprise. "Your dad kept searching to fill that hole in his soul from losing Carol. I'd bet my best spurs that Georgie is your soul mate, and you're going to spend a lot of useless years if you don't own up to it."

Austin wanted to reject their notions. "I can't believe the two of you can overlook the fact that he was married to both of you at the same time. Hell, he spread himself so thin he wasn't giving anyone the time they needed, including his six sons."

"You're absolutely right, sugar," Jenny said. "All the more reason for you to resolve the issues with Georgie and get busy spending time with your little boy."

His head had begun to spin from all the unwelcome advice. "I'll consider what you've said, but right now I have to take care of the horses. So if you two don't mind, I need to get on with my day."

"Okay." Maria came to her feet. "*Mijo*, you need to learn that if you really love someone, nothing they do or say is beyond forgiveness."

Jen rose from the sofa. "Sugar, the best holiday gift you can give yourself is a happy New Year with a new family."

Without another word, the mothers walked out the door, blanketing the room in stark silence. Austin leaned back in the chair and felt compelled to revisit his past. He stood and walked to the shelves flanking the white stone fireplace, then withdrew his final high school yearbook. He returned to the sofa and once again flipped through the pages, finding various photos of Georgie scattered throughout. He appreciated the one of her holding the volleyball district MVP trophy when everyone had told her she was too short to play. The one when she'd been voted to represent the junior class in the homecoming court was really something else, but then so was she dressed in that blue shiny dress, her long hair curling over her shoulders. He also hated that Rory Mills had been on her arm during the halftime festivities, while he'd escorted the senior queen, Heather Daws, who was about as shallow as a dried-up lake.

It suddenly dawned on him that not once had they

appeared in a picture together, all because of an ongoing family feud and his resistance to rocking the boat. If he'd only stood up to his father, and hers, things might have been different between them. Or not. Maybe they'd been destined to go their separate ways, choose their own paths, make their own lives. Maybe his failed marriage had taught him what he didn't want—a relationship that would never live up to what he'd had with Georgie. But did he really deserve her now?

When a knock came at the door, Austin set the book on the coffee table and shot to his feet, anxious to see if maybe Georgie had stopped by. He was sorely disappointed to find a sibling standing on the threshold.

"Did I miss it?" Worth asked.

"Miss what?"

"The family meeting."

Dallas obviously told every last Calloway about his plight. "Yep. It's over."

"Mind if I come in for a bit?"

"Why not?" He didn't have anything better to do except sit around, feeling sorry for himself.

Worth brushed past him, dropped down on the sofa and eyed the yearbook. "Looks like you've been reliving your glory days."

He hadn't found any glory in the experience. "Just feeling nostalgic."

"Mom tells me you were a jock. Something about all-district wide receiver."

Austin had never been comfortable talking about his accolades. "It wasn't a big deal. My high school was so small there wasn't a whole lot of competition."

Worth forked a hand through his blond hair. "I know what you mean. I went to a private school. We didn't even have a football team, but I did play basketball. Our team pretty much sucked most of the time."

Austin was growing increasingly irritated by the small talk. "It happens. Look, I hate to cut this conversation short, but I have some chores to tend to."

"No problem. But before I go, I just have one thing to say about your current situation."

Just what he needed, more sage advice from a self-proclaimed Louisiana rodeo cowboy surfer. "Shoot."

"I know you've had everyone coming at you with suggestions on how to handle this news, but I just want you to know that if you want to talk, feel free to find me. No advice. No judgment."

That nearly shocked Austin out of his boots. "I appreciate that."

"What are brothers for? Besides, you'll figure it out."

"I'm not so sure about that."

"You're a smart guy, Austin. In fact, intelligence is a Calloway trait, although some of us intentionally don't show it."

"You've got to be pretty smart to build a fleet of charter boats all down the coast, Worth."

"I've been lucky in business. I just thank my lucky stars I didn't head down my original career path."

"Rodeo?"

"Medical school."

Now he was downright stunned. "I didn't know that."

"Most people don't. I swore my mom to secrecy after she bragged I was accepted to every Ivy League school I applied to. She was damn disappointed when I decided to stay in Louisiana and went to Tulane. She was proud of my 4.0 GPA as a chemistry major."

Austin wasn't sure he could take any more revelations. "No offense, Worth, but I've never pegged you as a science geek."

Worth stood and grinned. "I figured out early on it's best to dumb it down a bit when it comes to courting women. Take care, bud."

Austin came to his feet. "You, too, Worth. Are you going to be around during the holidays?"

"Nope. I'm going to Maui. I'd invite you along but I figure you've got more pressing issues at the moment."

"You're right about that," Austin said as he followed his brother to the door.

Worth paused with his hand on the knob. "You know, Austin, we're not our dad. Not by a long shot. Except maybe Fort. As bad as he hated J.D., he's the most like him. Mom hopes he'll eventually come around, but I've given up on that ever happening."

So had the rest of the family. "Happy holidays and have a good trip."

"Same to you, and when I get back, I look forward to meeting my nephew."

He might have been mad at Worth for tossing in that veiled recommendation, but in all honesty, his half brother had been the most helpful.

Austin settled back on the sofa and rolled all his options around in his head. Truth was, he did love Georgie and probably always had. He wanted to know his son and to avoid all the mistakes his own father had made. He still wanted to marry the love of his life…but what if he failed?

That in itself was his greatest fear, but maybe the time had come to stop being a relationship coward. First he had to decide if, when and where he would present the plan to Georgie, and hope that he hadn't waited too long.

* * *

When Georgie pulled into the drive, she was thrilled to see her mother and Chance waiting for her on the front porch. She'd barely exited the truck before Chance ran to her and threw his arms around her waist.

He smiled up at her. "Hi, Mama."

She leaned down and hugged him hard. "Hi, sweetie. I missed you so much! I think you grew two inches while you were gone."

His eyes went wide as he stepped out of her grasp. "Did I?"

"I believe you did." She looked around but didn't see the motor home. "Where're Uncle Ben and Aunt Debbie?"

Her mother approached and ruffled Chance's hair. "They took off for Arizona to see the grandkids. They told me to tell you bye and what a pleasure it was to have your son along for the trip."

"I'm sorry I wasn't here to thank them," Georgie said as Chance ran back into the house. "I didn't expect you for another hour or so, and I had an emergency at the Rileys' farm. I had to treat a colicky mare."

"That's okay. You can give them a call later."

"Do you need a ride home?"

"No. Your father should be here any minute now."

Georgie was quite surprised by the news. "You mean he's actually going to step foot on his daughter's property?"

"Yes, and he wants to talk to you."

After everything that had happened with Austin, Georgie didn't have the energy for a fight. "I'm not up to that right now."

"Well, I suppose you should get up for that because this conversation is long overdue."

Before Georgie could respond, the familiar ancient white truck headed up the gravel drive, signaling her patriarch had arrived. She experienced a case of butterflies in the pit of her stomach and her palms began to sweat, despite the fact that the cold front had arrived in earnest, bringing with it forty-degree temps.

She had no clue what she would say to the man who'd raised her, and ignored her for five years. A hard-nosed man who could be as stubborn as a mule. A man who had never even seen his own grandchild. At least she had an ally in his wife.

Her mother began to back away as soon as the truck came to a stop in front of the house. "I'll keep Chance occupied while you two chat."

"But Mom—"

"You'll be okay, honey. Just hear him out."

Lila turned around and started away, while Georgie held her breath and waited for George Romero to appear. And he did a few moments later, looking every bit the brown-eyed hulking cowboy, only his hair seemed a little grayer and his gait a little slower. He'd always been larger than life, her hero, and she'd always been his little girl, until she'd shamed him by having a child out of wedlock. Heaven only knew what he would've done had he known the identity of Chance's father.

"Dad," she said when he walked up to her.

"Georgie," he replied, tattered beige hat in hand.

So far, so good. "You look well. How's your back?"

"Stiff as usual, but it's nothing compared to the scare I had with the old ticker last month."

That was news to her, and very disconcerting. "Mom didn't say a word to me about you having heart problems."

"I told her not to say anything until I could tell you myself."

"Is it serious?"

"Just some minor blockage. They did one of those angioplasty procedures and stuck some sort of tube in my artery. Now I'm good as new."

"I'm so sorry." And she was. "I wish I would've known."

"The only thing you need to know is I had a wake-up call. I've been a fool and prideful and a sorry excuse for a father. That comes to an end today."

"I appreciate that, Daddy."

That earned her a grin. "Been a long time since you called me that. I love you, princess. And I'm done being an old stubborn goat. I'm ready to meet my grandboy."

That earned him a hug. "I'm so glad we have this behind us. Chance needs his grandfather a lot. He hasn't had a solid male influence for five years."

Her father's expression melted into a frown. "No surprise there. Austin Calloway is a no-account tail chaser, just like his dad."

Clearly Lila hadn't hidden Georgie's secrets. "How long have you known?"

"When your mother told me you were coming back to town. She has some crazy idea that you and Calloway are going to set up house and raise your son together."

Considering she hadn't heard a word from Austin, that was highly unlikely. "Did Mom also tell you that Austin was unaware that he had a child?"

He inclined his head and studied her straight on. "Was?"

"I told him about Chance a few days ago."

"Is the jackass here?"

She shook her head. "No, he's not here. He's still trying to get over the shock."

He sent her a skeptic's look. "If you believe that, then I've got some swampland to sell you."

After what her father had done to her, Georgie felt the need to defend Austin. "You're wrong about him, Dad. He's a good man."

"He wasn't man enough to ask permission to date you when you two were in school. He just continued to sneak around behind my back."

Lila had evidently provided a wealth of knowledge. "Neither of us wanted to tell you or J.D. because you two were still acting like kindergarten rivals."

"That's because J.D. tried to…" Both his words and gaze faltered. "Never mind."

"Not fair, Dad. You apparently know about my life, now it's time you tell me more about yours. What did J.D. do to you aside from compete in the cattle business?"

"He dated your mother before me," he muttered.

Georgie couldn't hold back a laugh. "That's it? You two had an ongoing feud because J.D. went out with Mom? That's rich considering you married her. And best I can recall, he married Carol."

He shook out his hat and shoved it on his head. "I'm ready to get off this subject and get on with the business of meeting my grandson."

"I'm all for that."

Georgie led him to the house where he followed her through the front door. They came upon Chance hanging ornaments on the Christmas tree she'd purchased yesterday, a seven-foot fragrant pine that had been the last decent selection on the lot.

"Hey, little man," she said. "I have someone I want you to meet."

Chance hooked a red globe over one limb, turned around and stared in awe. "Are you my dad?"

Lila smiled. "No, sweetheart, but he's the next best thing. This is your grandpa."

"Grandpa George?" he asked without a hint of disappointment in his tone. "My grandma said you were gone a lot."

Her dad stepped forward and took off his hat. "Yep, I've been gone far too long. And you must be Chance."

Her son nodded his head and grinned. "Chance William Romero."

"Well, bud, looks like you've got my middle name," George said in an awed tone. "Do you like to go fishin'?"

"Haven't gone fishin' yet," Chance said.

Amazingly, the grandfather took his grandson's hand and led him to the sofa. "Let's sit a spell and I'll tell you all about how to cast a line…"

Georgie began to finish the decorating tasks, all the while counting her blessings over the scene playing out before her. She'd almost given up believing that her dad would accept his grandson, much less begin a precious relationship with him. And if any more time passed, she would be forced to give up on Austin.

She wondered if it might be too much to ask for one more holiday miracle.

Ten

It would take a miracle if Austin survived this visit without incurring Georgie's wrath. For the past five days, he'd developed a plan that could smooth over his disregard, if she didn't kick him off her rented ranch.

Before he could climb out of the truck, his cell sounded, and he didn't even have to look to see who might be calling. If he ignored it, he'd have hell to pay. If he answered, he would only be further delayed. He answered it anyway.

"Yeah, Jen?"

"Have you done it yet?"

"I just got here."

"Oh, good. If all goes well, Maria and I want you to invite everyone to dinner."

He might not even get in the front door. "You're jumping the gun a little there. I don't even know if Georgie will see me yet."

"She will, sugar. Best of luck and we'll see you, Georgie and the little guy soon."

Before he could debate that point, Jen, with her overblown optimism, hung up. Now he had to return to the starting line and begin the mental race to the finish.

Gathering all his courage, he exited the truck and sprinted up the steps to the porch. He checked his back pocket for the gift, rehearsed what he planned to say and then finally knocked.

He expected Georgie to open the door, but what he got was her mother. Not a good way to begin his groveling.

Lila laid a hand beneath her throat like she might start choking. "Oh, my. Hello, Austin."

He took off his hat and nodded. "Nice to see you ma'am. Is Georgie here?"

"Yes. It's Christmas morning."

Good going, Calloway. "Mind if I have a word with her?"

"Wait here and I'll go get her."

He wasn't exactly surprised that he hadn't been invited in, and that was probably best. If George Romero happened to be there, Austin would risk getting a right hook as a greeting.

He paced around the porch for a few minutes until he heard, "What are you doing here, Austin?"

When he turned around, Austin would swear his heart skipped several beats, and it had nothing to do with his giant case of the nerves. Just seeing Georgie again served to confirm he had done the right thing, even if the end result could include her rejection.

He decided to lay it all on the line, beginning with their child. "I did a lot of soul-searching over the past few days, and I've come to the conclusion that I've already missed too much time with our son."

She folded her arms across her middle. "I'm glad. He needs to get to know you before he's any older."

One issue resolved, several more to go. "I plan to start on that immediately, and you need to be aware that I'm going to be there to support him and not only financially. I want to be part of his life in every way, including school and whatever extracurricular activities he chooses to do, and I'm banking on teaching him to rope."

He saw a mix of happiness and disappointment in her eyes. "That all sounds wonderful, Austin. We can work together to give him a good life. You can count on me to be cooperative when it comes to visitation. We'll work out a schedule."

She didn't understand he didn't give a damn about a schedule, but she would. "I haven't covered the most important aspect of our arrangement."

"Then please, continue," she said in a frigid tone.

"First, I have a question. Is your dad in the house?"

She looked confused. "Yes, but—"

"Could you send him out here?"

"Are you sure you want to do that?"

Not really. "Yeah. I have to talk to him before we continue this conversation."

"All right, I'll try. But I can't guarantee he'll do it."

If Old George wanted to be pigheaded, he'd have to go in after him. Fortunately that didn't happen when Georgie went inside and returned with her dad in tow, looking none too pleased to be there.

"Merry Christmas, sir," Austin said, even though he realized the man didn't look like he embraced the holiday spirit.

"What do you want, Calloway?" George asked, confirming Austin's theory.

"I have a question to ask you before I finish my talk with Georgie."

"Let me make this easy on you. No, I don't want you here, and yes, you should get in that fancy truck and head for the hills."

"Behave, Dad," Georgie scolded. "You can at least hear what he has to say before you send him packing."

"Fine," George said grudgingly. "But make it quick."

He drew in a breath and released it slowly. "Mr. Romero, I've screwed up a time or two in my life, but my biggest mistake was letting Georgie go without a fight, even if it meant going into battle against you and my dad. Hell, when she didn't meet me that day I left for college, I should have come looking for her."

Georgie touched his arm. "What are you talking about?"

"I went to your house and gave your mom a card that asked you to meet me at the old windmill. I planned to invite you to join me at school once you graduated."

"I never got that card," she said, anger in her tone. "I definitely have a bone to pick with Mom."

"I tore it up," George muttered, drawing both their attention.

Now Georgie looked furious. "Excuse me, Dad?"

"You heard me. I took it from your mother, read it and shredded it." He pointed at Austin. "You should be glad I didn't know you were taking her behind the shed."

That explained a lot, and fed Austin's resentment toward this man. But in the interest of keeping the peace, he tempered his anger. "As pissed off as I am over your actions, it really doesn't matter now. What's done is done. We can't go back." Although he wished they could.

"Yes, it does matter," Georgie said. "I've always blamed you for not saying goodbye before you took off for college. Why didn't you tell me this before now?"

Austin shrugged. "I thought you had your reasons, the main one being we were on different paths. I figured you decided our relationship had run its course."

"If I had known, I would have been there."

Austin wanted to kiss her, but he still had business to tend to. "Back to the question at hand." He turned to Georgie's dad. "Mr. Romero, I'm going to ask for your daughter's hand in marriage, and if she decides to accept my proposal, I hope we have your and Mrs. Romero's blessing."

Georgie stared and George glared, while Austin just stood there, waiting for someone to speak. Her dad came through first. "I'd like to tell you hell no, you're not going to get my blessing, but you're going to do what you want anyway, so go for it. As far as my wife is concerned, she had visions of the two of you hitched the minute Georgie came back to town. Now get your proposing out of the way before your boy wakes up and wonders if his mama ran off with Santa."

When the man returned inside, Austin decided to proceed as planned, even though he worried Georgie's continuing silence indicated she wasn't too keen on the idea. He'd find out real soon.

He pulled the box from his pocket and set it on the railing, then withdrew the ring before turning to Georgie. "Darlin', there is no one else on this earth that I want to wake up to every morning and go to bed with every night. I've made my share of mistakes, but having you as my wife wouldn't be one of them. I'd be proud and honored if you would marry me."

"This marriage proposal isn't because of Chance, is it?" she asked, the first sign of tears in her eyes.

"No, sweetheart. I want to spend my life with you because I love you. Always have. Always will."

"And you're absolutely sure you want to do this marriage thing again?"

"Sure as sunrise."

"I can be a handful."

"So can I. But together, we're pretty damn perfect."

Finally, she smiled. "Then yes, Austin Calloway, I will marry you, with or without my father's blessing. I love you, too. Very much."

"That's all I need to hear." Smiling, he slid the sapphire-and-diamond ring on her finger and waited for her response to the surprise.

She studied it for a moment before recognition dawned in her expression and her gaze shot to his. "This is the ring from the silent auction. I had no idea you bid on it."

"I didn't. I had to hunt down the guy who won it and pay twice the amount to take it off his hands when I saw how much you wanted it that night. I may not have consciously believed it would be an engagement ring, but deep down I probably realized that it should be."

She threw her arms around his neck, then kissed him soundly. "You're too much. And this is too much."

The joy in her eyes said it all. "Darlin', nothing is too much for my future bride. But before we make this official, I probably need to ask the little man's permission, too."

She placed a hand to her mouth. "I hadn't thought about Chance. I think we should probably ease him into the idea. Meeting you on Christmas morning is a lot for a five-year-old to handle."

His first lesson in fatherhood. "Let's just play it by ear."

She let him go and reached for the door. "Are you ready?"

"As ready as I'll ever be."

Austin followed Georgie inside and surveyed the room, only to discover George seated in a chair, watching some cartoon on the TV mounted over a fireplace decked out with stockings. The Christmas tree positioned in the corner had been decorated in red and green, and a slew of unopened presents reminded Austin of what he'd forgotten.

"I'll be right back," he said as he headed outside and sprinted to the truck, then returned with the first gift for his son. He planned to give him many more—the most important, his time.

When he heard voices, a woman's and a child's, he clutched the package and waited anxiously for the moment he laid his eyes on his son. He didn't have to wait long before a brown-haired, hazel-eyed boy wearing pajamas dotted with bucking broncos padded into the room. Austin's first reaction—he looked just like his mother. His second—he couldn't have imagined the impact on his emotions. He hadn't known he would feel so strongly. He couldn't be more proud to be his dad. He only hoped his son shared his feelings.

With Lila following behind him, Chance pulled up short the second he spotted Austin, then he grinned. "You're that guy we saw at the calf roping. Mama's friend."

Before Austin could respond, Georgie gestured Chance to her, turned him around and rested her hands on his shoulders. "This is Austin Calloway, Chance. Austin, meet Chance."

He hesitated a moment before he approached slowly and knelt at his child's level. "It's great to finally meet you, bud. This is for you."

Chance took the offered present and looked it over. "Can I open it now?"

Austin turned his attention to Georgie who nodded. "Go ahead."

The boy tore into the package in record time, then pulled out the baseball glove from the box. "Wow. I don't have one of these."

"My dad gave me that when I was about your age," Austin said. "I figure we can play a little catch someday soon."

Chance wrinkled his nose. "Won't your dad be mad 'cause you gave it to me?"

He didn't have the heart to tell his son that he wouldn't ever know his grandfather. "Nope," he said as he straightened. "He'd be pleased."

Georgie ruffled Chance's hair. "Sweetie, before we open the rest of your gifts, we need to have a little talk."

Chance glanced back at her. "Aw, Mom. Do we hafta?"

She smiled. "Yes, but this has to do with something you wanted from Santa."

"A pony?" he asked.

"We'll get to that later," Georgie said. "Mom, Dad, do you mind if we have a few minutes alone?"

"Come on, George," Lila said. "You can help me make breakfast for a change."

George stood and muttered under his breath as he followed his wife out of the living room.

Georgie swept her hand toward the navy-colored sofa. "Let's have a seat."

After they settled in with Chance between them, Austin regarded Georgie. "Do you want me to go first?"

"I think you should," she said, wariness in her tone.

Austin shifted slightly so he could gauge his son's reaction. "Chance, I've known your mom for a long time. We went to school together."

"Kindergarten?" he asked.

"Yep, and all the way through high school."

"We were boyfriend and girlfriend," Georgie added. "Do you know what that is?"

Chance sent them both a sour look. "Yeah. That means you kissed and stuff."

After she and Austin exchanged a smile, Georgie continued. "Austin and I cared about each other very much. We still do."

When Georgie went silent and looked at him, Austin figured that was his cue. "I'm not only your mama's friend, bud, I'm your dad."

Chance stared at him without speaking, then his smile came out of hiding. "Santa sent you to me?"

Austin chuckled. "I guess you could say that, seeing how it's Christmas morning. How do you feel about this?"

"Are you a real live cowboy?"

"I guess you could say that, too."

"He's a calf roping champion, Chance," Georgie chimed in. "He has lots of trophies."

"Can I see them?"

"Sure," Austin said. "I plan to teach you how to rope and ride."

Then his son did something so unexpected, it shot

straight to his heart. Chance wrapped his arms around Austin, gave him a hug and said, "I'm glad you're my dad."

Austin swallowed around the lump in his throat. If someone would have told him a year ago that he would feel so much love for a child he'd just met, he would've called them crazy. "I'm glad you're my boy, too."

Chance climbed off the couch and faced them both. "Can we go to the barn and see my pony now?"

Georgie frowned. "What makes you think you have a pony?"

"Because if Santa can bring me my dad, he can bring me a horse."

Both Georgie and Austin laughed, sending Lila and George back into the room. "Everything settled?" Lila asked.

Chance pointed at Austin. "He's my daddy and he's going to teach me how to rope."

"Great," George groused. "Now you can traipse around the country chasing cows and women."

Lila elbowed her husband in the side. "Hush, George Romero. He can be anything he wants to be."

"I want to be a cowboy," Chance proclaimed. "And I want to see my horse."

Georgie pushed to her feet. "All right. Go get dressed and we'll go to the barn."

Chance hurried to the opening to the hall and paused to face them again. "Are you guys going to get married?"

"How would you feel about that if we do?" Georgie asked.

He shrugged. "Would we live here?"

Austin determined he should field this question. "Actually, I have a big house not far from here, with a barn and a room reserved just for you."

"Cool," he said. "Mama, you should marry my dad."

She smiled. "Then I guess it's official. We'll get married."

Seemingly satisfied, Chance took off and Austin grabbed the opportunity to take Georgie into his arms. "You heard our son. Let's get married."

"When do you propose we do this?" she asked.

"The sooner, the better. In fact, I'm thinking a New Year's Eve wedding would be good."

"That's less than a week away," Lila interjected. "We can't plan a wedding in a week."

"I don't need a fancy wedding, Mother," Georgie said. "Just family and friends and my dad to walk me down the aisle."

George stepped forward, looking less cranky than usual. "You can count on me to do that, princess."

"That's great, if we can actually find an aisle," Lila added. "Six days won't be enough time, not to mention it's a holiday."

A remedy to the time crunch entered Austin's mind. "We can have the ceremony at the ranch's main house. It's big enough to hold everyone, and I happen to know a woman who'd be glad to arrange everything, and she'll do it in record time."

"Do you mean Jenny?" Georgie asked.

"The one and only. If for some reason she can't get it done, then we'll just take a trip to the courthouse on Friday."

Lila looked mortified. "You can't marry for the first time at the courthouse."

"We did," George said. "And we're still married."

Lila scowled at him. "Don't press your luck, George Romero, if you really think you're going to force our daughter to marry in a county building."

Chance ran back into the room as fast as his boots would allow. "I'm ready to go."

Georgie slipped his hand into hers. "Then let's go."

To add to the joy of the day, Chance took Austin's hand and together they walked to the barn. They didn't talk about weddings, only the wonder of a boy's first horse, and plans for their future together. Austin executed his first duty as a father by helping Chance saddle up the pony, and keeping a watchful eye as his son rode the pen like a pro.

He draped his arm over Georgie's shoulder and pulled her close. "You've done a great job raising him, darlin'."

"It was easy. He's a great kid."

"You went to school and took care of him all by yourself. There had to be some hard times, and I'm sorry for that."

She pressed a kiss on his cheek. "The hard times are behind us. I love you, Austin Calloway."

"Let the good times begin, and I love you, too, Georgia May Romero."

"Are you serious about the wedding in a week?" she asked.

"Yep, I am. I think it's a good way to end the old year and welcome in the new."

"If we can get it together."

He kissed her in earnest then gave her a smile. "I'd bet my last buck that Jenny will find a way to pull it off."

Georgie couldn't believe Jenny had pulled it off. The downstairs parlor was fraught with floral arrangements, the food was ready for consumption by the guests and the mint juleps were chilling in the fridge. She was dressed in a short satin gown with a lace cutout in the back and a pair of three-inch matching heels that Paris had insisted Georgie wear because she couldn't. The last she'd heard, the groom was pacing nervously throughout the family homestead and her parents' appearance hadn't started another uncivil war. Everything seemed to be going as planned. Almost everything. The officiate was still missing.

Five minutes ago, Maria had announced that the local justice of the peace, Bucky Cheevers, had been detained by another duty for another hour. Georgie worried that if his reputation rang true, he might be holed up with a woman. That was okay, as long as he finally showed up, which he promised he would. She could think of far worse things to stall a wedding.

"My water broke."

She hadn't considered that one. Georgie turned to Paris, now standing in the doorway wearing a bathrobe, not her bridesmaid's dress. "Are you sure?"

She shuffled over to the bed and perched on the edge of the mattress. "Yes, I'm very sure. I started having some twinges yesterday afternoon, and now they're... Oh, lord, I think this baby is going to come very soon."

Georgie rushed over to her and said, "Lie down." She then hurried to the top of the stairs to sound the alarm. "Dallas, get up here now. Someone call 911 for Paris."

She returned to Paris and sat by her side. "Just take some deep breaths and try to relax, although that won't be easy under the circumstance."

Paris gave her an apologetic look. "I'm so sorry, Georgie. I'm ruining your wedding."

Georgie took her hand. "You don't need to apologize.

Besides, Bucky isn't even here yet. We can always wait a couple of days. Your baby can't."

The sound of pounding footsteps echoed through the corridor, followed by Dallas bursting into the room. "What's wrong?"

Paris lifted her head from the pillow. "We're going to have a baby."

He looked somewhat relieved. "I know that."

"Today," Paris added.

Now Dallas looked panicked as he rounded the bed and claimed a spot next to his wife. "Can you hold off?"

Paris grimaced and laid her hand on her belly. "I'm trying, honey, but maybe you should propose that to your son or daughter."

Maria rushed in with Jenny trailing behind her. "The paramedics are on their way. They should be here in five minutes."

"Five minutes I can do…" Paris sucked in a ragged breath. "I think."

"Should I boil some water just in case?" Jenny asked.

"Sure," Maria answered. "And while you're in the kitchen, have a drink. Or two."

Georgie peered behind the mothers, half expecting to see her future husband. "Where's Austin?"

"He's downstairs with Chance," Maria said.

"I told him it was bad luck to see the bride before the wedding," Jenny added. "If there's going to be a wedding. What am I going to do with all that food?"

"We're going to eat it," Maria muttered. "Now is not the time to worry about the nuptials or the catering. Austin and Georgie can still get married, even if we have to hold it at midnight after Paris delivers."

From the pain crossing Paris's face, Georgie doubted the next Calloway grandchild would wait that long.

Sitting in a hospital waiting room for five hours was not a part of Austin's plan. But here he was, dressed in suit and tie, with his almost-bride by his side and his son leaning against his shoulder, fast asleep. Jenny played games on her cell phone across from them while Maria focused on an Old West rerun playing on the TV suspended from the ceiling in the corner. George kept nodding off and, when he snored, Lila periodically shook him awake. Instead of a wedding, they'd inadvertently created a scene straight out of a weird reality show.

Austin had a good mind to go after Bucky Cheevers. If the jerk would have showed up on time, the wedding would already be over. Instead, they were clock-watching and coming to attention every time the Labor and Delivery door opened.

"What a way to ring in the New Year," he whispered to avoid disturbing Chance, who'd just settled down.

"We still have twenty minutes before the New Year is here," Georgie whispered back. "I'm surprised the baby is taking this long. I thought for sure Paris would have delivered in the ambulance."

That would've saved them this waiting game.

As good luck would have it, two minutes later, Dallas came through the door, holding a blue bundle in his arm. "I'd like you to introduce you to Lucas James Calloway."

Everyone scurried out of their seats to catch a glimpse of the newest member of the Calloway family. Everyone but Austin. He didn't believe for a minute that his own son would care to be disturbed from sleep to meet his cousin.

But as bad luck would have it, Chance stirred anyway, rubbed his eyes and asked, "Are we gettin' married now?"

"Not yet, bud," Austin told him. "That probably won't happen until tomorrow."

"Come see little Lucas, Chance," Georgie said. "He reminds me of you when you were born."

Chance looked like he'd rather eat dirt, although he grudgingly climbed off the couch to answer his mother's summons. Austin followed him over to Maria who was now holding the baby. Chance took a quick peek then frowned. "He's all wrinkly and his hair is sticking up."

Georgie smiled. "That's what babies look like when they're first born."

"Okay." Obviously disinterested, Chance returned to the couch, stretched out on his back and closed his eyes.

Georgie slid her arm around Austin's waist and regarded Dallas. "Is Paris okay?"

"She's not as tired as I thought she'd be," he said. "She is relieved it's over."

Jenny took the baby from Maria without asking. "Oh my. He looks just like Worth did when he was a baby, minus the blond hair."

Austin leaned over to verify that. As far as he was concerned, the kid looked like every other kid at that stage. And he wasn't as good-looking as *his* kid. "I think he looks more like Grandpa Calloway before he got his dentures."

Georgie pinched his side. "Stop it."

"I'm sorry we blew the wedding," Dallas said.

So was Austin. "We'll figure something out in the next day or so."

Jenny handed the baby to Dallas and uttered, "I'll be right back," then pushed out the door and disappeared into the lobby.

"I better get this guy back to his mother," Dallas said. "She's going to think we left without her. She's a little disappointed he didn't arrive after the New Year so he could be the first one born."

"When can we see Paris?" Georgie asked.

Dallas glanced at the clock. "I'll check, but she should be ready for guests in a few minutes."

After Dallas walked out of the room, Jenny returned with a tall man in tow. "Georgie, Austin, this is Chaplain Griggs. He'll be glad to perform the wedding ceremony so you won't have to wait."

Austin exchanged a look with Georgie. "Do you really want to get married in a hospital waiting room?"

Georgie shook her head. "No, but I wouldn't mind getting married in Paris's hospital room, if she's up to it. That way we can all be together as planned."

"I can do that," the chaplain said. "As long as medical personnel clear it."

"And Paris," Maria added. "She might not be up to it."

Lila stepped forward. "Georgie, honey, this isn't much better than the courthouse."

Georgie patted Lila's cheek. "It's okay, Mom. It's unique, like all of us."

"I'll drink to that," George said. "Too bad I don't have a drink handy."

"Before we go any further," the chaplain began, "I need to find out if we're cleared to continue. I'll let you know in a few minutes."

After the clergyman left, Austin turned to Georgie to find out if she was in fact serious. "If you're sure about this, I have the license."

"I'm very sure, but I don't have a bouquet."

Jenny crossed the room to an end table, yanked the

fake flowers from a crystal vase and handed them to Georgie. "Here you go. It's not perfect, but it should do. Hopefully they won't send you a bill."

Maria pulled her cell from the pocket of her plain blue dress. "I'll call the other boys, just in case."

Austin saw several problems with that. "Don't bother, Mom. Before we left the house, they told me they were going to have a few beers, and I don't see any one of them being a designated driver. Besides, if we're going to get this show on the road, we have ten minutes before midnight arrives. I'd like to stick to at least one of our original plans to be married before the New Year."

"You could also use the chapel, sugar," Jenny said. "If the room doesn't work out."

"It's going to work out fine." All eyes turned to the chaplain as he continued. "I have been instructed that we need to have a quick ceremony out of respect to the new mother. Now if you're ready, follow me."

Lila went over and nudged Chance. "Time for a wedding, baby boy."

Chance hopped off the couch and grinned. "About time."

Austin couldn't agree more.

As they wandered down the sterile corridor, their son between them, Austin took Georgie's hand and gave it a squeeze. When he imagined what they must look like to strangers, a bevy of guests dressed in their finest, he couldn't help but chuckle.

They arrived at Paris's room a few moments later, where George offered his arm to Georgie. "Son, I've waited a long time to give my daughter away, and even though we don't have an aisle, I'd like to at least walk her into the room."

He didn't dare argue with a man who had a grip on his future bride. "Not a problem, sir."

"Should I sing?" Jenny asked.

"Good heavens, no," Maria answered. "You'll wake every baby on the floor and every dog in the county."

They pushed through the door where the chaplain immediately claimed a spot near the window.

Paris was sitting up in the bed, holding the baby close, Dallas at her side. "I'm tickled pink you're doing this, you two," she said. "Just excuse my not-very-chic attire."

Georgie kissed her dad's cheek, walked over to Paris and gave her a hug. "I couldn't have a wedding without my maid of honor standing up for me. And don't worry about standing."

The chaplain cleared his throat. "Shall we begin?"

Austin checked the black clock on the wall. They had all of four minutes to get this done. "You bet."

He guided Georgie and Chance to the officiate, who started off by saying, "At times the best moments in life come in the face of a miracle. And it appears it took a miracle for you both to get to this point."

"Amen," George said from behind them, drawing more laughter.

"Would you like traditional vows, or do you plan to say your own?" the chaplain asked.

"Our own," Georgie replied before Austin could even think.

She turned to face him and smiled. "Austin, we've both traveled differing paths, but all my roads led to you. I feel blessed to have you as my husband, and the father of our child, for the rest of our life."

Austin could only come up with a few short and simple words to say. "Georgie, it's always been you. It will always be only you. Thank you for giving me our son, and the opportunity to make up for lost moments. I promise I will stay this time, forever. I love you."

She swiped at her eyes. "I love you, too."

"Do we have rings?" the chaplain asked.

"I do." Dallas stood, fished the bands from his pocket, then passed them off to Maria who handed them to the chaplain.

They slid the rings onto each other's fingers, sealing the deal, and Austin happily obliged the directive to kiss the bride. He responded to the tug on his hand with a grin aimed at his boy. "Are we married now?" Chance asked.

Austin scooped his son up into his arms. "Yeah, bud, we are. Now let's go home and get you to bed."

"To our home," Jenny said. "We still have all that food and drink."

George clasped Lila's hand. "I'm more than ready for that drink."

"I'm ready for sleep," Paris said. "Congratulations to both of you. We'll celebrate large when we come home."

After the marriage license was signed, and Austin paid the man who married them with a minute to spare, everyone said their goodbyes to the new mother and baby, then filed into the parking lot. Georgie settled Chance into his booster in the backseat then turned and slid her arms around Austin's waist. "Maria is going to put Chance to bed in your old room. That way, we can have our honeymoon at your house."

"Our house," he amended. "I believe we should forego the food and drink, unless you're hungry."

"Only for your attention," she said as she pinched his butt.

He faked a flinch. "You've got it. And you've got me from now on. Can you handle it?"

"I don't know. You can be pretty tough to take, but I'll

manage." She studied his eyes, her expression surprisingly sober. "We have a lot of catching up to do, Austin, and it's going to take a lot of adjustments to our lives, raising Chance together."

He cupped her pretty face in his palms and brushed a kiss across her lips. "We can make it through anything together, sweetheart. Just look how far we've come to get to this point."

"And look at what we've got."

When they turned their attention to their sleeping son, a host of emotions ran through Austin. Awe. Amazement. The fierce need to protect him. Above all, an unexpected, abiding love.

Yeah, he'd made more than a few mistakes, failed at a few endeavors, feared he might continue that pattern. But with his cherished Georgie by his side, Austin no longer worried if he would falter because he knew he would. And that was okay. For the first time in his life, he knew what it took to be a deserving husband and father, a real man, and it had nothing to do with how much money he made, or how many championships he'd won. It had everything to do with opening himself to love, and that much he had done. And damn if it didn't feel good.

A year ago, if anyone would've told him he'd be married and have a kid, he would've called them crazy. But now, he called himself blessed.

* * * * *

YOU HAVE
JUST READ A
HARLEQUIN®
DESIRE
BOOK.

Discover more sensual stories starring **powerful heroes, scandalous secrets**…and **burning desires**. Be sure to look for all six Harlequin Desire books every month.

HALO2018

*Wealthy Texas politician Chase Ferguson ended things with his
ex to protect her. Yet now she's crashed his isolated vacation
house in a snowstorm. And when a stormbound seduction has
real-world repercussions, he must make a stand for what—and
who—he truly believes in.*

*Read on for a sneak peek at
A Snowbound Scandal by Jessica Lemmon,
part of her **Dallas Billionaires Club** series!*

Her mouth watered, not for the food, but for him.

Not why you came here, Miriam reminded herself sternly.

Yet here she stood. Chase had figured out—before she'd
admitted it to herself—that she'd come here not only to give
him a piece of her mind but also to give herself the comfort of
knowing he'd had a home-cooked meal on Thanksgiving.

She balled her fist as a flutter of desire took flight between her
thighs. She wanted to touch him. Maybe just once.

He pushed her wineglass closer to her. An offer.

An offer she wouldn't accept.

Couldn't accept.

She wasn't unlike Little Red Riding Hood, having run to the
wrong house for shelter. Only in this case, the Big Bad Wolf
wasn't dining on Red's beloved grandmother but Miriam's
family's home cooking.

An insistent niggling warned her that she could be next—and
hadn't this particular "wolf" already consumed her heart?

"So, I'm going to go."

When she grabbed her coat and stood, a warm hand grasped
her much cooler one. Chase's fingers stroked hers before lightly

squeezing, his eyes studying her for a long moment, his fork hovering over his unfinished dinner.

Finally, he said, "I'll see you out."

"That's not necessary."

He did as he pleased and stood, his hand on her lower back as he walked with her. Outside, the wind pushed against the front door, causing the wood to creak. She and Chase exchanged glances. Had she waited too long?

"For the record, I don't want you to leave."

What she'd have given to hear those words on that airfield ten years ago.

"I'll be all right."

"You can't know that." He frowned out of either concern or anger, she couldn't tell which.

"Stay." Chase's gray-green eyes were warm and inviting, his voice a time capsule back to not-so-innocent days. The request was siren-call sweet, but she'd not risk herself for it.

"No." She yanked open the front door, shocked when the howling wind shoved her back a few inches. Snow billowed in, swirling around her feet, and her now wet, cold fingers slipped from the knob.

Chase caught her, an arm looped around her back, and shoved the door closed with the flat of one palm. She hung there, suspended by the corded forearm at her back, clutching his shirt in one fist, and nearly drowned in his lake-colored eyes.

"I can stay for a while longer," she squeaked, the decision having been made for her.

His handsome face split into a brilliant smile.

Don't miss A Snowbound Scandal *by Jessica Lemmon,*
part of her **Dallas Billionaires Club** *series!*

Available August 2018 wherever
Harlequin® Desire books and ebooks are sold.

www.Harlequin.com

HDEXP0718

HARLEQUIN *Desire*

Family sagas…scandalous secrets…burning desires.

Save **$1.00**

on the purchase of ANY
Harlequin® Desire book.

Available wherever books are sold,
including most bookstores, supermarkets,
drugstores and discount stores.

✂ - - - - -

Save $1.00

on the purchase of any Harlequin® Desire book.

Coupon valid until September 30, 2018.
Redeemable at participating outlets in the U.S. and Canada only.
Not redeemable at Barnes & Noble stores. Limit one coupon per customer.

52615854

Canadian Retailers: Harlequin Enterprises Limited will pay the face value of this coupon plus 10.25¢ if submitted by customer for this product only. Any other use constitutes fraud. Coupon is nonassignable. Void if taxed, prohibited or restricted by law. Consumer must pay any government taxes. Void if copied. Inmar Promotional Services ("IPS") customers submit coupons and proof of sales to Harlequin Enterprises Limited, P.O. Box 31000, Scarborough, ON M1R 0E7, Canada. Non-IPS retailer—for reimbursement submit coupons and proof of sales directly to Harlequin Enterprises Limited, Retail Marketing Department, 22 Adelaide St. West, 40th Floor, Toronto, Ontario M5H 4E3, Canada.

U.S. Retailers: Harlequin Enterprises Limited will pay the face value of this coupon plus 8¢ if submitted by customer for this product only. Any other use constitutes fraud. Coupon is nonassignable. Void if taxed, prohibited or restricted by law. Consumer must pay any government taxes. Void if copied. For reimbursement submit coupons and proof of sales directly to Harlequin Enterprises, Ltd 482, NCH Marketing Services, P.O. Box 880001, El Paso, TX 88588-0001, U.S.A. Cash value 1/100 cents.

5 65373 00076 2   (8100)0 12375

® and ™ are trademarks owned and used by the trademark owner and/or its licensee.

© 2018 Harlequin Enterprises Limited

HDCOUP0718

Want to give in to temptation with
steamy tales of irresistible desire?

Check out **Harlequin® Presents®**,
Harlequin® Desire and
Harlequin® Kimani™ Romance books!

New books available every month!

CONNECT WITH US AT:

Facebook.com/groups/HarlequinConnection

 Facebook.com/HarlequinBooks

 Twitter.com/HarlequinBooks

 Instagram.com/HarlequinBooks

 Pinterest.com/HarlequinBooks

 ReaderService.com

**ROMANCE WHEN
YOU NEED IT**

PGENRE2018